# ZENITH

ZENITH

# ZENITH

#1 *NEW YORK TIMES* BESTSELLING AUTHORS

## SASHA ALSBERG
## & LINDSAY CUMMINGS

YOUNG
ADULT

HQ

HQ
An imprint of HarperCollins*Publishers* Ltd
1 London Bridge Street
London SE1 9GF

This paperback edition 2018

1
First published in Great Britain by
HQ, an imprint of HarperCollins*Publishers* Ltd 2018

Copyright © Sasha Alsberg and Lindsay Cummings 2016

First published by Mirabel Inc., 2016
This edition published by HQ YA 2018
Sasha Alsberg and Lindsay Cummings asserts the moral right to be
identified as the author of this work.
A catalogue record for this book is
available from the British Library.

ISBN: 978-0-00-822833-0

MIX
Paper from
responsible sources
FSC
www.fsc.org
FSC™ C007454

This book is produced from independently certified FSC™ paper
to ensure responsible forest management.

For more information visit: www.harpercollins.co.uk/green

Printed and bound by CPI Group (UK) Ltd, Croydon CR0 4YY

*From Sasha:*
To my amazing father, Peter Alsberg
for always telling me to shoot for the stars.

*From Lindsay:*
To my dad, Don Cummings,
who gave me a love of sci-fi!
Here's to #7!

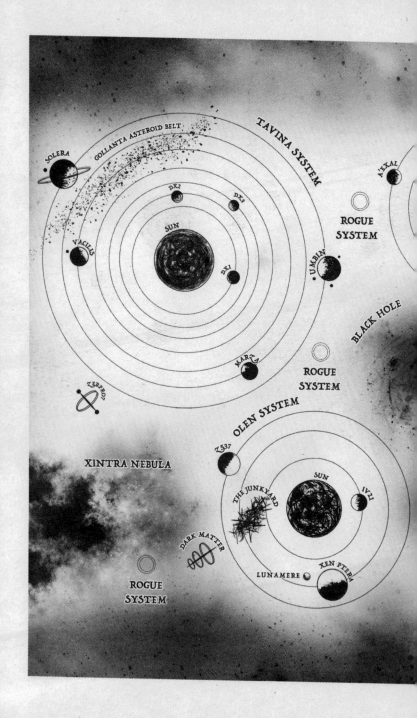

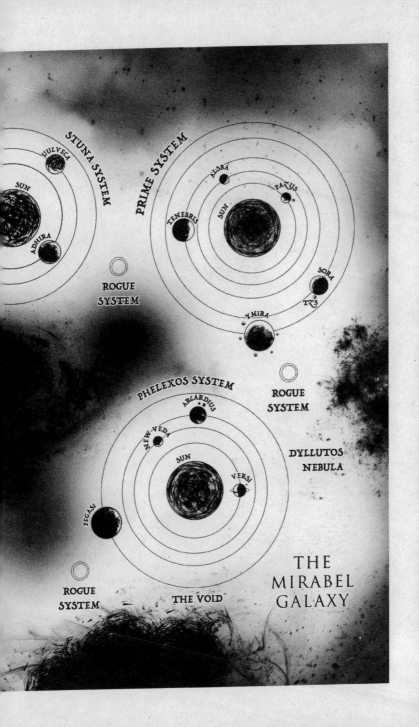

# CELL 306
## THE PAST

ENDLESS DARKNESS.

It surrounded him in Cell 306, twisting and turning itself into his bones until he and the darkness became one.

His thoughts had long since stopped running wild with every groan and creak of the prison walls. A thinning blanket, his only companion, was wrapped tightly around his shoulders, but it failed to block out the cold kiss of air that snuck through the threads.

*I am Valen Cortas*, he thought, rolling the words over and over in his mind. It was the only thing that kept him going, leashing a sharp coil of courage around his veins. *Vengeance will be mine.*

What he would do, what he would give, to have a single moment of time in the light. To feel the touch of a warm midday breeze on his skin, to hear the rustle of leaves on the trees of his home planet, Arcardius.

He had lived on Arcardius all his life, and yet in Cell 306 the memories of his home had begun to grow dim. Valen had always looked at the world and seen it in a thousand colors, his fingers itching to paint each turn of the light, each curl of the wind sweeping through the silver streets.

Every shade was unique in his eyes.

And yet...he was losing the colors.

Try as he might, Valen couldn't remember the precise shade of purple that spiraled across the Revina Mountains. He couldn't recall the exact hue of the blue and red moons that mingled together in the sky. The sparkle of starlight when true night fell, a constant, glowing guide through the sky. As each moment in this abyss passed, the colors all melted into a single shade of black.

He shivered and pulled the blanket tighter around his emaciated frame.

The pain of remembering things loved and lost had sunk its claws into him, threatening to crush his bones.

Somewhere in the dank prison, a scream rang out, razor-sharp, like the tip of a blade scratching its way down Valen's spine.

He rolled over, pressing his hands to his ears.

"I am Valen Cortas," he whispered through cracked lips. "Vengeance will be mine."

Another scream. The sizzle and pop of an electric whip, a flash of blue light that ghosted across the bars. Valen gasped, his eyes aching, head throbbing, memories churning. Color. A blue like the powerful sea, a blue like the open, cloudless sky. And then...darkness again, and silence.

The new prisoners always screamed for days, until their throats went ragged. They cried out the names of loved ones and tried to hang on to who they were.

But on Lunamere, everyone became a number in the end.

Valen was 306. Deep in the belly of hell incarnate.

The cold was endless. The food was enough to keep skin hanging on bones, but muscles atrophied and hearts slowed. The stink of bodies rose up like a wave, a scent that had long since sunk into the obsidinite walls and bars.

Those walls of obsidinite were the only thing separating Valen and the other prisoners from the void of space and their untimely deaths. He'd thought of escape, as every other prisoner had. He imagined leaping through the wall, diving out into the airless abyss.

Death had once scared Valen, but with each day that passed, it grew closer and closer to becoming his greatest wish.

Still, deep within his tormented soul, he knew he had to survive.

He had to bide his time and hope that the Godstars had not forgotten him.

And so he sat, dreaming of darkness, wrapped up in its cold arms.

*I am Valen Cortas.*

*Vengeance will be mine.*

# CHAPTER 1
## ANDROMA

HER NIGHTMARES WERE LIKE BLOODSTAINS.

They were impossible to get rid of, no matter how hard Androma Racella tried to scrub them from her mind. On the darkest nights they clung to her like a second skin. In them, she could hear the whispers of the dead threatening to drag her down to hell, where she belonged.

But Andi had decided, long ago, that the nightmares were her punishment.

She was the Bloody Baroness, after all. And if surviving meant giving up sleep, then she would bear the exhaustion.

Tonight the nightmares had come as they always did, and

now Andi sat on the bridge of her ship, the *Marauder*, scratching a fresh set of tallies into her twin swords.

The glowing compression cuffs on her wrists, which protected skin burned in an accident years before, were the only light in the otherwise dark space. The press of a button was all it took to power them up.

Her fingertips were white beneath red-painted nails as she gouged a piece of steel against the flat of one blade, creating a thin tally the length of her smallest finger. Without its spirals of electricity, the sword looked like any other weapon; the tallies, any other soldier's lucky mark. But Andi knew better. Each line she etched into the metal was another life cut off, another heart stopped with a slice of her blades.

A hundred lives to cover up the pain of the very first. A hundred more, to shovel away the hurt into a place that was dark and deep.

Andi glanced up as an object in the sky caught her eye.

A piece of space trash, hurtling away among thousands of stars.

Andi yawned. She had always loved the stars. Even as a child, she'd dreamed of dancing among them. But tonight she felt as if they were watching her, waiting for her to fail. Mocking little bastards. Well, they'd be sorely disappointed.

The *Marauder*, a glimmering starship made from the rare impenetrable glass varillium, was known for its devilish speed and agility. And Andi's crew, a group of girls hailing from every hellish corner of the galaxy, were as sharp as Andi's blades. They were the heart of the ship, and the three reasons why Andi had survived this long so far from home.

Five days ago, the girls had taken on a job to steal a starload of sealed BioDrugs from Solera, the capital planet of the Tavina System, and deliver them to a satellite station just outside the planet Tenebris in the neighboring system.

It wasn't an abnormal request. BioDrugs were one of Andi's most requested transports since these particular drugs could burn someone's brain to bits or—if used correctly—carry one into a blissful oblivion.

*Which*, Andi thought, as she resumed her death-mark scratching, *I wouldn't mind experiencing right now.*

She could still feel the hot blood on her hands from the man she'd slayed on the Tenebris station. The way his eyes had locked on to hers before she'd run him through with her blades, silent as a whisper. The sorry fool never should have tried to double-cross Andi and her crew.

When his partner had seen Andi's handiwork, he eagerly handed over the Krevs her team was owed for the job. Still, she'd stolen another life, something she never relished doing. Even killers like her still had souls, and she knew that everyone deserved to be mourned by someone, no matter their crimes.

Andi worked quietly with only the hum of the ship's engines far beneath her for company, the occasional hiss of the cooling system kicking on overhead. Outer space was quiet, soothing, and Andi had to keep herself from falling asleep, where the nightmares would be lurking.

The sound of footsteps brought Andi's gaze up once more.

The rhythmic tapping made its way down the small hallway that led to the bridge. Andi continued her scratching, glancing up again when a figure stopped in the doorway, her blue, scaled arms poised on narrow hips.

"As your Second-in-Command," the girl said, with a voice as smooth as the spiced Rigna they'd shared earlier, "I demand that you return to your quarters and get some sleep."

"Good morning to you, too, Lira," Andi said with a sigh. Her Second always seemed to know where she was—and what she was doing—at all times. Her sharp eyes caught every detail, no matter how small. This quality made Lira the best damned pilot in the Mirabel Galaxy, and it was the reason they'd managed to succeed with so many jobs thus far.

It was one of many peculiar qualities Lira had, along with

the patches of scales scattered across her skin. When she experienced strong emotions, the scales began to glow, giving off enough heat to burn through the flesh of her enemies. All of Lira's clothing was sleeveless for this reason. But this defensive mechanism also took a lot of energy from her, occasionally rendering Lira unconscious when activated.

Her scales were a trait many from her home planet desired, but few had. Lira's bloodline traced back to the first Adhirans who colonized the terraformed world. Soon after the colonization, the planet experienced a radioactive event that transformed its earliest settlers in a number of strange ways, including the scales Lira had inherited.

Andi's Second stepped into the starlit bridge and lifted a hairless brow. "Sooner or later, you're going to run out of space on those swords."

"And then I'll turn my tallies on to you," Andi said with a wicked grin.

"You should take up dancing again. Perhaps it would ease some of that deadly tension you're carrying around."

"Careful, Lir," Andi warned.

Lira grinned, swiping two fingers across her right temple to activate her internal communication channel. "Rise and shine, ladies. If the captain can't sleep, we shouldn't, either."

Andi couldn't hear the response Lira chuckled at, but soon enough, two more pairs of footsteps sounded from the deck above, and she knew the rest of her crew was on their way.

Gilly arrived first, her fire-red braids bouncing on her shoulders as she approached. She was small for her age, a girl no older than thirteen, but Andi wasn't fooled by her wide, innocent blue eyes. Gilly was a bloodthirsty little beast, a gunner with plenty of death on her hands. She had one hell of a trigger finger.

"Why do you insist on ruining my beauty sleep?" she exclaimed in her fluid little voice.

A tall, broad-shouldered girl appeared behind her, bending so as not to hit her head on the doorway when she entered. Breck, Andi's head gunner, rolled her eyes as she placed a large hand on Gilly's small shoulder.

"Kid, when are you going to learn not to question Lira? You know she won't give you a reasonable answer."

Andi laughed at Lira's sharp glare. "If you would only look up from your gun sights long enough to listen to me, you'd know that my answers are, in fact, quite reasonable." Lira winked at the girls before settling into the pilot's seat next to Andi's captain's chair.

"Adhirans," Breck said with a sigh, crossing her thick arms over her chest. At seven feet tall with choppy black hair that just brushed her muscled shoulders, Breck was the most intimidating member of the crew. They all assumed she was a giantess from the planet New Veda, where Mirabel's greatest warriors were born.

The only problem with that assumption?

Breck had no memories of her past. She had no idea *who* she was, or even where she'd come from. She'd been on the run when Andi picked her up, a bruised and beaten ten-year-old Gilly at her side.

Gilly, plucked from the market streets of her home planet Umbin, was struggling to escape from a couple of Xen Pterran slavers when Breck found her. The older girl had saved Gilly from a fate worse than death, and now the two girls were as close as kin. To them, it no longer mattered what life Breck couldn't remember or what past Gilly tried to forget. All that mattered was that they had each other.

Breck tugged on one of Gilly's red braids, then lifted her chin and sniffed the air. "I don't smell breakfast. We need a cook, Andi."

"And we'll get one as soon as we have the funds to buy a culinary droid," Andi said with a curt nod. The girls usually traded off on kitchen duty, but Breck was the only decent cook among them. "We're down to less than three hundred Krevs. *Someone* spent a little too much on hair products on TZ-5."

Breck's cheeks reddened as she touched the new crimson streaks in her black hair.

"Speaking of Krevs," Gilly added, her tiny hand grazing the golden double-triggered gun at her hip, "when's our next job, Cap?"

Andi leaned back, arms crossed behind her head, and surveyed the girls.

They were a good crew, all three of them. Small, but mighty in the best of ways, and better than what Andi deserved. She stared at her blades once more before putting them back in their harness. If only she could put her memories away just as easily.

"I've got a tip for a possible job on Vacilis," Andi said finally. It was a desert world where the wind blew as hot as the devil's backside and the air was choked with the stench of sulfur, just a few planets over from ice-locked Solera. "But I'm not sure how many Krevs it'll haul. And it'll be messy, dealing with the desert nomads."

Breck shrugged her broad shoulders. "Any money is good money if it brings us more food stores."

"And ammo," Gilly said, cracking her knuckles like the little warrior she was.

Andi inclined her head at Lira. "Thoughts?"

"We will see where the stars lead us," Lira answered.

Andi nodded. "I'll get in touch with my informant. Take us away, Lir."

"As you wish." Lira punched the destination into the control panel's holoscreen. A diagram of Mirabel illuminated the room with blue light, stars floating around their heads and the little planets that made up each major system orbiting their suns. A bright line traced from their current location near an unnamed moon, too barren for habitation, to Vacilis, almost half a galaxy away.

Lira scrutinized the route, then minimized the map and readied the ship for hyperspace travel.

Andi turned in her seat. "Breck, Gilly, go to the vault and do a weapons check. Then make sure the Big Bang is fully loaded. I want you two ready in case we run into any trouble once we arrive in the Tavina System."

"We're always ready," Breck said.

Gilly giggled, and the two gunners nodded at Andi in salute before exiting the bridge. Gilly skipped along behind Breck, her golden gun bobbing against her tiny frame.

"Engines are hot," Lira said. "Time to fly."

The *Marauder* rumbled beneath Andi as she slumped down in her chair, exhaustion worming its way in.

The expanse of space stretched out before them, and Andi's eyelids began to droop against her will. With Lira by her side, she sank into the warm folds of sleep.

*Smoke pooled into the ruined ship, unrelenting as Andi gasped for air. She glanced sideways, where Kalee's bloody hand twitched once, then hung motionless over the armrest.*

*"Wake up," Andi rasped. "You have to wake up!"*

Andi awoke to a rough shake of her shoulder from Lira. Her heart hammered in her chest as her eyes adjusted to the dim light of the bridge. Starlight ahead, the glowing holoscreen on the dash.

She was *here*. She was *safe*.

But something was off. A light on the holo blinked red, a silent prox alarm beside the markers that showed not only the *Marauder*'s location, but three ships behind them, catching up fast. An unwelcome sight to any space pirate.

"We have a tail." Lira curled her lip in annoyance. She tapped a blue fingertip on the holoscreen, changing it to the rear-cam, showing Andi a faraway look at the ships soaring behind them. "Two Explorers and one Tracker."

"The stars be damned," Andi said. "When did they show up?"

"Seconds before I woke you. We came out of light speed just

outside the Tavina System, as planned, and the alarm activated not long after."

Andi's mind raced, calculating all the possible scenarios. Lira never let anyone get the drop on the *Marauder*. They had to have been cloaked with technology the likes of which Andi's crew could only dream of getting their hands on. She told herself this was just like any other night, any other chase, but she couldn't shake the ominous feeling that this time might be different.

"Do we know who they are? Black market, Mirabel Patrol?" Andi asked, staring at the radar as it blinked, the three hellish red dots slowly gaining on them.

Lira glowered. "With this tech, it has to be Patrol. They didn't show up on our radar until they were practically on top of us."

Andi chewed on her bottom lip. "Which branch?"

*You know which branch*, her mind whispered. She shoved the voice away.

"We won't know until they're in our close-range sights, and by then, it'll be too late for us to escape," Lira said.

"Then don't let them get that close."

The Patrolmen, those bastards. The government lackeys had been after Andi's ship for years, but they'd never once come close enough to appear on the *Marauder*'s radar.

Their last job shouldn't have been enough to capture the attention of the Patrolmen. It was a black-market operation, a simple grab and go. All they'd done was haul a few crates' worth of meds for a drug lord, nothing significant enough to bring the Patrolmen down on them.

The girls had taken on more high-profile jobs than *that*—like the time they kidnapped a rich Soleran's mistress and left her on a meteor, the job requested by the man's furious wife. She paid a pretty penny for their services. It wasn't until days later that they found out the woman was not only a mistress, but a prominent politician's daughter from Tenebris. The politician tore the galaxy apart looking for his daughter. When he eventually found her withered corpse on that barren rock, word got back about who put her there.

Andi screened their jobs much more carefully now. Her crew was still on the run from that politician to this day.

It *could* be he'd finally caught their scent. She closed her eyes. Black holes ablaze, she was screwed. The ship rumbled beneath her, almost as if in agreement.

"Cloaking is useless at this point," Lira said as she readied the gears, slamming buttons, tapping in codes. "Engines are still too hot to go back into hyperspace. Damn their tech."

In the distance, Andi could just barely make out the ghostly forms of their pursuers. They were still far out, but heading closer with each passing breath. "Get us out of this, and I'll see to it that we get devices of the same caliber."

"And bigger guns?" Lira asked, her blue eyes wide. "We'll barely scrape by if we have to turn and fire on them. We only have one Big Bang left."

Andi nodded. "Much bigger guns."

"Well, then," Lira said, a dangerous grin spreading across her face. "I think the stars may align for us, Captain. Any last words?"

Someone else had said that to her once, long ago. Before she escaped Arcardius, never to see her home planet again.

Andi chewed on her lip, and the memory fizzled away. She could have given her Second a thousand words, but instead she simply strapped herself in, turned in her seat and said, "Fly true, Lir."

Lira nodded and took the ship's wheel, her grip steady and practiced. "Fly true."

A humming vibration filled the bay before the ship shot forward, like the tip of a crystal spear hurtling through the black expanse.

# CHAPTER 2
## ANDROMA

ON A GOOD DAY, THE *MARAUDER* AND HER crew could lose a tail as fast as an Adhiran darowak could fly, but when Andi glanced at the radar, three little dots continued to blink back at her.

She suppressed a groan and tapped on the viewport in front of her. The glass melded, colors morphing to show a live image from their rear-cam.

Her stomach dropped to her toes.

The approaching ships were still behind them. Two black Explorers, angular and sharp, and in between, a giant Tracker ship. A monster in the sky that tore a memory from Andi's mind.

*A hundred pairs of polished Academy boots clacked on the ground of a brand-new, state-of-the-art facility in the sky. A rigid man in a royal blue suit stood before the crowd, announcing the specs of the new Tracker ship. Andi raised her hand, wincing as she disturbed a bruised rib from a fight, but she was hungry for knowledge, already in love with flying.*

"I still can't see a sigil on them," Lira said, drawing Andi back to the present. The memory faded like mist. "We don't know which planet they've hailed from yet."

Andi leaned forward, sliding two fingers against her temple and linking with her crew's channels. "We've got a tail, ladies." She swallowed and cast a sideways glance at Lira, who sat calmly steering the ship. "Three of them, coming in from the rear. Get to your stations and prepare for immediate engagement. We're going dark." She switched the channel off and looked at Lira. "Ready?"

Lira nodded as Andi typed in the codes that would activate the *Marauder*'s outer shields.

The stars winked goodbye as the metal shields slid out from the belly of the glass ship, like hands wrapping them in darkness. Over and around, until only three viewports remained. One large for the pilot, and two small for the gunners, decks below.

"I warned you before the last job about leaving bodies behind," Lira said suddenly, banking them left to avoid a cluster of space trash cartwheeling endlessly through the black. Her voice wasn't harsh. And yet Andi still felt the painful truth of Lira's words.

Blood trails were far easier to follow than any other. And after all these years of running, it was possible that the Patrolmen had finally caught up to them because of Andi.

"I had to kill him," Andi said. "He almost shot Gilly. You know that, Lira."

"The only thing I know for sure is that the ships behind us are closing in," Lira said, glancing at the radar.

The patrol ships could have come from anywhere in the galaxy, but a nagging in Andi's gut told her they hailed from

Arcardius, the headquarters of the Unified Systems. A planet with cities made of glass and buildings towering on floating fragments of land in the sky, where military life reigned supreme and a pale-haired general ruled with an iron fist.

Home. Or at least it used to be.

After years of work, the Arcardian fleet had finally been rebuilt after the war against Xen Ptera, the capital planet of the Olen System.

These new ships were faster, better equipped.

Lira laughed. "It's too bad we'll have to miss their party."

"Maybe that's why they're here," Andi said. "To hand deliver our invitations."

"They won't catch us." Lira dug her fingers into a metal cup soldered to the ship's dash, the words *I Visited Arcardius and All I Got Was This Stupid Cup* inscribed on the side. Andi grimaced as Lira pulled out a hunk of Moon Chew and popped it into her mouth.

"That stuff can kill you, you know," Andi said as the ship groaned and lurched. She was thrust sideways against her bindings as Lira quickly steered the ship to the right.

"I enjoy flirting with death." Her Second smirked.

They fell silent as the *Marauder* soared on, Lira navigating the ship left and right, up and down, the tails trailing them as if this were a mere game of chase.

But this game they were playing rarely ended with laughter and fun. It would end with bodies burning in the sky, the air sucked from their lungs as they succumbed to the void of space.

Andi rapped her fingertips on the armrests. Her rouged nails looked tipped in blood, a playful nod to those who had given Andi her pirating name.

She was frustrated and hungry and, thanks to the nightmares, reaching a level of exhaustion that shouldn't have been humanly possible to survive. Usually she would've been up for the challenge because, in Lira's terms, she lived for the thrill of a life dangling on the edge of death.

But as she looked at Lira's hands guiding the ship, a very different image took their place.

In her mind's eye, Andi saw her old home's moons, those beautiful orbs of red and blue beside Arcardius, the ice rings circling them like frozen guardians. She saw her younger, gloved hands, the Spectre sigil on them winking in the light as she clutched a traveler ship's throttle. She felt the rush of adrenaline coursing through her veins. Then that fateful crash of fire and light, the screech of machinery and a girl's piercing scream. And blood, rivers of it, drying on hot metal…

A voice buzzed into the pilot's com system, and Andi flinched back into the present.

"What is it?" she barked.

Beside her, Lira punched the engine, the *Marauder* screaming as it rocketed forward.

"I got 'em comin' in hot!" Breck shouted. Andi could imagine her gunner several decks below, lying flat before her massive hull gun. "Almost in my sights now. Can't outrun 'em?"

"If we could, don't you think we would have done so already?" Andi growled.

"Godstars, Andi." Breck's voice was deep and throaty. "I can see the sigil now. They're Arcardian Patrol. We're gonna be space bits."

Andi tapped the rear-cam, zooming in as the ships gained speed. The exploding star of Arcardius stared back at her. Her insides turned to ice. There was only one reason they would have traveled so far from their domain.

So this was it, then. The enemy she'd run from all these years had finally found her.

Though dread threatened to freeze her insides, Andi straightened her spine and steeled herself. She wouldn't go down without a fight.

Andi reached up and pressed her responder, ignoring Breck's final words. "You girls in position?"

"Gilly's on Harbinger, I'm on Calamity. Permission to engage?"

Andi smiled through her fear. "Granted."

The channel fell silent, and then it was just the captain and her pilot, hearts racing in their throats, stars streaking past them like rips in the fabric of the universe.

And then Andi felt it.

The lurch.

The *bump*.

A knife of rage sliced through her. "Those bastards just shot at my ship."

"Test fire?" Lira asked, but then she cursed, and suddenly they were spiraling to dodge blasts as the sensors screamed warnings. "On second thought…"

Andi gritted her teeth. Too many shots.

"Cap, they're turning up the heat."

This time the voice was Gilly's. In the background, Andi could hear the familiar *tick, tick, tick* of Gilly's gun firing from down below, the *BOOM* of Breck's right after, one shot after another at the oncoming ships. "They're closing in, starboard side."

"Faster, Lira," Andi growled.

She pulled up the radar and zoomed in on the other two blinking red dots, ignoring the shaking in her hands. They were growing ever closer, and now the *Marauder*'s prox alarms were blaring. What in the blazes were they using to run their ships?

*Tick, tick, tick.*

*BOOM.*

Shots blasted, piercing whines that shook Andi down to her bones.

It was all she could hear, all she could *feel*, louder and louder with each blast that sent the *Marauder* careening off course. She switched to the ship's rear-cam again.

The three ships were directly behind them now. Two sleek

black triangles with massive guns on their hulls, the other crisp and purple with smoke stains from Breck's magnetic ammo, birdlike in its wingspan, with enough space to swallow Andi's ship twice over.

The Tracker.

Her brain screamed stats about it—designed for speed rather than agility. She'd spent months studying the ship at the Academy, desperate to explore every inch of its well-designed insides. Even the best tech had its flaws, and if they weren't also being chased by the two Explorers, they might've stood a chance against the Tracker. But truth be told, smaller ammunition wouldn't be able to affect the reinforced siding. And with its dodging tech, they'd have one hell of a time hitting the beast with the Big Bang.

"Take them down!" Andi commanded. "Go *faster*, Lira." She clenched the armrests, leaning forward as if her body could help her ship pick up speed.

"I'm trying," Lira said. "We haven't refueled in weeks, Andi. At this rate, we'll burn out. We'll have to lose them instead of outrun them."

"But without the cloaking system, we're flying loose as a…"

Lira stopped her with a sly grin. "I wasn't talking about cloaking."

She straightened the ship and gave the engines a final push. The ships behind them fell back as the darkness around them heightened, like something monstrous was blotting out the stars.

It was then that Memory, the *Marauder*'s mapping system, came on, a cool female voice that usually guided their path, a comfort in the void of space. But today, Memory's words filled Andi with a cold, trembling dread.

*Now approaching Gollanta.*

"Starshine, Lir," Andi said, the darkness approaching more quickly now. She remembered the last time they'd come through Gollanta—they almost became space junk that day. They'd tried to avoid the area ever since. "You can't be serious."

Lir raised a bare brow. "Have you no faith, Captain?"

It was death behind bars or death by the sweet black sky.

Andi loosed a breath and ran her fingers through the ends of her purple-and-white braid. It had been months since they'd made a good purse, and their stores were depleted. If they were going to escape, things would have to get a little dirty before the Marauders got away clean.

"Not at present," Andi said.

"You always did know how to make a girl blush." Lira grinned, her sharp canines flashing in the red lights of the prox alarm. "You should see the last ship I piloted."

"Just do it...before I change my mind." Andi tightened her harness, silenced the prox alarms and settled back as Lira navigated the *Marauder* toward the Gollanta Asteroid Belt. It was a massive expanse full of thousands of giant space rocks, tumbling endlessly, just waiting for a target to obliterate.

The Graveyard of the Galaxy.

The place where ships went to die.

The *Marauder* hurtled past an asteroid double its size, an ugly thing full of deep impact holes. Beside it, spinning slowly on its side, was a hunk of burned and blackened metal that looked like the hull of an old Rambler.

"Lir?" Andi asked. "What was it that happened to your last ship?"

Lira grimaced and popped another wad of Moon Chew. "We may have just passed it."

"Godstars guide us," Andi prayed. She glanced up. "Memory? Some accompaniment, please, as Lira tries not to fly us to our deaths."

A moment later, music flooded the bridge. Strings and keys and the swelling feeling of peace, control and calm.

"I will never understand how you can listen to this stuff," Lira muttered.

Andi closed her eyes as Lira gunned the engine and they slipped into the tumbling black abyss.

# CHAPTER 3
## KLAREN
## YEAR TWELVE

*THE GIRL WAS BORN TO DIE.*

*In darkness she stood with her palms pressed to the cold glass of her tower. She was alone, protected as all of the Yielded were, staring out at the Conduit below. Swirls of black and silver and blue. An endless, starlit sea.*

*Each morning, she found herself here before the sun rose, imagining what it would feel like to touch the abyss. To feel the freedom of a single day where she could make her own choices, choose her own steps, one delicate moment at a time.*

*Her palms slid from the glass.*

*It was a gift, this body. A way to change her world, and the others beyond.*

*As the girl stood there, she thought of her dreams. Nameless faces, uncertain futures, deaths she couldn't stop, births she had predicted before the dawning of their times.*

*The Yielded were special.*

*The Yielded were loved.*

*Outside, the darkness shifted. The girl gasped and pressed her hands back to the glass, heart racing as she waited.*

*It began slowly. A flicker on the dark horizon, far beyond the swirling Conduit. A flame, fighting for life. Then it sprung forth, veins of crimson light stretching into the sky, spreading to yellow, orange, pink the color of laughing cheeks.*

*The girl smiled.*

*It was a new act. Something she'd only just begun to discover how to do.*

*She loved the way it made people listen to her. Loved the way it made their minds seem to bow in her midst.*

*If her dreams were true, then someday she would use this smile for greatness. For glory. For the hope of her people.*

*Today she stood watching, far above the Conduit, as the red sun rose.*

# CHAPTER 4
## DEX

THEY FLEW LIKE DEMONS SPRUNG FROM A PIT of fire.

Whoever the pilot was, she had one hell of a handle on the *Marauder*. Leave it to the Bloody Baroness to get the best of the best. Memories of their history together tried to spring their way forward, but he quickly suppressed them, knowing such thoughts and feelings would only stand in the way of his big payday. This was a job, not a social call.

"Androma Racella." Dex tested her name on his tongue. "I've been searching for you for quite some time."

Two months, to be exact. The longest Dex had *ever* spent trying to capture someone on the run. He'd been to countless planets in search of her and gotten lost for two weeks inside the Dyllutos Nebula before eventually picking up a blood trail that stretched from one end of Mirabel to the next.

Now he sat on the bridge of an Arcardian Tracker ship, the flashes of fired shots illuminating his face.

*Also leave it to the Bloody Baroness to force me to work with the Arcardian Patrolmen,* Dex thought as he stared at her image on the holo before him.

In his hands sat a document that included all the information about the *Marauder*'s captain, including a snapshot of her face. The photograph had been taken by Dex himself when he'd *almost* caught up to Androma on TZ-5 last week. Unfortunately, she'd disappeared before he could reach her.

She was standing in the shadows of a pleasure palace, a cyborg dancing in the window behind her. Androma's pale, ghostlike hair was now streaked with purple and peeked out from beneath a black hood pulled low over her face. He could just barely make out her gray eyes and the smooth metallic plates on her cheekbones, a defensive body mod she'd had done years before. But he could certainly see the rest of her: perfect curves beneath a sleek, skintight leather bodysuit, the hilt of a knife sticking out from her black boots. And, of course, outside the hooded cape, her trademark glowing swords were strapped across her back like an X of death.

The ship rumbled from a weapon blast, and the screen flew from Dex's fingertips, the holo winking out.

"Blazing hell!" he cursed as the ground seemed to fall out from underneath him, then shifted sideways until he was practically dangling from his harness. "Settle her!" he shouted to the pilot.

His borrowed crew scrambled to control the ship as Dex clutched the armrests, gritting his teeth. A little mechanic droid wrapped its hooked arms around Dex's ankle, squealing as it tried in vain to stay in one place.

Dex growled and shook it away. What good was being the captain when you couldn't get your crew to do anything worthwhile? And he didn't even want to *think* about the Tracker they were flying. Dex swallowed his revulsion.

*Here I am*, the ship seemed to say. *Large and in charge and as undercover as a Xen Pterran carriage slug.*

They'd never catch the *Marauder*. Not like this.

The Tracker was fast, but the "seasoned pilot" General Cortas had provided for this mission had no style. A starship was meant to fly weightless, limitless and free.

Just like the one they were pursuing now, its belly full of lying, cheating lady thieves.

He stared out the viewport, past the laughable pilot and co-pilot, their heads pressed together as they tried in vain to discover a way to outsmart their prey.

The *Marauder.*

Dex could see her tail up ahead. Each blast of gunfire illuminated her outline.

A sleek, beautiful beast that looked to be made of the stars in which it swam. Deadly and delicious, all varillium glass in the shape of an arrowhead, now concealed by metal shields to protect it during the chase. The Aero Class ship was one of a kind.

He'd catch that damned ship and finally reclaim it for his own. And when he captured Androma, he'd bring her to her knees, get her to agree to his employer's terms...

"Sir." A trembling voice pulled Dex from his thoughts. He looked up at the youngest Patrolman on the ship, a boy no older than fifteen with slitted reptilian nostrils. A boy who'd never seen battle. Who didn't know the feeling of blood on scarred hands. His glowing yellow eyes were wide as he spoke. "They're making an interesting move."

"What move?" Dex sighed. "Use your words."

"It seems they're charting a course for the asteroid belt."

"As I said they would," Dex snapped.

"What should we do?" the boy asked timidly as he took a step back, sensing Dex's imminent explosion of outrage.

The ship rumbled.

The pilot cursed.

Dex pressed a palm to the bridge of his nose. *"You,"* he said, glaring at the youngling between his fingers, "will do yourself a favor and go to the passenger bay so you can crap your pants in private. I can smell your fear from here."

The boy tripped over his own webbed feet as he raced from Dex's view.

"The rest of you," Dex said, unbuckling his harness and standing up from his seat, voice rising to a roar, "will *catch me that damned ship!*"

The glory of his rage was lost in another explosion.

This time, it was so bright and so loud that it lit up the skies. A lurch resonated all around him as the ship went sideways. The little mech droid tumbled past.

"Engine one has been hit!" the pilot yelped.

A lucky shot.

Dex's temper rose as he unclasped his harness and toppled against the metal siding. This job was the answer. It was *everything*. It could make or break his career.

And if Dex lost this opportunity now, when his prey was so close, General Cortas would have someone pulverize him when they docked back at Averia—and then Dex would be sipping from a straw for the rest of his life.

Enough was enough.

Dex raced forward, boots clacking on the grated floor.

The pilot looked up as Dex hovered over him, leather gloves squealing with each shift of the wheel.

"Move," he commanded.

"Sir, I am under direct orders from General Cortas to…"

Dex squeezed his fists. The pilot flinched back as four crimson triangular blades sprung out of each of Dex's gloves, just over his knuckles. "Move over."

The pilot stumbled as he leaped from his chair.

Dex took the throttle, his bladed knuckles shining as another streak of gunfire shot past. He could hear a commotion in the background, the sound of the pilot's whining voice as he commed the general. Pathetic tattletale. Dex blocked it all out as he tapped on the screen, losing himself in the motions he'd grown so used to.

This was where he belonged, in the pilot's chair. Behind the throttle of his own ship.

The copilot, a man covered in purple spikes, stared at Dex openmouthed. "You were right," he said, his massive canines visible. "They're heading for Gollanta."

*Of course I'm right*, Dex wanted to say. *Androma always runs until she finds a place to hide.*

Through the viewport, Dex caught a perfect, shining glimpse of the *Marauder*, its jagged, dagger-like shape heading right into the mouth of hell.

"Alert the fleet near Solera," Dex said as he angled the Tracker to follow them. Solera was the closest planet, just on the outskirts of the asteroid belt. They could make it in time to intercept the *Marauder* if they sent their fastest ships.

"Alert them of what, sir?" the copilot asked.

Dex sighed. "They need to meet us in the center of the belt. Cloaked." If he was wrong, well, he was already under the general's control. He may as well use it to his advantage. "Tell them the *Marauder* is heading their way."

Dex closed his eyes and allowed himself to *hope*. Then he begged the Godstars that his last-minute plan would fall into place.

Androma was good at what she did. But so was Dex.

And a protégée could only outrun her master for so long.

# CHAPTER 5
## ANDROMA

*GOLLANTA.*

A world of space rocks dancing around them with death knocking at every viewport.

Andi stared out at them, her eyes wide and bright against the dimness of space. Darkness surrounded them, lit only by the faint shine of Tavina's distant stars. And, of course, the telltale flashes of the three ships still trailing them.

She'd make them regret coming after the Bloody Baroness. It was time to end this.

Andi turned on her com. "Breck, Gilly." The permanent lens in her eye, activated by a light tap to her temple, allowed her to patch into another crew member's visual feed.

They'd installed them months ago, and the blessed coms had saved their skins several times over. They were well worth the expensive visit to the shady doctor on the satellite city near Solera.

She patched into Breck's com first, revealing the gunner's targeting screen, the glowing crosshairs focused on the nearest ship's wing. Andi clenched her teeth as an asteroid resembling a skull came hurtling toward Breck's viewport. Breck took a shot, and it exploded into space dust.

Andi blinked, shutting off the eye connection and returning to her own view of the asteroids. Lira sat beside her, the scales on her arms flashing as she tried to keep her nerves under control. Music still filled the space, calming Andi, allowing her to concentrate.

*This is just another day*, she told herself. *Just another chase.*

"We're low on fuel, low on ammo," Gilly yelped into the com.

"Shoot the small stuff and wait for my command," Andi said. "Then we'll use the Big Bang and turn their bones to dust." The weapon sent out a pulse, crippling an enemy ship's defensive systems, followed by an explosive that could obliterate an entire ship with one shot.

It wouldn't be able to hurt the Tracker, but the other ships would be perfect prey, if Gilly and Breck played their cards right. They only had one Big Bang left on board, so they'd have to make it count.

Gilly answered with a giggle sharp as a knife. "Done."

*Tick, tick, tick.*

*BOOM.*

An old spacesuit floated past the window to her right. Andi wondered if a corpse was still inside and shivered slightly.

Death was Andi's closest friend, a little demon that whispered in her ear on dark nights. And here in this wasteland, a graveyard where many had met their demise, death felt closer than ever.

"We need to single out the Explorers," Andi said. She'd never flown one herself, but she'd seen plenty of demonstrations at the Academy. They were designed for agility and speed, which meant they were somewhat lacking in armor.

"I'm on it," Lira answered.

The Tracker was a beast as it followed. The smaller asteroids bounced off its sides, barely scraping the reinforced material. The Explorer ships followed behind, protected from the brunt of the asteroid attacks.

The girls had to separate them, get the Explorers alone in the sky.

A massive, hulking rock appeared ahead of them, easily the biggest asteroid they had seen so far.

"Lira," Andi said, a plan brewing in her mind as she pointed at the asteroid, "circle us around that thing."

"Circling will slow us down." Lira cocked her head, orange light dancing across her face as Solera's distant sun came into view.

Andi gritted her teeth. "Do it, Lira."

Lira nodded, clenched the throttle and sent the *Marauder* careening right around the massive asteroid.

The *Marauder* swung in a great arc, the music rising in volume as cymbals crashed. In the rear-cam, the ships pursued, flashes of silver and black, shadows that just wouldn't quit. But as they angled farther and farther around the outer edge of the asteroid, the Tracker ship slowed too much and pulled out of the race.

Now it was just the Explorers and the *Marauder*, odds Andi knew her crew and her ship could handle.

"Wait for it…" she whispered, her breath hitching in her throat. In the rear-cam, the Explorers followed like streaks of light, their guns firing as they tried in vain to catch up to the *Marauder*. What was their plan? Even if the two Explorers caught them and tried to dock, ships that small wouldn't be able to haul the *Marauder* across the skies.

A flash darted behind them, a short distance away.

"They're getting closer!" Breck shouted in the com. "Ready for the command!"

Andi bit her tongue, the metallic tang of blood strong enough to keep her fear at bay.

Out of the corner of her eye she saw another flash, closer now.

Prox alarms blared in her ear. The music was too loud, the whine of the strings too piercing.

"Incoming!" Breck shouted. "They're almost on us!"

"Anytime, Cap!" Gilly yelped.

Close.

Closer.

"One more second," Andi whispered.

"Andi, we should shoot." Lira's blue eyes looked black in the shadows.

Andi hissed in a breath.

"Now?" Gilly asked.

Andi could imagine her, tiny and fire-headed, seated in her gunner's chair several decks below, the whole crew's fate at her fingertips.

"Now," Andi commanded.

A breath of a second. Andi stared at the Explorer ships on the rear-cam, thinking of the men and women inside. Knowing that here and now, they were facing their final moments. She felt a flash of pity for them, the pang of regret Andi always felt before she took a life.

Then came the hiss of Gilly's *Big Bang* sliding loose from its chamber, a death rocket that Andi knew would fly true.

She watched as it struck the Explorer on the left first, the blast taking out both ships. The explosion was a work of art. Two ships in one shot, bits of metal and blood and bodies. Carnage stained the skies.

The *Marauder* whined as the blast knocked it off course, as if the dying ships had laid bleeding hands on them and *shoved*.

Then there was a strange, still silence. Even the song had stopped playing.

"Explorers are down," Breck said. "Nice one, Gil."

Andi loosed a breath, her fingertips releasing their hold on the armrests. But it wasn't over yet. She glanced sideways at Lira. "Take us to the center of the belt. Bigger asteroids."

Lira caught on. "We can lose them there and fly out the backside, hide somewhere on Solera."

"Fuel?"

Lira spat a wad of Chew into her mug. "Low. But we can make it. We just lost a lot of weight from that ammo."

Andi felt the swell of victory like a star exploding in her chest. But beside it, eating away at the feeling of triumph, was the knowledge of what she'd just done. How many lives had she stolen? How many families back on Arcardius would don shades of gray in mourning for weeks to come?

She loosened her harness, allowing herself to breathe a little deeper, and was just leaning back against the headrest when Lira cursed.

Breck's and Gilly's voices shouted into the com, and somewhere, down in the pit of Andi's dark soul, she knew she'd missed something.

"There are more of them," Lira said breathlessly. "Andi, they're *everywhere*. It's not possible. Where did they come from?"

Andi's heart rocketed into her throat as the bleating prox alarms went off again.

Seven ships waited for them, uncloaking themselves, materializing before her eyes.

"Turn around, Lira! Get us the hell out of here!"

"I can't!" Lira shouted. "The Tracker is still behind us."

She furiously typed in codes, her fingers flying across the screen. Then Lira yelped as the holo sparked, and a strange hiss fizzled out of the dash. The ship itself seemed to release a deep, rumbling sigh.

And then…darkness.

The only light came from Lira's scales, glowing a bluish-purple in the dark.

*Oh, Godstars.*

*No.*

They'd been hit by an EMP. Andi watched as Lira tried to repower the ship with the backup system but to no avail.

Everything went still and silent, as if the *Marauder* itself had lost all life.

"They shut us down," Lira whispered, her features turning to stone. Smoke streamed from her scales, but even *they* had gone dark now. As if shock had paralyzed her emotions. Her voice cracked as she tried to bring the dash back to life, tried to restart the emergency engines. "Oh, Andi. They shut *everything* down."

Andi shook her head. "That's not possible. We have shields against that, nothing could… No one knows how to get past them and stop this ship!" Andi had the special defensive shields installed shortly after taking possession of the *Marauder*. They were meant to prevent EMPs and other such attacks from affecting the ship's internal systems.

Lira's blue eyes were haunted, her fingers still as stone on the throttle. "*He* could, Andi."

Andi's heart turned to ice.

It wasn't possible.

He was supposed to be *dead*, cast away into some deep, dark hell where he'd never be able to claw his way back out.

This wasn't happening. This *couldn't* be happening. She leaped to her feet, tuning into the crew's audio channels. "Escape pods. Now. Move."

Andi grabbed her swords from the back of her captain's chair, where she stowed them during flight, and strapped the harness around her back, clicking it into place.

Lira sat frozen in her chair.

"Lira! I said *move*!"

Lira's voice was as dead as the *Marauder*. "We can't leave, Andi. When the ship goes dark, the pods go dark, too."

Footsteps rang out, boots clacking on metal. Breck and Gilly appeared in the doorway.

"What do we do?" Breck asked. "They'll kill us all."

"Not if we kill them first," Andi hissed.

"We could hide," Breck suggested.

"*We* don't *hide*," Lira said hotly.

Andi felt torn in two. This was her crew, broken and battered though it was, criminals from all sides of the galaxy waiting for her to save them. But with a dead ship, what could she do?

"I don't want to be taken again," Gilly whispered. Gone was the bloodthirsty little fairy. In its place was a frightened young girl. She burst into tears, fat droplets splashing on the dead metal at their feet. Breck dropped to her knees and pulled Gilly forward into a crushing hug.

She whispered soothing words, but Andi didn't hear them. She wasn't listening.

She turned and looked out the viewport at the waiting ships. So many of them—Solerans, by their sigil. And then, all around her, a rumble. It seemed to shake the very bones of the ship, rattling the walls. A deep, dark sound that made Lira drop her hands from the throttle and rush to Andi's side.

"They're pulling us in," Lira whispered. "If you have a plan, Andi, you'd better tell us now."

But there was no plan.

For the first time in her pirating life, someone had bested her.

*It's not him*, Andi's mind whispered. *It can't be him.*

And yet the *Marauder* was a corpse. It was already growing cold on the bridge, Andi's breath appearing before her in tiny white clouds.

*Do something*, her mind screamed. *Get us out of this. You can't be captured, Andi, you can never go back.*

Fear spiked through her, in and around, threatening to freeze her, just like the ship.

But she was the Bloody Baroness. She was the captain of the

*Marauder*, the greatest starship in Mirabel, and she had a crew waiting on her word.

So Andi settled her nerves, shoved them down deep. She turned, unsheathed her swords and held them at her sides.

"Stand up," Andi said to Breck and Gilly.

They stood, Gilly wiping tears from her small face, Breck keeping a hand squeezed on the younger gunner's shoulder.

"Weapons," Andi said.

The girls lined up side by side, Andi with her swords, Gilly with her gun. Breck unveiled a black short-whip that crackled with light. Lira stood with her fists clenched, appearing weaponless to those who did not know the ways her body could move, lithe as a predator on the hunt. Her scales flashed as she glared at the bridge's exit.

They waited, determination the only thing keeping them on their feet. On the deck below, the main door of the *Marauder* opened.

Andi heard the echo of heavy footsteps moving through the narrow halls, climbing up the stairwells. A faint male voice mingled with the footsteps, whispering a command as they drew closer.

Andi saw the first man's head as he came around the corner. Others followed close behind, soldiers filling the hallway that led to the bridge, all clad in blue Arcardian bodysuits, the white three-triangle badge of the Mirabel Patrolmen on their chests. They held silver rifles against their stomachs and satisfied grins on their faces.

Andi was all too familiar with those rifles and the small electric orbs they released. One shot would paralyze its victim, rendering them helpless against capture by the Patrolmen.

"Hello, boys," Andi said.

Arcardian or not, she'd see the badges of those who wouldn't back down stained with blood. It was her crew or her past and— her soul be damned—she would *always* choose her crew.

"We can do this the easy way or the hard way," the soldier in front said, his voice calm and cool, as if he were making pleasant conversation.

"Ah," Andi laughed. "But see, you just interfered with my ship. I don't take too kindly to that."

Her attention was pulled away from the man in front of her by the sound of boots tapping against metal. The Patrolmen turned sharply to attention as their commander approached.

*This* was the man who'd bested her.

*This* was the man she'd have to kill today.

As he approached, Andi's chest tightened at the sight of him, tall and muscular and perfectly honed for fighting.

*It's him*, said a small, frightened voice in her mind.

Then, as if confirming her suspicions, *he* stepped out of the darkness, like a demon emerging from hell.

The purest shock spiked in Andi's veins. Then it melted into fury.

*"You,"* she growled.

"Me," Dex said with a shrug.

"You're supposed to be dead," Andi whispered. "I left you..."

"Left me to die?" Dex lifted a brow.

She remembered every inch of the angular white constellation tattoos twisting their way across his brown skin, the feel of his strong hands on her body. The memory of him, the *pain* of her shattered heart. It all twisted into boiling rage as she stared at him, alive and *free*, on *her* ship.

Andi's swords crackled, purple light arcing around the fierce blades. Beside her, the rest of the Marauders tensed and readied themselves for a fight.

"I'm going to kill you," Andi whispered.

"You can try," Dex said, shrugging, his once-captivating brown eyes sparkling with laughter. "But we both know how that will turn out."

She screamed and charged straight at him, not giving a damn if there were twenty or even a hundred heavily armed Arcardian soldiers blocking her path.

She was going to drown Dex Arez in his own blood.

# CHAPTER 6
## DEX

IT WASN'T EXACTLY THE REUNION DEX HAD hoped for.

It's not like he'd imagined Androma running into his arms and kissing him with the passion of lovers parted for years. Their last moments together hadn't exactly gone well, what with the whole "Andi soaring away with Dex's ship, leaving him bleeding and dying on a barren moon" thing.

Then again, he *had* sold her out to the Patrolmen for her crimes, knowing she'd be sentenced to death upon returning to her home planet.

Love was all well and good, but money was the true key to Dex's heart.

Still, for what Androma did to him, he should hate her, should want her dead.

But seeing her before him, melting into rage and riot, the smooth metal implants on her cheekbones reflecting the electricity that swam around her swords...

Godstars, she was magnificent; a creature who had released her wrath on the world. It would be worth every drop of blood about to be shed to be the one who finally brought her to the general's feet.

But as her blades crackled in the too-quiet room, and waves of electricity spiraled around them, Dex wondered if he'd made a mistake. He hadn't seen her in years, but he'd heard the rumors. He hadn't known if she truly could wield those weapons with a glory and grace that drew blood and split bones.

But now, as Androma rasped, *"I'm going to kill you,"* and her words sent a slice of regret cutting through Dex's heart, he *knew*.

Gone was the young woman he'd once known, that shivering thing he'd found bruised and broken in the markets of Uulveca.

In her place stood the warrior he'd trained and hardened and turned into something devilishly delicious.

Dex reached for his gun as the Bloody Baroness attacked.

The world slowed, but Andi moved like a flash of light.

She hurtled her way through the first wave of Patrolmen before they could blink, lashing out her swords, removing smoking limbs from bodies as they screamed and succumbed to the trademark agony of the Bloody Baroness.

Her white hair sprung loose from its braid, the dyed purple streaks almost a blur as she whirled and leaped. She knocked her varillium cuffs into faces, drawing bursts of blood, and kicked her legs out, toppling her opponents like stars falling from the sky.

The Patrolmen finally regained their wits and lifted their rifles to shoot.

An unfortunate weapon they'd chosen. For as soon as they

loosed their bullets, the girls dove behind Breck's towering form. The bullets pinged off her skin, flattening and falling to the floor.

Bless her New Vedan blood, her bulletproof skin.

"You're going to have to do better than that, gentlemen," Breck said, hands on her hips, the girls still protected behind her. "What? You've never shot at a New Vedan before?"

"Take them out!" Dex shouted. "Save Androma for me."

His words sent a spike of rage straight through Andi's heart.

He'd threatened her crew. For that, his life—and the lives of the Patrolmen—were now forfeit.

"Forward!" she shouted. Breck moved, and the girls followed behind as bullets continue to barrage her chest, useless.

A ball of white light shot past Andi's shoulder. An enemy was blasted backward, already a corpse as he slammed into the door frame.

"Oh, that was a good shot," Gilly said, giggling and brandishing her double-trigger gun. One trigger killed, one disabled. She blew smoke away from the barrel and grinned as she ducked back behind Breck.

"I want the floor stained with their blood!" Andi yelled to her crew above the chaos.

Gone were her emotions, gone was her heart.

The killing mask of the Baroness slid into place.

Patrolmen dropped around them as the girls attacked, lunging out from behind Breck's body at random. Andi swung her swords, lashing out with a fury she kept locked inside for moments just like this. Years of dancing and training at the Academy had turned her body into a fluid, ferocious thing.

A Patrolman turned his rifle around and swung it at Breck's head.

"Take him!" Andi roared.

Gilly unloaded her gun on the man.

Behind them, Lira flipped, twisted. She was a blur of glowing scaled skin and black bodysuit, fists cracking jaws, legs locking around throats. They moved forward, leaving moaning bodies in their wake, silenced soon after by Gilly's gun and Breck's whip as the fight carried on into the hall.

Still, the remaining Patrolmen fought on.

"Take them all down," Andi commanded her girls as she sliced a Patrolman's hand off at the wrist. Breck scooped up the gun still clutched in the hand before it could hit the floor and fired it. Silver blood exploded against the metal wall beyond. "But remember, Dex is *mine*."

He was standing there, beyond the wave of his fighting men, staring at her as she came out from behind Breck's protection.

A Patrolman shot.

Andi lifted her arms. The bullet slammed against her varillium cuffs before it could lodge itself into her throat.

"Take care of him," she said as the bullet clattered to the floor. Breck was suddenly beside her, twisting the man's neck with a glorious *pop*. Music to Andi's ears.

Now there were only three men between Andi and her enemy.

They stood at the ready, guns out, a solid line in front of Dex.

She could see his shadowed outline leaning up against the metal wall of the hallway beyond, his stance so cool and casual it made her want to tear his eyes out.

"What's wrong, Dex? You don't want to come out and play with me?" Andi said, her voice a dangerous purr.

Dex chuckled, his mahogany hair falling across one brown eye as he stepped forth to meet her gaze. "You were always one for theatrics, Androma. My little bitter ballerina."

"I am not—and never will be—*yours*."

"We'll see about that."

"These three can live," she said, nodding her head at the final Patrolmen. "It's you I want a fight with, Dextro."

She saw his brow furrow at the use of his full name. Definitely not a name one would associate with a Tenebran Guardian, let alone with the most notorious bounty hunter in Mirabel.

"Is that mercy I hear?" Dex smiled as he walked backward, stopping at the silver ladder that led to the deck below. His fingers curled over the railing, his boots poised over the hole in the floor. "Surely not from the Bloody Baroness."

"Don't pretend you know me," Andi retorted. "Though they did invade my ship, and since they insist on protecting you…"

With a crackle of her swords, she lunged forward and cut off three heads in one scissoring slice. The bodies sagged, then landed in a heap at Andi's feet. The familiar scent of singed flesh wafted up to her nose. And with it, a stab of regret that she buried deep.

Dex blinked once, his only reaction thus far, and Andi's blood *raged* at his air of nonchalance. "They were a terrible crew," he said.

Then he slipped down the ladder. Andi, after holstering one blade, charged after him, not even bothering to use the footholds as she slid down. She landed with a slight thud before turning toward the long corridor behind her.

"Andi, Andi," Dex said. "So predictable."

She froze.

*Your running is over*, a little devil in her mind hissed.

In front of her was another cluster of Arcardian guards, guns trained on her. At the head of them was Dex, a smug grin plastered across his face.

She'd walked right into his trap for the second time today.

Dex would have patted himself on the back, if not for the crowd of Patrolmen around him.

"Are you ready to talk, or do you want to kill a few more of my men?" he asked, knowing Andi had no choice but to obey. She was vastly outnumbered, no matter how skilled she was with those swords. Not unless she wanted to be shot by hundreds of paralyzing light bullets before she could take a single step.

The look she gave him would've made a lesser man cringe, but he stared straight into those light gray eyes, meeting her challenge head-on.

She said nothing. Instead, she holstered her remaining blade and crossed her arms over her black suit, the glowing cuffs on her forearms catching his eye. He'd paid for those varillium cuffs himself, a gift that had saved her life ten times over. They were unbreakable, just like her swords. But the cuffs weren't just an accessory. They held together the burned flesh on her wrists from an accident long ago. She didn't have the privilege of seeing a doctor at the time, so her skin had become damaged beyond repair.

Without Dex's gift, she wouldn't have the full function of her wrists and forearms—likely wouldn't have the strength to lift those swords she was so fond of.

It gave him a sick kind of pleasure to know she still had the cuffs, a reminder of his kindness to her when she was at her weakest. A part of him she could never shed from herself.

Dex turned to the blue-uniformed guard standing closest to her.

"Take her weapons." The burly, horned man looked like he would rather jump out the airlock. "Now," Dex said more sharply, and the guard rushed to action.

Andi spat in the man's face as he pulled her swords out of their harness and the gun out of her thigh holster.

"You're going to regret this," Andi said, her voice low and menacing.

He glared at her with red-and-white striped eyes. "I'm not so sure that I will."

She looked up behind her to where the rest of the Marauders were grouped at the top of the ladder.

"If they move, my guards will shoot." Dex waved a hand,

and half the men angled their light rifles upward toward Andi's motionless crew.

The pilot from Adhira, the giantess beside her. And the red-headed child, glaring down at Dex with all the cold calculation of a seasoned killer.

He wouldn't show mercy toward them if they continued to fight, and he knew Andi sensed that. She looked up at her crew and said, "Stand down. Do what he says."

"We can take them, Andi, they're not—" Lira started.

"That's enough, Lira," Andi growled. "It's over." He knew she hated to say those words.

Dex clapped his hands.

"Now *that* is the drama I've been waiting for." Satisfied, he turned toward two guards with badges adorning their uniforms. It took a hell of a lot of work to attain Arcardian officer status, and yet here these two were, bowing their heads to Dex's every command. "Officer Hurley, your squad will guard the crew. Officer Fraser, follow me and bring your men to guard *Captain* Racella."

They made their way down the long metal corridor. The blue light from Andi's cuffs bounced along the hallway. Four guards surrounded Andi like a box, while the other two were positioned on each end of the line.

Six men, plus Dex, would be enough. She wouldn't fight while her crew was in danger. As they walked, Dex's memories took over, his body moving on instinct through the familiar halls of the ship. They passed several doors before stopping at the glass door that led to the meeting room. Dex placed his hand on the scanner next to the door, but it remained as dead as the rest of the ship.

Andi grinned smugly. Dex smiled back, lifted his gun and shot the glass.

A growl rumbled up through her chest, but Dex simply shrugged and said, "I can replace it. The *Marauder* is mine again."

Then he stepped over the shattered glass and into the room. "Set up the Box." He stepped aside as the guards brought in a thin silver box no longer than his forearm. The symbol of Arcardius, an exploding star, was engraved on the side. They set the Box on the table and lined up against the back wall of the room, hauling Andi with them.

"Please, do take a seat," Dex said to Andi, sweeping his arm out in a grand gesture. "I am nothing if not a good host."

Disgust flashed in her eyes. She did not sit. Instead, she stood with her back up against the wall, her gray eyes roving left and right.

Dex *had* taught her well.

"Suit yourself," he said, walking to the opposite side of the conference table, where he plopped down into a chair.

The tension in the room was a living beast. Dex could practically feel it breathing down his neck. So he leaned back in his chair, propped his boots up on the glass table next to the Box and focused all his attention on Andi.

She glared at him, cold as the metal wall she leaned against. "What the hell do you want?"

Oh, this was good. Better than good. It was the best damned thing Dex had experienced in *years*.

For four years, Andi had been on the run from the fate that awaited her on Arcardius. High-ranking, war-hardened soldiers had been sent to track her down. Other criminals, capable of slinking through the shadows, had tried to find her. Even the general himself, and his personal Spectre guards, had gone out looking a time or two. But after every effort, every Krev spent to discover the fugitive, *Dex* had been the one to catch her.

Fate was a beautiful thing.

"Just a moment now," he said, relishing this time, the feel of Andi's eyes boring into his. "We have another guest joining us before we start."

Dex waited for her onslaught of questions and was surprised when none came.

She simply stood there, hands balled into fists at her sides, stabbing at him with her cold, unfeeling stare.

"Relax, Andi," Dex drawled. "You used to love spending time alone with me."

He knew they were anything but alone, with four guards stationed around the room and two just outside the shattered door, but it felt as if they were. Just like that fateful day on the fire moon.

"You don't know anything about what I used to love," Andi said.

She narrowed her eyes, and he waited for her to serenade him with the list of colorful words she loved using—some that Dex had taught her himself—when the Box suddenly chimed. A funnel of light shone out of its side onto the blank wall at the front of the room.

This pulled their attention away from each other and toward the man whose face appeared across from them on the wall.

Andi went rigid.

For the first time today, despite everything Dex had thrown at her, she actually looked stricken. Shocked. *Pained.*

"Hello, Androma," the man on the screen said. "I've been searching for you for a very, very long time."

Dex smiled. *This* was worth more than all the Krevs in the galaxy.

# CHAPTER 7
## ANDROMA

"GENERAL CORTAS," ANDI GASPED.

She practically fell into a chair, her legs going weak beneath her.

The general's face had haunted Andi for the past four years, sworn to destroy her in every dream—sometimes in her waking moments, too.

She was at a loss for words.

The last time she'd laid eyes on General Cyprian Cortas, she'd been a desperate girl in chains, seated alone at the trial where she was convicted for the death of his daughter.

*Kalee.*

All the tallies on her swords combined couldn't cover up the pain of that first death.

Guilt brewed in her gut, and Andi was sucked back into her memories, back to that fateful night on Arcardius.

*Wind in her hair, the kiss of freedom coating her skin as she sprinted through the hallways, Kalee beside her.*

*Laughter bubbling between them as they snuck onto the general's personal transport ship.*

*The click of Kalee's harness, buckled tight in the copilot's seat, and Andi's nervous laughter again as she looked at her charge, the girl she was sworn to protect.*

*"Are you sure about this?" Andi asked, her fingers curled over the throttle.*

*Kalee lifted a pale brow, a smile tugging at her lips. "As my best friend and personal Spectre, I command you to do this, Androma."*

*The engine purred as Andi started it up. A feeling of excitement coursed through her at the sound.*

*Kalee smiled. "For once in your life, have some real fun."*

"I have to admit, you've looked better," General Cortas said, yanking Andi back into the present, leaving her breathless beneath the man's stare. The burn scars on her wrists ached beneath her cuffs.

*Stars above.*

All these years, she'd tried to suppress the memories, only to have them brought back with a sudden cruelty as sharp as a whip. The man in front of her was a victim of her foolishness. Beside her was the man who'd rejected her love.

The two of them, together? It was nearly enough to shatter Andi.

She forced her eyes up at the screen, grateful her crew wasn't here to share this moment. She could feel them now, trying to reach her, but she denied them access each time a request pinged in to her com.

Some things a captain had to face alone.

The general had aged since she last saw him. His once-brown hair was now peppered with gray, and wrinkles creased his sun-worn skin. His body looked tired, though his brilliant blue eyes sparkled with the very same scrutiny he'd always had.

"You're the one behind all of this?" Andi asked, forgetting the formal deference she'd been trained to show this man since birth.

"I'm a very powerful man, Androma."

The general of Arcardius was seated at a silver desk. Behind him, a large window showed a spectacular view. The sight pained her, and yet she couldn't look away.

*Arcardius.*

Waterfalls flowed over a floating gravarock into streams far below. A vast landscape of color stretched as far as the eye could see, dotted with glimmering glass structures that made up the capital city of Veronus. This was the planet she was no longer able to call home. Even from here, she could see the domed glass building in the center—the Academy, where she and thousands of other military students had trained. It was also the place where she'd learned to dance. Where she'd been introduced to the throttle of a ship after she'd chosen piloting as her military training path. It was there, at the Academy, that her greatest dreams were born. She'd been handpicked to become a personal Spectre for the general's daughter, a status most Arcardians only dreamed of achieving.

She'd spent every second by Kalee's side afterward.

Until the crash.

Until her very public death sentence, with millions of hateful eyes watching, deeming her a traitor.

"What do you want from me?" Andi asked now.

For a while, the general said nothing. He worked his stubbled jaw back and forth, as if chewing on a thought he wasn't sure he should share. His chest was peppered with glowing silver and gold beacons, heavy with the weight of the accomplishments and medals he'd acquired during his long reign as the military leader of Arcardius.

*I'd like to kill you, the way you killed my daughter,* Andi imagined him saying.

*I'd like to give you the traitor's death sentence you truly deserve.*

A million possibilities, all of them grim.

And *all* of them well deserved, filling Andi's gut with another layer of guilt. Another bit of heaviness to carry with her to the grave.

But when the general spoke, his words weren't of punishment or death.

"You've been quite busy since we last met." He snapped his fingers, and a cyborg woman shuffled forward from the corner of the room. Her head was bald and smooth, bits of metal interspersed with artificial flesh, similar to Andi's cheekbones. The cyborg held a holoscreen out to the general, which flickered to life in his hands.

"'Blood Stains the Skies above Pazus,'" General Cortas read from the screen. He tilted it ever so slightly, and Andi could make out the telltale red-and-gold title of a news feed. She sunk low in her chair, remembering that story. It had gone viral across Mirabel.

The general sighed before continuing. "Two black market ships were shot down in the sky sixteen months ago, which ended many lives when the debris fell onto a Pazian village. Black market arms dealers paid you a large sum to haul their weapons for them, and when things got a little complicated… you attacked your enemies' ships without thinking twice about what destruction it would cause."

She took complete responsibility for those deaths. She'd never thought the debris would get through the atmosphere in such large pieces, let alone hit one of the few settlements on Pazus.

"You were never caught," General Cortas said, his voice low, "but I knew it was you. That's what you do, Androma. You leave a path of chaos in your wake, and you don't ever look back to see whose lives were ended because of it." His blue eyes flashed at her.

Worlds away, and Andi still withered beneath that icy stare. But she refused to take his bait, to breathe out a word that this man could twist and turn on her in an instant.

The general tapped the screen again, and another headline materialized, this one with a photograph of the *Marauder* in all of its varillium-sided glory. "The Bloody Baroness," General Cortas said, setting down the screen, "is mentioned in thirteen cases since last year, six of those involving numerous deaths. And I have no doubt, Androma, that there are many more cases that went unnoticed. You are one of the most notorious criminals in all of Mirabel." He sighed and shifted in his seat. "Which is why I hired Dextro to find you."

"Then get on with it," Andi said. The words poured out of her, unable to stay locked inside any longer. "Give me the injection, like you really wanted to do all those years ago." It was her mistake that led to Kalee's painful death, and it was only by a twist of fate that Andi escaped joining her charge.

Andi looked back at the general. "If you wish to kill me, go ahead. But let my crew go free. I'll take the blame for our crimes in Mirabel. All of them. If this is about…" She couldn't bring herself to say the name. Her scars ached again at thoughts of the past. "If this is about your daughter…it was an accident, General. A mistake."

"I'm not here to speak of the past," the general snapped. His voice was pained, and he took a deep breath before speaking again. "I'm a powerful man, Androma, but a desperate one."

"Desperate for what?" Andi asked. "To finally see me die?"

General Cortas leaned back, wincing as if in some hidden pain, and folded his hands on top of the silver desk. "I'm not here for revenge," he said.

Andi blinked in surprise. "Then…what is it you want?"

The general sighed. "I'd like to offer you a job."

Andi almost fell out of her chair. "I'm sorry—what?" She didn't know what else to say, or even what to think, so she waited for him to continue.

"It is desperation, Androma, that brings me to this. And believe me," the general said, glancing at Dex, who had been sitting silently with his feet still propped up on the table, "I have exhausted every other option."

Dex winked, and Andi couldn't fathom why General Cortas wanted Dex to be his personal bounty hunter on this job. Probably just to spite her. He was the general of the strongest military planet in Mirabel. Surely he had other operatives.

The general continued. "My son, Valen, went missing two years ago."

"I remember," Andi said with a curt nod. How could she forget?

Valen, Kalee's older brother, with his dark hair and soft hazel eyes. He had always been kind, but he'd never spoken more than a few fleeting words to Andi each time she visited Kalee's floating estate on Arcardius.

Except for *that* night.

He'd seen them sneaking out and tried to stop them, only for Kalee to put him in his place as they slipped out the door of the sprawling Cortas estate. That was the last time Andi ever saw him—he hadn't shown up to court when she was on trial for Kalee's death.

Two years later, Valen Cortas disappeared in the night, all traces of him whisked away. Though there was no sign of a struggle, General Cortas swore it was a kidnapping, carried out by a skilled group trained to leave no trace behind.

The news had spread like wildfire across Arcardius, and then into the skies to the leaders of every other inhabited planet, moon and satellite city in Mirabel.

"We suspected a mercenary from Xen Ptera took him," General Cortas said, "but there haven't been any ransom demands.

No responses to our inquiries. I would've stormed their planet when he was first taken, but we couldn't risk upsetting the peace treaty between our part of the galaxy and theirs. Ten years still remain until the treaty ends."

He paused. Grief made his voice heavy. Two years after losing one child, the other had been snatched from him, too.

Again, the guilt clawed at Andi from inside.

"So what do you want me to do?" she asked carefully. "If I remember correctly, there was never much of a trail to begin with, and surely all traces of him are long gone by now."

The general leaned forward in his chair.

"Two months ago, one of our satellites picked up a signal from Xen Ptera's prison moon, Lunamere. The message was in Arcardian military code, which you no doubt remember from your time serving."

Andi inclined her head. "I remember." So many nights, she had stayed awake inside her quarters in Averia while Kalee was asleep. Glowing screens laid scattered across her desk alongside military manuals and scribbled notes and failed attempts at decoding the strange ancient symbols. She'd always excelled at weapons training, but hadn't taken as much care in honing her mind. But a Spectre was expected to learn *all* things, and learn them well.

"I was teaching the code to Valen before the kidnapping." General Cortas ran a hand through his graying hair. "There has been no word since, but we feel strongly it is Valen. The message was a specific word I gave him to decode just before he was taken."

Andi listened intently. After all this time, most believed Valen Cortas to be dead. There were rumors that he'd run of his own accord and was hiding out on some distant tropical moon, far from his father's clutches and the strict military life of Arcardius. Others suspected he'd been too wounded by his sister's death and simply hid away in the darkness of the estate. The kidnapping, Andi had always suspected, was the real truth.

"Why are you telling me all of this?" she asked.

"Because I want you to recover him."

It was an effort not to let her jaw drop.

"I don't..." Andi fumbled for the right words. "I can't..."

"You *can't*?" The general barked out a laugh. "The Bloody Baroness does whatever she wants. Even stealing a starship in the middle of the night, crashing it into the side of a mountain and slaughtering an innocent girl in the process. One she was sworn to protect."

Andi sucked in a breath.

Her chest felt split in two.

"She was to be my heir," General Cortas whispered. "And you stole her from me. From my wife. From *my people*."

*My people*. They were once Andi's people, too. Her throat was dry as a husk, her heart hammering against it.

But killing Kalee, even by accident, had been an act of treason. There was nothing to say, nothing she could do to take back what she'd done.

So she focused on the present.

"Why me?" Andi asked. "There are a million Patrolmen or soldiers you could offer the job to."

"Not without starting a war," the general said.

It made sense. The Mirabel Patrolmen couldn't just waltz into a Xen Pterran prison and steal a prisoner out from under the guards without violating the terms of the treaty. The agreement was meant to prevent further war between Xen Ptera and the galaxy's other major systems, Prime, Stuna, Tavina and Phelexos. Galactic peace had always required a careful balancing act between each system, and when the Olen System rebelled, it had upset that balance.

The Unified Systems couldn't risk an upset again.

But a pirate, not officially affiliated with any side...

The general tapped his fingers against the desk, drawing Andi's attention back to the screen. "There is, of course, another option."

Andi raised her eyebrows, and General Cortas smiled.

"I could send you and your entire crew to the Pits of Tenebris to serve out a life sentence for the crimes you've committed. Murder, robbery, forgery, arson." He ticked off each word on the tips of his fingers. "Dare I go on? I can bury you all, so dark and so deep that you will never see the sun again."

Andi sucked in a breath. The Pits of Tenebris were where the hardest of criminals were imprisoned, those even worse than Andi. Men and women who took sick pleasure in torturing and killing innocents.

"*Or,*" the general said, "your slate could be wiped clean. If, and only if, you bring my son back to me. *Alive.*"

"Clean?" Andi asked. "You mean…"

General Cortas met her eyes. "I will pardon you for your crimes. Lift your death sentence. You could return to Arcardius, Androma."

*Home*, Andi's mind whispered.

A thousand memories suddenly unlocked, poured into her from the place she'd kept them safely hidden away.

*Her mother, twirling in a circle as a silver gown blossomed around her. Her freshly painted nails shining under the chandelier light as she pressed a soft hand to Andi's cheek and whispered, "My daughter, protecting the general's heir. A true Arcardian dream."*

*Her father, later that night, praising Andi as she blocked his attack. "You've been practicing without me," he said, hands flexing as he lunged forward and she slipped easily past him.*

*Arcardius, full of warmth and laughter and beauty.*

*Arcardius, full of Kalee's screams and blood on Andi's hands, hot and wrong and…*

Andi blocked the memory like a hit, before it could fully form.

For years, she had been a soldier without a home, always on the run, too afraid to slow down for fear that the past would catch up to her. She'd turned herself into a criminal to survive. Set aside her honor in exchange for her life. Now she had a chance to eliminate the past. To find some honest work and stability for her crew.

"That's it?" she asked. She crossed her arms over her chest.

The general nodded. "That's it."

Andi narrowed her eyes. There had to be a catch, some hidden detail that General Cortas wasn't revealing. But she was out of choices. Her crew was somewhere in this very ship, surrounded by armed guards. One wrong move, and she'd have their blood on her hands, too.

She wouldn't be able to come back from that.

"Swear it," Andi said.

The general raised a brow. His lips tightened together.

"Swear it as you once made me swear," Andi continued. "The Arcardian Vow."

For a time, General Cortas simply stared at her. She imagined he was living through the same memory she was. A different time, a very different place, the two of them standing face-to-face inside the Shard—a sharp, crystalline tower that captured the sun and cast it across the room like living fire.

*"I vow my life and my blood to protect Kalee Cortas," Andi said.*

*General Cortas turned to face her, pride blazing in his eyes. She would not let him down.*

The memory faded, and Andi met the general's eyes as he recited the Vow. "I vow my life and my blood to honor the terms of our deal."

Andi crossed her arms, cuffs clinking together.

"When do we leave?"

The general signaled for the cyborg woman again, who glided back to his side and straightened his sleek jacket as he stood. "I want my son back as soon as possible."

"My ship needs repairs," Andi said. "And we'll need supplies. Enough for twice the haul to the Olen System and back, just in case we run into problems." The job wasn't going to take that long, but she might as well get supplies while she could.

"You'll have what you need," General Cortas said with a curt nod.

"I'll also need more ammunition," Andi said, remembering her promise to Lira before this all began. They would need it if they encountered the Olen System's Rover ships. "There's no telling what Queen Nor will throw at us once we gain entry to her system, let alone when we reach Lunamere."

At that, the general smiled and looked not at Andi, but at Dex.

"The bounty hunter will take care of that for you," General Cortas said, his voice dripping with sick satisfaction, "since he'll be joining you on your mission."

# CHAPTER 8
## KLAREN
## YEAR SIXTEEN

*THE GIRL STOOD IN HER TOWER, BATHED IN* darkness.

So many years she'd waited. So many dreams she'd endured.

The girl had grown, eighteen years strong. Tonight, she was a willing, worthy sacrifice, with blood the color of the silver weapon hidden in the folds of her cloak.

She could feel, more than see, the other Yielded around her. A trio of bodies each to her left and to her right as they all watched the Conduit swirl far below.

The girl lifted her chin a little higher. She would not tremble, like the Yielded to her left. She would not boast, like the Yielded to her right.

*Tonight, she would conquer the Yielding.*

*And then she would conquer the world beyond this tower, the wind at her back, the fire of hope igniting inside her veins. From the moment of her birth, the girl had known it would be her path to pave.*

*Her journey to take, through the Conduit.*

*"When will it begin?" one of the others asked. "When will we be chosen?"*

*The girl waited, watching the swirling sea below. It spread as far as she could see, a blanket of black, made thicker by the absence of the moon.*

*She sensed it a moment before it began.*

*"There," one of the Yielded whispered. "It begins."*

*A single blue flame flickered to life in the center of the sea. The color spread, churning, until the Conduit looked like a raging whirlpool of hues. A sea of darkness transformed into sweeping, glittering light.*

*Around her, the Yielded shifted. Breaths released. Hands began to shake. But the girl's heart simply fluttered, as if sensing what was soon to come. She'd already seen it in her dreams.*

*She watched, eyes unblinking, as the Conduit began to stretch, sending floating orbs of its light into the sky.*

*They trailed higher, catching the wind. Dancing like souls released to the stars.*

*Soon, the orbs would shift. Soon, they would choose the one worthy of the journey.*

*The girl was ready, reaching into the folds of her cloak as the orbs began to form a trail in the sky. They rose, higher, higher, like the tail of a blazing star. When they got high enough, they would reach the top of the tower. And then they would choose.*

*The girl's dreams told her it would be her. But she had to be certain. She would not leave the hope of her people up to fate.*

*As the first orbs began to reach the top of the tower, she slid the blade from her cloak. It was silent, not even a hiss as it grazed across the sleek fabric.*

*"The dreams are true," she whispered.*

*Then she went about the room, sliding her blade across Yielded throats.*

*Taking precious lives.*

*It was too easy, just as her dreams had promised. Each year, there would be more Yieldings, more chosen. But she would now be the first.*

*When the girl was done, crumpled bodies silent at her feet, she stepped over them. As she pressed her bloody palms to the glass of the tower, steam swam across it like a cloud.*

*Outside, the orbs from the Conduit had gathered in the sky to form an arrow, lighting her up like a beacon. Revealing her to the thousands of beings gathered far below. She could feel them roar, so loudly the glass trembled, as she was chosen.*

*The Yielding was over.*

*The Conduit had chosen.*

*And only the girl remained.*

# CHAPTER 9

## DEX

"THE HELL I AM!" DEX LEAPED TO HIS FEET.

That old, sagging, sneaking bastard.

"Will that be an issue, Dextro?" The general smiled like a Soleran ice wolf, pale blue eyes crinkling at the corners as he looked to Dex. "You will be joining Androma on her mission to make sure she stays in line and doesn't escape. I've already lost one child to her foolishness. I won't lose another."

Dex cursed inwardly.

He should have known better than to scheme with the general of Arcardius after all that he'd heard about the man—the decorated soldier with the ability to weasel his way into getting what he wanted by twisting words and blackmailing anyone who stood in his way. An ability few witnessed, but many whispered about. General Cyprian Cortas was a walking, talking hypocrite of the Arcardian way of honor.

"We had a *deal*," Dex said through gritted teeth.

"And the deal will still be honored. The terms have simply been…" the general waved a hand, as if dismissing their old agreement "…extended."

"I could kill her," Dex snarled. "And then what would you do to get back your precious son?" He glanced sideways at Andi, who was now on her feet, too, hands balling into fists as if preparing for a fight that Dex wasn't sure he would actually win.

"Ah," Andi said, "but we both know how that would go." She smiled at him mockingly.

Dex felt his own hands curling up, the blades in his gloves begging to slip free and find their mark across her throat.

Instead, Dex turned back to the general.

"She's plenty capable of doing this job on her own. I am not a babysitter." He'd played his part; the job was supposed to be done.

General Cortas raised a graying brow. "Do you want your money or not, bounty hunter?"

So he was going to play it that way. Dex sighed. "You have thousands of men and women at your command. Why not pick one of them to escort her? She'll probably eject me from the ship the moment we get out of range. You know that." It would be an incredibly *Androma* thing to do.

"Then you'd better stay alert," the general suggested.

"Do I get any say in who is coming onto my ship?" Andi said, arms held up in exasperation, cuffs glowing bright.

Dex whirled on her. *"It's not your ship."*

"Finders, keepers, Dextro."

"Enough!" General Cortas barked out. He approached the camera on his side, his face growing large enough on the screen that Dex could see his eyes give a sudden twitch.

"You can go with her, Mr. Arez, and get your money and stay in the government's good graces when the job is done, or you can leave here with nothing. Keep in mind that I am your greatest hope of being reinstated as a Guardian. The choice is yours."

Dex was truly and thoroughly screwed if he rejected this job. Not only would he lose a cargoload of Krevs, but everything he had gone through to get to this moment, when he was so close to regaining his Guardian title that he could almost *taste* it, would all have been for nothing. Not unless he played the general's awful little game and teamed up with the very person who'd gotten his Guardianship stripped from him in the first place.

His guts roiled just thinking of soaring away from here with Androma Racella at his side, on board *his* ship. The very same one that she'd stolen from him three years ago, when she left him bleeding on that moon.

He'd survived. But she'd taken everything he loved.

This time, he was looking forward to taking back his ship and blasting off into space, leaving her behind to watch it go, to feel what he had felt.

He turned, slowly, to look at Andi now.

She seemed frozen. Trapped. And yet he knew, deep in that mind of hers, she was coming up with some sort of plan for revenge against him.

Dex sighed.

This was a battle he'd lost against the general. But there was payment and his reputation on the line, two things he valued more than anything else in this life.

He wouldn't go down without a fight.

He'd caught her, just as he'd set out to do. Now he just had to keep her in his grasp a little longer, until the job was done.

And ensure that she didn't try to kill him. Again.

So Dex Arez, the greatest bounty hunter in the Mirabel Galaxy, stared deep into Andi's moonlit eyes and winked at her as he said, "It'll be just like old times, love."

# CHAPTER 10
## LIRA

THERE WEREN'T MANY THINGS IN THIS GALAXY that Lira Mette hated.

A slow ship, though annoying at first, could always be altered to run faster, if she had the right parts and the right crew.

A wad of expired Moon Chew, though bitter as a cold Soleran night, could still give her just enough of a buzz to lift her spirits during a dull flight.

Even her captain's temper, which was as vicious as an electric whip, could be channeled into something that made the crew of the *Marauder* great. Terrifying enough, even, to make people quake at the mention of their names.

But when it came to Dextro Arez?

Hate wasn't a strong enough word to describe Lira's feelings.

He was a merciless bounty hunter with no honor. A man who had shredded her best friend's heart and left her bound in chains, leading her to escape and take up a life on the run. A bastard who could barely call himself a Tenebran Guardian after everything he'd done. She was glad he'd lost his title and his ship that night.

"That fool will never be a worthy Guardian," Lira muttered under her breath, hatred swimming through her veins.

The sensation threw her off balance.

Hatred was a newer feeling to Lira, something she'd always been taught to extinguish the moment it tried to flicker to life. But now, in this moment, she latched on to it.

There were a lot of things she'd latched on to since leaving her home planet of Adhira.

"I hate him," Lira said, testing the words on her tongue. "I find that I hate him very, very much."

"Newsflash, Lir. We all do," Breck said from her left. And though it was too dark for Lira to see her crewmate, she could imagine the snarl on Breck's face. "We need to escape. We should be down there with Andi, setting her free."

"And how do you propose we do that?" Lira asked.

The words weren't harsh, but rather, inquisitive.

Knowledge, along with peace, was another trait Adhiran citizens were encouraged to pursue above all else. The desire to learn and grow, questioning the world around them at every given moment.

"I think," Gilly said across from them, somewhere in the darkness, "that we should shove Breck down the ladder and let her crush those Patrolmen until all that's left is their awful souls."

"There's a minor problem to that solution, Gil," Breck said. "The cuffs."

The little girl huffed in response. "We've gotten out of cuffs like these before."

"Not with our captain imprisoned below," Lira said.

All three of them were bound in electric cuffs, seated with their backs pressed up against the cold steel walls of the hallway that led to the ship's bridge. Bodies still littered the floor around them from the fight, the smell of death starting to flood the narrow space.

Lira's stomach quivered with equal parts disgust and frustration.

She didn't believe in killing, didn't believe in taking lives senselessly and sending the souls on to their next lives. That was for the Godstars to decide. Killing just wasn't the way of Adhirans—many times growing up, Lira had heard her aunt recite the words that bound her people to a life of love and harmony. *Peace, stretching as deep as the roots of the trees of Aramaeia. As tall as the Mountain of Rhymore.*

But that was then, back on her home planet. This was now.

And life on the *Marauder* was a very, very different sort of thing. It had changed Lira little by little, marking her the way Andi marked death tallies on her swords. Lira doubted her family would even recognize the girl she had become in recent years.

And besides, these fallen Patrolmen around Lira hadn't been killed by her hands. Andi, Breck and Gilly, sure. Lira aided them in bringing down their opponents. What happened after that was for the other girls to decide.

This was their ship. Their home. The Patrolmen had invaded it, threatening their hard-won freedom.

And as much as Lira's old self frowned upon her to think it… those Patrolmen had deserved what they got.

"Well?" Breck asked. "What's the plan, Lira?"

"We wait," Lira said. Because for once, her mind had drawn a blank. She'd never been separate from her captain on a mission. Never had to *actually* take up the title of Second-in-Command. Especially not with invaders on their ship. And especially not while in restraints.

"Like hell we wait!" Breck rasped.

Down below, the sound of laughing guards trickled up through the hole in the floor where the ladder stood.

*Mountain of Rhymore*, Lira thought. *How can they actually be laughing at a time like this?*

There was no humor in Andi being captured, a prisoner to Dextro Arez somewhere on one of the lower decks, separated from her crew and facing the stars knew what. Even now, Lira could feel the hole in her chest where Andi was missing. Like a stitch had come loose in her heart, and soon she might unravel. The other girls, too.

Blood relation or not, Andi was part of their family. And families were never meant to be torn apart.

*Lon would agree with that statement*, Lira's old self whispered from the back of her mind.

She shook that whisper away. This wasn't about Lon. This wasn't about the past. This was about here and now.

About getting free.

They *would* get out of this. Wouldn't they? Lira racked her brain, searching for a solution, a way *out*. But she came up empty each time.

Gilly sighed. "I'm losing feeling in my ass, you guys. I need to move."

"Don't say *ass*, Gil," Breck chided.

"But you called Dex one!"

"That's because it's his name. Along with brainless bastard and soulless shite and…"

The girls' words trailed off as Lira retreated back into her mind. It was a silent place, calm and controlled. Just like her hands guiding a ship's throttle, nothing but space and stars spread out before her.

With her eyes closed, her head leaning back against the cool metal, Lira cycled through the timeline of today's events, wondering where she'd gone wrong. Wondering how she could have saved the crew from this fate. If only she'd flown the ship with more finesse. If only she'd figured out a way to enhance the rear thrusters or shed more weight from the cargo bay or…

She clenched her fists. The blue scales scattered across the surface of her arms and neck began to glow a deep purple, shedding light into the cramped space. Steam rose from her skin as the heat intensified.

*Anger.*

An emotion that sidled up against the hatred like an old, cherished friend. Lira hadn't felt anger in months. She'd always worked to control it, because deep emotions like anger led to a reaction in her blood, and that reaction led to Lira burning holes in her clothing as the scaled patches on her skin got hotter.

Lira's brother's voice slipped into her mind again. *Anger is never your friend, little bug.*

Damn the ache in her chest that came with it. Why was it always Lon's words that accompanied her in her darkest moments? Reminding her of home. Reminding her of another past failure.

She focused back on the issue at hand.

"We need that Soleran ice mare who tried to eat Andi's throat with her teeth a few months ago," Gilly said. "These cuffs would be nothing to her."

"The ice mares eat people, Gilly," Breck said. "Not metal."

Lira sighed. If only the cuffs on their wrists were made of rope. Then she could burn her way out of them and tear through the barrier of Patrolmen below with her bare hands.

She winced as her scales heated to a boiling point.

"Lir," Gilly said, the light from Lira's scales illuminating her worried face. "It's okay. We'll figure this out."

"She's right," Breck added. "Just…calm down, before you exhaust yourself. The last thing we need right now is to lose you, too." She plastered on a smile. Her teeth glowed a ghostly purple from Lira's light. "Andi will be fine. She's smart. And Dex is…"

"An ass," Gilly said with a wicked little grin.

Despite everything, Lira laughed.

Lon would love this child. If they ever got out of this, maybe someday Lira would introduce the two of them.

"So what now?" Breck asked, drawing Lira's attention back to her. The gunner's nose dripped blood from both nostrils. One of the Patrolmen had gotten brave and slammed her face with a rifle butt. *He* was now unconscious, thanks to Lira's rapidly bruising fist.

"We wait," Lira said again, as her skin cooled, as she locked the anger back into herself and buried it deep. "There is no plan other than patience. Because if we move, Dextro's men will put a bullet in Androma's brain. And then we will be the cause of our own captain's death."

It had taken everything in Lira not to dive down the stairwell and stick a blade in Dex's back as he led Andi away through the halls of their ship. Even his posture had been smug. Lira couldn't fathom—save for the possibility that he might have a stick up his backside—how or why anyone would walk that way.

"We wait," Breck said.

"We wait," Gilly echoed.

And so the girls waited.

And waited.

For hours, it seemed, until Gilly, sufficiently bored, fell asleep, her snores echoing through the hallway. Until Breck's stomach began to growl and Lira stopped counting the minutes since Andi had been gone. A thousand scenarios ran through her mind.

A thousand solutions, too, soon followed by reasons why they wouldn't work. They bit and tore at her as her scales lit up, dimmed, then ignited again.

Useless. So incredibly useless, this ability.

Lira nearly succumbed to the exhaustion of wasted energy. Her eyes were just beginning to close, sleep tugging at her like a poison, when a voice pierced the darkness.

"Ladies?"

All three of them snapped to attention.

The ladder below them clanged as someone began to climb up.

"Protect Gilly first," Breck whispered to Lira.

"At all costs," Lira agreed.

Then a creature appeared, stopping about halfway up the ladder. It held a lantern in its fist, the light casting a strange, otherworldly glow on its face.

Its body was made up of metal and gears and blinking lights behind a clear casing, like a skeleton clock. Its face was stark white, with strange, unblinking eyes.

An AI.

"Who the hell are you?" Gilly yelped.

"My name is Alfie," the creature responded, his voice clear and clipped. Diplomatic. "I am the personal assistant to General Cyprian Cortas, an Artificial Lifeform Intelligence Emissary, Version 7.3." As he pulled himself the rest of the way up the ladder and into the hallway, Lira noticed a shining silver key clutched in his other fist.

She could make her move now. She could set the girls free with the help of this strange new arrival, this fateful turn of events. The creature's white face turned to Lira. "Captain Androma Racella has agreed to a deal with the great General Cortas."

"A deal?" Lira asked, not taking her eyes from the key. Her body tensed, ready to spring. Andi hated General Cortas. He was the only person she feared in all of Mirabel. "What are the terms?"

"Soon to be discussed, Lira Mette." The AI tilted his head, as if staring at something he could not quite understand. "But first," he said, lifting the key, the movement strangely smooth, "my orders are to set you all free."

"Well…hell," Breck said. "That's unexpected."

Lira could only stare as the strange AI stopped before her, dropped to a metal knee and slipped the key into her cuffs.

# CHAPTER 11
## NOR

XEN PTERA WAS DYING.

Queen Nor Solis had known it for years, had witnessed her planet's pain with her own eyes—but knowing the truth didn't make facing it any easier.

For years, she'd known it was coming.

She felt it in the tainted air she breathed, the sting of pollution scraping its claws against her lungs as she stood on the balcony of the Nyota Room, overlooking the once-beautiful remains of her kingdom.

She and her advisers had tried to restore beauty to Xen Ptera since the end of The Cataclysm, but radiation had left the ground barren. Crops withered the moment they tried to sprout from seed. Streams dried up. Creatures became extinct, while others mutated, their blood becoming acidic, impossible to eat.

Xen Ptera was once a prosperous planet, rich with varillium mines that brought trade and wealth to the Olen System. But as more mines were exhausted and sealed up, the future of Xen Ptera began to look bleak.

Businesses collapsed. Trade between Olen and the other systems ceased as the varillium ran out. Xen Pterran homes fell to starvation, which gave way to weakness, which allowed filth and disease to spread more with each passing year.

Nor's father had turned to the other systems for help, but the Unified Systems refused to offer enough.

And so The Cataclysm began.

Now, fifteen years later, the fighting had long since ceased, but despite everything she had done, Nor was out of options.

Until recently, Xen Ptera had been relying on food and water sourced from Iv21, a small neighboring planet. But Iv21's resources were far from sufficient to sustain the population of Xen Ptera for an extended period, and the limited food stores harvested from that planet had run out months ago.

Death filled the void left behind.

Mechanical noises hummed across the bustling city. From her vantage point miles above the ground, Nor had an unobstructed view of the land. Black plumes of smoke billowed over the gray landscape. Buildings, ranging from a few stories tall to some towering miles high, suffocated each other in the claustrophobic capital of Nivia.

Flowers ceased to bloom, and real water was now a dream as artificial water tablets took its place. The burnt orange sky rained acid, the kind that burned both flesh and metallic skin.

Nor grasped the railing as the ground beneath her gave a great shuddering breath. The quakes were near constant, cracking open the ground and devouring anything in their path. Her people used to mourn the lives lost to the molten crust, but over the past few years, the quakes had become too regular for anyone to care.

The Xen Pterrans were growing numb to the destruction around them.

Nor heard the chorus of death in the cries of her starving people, saw it in the green fog that burned their skin as it swept its way through the crumbling city streets with each bitter gust of wind.

For years the suffering of her people, her planet, had torn her apart.

But she knew, deep in her soul, that soon she would have the power to stop it all.

"Your Highness?"

Nor stiffened at the sound of a girl's voice behind her. She turned from her spot on the balcony, abandoning the view of her capital city and the pain it struck in her chest.

Like a poison.

A cyborg girl stood in the doorway, patches of metal spiraling across her burned skin, a whirring gear where her heart should be. She was one of the few who had been saved from radiation exposure even after it had done its damage.

"You dare approach me in my private quarters?" Nor said. The wind howled in from the open balcony doors, whipping at her midnight waves of hair. "What is the meaning of this?"

She smiled to herself as the girl took a step back and bowed her head, silver hair falling into her face.

Nor had always loved the sound of her own voice—powerful, yet pure. A voice that brought even the strongest, bravest men to their knees. A voice that could make heads roll, should anyone speak a word against her.

"Apologies, Your Highness," the girl whispered. She cast her gaze down to her bare toes. "Darai has called upon you, and…"

Nor lifted a hand. The girl's words stopped at once.

"Take me to him," Nor commanded.

"He is in his office, Your Highness. I will escort you there, if you should wish it."

Nor nodded once, and the girl turned, the gears in her metallic chest whining. Human, but barely so.

She briskly followed the servant girl down the tapestry-lined hallways and into the elevator. They stood in silence during the ten-story descent before coming to a halt at the floor that housed her adviser's office.

Nor brushed past the trembling girl and swept into Darai's room, not bothering to knock.

Stars winked at her from the inside. Hundreds of thousands painted on the walls, a replica of the sky that Xen Ptera had not been able to see for years. And in the center of the room, seated at his white desk, was Nor's most trusted adviser.

"You think so highly of yourself, Darai, that you dare summon *me* to *your* quarters?" Nor hissed. She approached the pristine white desk.

"Apologies, Your Highness," he said, standing and giving her a deep bow, gray hair falling across his weathered face. Half of it was mutilated, skin shriveled and burned from a childhood accident, bits of metal poking through where permanent stitches helped hold the skin in place. He rarely spoke of the accident and never gave much detail in response to Nor's questions about it.

"What is the meaning of this?" she asked.

"I have news regarding the weapon. I just received word from Aclisia that it is in the final stages of development."

Nor smiled, her mood lifting immediately. For years, she'd been waiting, imagining the glory of her greatest creation. And now it was nearly complete. "Then we should prepare ourselves at once."

Darai stood from his desk, his long robes sweeping behind him like a curtain. "Nor, if I may suggest…"

"Speak your thoughts now, Uncle, before I grow tired of you."

His lips pressed together in a thin smile. He was a proud man, but he himself had taught her to wield her rule like a mighty sword. He'd been a part of her life for as long as she could remember. The only surviving member of her family—not by blood, but through his years of loyalty to Nor and her mother before her.

Darai bowed his head and approached her slowly. "The timing, of course, is of the utmost importance. We must remain patient to ensure all of the pieces fall into place before making our move."

"The final piece is already in place," Nor said with a wave of her gold prosthetic hand.

Seeing it reminded her of the past. The explosions. The loss. The need for revenge that empowered her.

The past was what fueled her present.

Nor turned away, her spiked collar grazing her jaw. Across the room, the painted stars glared back at her like devil's eyes.

"When we bring the galaxy to its knees," Nor said, a smile slowly appearing on her rouged lips, "I'd like to repaint this room. With the blood of every man, woman and child who has ever lifted a finger against my planet."

Darai swept across the tiled floor to stand at her side.

"My dear." His voice was slippery, as if drenched in oil. "When we bring the galaxy to its knees, you can paint the entire palace in blood, if you wish it."

Nor closed her eyes and smiled.

She could see it, *taste* it.

And it pleased her.

# CHAPTER 12
## ANDROMA

ANDI CROSSED HER ARMS OVER HER CHEST, fingers digging into her biceps as she tried to keep her anger in check. She sat in the captain's seat on the bridge, staring out the viewport of the newly repaired *Marauder* and into the Tracker ship's massive cargo bay. The internal damage had been a relatively quick fix, but it was the exterior of the ship that showed the most damage from their fight with the Patrolmen. She'd make sure General Cortas paid for that, too.

Her ship wasn't a junker. She refused to let it look like one.

Andi spun in her chair to face her crew, giving them each a once-over. No serious injuries, though there was a nasty cut on

Gilly's collarbone and dried blood beneath Breck's nose. Lira, graceful as ever, perched on her pilot's seat like a bird.

Andi's heart unclenched slightly knowing they were all in one piece.

"Are we really going to go quietly into this job?" Breck asked, leaning against the entry door behind her.

"This team is never quiet," Lira said. "We slaughtered them. I'm still surprised they allowed us to keep our heads after that."

Breck made a sound in the back of her throat. "I wouldn't be surprised if the general goes back on his word to pardon us after we deliver his son, safe and sound, back to Daddy. How do you even know he's going to keep his promise, Andi?"

Andi grimaced as she watched the Patrolmen outside, in their perfectly polished boots, their pristine blue uniforms. "He made the Vow." All the Patrolmen out there had made vows, too, when they joined the Arcardian ranks. Several of them had followed Dex to their deaths because of those vows. The Arcardian Vow was as binding as two souls becoming one. "He'll keep his word, as long as I keep mine."

"Making deals with the devil," Lira said with a sigh. "Whatever will we do next?"

"Let me shoot the old man, Cap. We can swing over to Arcardius now, and I'll make it quick," Gilly whined from beside Breck. Her red braids had come undone, and curls tumbled over her shoulders, making her blue eyes pop. "Then this will all be over. You don't want to go back to Arcardius, anyways." She seemed to shrink back into herself for a second as she thought that over. "Right?"

"No one," Andi said, glaring at Gilly over Breck's massive form, "is shooting anyone else. Not yet, at least."

She didn't answer Gilly's second question.

She'd already thought about it, imagined all the ways a life back on Arcardius could play out.

Even with a pardon, it would never be the same. When Kalee died, people had looked at Andi as if she were the scum of the planet. As if, by choice, she'd taken a knife to Kalee's throat and slit it herself. As if she'd wanted to become a traitor.

Pardon on the line or not, Andi knew she wouldn't be able to get herself and her crew out of this. Right now, they were boxed in like the blue cattle she'd once seen on a farming satellite.

"I don't like it any more than any of you," Andi said, "but we don't have much of a choice. Our ship is in his hands, and he has an entire Tracker full of armed guards surrounding this cargo bay right now." She tapped her red-painted nails on the armrest. "I don't doubt he'll keep the Vow…but that's not our biggest concern right now. We're headed to the Olen System."

"And this is Xen Ptera we're talking about," Gilly said. "We've never stolen anything from there. We've never even *been* to the Olen System, Cap!"

Traveling to Olen had become a fool's journey ever since The Cataclysm ended. There was still the peace treaty in place, preventing the massive Olen System, with its capital planet of Xen Ptera, from attacking the other Unified Systems of Mirabel. But those living in the Olen System weren't exactly friendly with the Unified Systems.

Andi didn't blame them. It was a miracle anyone had survived the explosive final battle that took place on Xen Ptera in the final days of the war.

"We can't think of it like that. If we do, we'll end up overthinking every move we make. It's just another job. A grab and go." But Andi had a hard time believing that herself. She'd been to plenty of dingy, destroyed places in Mirabel. Pirating had a way of drawing her and her crew to the darkest sides of the various planets and moons they'd visited. But if half the rumors she'd heard about Xen Ptera were true, then she had to be strong. If not for herself, then for her crew.

Her past actions had gotten them into this mess. She had to keep them alive to the end.

"Whatever you say, Androma," Breck said. "If you don't

mind, I'm going to take little Gilly here down to check out the new weapons. With the supplies the general gave us, we can make Sparks large enough to destroy an entire moon."

"Go ahead," Andi said. "But I want you both back here before we take off."

A selfish part of Andi wished General Cortas hadn't been the one to give the gunners their new weapons. For the past several months, they'd been low on their most beloved supplies. She wanted to be able to provide for her girls, but so far, all she'd done was put them in danger.

Andi sighed, knowing this line of thinking was foolish. Gilly was grinning ear to ear as she and Breck left the bridge, and as long as they were both happy with the new weapons, it didn't matter who actually supplied them.

Lira remained behind, watching Andi with those all-seeing Adhiran eyes of hers. They'd been together the longest, shared countless stories over bottles of fizzy Cosmic Cram until their eyes became as glassy as the stars.

Andi would never forget the day she met Lira at a fighting ring on Zerpro7. They'd stood side by side, two girls intent on winning their bets. But the fights were slow that night, the brawlers not very skilled, and soon Andi found herself conversing with Lira.

*They should put me in the ring*, Lira had said, sighing as she leaned over the dirty railing, peering at the fight below.

*You sound confident*, Andi had answered.

*I'm confident enough when it comes to fighting*, Lira said, *but flying is my true gift*.

They'd talked long into the night, and hours later Andi had offered Lira a test run with her ship. They'd flown away from Zerpro7 and never looked back.

"You're not okay, Andi," Lira said now. "I can see it as clear as varillium, so stop trying to pretend that you are."

Andi sighed, running her hand through her tangled white and purple hair. It was going to take her hours to work out the knots.

"I'm fine." But she knew Lira sensed the lie the moment it left her lips. "I'm just…" She sighed. "I need some time with my thoughts, Lira."

Lira looked at her doubtfully, but obliged. "I'll be in my quarters if you need me."

Andi watched Lira leave the room before turning to look past the clear glass wall and at the inside of the Tracker ship. Men in blue Arcardian Patrolmen uniforms scuttled around like ants as they finished their final checks on the *Marauder*.

Andi was exhausted, both mentally and physically, the kind of exhaustion she doubted sleep could fix. For once, she wasn't positive what the next step would be, besides rescuing the general's son. Beyond that was an expanse of complete uncertainty.

A death sentence pardoned. An entire planet waiting for her. But after all that had transpired and with the wounds she still held inside…could she ever really return?

With a sigh, she picked up her swords and began tallying the day's kills. As she dug into the metal, Andi's thoughts drifted to the past.

She wished, desperately, that she'd never been chosen for the sacred Spectre position, that she'd simply become a regular soldier like her father. Her earliest memories of their time together were of training days, bruised fists and bloodied knuckles. *Fighting is in our blood, Androma. We will always defend Arcardius, at all costs.*

It was because of her father's training that she so often wound up in the commandant's office after fighting with other students at the Academy when her anger got the best of her. It was because of her anger that her parents put her into dance classes, in hopes they would help soften her edges.

And it was because of dancing that she'd met Kalee. If she'd only kept quiet at the Academy, hadn't made Kalee laugh in their dance classes, hadn't invited her to eat lunch in her pod... their friendship would never have begun.

General Cortas never would have seen the bond they shared. The fierceness with which Andi defended Kalee from the teasing of their classmates. The way she could so skillfully break a nose and slip back into the shadows without another word. How she excelled in every military class and received top marks in physical combat classes.

It was a series of small choices that led to one large mistake, and because of it, because of *Andi*...Kalee had died.

The painful truth still clung to Andi after all this time.

This ship and these girls were her only solace. And now they were heading into the mouth of hell.

Gilly was right. This job was bigger than anything they'd ever done before. It was rare moments like these when Andi wished she had a simpler, easier life.

If only she could believe that a pardon from General Cortas would take the pain of the past away. But she knew, as well as the general did, that her future was destroyed when Kalee took her last breath.

"Hello, Androma Racella."

Andi whirled in her chair, lifting her swords and finding herself face-to-face with someone unexpected.

*Some*thing, *more like.*

Confusion riddled her brain before she put the pieces together. She hadn't met many AIs in her life, though she'd seen them on the feeds years ago attending to the deep-pocketed aristocrats across Mirabel.

The AI's face was white like the snowcapped mountains on Solera. It had two eyes and a mouth, legs and arms, but besides that, it was absent any other humanoid traits. The AI's body was see-through, like the *Marauder*'s walls, and Andi could see all the gears and wires inside, clicking and whirring silently like an old-era clock.

AIs had been exceedingly rare since The Cataclysm ended fifteen years ago, when they were outlawed across Mirabel. The Olen System had weaponized AIs during the war against the Unified Systems, and if not for the advanced military tech developed by New Veda and Tenebris to combat the AI army, the Unified Systems would've fallen. It wasn't until six years ago that the artificially intelligent beings had been integrated into society again, primarily as servants and errand-goers and mechanics—and sometimes chefs, which Breck had so often begged Andi to obtain for the *Marauder*.

After staring at the AI for a few more seconds, a whistling from down the hallway pulled Andi's attention away. Dex strolled into the bridge with a smug grin on his face.

"Oh, I see you've met Alfie," he said, looking between the two of them.

"Alfie?" Andi asked, confused by the name.

"It stands for Artificial Lifeform Intelligence Emissary," the AI said, staring at Andi with those strange eyes. "But you may call me Alfie." He bowed slightly.

Dex patted Alfie on the shoulder. "He's the general's. His job is to babysit us on this trip and report back to the big guy on Arcardius."

"Wonderful," Andi said. "I've always wanted a babysitter on my ship."

Dex crouched down next to her, lips level with her ear. "You know, you were a lot more fun three years ago."

It was like he *wanted* her to kill him.

She turned and immediately felt flustered when she realized they were separated by mere centimeters. He was so close she could see the pores in his soft brown skin, the deep brown of his eyes and the raised scar on his temple, a souvenir from a fight he got into with an ex-convict just after he and Andi met.

That scar was nothing compared to the one she must have given him on his chest the day she stole this ship from him.

Tenebran Guardians were known for taking pride in their battle marks, but the scar she gave him—whether it still existed or not—was not one he should be proud of.

It was a sign of his weakness. A disgusting reminder of how he'd chosen money over love.

Her heart, the traitorous thing, fluttered for a moment like it used to when he looked at her. She used to love his eyes, the unspoken words in their depths. The feel of his skin against hers during their passionate nights.

Now those thoughts made her cringe. She guarded herself against those memories, which were no longer part of a blissful present, but a hurtful past.

"A lot has changed in three years, Dextro," Andi said calmly. "Now, if you don't move, I'll give you a new scar, and this time, it will be across your neck."

He put his arms up in defense before rising, distancing himself from her.

"Alfie, grab my bags, please. Let's get settled in." He glanced back at Andi with a faraway look in his eyes. The thoughtful gaze unnerved her momentarily, but then he smirked and said, "It's great to be back on *my* ship."

"My records tell me," Alfie said, trailing after Dex, "that the *Marauder* belongs to Androma Racella."

Andi laughed in satisfaction as they disappeared.

*Dex.*

Even his name was poison in her mind.

At another time in her life, Andi would've felt guilty for her coldness toward him. But that time was long gone. Now she was made of ice, too full of anger and regret to get close to him again.

He'd betrayed her, and so she'd betrayed him.

One shredded heart for another.

She remembered the way Dex's eyes had burned, how the hilt of her dagger stuck out from his chest as he lay there on that scalding, barren moon. It was the day she'd claimed the *Marauder* as her own. The day she'd claimed her heart back, too.

Hearts were pathetic things, too easily broken. The Bloody Baroness couldn't afford such weakness. *Especially* not now that Dex was back at her side.

*It's one job*, Andi told herself. *You can shoot him out the airlock the second you recover Valen Cortas.*

She smiled at that thought, then settled back down into her seat, where she resumed her tallying.

There would be another tally added soon, accompanying the others on her blades.

It had Dex's name written all over it.

# CHAPTER 13
## DEX
### FOUR YEARS AGO

*DEX HATED COMING TO UULVECA DURING* their annual harvest.

It was a minor planet in the Stuna System, a place where the pungent smell of the dung of feathered uhven filled the air. Dex covered his nose and mouth with a cloth to suppress the odor, but it failed to block the nauseating stench entirely.

He wouldn't be here long—all Dex had to do was check in on a suspected bounty who was rumored to be making some under-the-counter deals and take a few snaps of the evidence. If he caught the scheming bastard in the act, it would mean a load of Krevs, and another constellation tattoo added to his body. Another mark of his Guardian status.

*If not, well… Dex didn't want to think about the look on Raiseth's face if he came back empty-handed.*

*This was his opportunity to prove to the leader of the Bounty Hunter's branch that he was more than just some seventeen-year-old student with stars in his eyes. He was a Guardian, born and raised, newly adorned with the title he'd worked his entire life to obtain.*

*Life as a Guardian after graduation wasn't easy. You weren't offered free room and board or given a steady mission.*

*You could work a desk job, damning yourself to a life of boredom while you waited to be called upon for something greater.*

*Or you could be like Dex.*

*Desperate to live in action, to collect riches, he had joined the Bounty Hunters' branch of the Guardians in hopes of getting his hands on the worst criminals in Mirabel and placing them behind bars. To keep himself busy, honing his skills, while he waited for further orders.*

*With the peace treaty between the Unified Systems and the Olen System, Dex guessed it would be a long wait before he saw any real action.*

*He was just as good as any of Raiseth's other bounty hunters. Better, even. If this had been the Guardian Academy, he would have aced every skill test. Dominated in the fighting classes. Destroyed all the other ranks when it came to intel.*

*But Raiseth didn't care about Dex's hard-earned title. Raiseth himself was a war hero, a retired Guardian of the highest status. To him, bounty hunting was about proving your worth, catching a criminal prize with ease.*

*Dex was determined to do so.*

*Now, on his first mission, Dex wove his way through the crowds of people selling their goods in rickety tents. Some offered ripe senada fruit, a rarity that only grew in the southern rainforests of the planet, while others hoisted chunks of freshly slaughtered meat on hooks, blue blood dripping into pans beneath.*

*"Drink the blood to find the woman of your dreams," an elderly shopkeeper called to Dex, her one eye twitching as he passed. It was pure*

*purple, a shade that reminded him of the moons outside New Veda. Her eye twitched again. "Five Krevs a pint, dear boy."*

*Dex laughed as he sidestepped her booth. "There isn't a woman in the galaxy who would put up with me."*

*Her cackles trailed after him as he faded deeper into the crowd.*

*All around him, laughter bubbled up like a wellspring. Music drifted through the air, the different songs sounding out of time—yet somehow it all wove together as if played by one hand. Despite its stench, this small planet was a place of growth and love and life, and somewhere in the midst of it all was his target.*

*Dex kept his head on a swivel as he walked, searching for his target's telltale shock of red chest fur. Raiseth had said the Stramh man would be here, peddling illegal brainworms. Striding past a leather maker's stall, Dex hastened his pace, boots gliding effortlessly over the rocky ground. He could see his target's shop in the distance, a ramshackle booth made of canvas and rusted metal poles.*

*But as he drew closer, Dex frowned. The booth was empty, its owner nowhere in sight.*

*Almost as if he'd packed up and left, knowing Dex was on his way.*

*Raiseth had warned him about this—targets with their own informants, too quick and too clever to be caught on the first try.*

*Since the beginning of his mission, Dex had been imagining the moment when he'd reach out and hold a knife to the peddler's furry red side, whispering words of defeat in his pointed ear. That moment was now dead and gone. Instead, he strode over to the booth and slipped inside, kneeling down to the inspect the dust-covered shelves nailed together within.*

*Dex needed a sign, any indication of where the target had fled, but he was greeted with only dust and dirt.*

*He'd have to come up with a new plan. But first, he needed to trek back to his ship and contact his informant.*

*Dex was just sliding back into the crowd when he felt it.*

*A shift in the weight against his belt where he kept his bag of Krevs.*

Dex whirled, flipping out his blade and simultaneously wrapping a fist around the would-be thief's neck.

It was a young woman. She had white hair the color of stardust, tangled and matted as if she'd just been caught in the midst of a storm. Gray eyes stared out of a face masked by filth and grime. Dex's bag of Krevs was clutched tightly in her fist.

He snatched the bag away from her, but didn't release his hold on her throat.

"Nice try," Dex said. "On any normal person, you would've gotten away with that."

He'd dealt with street rats before, knew all of their tricks and, as Dex tightened his hold on the young thief, he expected her gray eyes to well up with tears. He expected a kick to the groin, or for her to sink her teeth into his hand. "I could kill you with one twist of your neck," he added, waiting for her to make a move.

Her eyes narrowed. It was his only warning that she was going to react before her body twisted. He felt her foot hook around his ankle, and before he knew it, they were on the ground.

She held a small knife to his throat. His knife, which she must have stolen from his belt.

"Impressive," Dex said.

Then he shifted his weight and used his momentum to roll them sideways, where he landed on top of her, the knife discarded, twin snarls on both their faces.

His pouch of Krevs sat several feet away, a few of the golden coins loose and glittering under the sun.

"Get off," the young woman said.

There was no fear in her eyes. Only a burning anger as hot as a flame.

She tried to wriggle away, but she was weak. He could see now how frail she was, how her worn clothing hung from her frame and danced in the wind. Her wrists were wrapped in thick cloth and tied with leather strips. Dark stains, possibly blood, stained the material.

She was too old to be a street rat, and too filthy to be working for a *pleasure palace. The palace owners on Uulveca liked to keep their workers clean and enticing.*

*A nagging in Dex's brain told him he'd seen her before. But he'd seen hundreds of people in this market today. Perhaps she'd been following him?*

*Curious, Dex lifted some of his weight from her, but didn't let her go. "You should learn how to pick your targets more wisely."*

*Her eyes narrowed, her gaze raking over his body. "I should say the same to you. You don't look nearly strong enough to capture that dealer you were going after."*

*"You know about him?" Dex asked curiously. If he could get information from her, maybe he wouldn't have to contact his informant. He could avoid the digs from Raiseth's other recruits and salvage the mission before it was too late.*

*The young woman tilted her head, a slight smile pulling at her cracked lips.*

*"It's going to cost you."*

Two can play at this game, *Dex thought. "How about instead of my turning you over to the Patrolmen, you tell me what I want to know?" He had her there. Or so he thought.*

*She shrugged her bone-thin shoulders and laughed. An empty one, the kind that came from a person with little hope left in life. "They don't care about me."*

*As Dex stood, pulling her with him, he caught the flicker in her eyes. A hint of fear as she glanced over his shoulder, as if she expected the Patrolmen to come running.*

*What had she done, Dex wondered, to end up in this stinkhole? Beyond the grime, he could see someone chased by the ghosts of her past. Someone broken, but clever and quick enough to play at his games. Certainly a strong fighter, likely stronger when she was well fed.*

*He thought for another moment before responding. "If you give me the information I need, I'll buy you a meal. By the looks of it, you need one."*

*She stared at him, eyes squinting as if trying to seek out an ulterior* motive. "I'll choose the place," she said finally. "And I want a week's worth of meals. And all the Krevs in your pouch."

He paused. If it weren't for his pride, he would happily walk right back to his ship and contact his informant. But he had a reputation to uphold, so this seemed the better option. "Half the Krevs," he said. "And if I find out you're lying to me, I'll kill you."

"That's the funny thing." She smiled, but it didn't reach her eyes. "I'm already dead."

Then she turned, fading into the crowd. Dex scooped up his pouch of Krevs and trailed after her, a nagging feeling in his mind as he wondered who she was.

And who she used to be.

# CHAPTER 14
## ANDROMA

IT WAS STARING AT HER AGAIN.

"Are you incapable of blinking?" Andi asked.

The AI sat across from her in the meeting room of the *Marauder*, where it had been since the beginning of their meeting.

"Since I am not a living being, I do not require eyelids to block damaging particles from entering my ocular lens. This means that I am incapable of blinking, Androma Racella."

If the infernal AI hadn't belonged to General Cortas, Andi would have unscrewed its head and pulled its wiring out through its neck. Instead, she turned to the second most kill-worthy member of her new crew.

"Silence him, Dextro, before I do it myself."

SASHA ALSBERG & LINDSAY CUMMINGS

Dex tsked, shaking his finger. "Now, now, Androma." He drawled out her name. "You of all people should know how the general likes his little pets to be."

Andi's fingertips flinched toward her sheathed blades.

"What is that supposed to mean?"

He held up his gloved hands. "Relax, Andi. I'm just trying to have a conversation. That's what people do."

"I don't want to have a conversation," Andi said. "Not with you."

It had only been a day since Dex took up residence on her ship, but it seemed much longer. Not for a single second had Andi been able to escape Dex's presence. The ship may have been small, but it wasn't *that* small. Yet no matter where she went, Dex managed to find her. In her room, where she pored over her photographs of planets, all the places she'd explored, he'd found her. He'd flipped through her classical music collection, then chuckled at the calendar screen flickering on the glass wall. The handsome models from all corners of Mirabel rippled as he flicked through the images, whistling at each one.

"So *this* is what you like, Androma?" he'd asked, waggling his dark brows suggestively. "I guess I understand why you left me."

"What do you want, Dextro?" she'd asked.

"We need to talk." Standing in the doorway of her room, a half smile tugging at his lips, he had looked for a moment exactly as he had long ago, when they'd shared this very space. She'd slammed the door in his face before her memories, and her heart, could unravel her.

How he could make light of their situation, how he could simply come here and want to just *talk*, after all that they'd been through and all that they had done, she couldn't fathom.

But she knew that the moment they delivered Valen Cortas back to his father, she'd be rid of Dex forever.

"Your heart rate is increasing dramatically," Alfie's soothing voice sounded from across the table. "Do you require a moment to rest?"

She required a lot more than that, but Andi simply shook her head and turned back to the task at hand.

A map of the Olen System filled the air of the room, three glowing orbs rotating slowly around a single sun. To the left of Xen Ptera, the capital planet of Olen, was a mass of gray: the Junkyard, where old ships were cast out into the skies, left for traders to pick over—but more notably, where the last real battle of The Cataclysm was fought, the Battle of Black Sky. It was rumored that Queen Nor's father, the previous king, had sent hundreds of ships to fight, only to watch them fall from the sky as thousands of Olen soldiers died at the hands of the Unified Systems.

The Junkyard was the perfect place for the *Marauder* to disappear.

Andi glanced up as the newly repaired door of the meeting room slid open and the rest of her crew walked in. The holographic map flickered as the girls walked through it, then bounced back into place.

Gilly was preoccupied with eating a chunk of bread from dinner. *If she had the chance*, Andi thought, *Gilly would eat all our food stores*. Andi often wondered if her stomach was a bottomless pit. The thirteen-year-old was growing fast and had an appetite to match her growth spurt.

The ship's system, Memory, beeped overhead.

*"Incoming message,"* the cool female voice said.

Alfie looked up, tilting his head sideways. "An Artificial Intelligence on the mainframe of a pirating ship," he said. "I have never observed such a thing."

"We stole her on a job last month," Gilly explained. "Breck installed her."

*"Incoming message,"* Memory said again, *"for Dextro Arez."*

Dex stood, the legs of his chair scraping like a wailing ghost against the cool metal floor. "My informant awaits."

They'd been going back and forth with different plans for hours, finally settling on one that pleased everyone—and most importantly, General Cortas. The general had his claws sunk deep into Andi's back, even from halfway across the galaxy. He'd already rejected several plans, which seemed to defeat the purpose of hiring Andi and her crew to do a job that he lacked the experience to carry out himself. Their short, often heated calls made Andi long for her days as a Spectre. Back then, he'd respected her, even praised her during rare moments when he'd let his general's mask come loose. She'd seen him through a soldier's eyes, trained to gain his approval. He'd given her the freedom to do her job, even allowing Andi to take up residence in Averia so she could stay by Kalee's side at all hours.

How far she had fallen since then.

Like it or not, General Cortas had to bow to her will on this mission, to respect her methods. She'd told him as much on their most recent call.

"Bring him back to me, Androma," the general had said, "and perhaps I will."

Now Andi and Dex had finally settled on a plan. Her crew surrounded the table as Dex left the room, Alfie trailing after him, saying something about conversing with his fellow AI.

The girls waited until they were gone to speak. Lira stood across from Andi, blue eyes searching her face. "You're looking a bit troubled."

"I'm fine, Lir," Andi said with a growl as she examined her chipped red polish. She'd have to ask Gilly to repaint her nails soon. "I thought you said you were going to keep Dex busy. He won't leave me alone."

The pilot shrugged. "Dextro is a man with many talents, the most obnoxious of which is that he knows this ship inside and out."

"That," Breck added, her massive hands curling into fists as she slumped back into a chair too small for her muscular frame, "and his little leech, Alfie, seems to always be ten steps ahead of us."

Gilly giggled and wiped bread crumbs from her face. "I'm going to lock the AI in the waste bay."

Andi smiled at the thought. "The sooner the better. You could lock Dex in there, too."

This was how it should be, just her and the girls making plans to strike it big. Without a self-righteous, Krev-worshipping *man* on board.

"We'll make our first move soon," Andi said, filling the girls in on the latest part of the plan. She glanced at her Second. "Lira?"

Lira nodded and reached out to swipe a hand across the map over their heads, which was programmed to respond to her and Andi alone. *Much to Dex's dismay*, Andi thought with a smug smile. He'd asked her to give him access at least a dozen times already, and she'd shut him down each time. With pleasure.

At Lira's touch, the planets on the map began to swirl, their muted colors deepening, the sun blazing bright as it spun around the room. Lira tapped a black spot on the map, enlarging the space before using her fingertip to trace a glowing red circle around it.

"That," she said, pointing to the circle, "is where we are now, in the Junkyard." The *Marauder* was currently hidden within the large husk of a fallen warship. If anyone happened to come through this area, their ship would easily be mistaken as a piece of the larger one. That had been Lira's bright idea, and the exterior damage the *Marauder* had recently sustained *was* helpful camouflage.

She drew a line from their current location to Lunamere, where Valen was being held captive.

"This is where we need to be," Lira said, right before Andi took over.

"The plan is that in two days' time, we will be meeting Dex's informant, Soyina Rumbardh, at the Dark Matter Pub, located just outside the security border of Xen Ptera." Andi tapped a spot on the map just to the left of Lunamere, where a small silver orb hung in the darkness. The satellite pub. "There, we'll finalize the escape plan with Soyina and initiate the rescue. Dex and I will enter Lunamere while the rest of you head to the rendezvous point." Andi looked at Lira, catching her in the middle of an eye roll.

Her Second wasn't happy that Dex and Andi were going in to Lunamere without her, *especially* with the plan they'd come up with. High risk, *possible* reward. But it was the best option they had, and they needed Lira to pilot the ship. Plus, as much as Andi hated to admit it, she and Dex did know how to work a job together.

It was what first brought them together, and later tore them apart. They simply had to get through this without killing each other first.

Andi swallowed hard and continued. "At this point, all we need is a map of the prison. Without that map, we'll be screwed. But luckily for us, our informant should be sending it to Dex as we speak."

Soyina could be described as a shadow hiding in darkness with few records to be found about her on the galactic feeds. She was a tricky woman who had refused to let anyone but Dex see her face, which meant Andi had to go in blind when she met the woman in person. It wasn't an ideal situation, but she'd faced worse before.

"I know I'm not the most experienced at this stuff," Gilly said from across the table as she polished her golden gun, "but it all seems a little too easy. How do you know we can even trust this so-called informant Dex has?"

Breck barked out a laugh. "How can we even trust *Dex*?"

"We can't," Andi said. In her mind, she saw Dex's face years ago on Uulveca, the very first time she'd met him. That sideways smile, his hand wrapped around her throat. His pouch of Krevs coiled in her fist. She should have known that day what he was. What he'd push her to become.

"Dex's trademark is double-crossing people," Andi continued. An old dent in the wall of this room was proof of that. Andi still remembered the brain-bashing she'd saved Dex from in the days they'd shared this ship. "That's why I have a plan B."

"And that is?" Breck asked, raising a brow.

"Well, ladies," Andi said as she leaned forward, face glowing in the light of the map. The stars rippled out and away from her touch, as if made of water. "I think Dextro needs to be taught a little lesson in the element of surprise."

# CHAPTER 15
VALEN

*THE HISS OF THE WHIP SANG THROUGH THE darkness.*

*A crackle, a pop, and with it, the stench of singed flesh.*

*The electric whip bit into Valen's skin, over and over, until he couldn't suppress his screams anymore, until his throat felt ragged and blood coated the floor like a warm, wet carpet.*

*They were unraveling him, bit by bit.*

*I am Valen Cortas, he thought. But as the whip came down again, a crackle of blue that lit up the splatters across the stone walls, it drowned out his own voice in his head.*

*His torture had begun three months prior, when he arrived at this prison—first with starvation, a hunger so deep he'd felt as if his stomach was shredding itself apart. Then came the questions, the beatings and, shortly after, the floggings.*

*Since then, Valen had lost track of the times he'd been slashed by the whip or pummeled by the guards' electric gauntlets.*

*If he sunk into the blissful oblivion of unconsciousness, they would bring him back with an injection, a prisoner to the horrors he couldn't escape. The cycle continued without end, until Valen thought the walls had grown claws that tore at him. Until he thought he'd drown in his own blood. Until the very mention of his home planet of Arcardius brought forth maniacal laughter from his lips. Home was nowhere as he drowned in pain in the darkness of Cell 306, a place without color or laughter or light.*

I am Valen Cortas, *he thought as the whip kissed his skin again, tearing at the tendons beneath.* Vengeance will be mine.

*More than once, he'd wondered if he had died and been dragged down to hell. But even hell couldn't possibly be this cruel.*

Hiss, rip, singe.

*On and on it went until his mantra was replaced by something else.*

Why are you taking it? Fight back! *a small voice said in his head. Valen nearly laughed as the whip came down again, drowning out the voice. But then it came back, stronger this time.*

Don't be weak like your father thinks you are. Fight back!

*How could he fight when he was nothing? How could he shout when they'd stolen his voice, when his body was too weak and too mutilated to move?*

Hiss, rip, singe.

*Then, as if right next to Valen's ear, the voice screamed,* You will never get vengeance if you allow them to have their way. You have to fight, Valen. Fight back!

*As if he'd been plunged into arctic waters, a feeling radiated through him, something he had never felt before.*

*A power, a want, a need.*

*The crackle of the whip hissed overhead, promising a swift return. He couldn't take it. He wouldn't take it.*

"STOP!" Valen yelled. His voice reverberated against the room's obsidinite walls.

He waited for the next slash, but when it didn't come, he craned his neck to the side. Even that slight movement sent a wave of pain through him, like he was being dragged across a bed of nails. His vision flickered in and out, unconsciousness tugging at him like a welcome friend.

But what he saw puzzled him.

His torturer, a large man with arms the size of Valen's torso, had paused midswing. The whip still crackled overhead, bathing the room in an eerie, flickering blue.

Valen didn't have time to make sense of it before the heavy door groaned open, two soldiers standing guard.

Between them, a robed figure glided in.

"Hello, Valen," the figure said, and Valen gasped as she drew back her hood. Dark ringlets fell across her shoulders, where a collar of ruby red encircled her throat. And her eyes, Valen saw, were a gold so bright that in his delirium, Valen smiled and imagined painting them. She stopped before him, reaching down to slide a lock of hair off his forehead with a golden metal hand. The fingertips were designed to look like delicate claws.

She was an angel of darkness, come to him in the pits of hell.

When she looked down at him, her smile was as bright as fire.

# CHAPTER 16
## ANDROMA

FROM FAR AWAY THE DARK MATTER PUB looked like a glowing beacon among the stars. Beside it, a short ship ride away, was Lunamere.

The prison moon was an inky black the color of outer space, pocked with scars from asteroid collisions and impact zones from The Cataclysm. But Lunamere had survived that war, a proud symbol of the system in which almost everything was destroyed.

As the *Marauder* soared closer, Lira guiding it effortlessly past the few ships that dared come out to this edge of the Olen System, the satellite pub revealed its darker side.

There were entire sections missing, as if a giant mouth had taken a bite out of it, or a series of bombs had simultaneously gone off, ripping it apart from the inside out. Starlight shone through the gaps like winking eyes. It was a wonder the ringed satellite was still in one piece.

*Not such a wonder, though*, Andi thought, *that it's the perfect place to find Dex's little friend*.

"That can't be the pub. It's a pile of space junk," Gilly said to the crew as they looked out the *Marauder*'s viewport.

"Wrong, little girl. It has style. Things that have style aren't junk," Dex said, looking down at her.

"That confirms my theory then," Breck said from beside Gilly.

Dex glanced sideways at her, raising a brow in question.

"Since *you* don't have any style, you're clearly just space junk."

Andi bit back a laugh and turned back to the view ahead of them. The landing dock was loaded with ships of all makes and models. Silver Thrashers with tails like fish, perfect for carving through the stars. Ice-blue Indigos, with four outspread wings like a giant bird. Then a rare beauty, a Red Recluse. Its sleek burgundy frame could become completely invisible to the eye, not just radar. All of the ships were lined up like multicolored gifts, ripe for the taking.

Too bad they didn't have time for a joy ride.

It was prime-time for Dark Matter, the end of the sun cycle. Everyone from bounty hunters to prison workers frequented the pub, according to Dex.

Dex slipped up beside Andi to stare out the viewport. "We need to talk," he said. His smell was the same as it had always been. Like Tenebran mountain trees, fresh and strong. Her pulse heightened at his nearness, and for a moment, things between them felt like they used to.

She took a step away, reminding her foolish heart that this man had been the one to break it.

"We don't have time to talk, Dex," Andi said with a sigh. "We're landing soon."

"That's exactly my point," he said. "We're about to go into this job together, and I'd rather go in as partners, not enemies."

Andi turned to face him, arms crossed. "You and I will always be enemies," she said, her voice low.

"You don't know the whole story, Androma."

"I know enough."

He huffed out a laugh and ran a hand through his mussed hair. "Five minutes. Just…five minutes, to let me say my piece."

Andi opened her mouth to respond, but Gilly's voice filled the void between them.

"Cap?" She bounded over, her hair freshly braided. "It's almost time."

Dex sighed. "Later," he whispered to Andi. "We're going to have that talk."

Andi turned away as Gilly took her hand and hauled her back toward the waiting crew. This was the second time Dex had tried to talk to her about what had happened between them, and while she had no desire to revisit the memories of the past, she couldn't help being curious about what he had to say.

She shook her head. Now wasn't the time to be thinking about such things. They had a job to do.

Andi turned her attention back to the view of Dark Matter. She had never been here before, but she could imagine that if anyone found out a girl with her reputation was near, they would happily kill one another to turn her in for the biggest prize. She'd been on Mirabel's wanted list for years, ever since she'd escaped Arcardius and taken up a life of pirating. Most didn't even bother looking for her at this point, because too many had already lost their heads trying to chase her down. But here, in a den of enemies, she was walking right into their hands. One would be stupid not to take a chance at capturing her.

She tucked her hair beneath her hood, cloaking her face in shadows.

"You'll keep a low profile," Andi commanded her crew. "Eyes

on us at all times. You smell trouble, you see anyone step out of line, you sound the alarm and get the hell out. No mistakes." She glared sideways at Dex as the girls nodded. "No surprises."

He crossed his tattooed arms and smiled. "I wouldn't dare."

He would. *Oh, he would*. She turned away from him, biting the inside of her cheek to keep from saying another word. "Lira?"

Lira sat in her pilot's chair, hands loosely gripping the throttle as she guided them closer to the docking bay. "You don't need to say what you're thinking. I am fully aware of what must be done in there."

"Good," Andi said. "We'll have to move quickly once we get inside. No more than forty minutes."

"Plenty of time to raise hell," Gilly said as she bobbed up and down on her toes. Her golden gun was sheathed on her hip beside a belt loaded with handmade Sparks. Breck had a matching one—the two girls were plenty capable of igniting chaos with them, if their past jobs were any indication.

"Then we're all set," Andi said. A flutter of nervous excitement winged its way through her chest. It was quickly replaced by nausea as she removed her blades. Dex sighed as he removed his gloves and slapped them down on the dash.

"If anyone messes with these while I'm gone..."

"Nobody wants your disgusting palm juice," Gilly said.

"What the hell is palm juice?" Breck asked.

Gilly sighed. "Man sweat."

"Where's Alfie?" Dex asked, ignoring their comments as Lira eased back on the throttle and the ship slowed in response. "I need him to send a check-in to General Cortas before we move."

Nobody answered.

Andi turned to Gilly, who was clearly trying to hold back a laugh.

"Why are you looking at me? I have no clue," Gilly said.

Andi raised a brow.

Gilly smiled innocently back at her.

"I'll just com the general myself," Dex grumbled as he walked out the door.

The *Marauder* angled toward Dark Matter, slipping through the liquid darkness like a weapon ready to unleash itself upon the world.

Meanwhile, deep in the belly of the ship, Alfie sat alone in the locked waste bay, staring out at the stars.

*"Hello, Alfie,"* Memory said. *"Would you like some company?"*

At the sound of her voice, Alfie looked up and smiled.

# CHAPTER 17
## ANDROMA

ANDI HAD BEEN IN PLENTY OF BACK-ALLEY
bars, unruly clubs and pleasure houses that had more going on
behind closed doors than what was expected.

The atmosphere inside Dark Matter, however, had a particu-
larly unpleasant feel.

The metal doors screeched as they slid open, unleashing a thick
wave of recycled air that smelled a little too much like vomit for
her taste. The room was curved, the metal walls dented at random, as if bodies had been thrown against them, leaving their
mark. A rusted bartop, thick with stains of both the bodily and
the brew type, stood in the center of Dark Matter. The patrons
littered around it were all in different states of drunken disorder,

some of them slumped haphazardly on their stools, others shouting at the four-legged, six-armed bartender for a refill.

She doubted they'd notice who she was even if she stared them straight in the face with her name tattooed on her forehead.

Andi took note of the exits as they stepped inside. One directly behind them, where they'd just entered. The other was straight across the crowd, the dimly glowing red sign half blocked by a bald man nearly triple Andi's height. No doubt from New Veda, a planet where the inhabitants were built like giants. Years from now, Breck would likely grow to close his height, a warrior woman that none would dare cross. Andi smiled at that thought.

She hoped Breck, Gilly and Lira would get their exploding Sparks in place quickly, then move out before their plan shifted into high gear.

Across the bar were others Andi recognized from the intel they'd gathered on the ship. A table full of Lunamere guards, likely off-duty, as they guzzled pint after pint, yellow foam dripping down their unshaven beards—or in one case, a spiked jaw. She knew that they all had electric whips on their hips, ready to stun or kill at the flip of a switch, and heavy electric gauntlets to match.

And eyes constantly on the lookout for someone to toss behind bars.

*We'll see you later, boys*, she thought. That was, of course, if everything went according to plan.

Beside the Lunamere guards, a woman playing cards whistled and signaled for the bartender to refill her ale. Burns covered half her body, forming a line that neatly bisected her face. Beside her, a four-legged male Tambaruun was puffing on a piece of Adhiran rainforest bark, the cloud of smoke changing colors each time he exhaled. He, too, was covered in burns that ran up his six muscular arms, turning his hands into swollen hunks of skin.

Most of the patrons had burns or scars, mutilated limbs, empty eye sockets sitting like black holes. They were survivors of The

Cataclysm's bloody ground battles, almost every one of them, with the marks to prove it. Since the war, Andi had seen her fair share of people with souvenirs from battle, but this scene was different. This was an entire *room* full of them at once, broken and bruised, guzzling alcohol to keep the pain of the past at bay.

Andi had an inkling of how that felt. She'd tried it many times herself.

War was a heartless thing, claiming lives left and right. But it was the survivors who had to continue battling even after the fight was over.

*"This,"* Dex said, spreading his tattooed arms wide and pulling Andi from her thoughts, "is the gem of the Olen System."

"You haven't seen very many gems, then." Andi pulled her hood low over her face as she wove her way through the throngs of people heading toward the bar. "Let's get on with it."

Dex followed in silence, his head held high as if he owned the pub. She'd always admired his zest for life, a quality that few had. Andi was not one of those people. She'd choose solitude and silence any day over going out in public.

Dex could enjoy this place for the both of them—Andi was used to finer places in brighter systems, spoiled by all the extravagant balls she'd had to attend on Arcardius, a constant shadow at Kalee's back. And in the mere seconds they'd been here, she already feared she'd never get the stench of Dark Matter out of her bodysuit and cloak.

The fact that she'd had to leave her blessed, beautiful swords on the ship only added to her annoyance. She'd have to make do with her cuffs as her weapon. They were heavy enough to suffice for now.

"We should split up." She sidestepped a man hobbling past on a golden crutch made from an old android's leg. "We'll find your informant faster that way."

"We'll find her eventually." Dex stopped to survey the room. "I'd rather we stay together."

Over his shoulder, Andi saw Breck, Gilly and Lira slipping among the crowd. One by one, they'd set their Sparks in place—slipped under tabletops, wedged in dark holes in the metal framing of the room, stuffed into the air vents in the floor. Andi smiled as she glanced away. When the girls detonated them, they'd cause one hell of a scene.

Enough to distract, but not enough to destroy.

"Soyina can be a little…off-putting," Dex said. "The two of you have that in common."

Andi gave him her trademark glare.

"I simply meant that you can both terrify any man with a single glance."

She flashed him her teeth.

He shook his head and signaled for a waitress to join them. A cyborg woman tottered over on mismatched feet, one metal and one skin, both covered in strappy silver heels.

"What can I do for you, Tenebran?" the woman asked, leaning against the bar, giving his marked skin a curious glance. "Haven't seen you around these parts before."

"I'm looking for a frequent patron of yours," Dex said. He took a step closer as Andi took a step away, missing the weight of her swords on her back. "Migratory tattoos, big mismatched moon eyes?"

The cyborg shook her pink curls. "Sorry, Tenebran, haven't seen anyone who fits that description." Her eyes flashed as they raked Dex up and down. "But I might be swayed to look a little harder if…" She held out a hand.

Andi sighed and stepped forward, ready to pummel the answer out of the woman. But Dex lifted an arm.

"I'll take your knowledge, and a pint of Griss." He tossed the woman a golden Krev. "And while you're at it, add on a double stack for my lady friend. She could use it."

Andi scowled at him from the shadows of her hood.

The waitress smiled, tucking the Krev into the space between her breasts. She flicked her head toward a dark corner at the back of the room. "You're looking for Soyina. She's over there. Though I should warn you…she doesn't like to be bothered. When you're done with your business, feel free to come back. I'll buy you a drink when my shift's over." With a wink, she went back to take orders from her other customers.

"There are other ways to get information, you know," Andi said as Dex turned back to look at her.

He threw his head back and laughed so hard, she got a glimpse of a chipped tooth in the back of his mouth. Andi was pleased to see it. She'd broken it with her elbow long ago, and it was worth the tiny scar she still had as a trophy. That was the day she'd completely disarmed him during training for the first time. The day that led to their first kiss, which led to more kisses, and a night spent…

"Why are you laughing?" Andi growled.

Dex held out a hand for her to pass by, feigning courtesy she knew he didn't possess. "There's one thing you never did learn from me, Androma."

"Loyalty?" Andi asked. "How to keep my mouth shut?"

"No." Dex patted her on the cheek, then sidestepped her swing at his face. "How to have *fun*."

With a laugh, he shot past her and headed toward the dark corner of the room, where their shadowed informant sat waiting.

"Well, if it isn't my favorite small-balled bastard."

"Dearest Soyina," Dex said as he pulled up a chair across from the woman and slid into it backward, arms folded over the top. "How I've missed your heartfelt compliments."

The last time he'd seen Soyina, they'd shared three bottles of Griss and locked themselves in the bathroom of a wealthy Tene-bran's mansion until morning.

The night had been glorious, but when he'd woken the next day, his Krevs were missing, and his pants along with them. He was tied to the golden toilet pipes, all his glory out for the poor servants to see.

Oh, what a lover she'd been. A little off course, but wasn't everyone in Mirabel? Dex had never been one to choose his companions with care. His past with Andi was proof of that. Of course, he'd done plenty of wrong. More than he'd been able to stomach. He'd hated himself for it, and still did. If she would just *talk* to him, listen to his side of the story...

*Focus, Dextro*, he told himself.

He smiled now as he drank Soyina in.

She sat lazily across from him, her legs casually propped up against the table. Bloodstains—of that Dex was sure—marred her worn boots, equally as menacing as the smile on her rouged lips. Her hair was braided back from her face to reveal her lovely eyes. One brown, like Dex's, the other a pale, ghostly white to match the lost souls of the prisoners she'd brutally tortured and killed on Lunamere. Writhing migratory tattoos swam across her skin, the patterns twisting and turning as they chose new locations on her body at random.

"You're a brave woman, agreeing to meet me like this, Soyina," Dex said now. "The last time I saw you..."

Laughter bubbled from her painted lips. "All fun and games, Dex." She stared him down for a moment with those unsettling eyes. Then she downed her drink and turned to look at Andi. "*You*, little miss starlight," she said, eyeing the tips of Andi's white and purple braids, hanging from beneath her hood. "*You*, I have heard stories about. Let me get a look at that pretty little face."

Andi didn't move, a silent statue in the darkness.

"You're better off trying to get in the good graces of the queen of Xen Ptera," Dex said.

Godstars, what was he doing here, with two of the most fearsome women he'd ever been with? They were so similar it sent a shock running through him. One wrong move, and it was possible they could become…

He shuddered to think it.

…*friends.*

He could only imagine the hellstorm they'd rain down on him then.

A squeaky yellow droid rolled over and refilled Soyina's mug, then turned to fill Andi's.

She lifted a hand to stop it, the silent movement enough to send the droid rolling away into the crowd.

"My brainless colleague and I are not here for idle chitchat," Andi said, hood still covering her face in shadows. "I believe Dextro here filled you in on the problem at hand?"

Soyina nodded. "He did."

"And do you have what we require? Dex says you're in the mood to cause a little trouble."

Soyina giggled in a way that reminded Dex of the little gunner on Andi's crew. To his surprise, he'd begun to like having her around. But he'd always had a soft spot for kids with attitudes.

"Show me your face, girl," Soyina said, "and I'll be your faithful servant."

Andi sighed. Dex searched the room for something he could use as a weapon. He knew she could turn on Soyina in a flash, and they couldn't afford that today.

To his surprise, Andi reached up and slid her hood back from her face, revealing herself to the other woman.

"Ahh," Soyina said. She swung her feet off the table, then leaned forward to stop with her nose a mere inch from Andi's face.

Soyina had a passion for darkness, and Androma Racella's soul was the darkest of them all.

"Beautiful," Soyina whispered, her breath blowing the hair back from Andi's face. She ran a sharp fingernail down Andi's metal cheek implant, the migratory tattoos swimming down her arm as if afraid.

Dex had to hand it to Andi. She didn't flinch beneath Soyina's stare. He allowed himself a moment to admire her finely sculpted face before looking away. She *was* beautiful, but he wasn't allowed to think of her that way anymore. Not after what he'd done.

"I can almost taste the death on you," Soyina breathed. "How many lives have you stolen, Bloody Baroness?"

Andi whirled on Dex. "You *told* her who I was?"

He shrugged, giving her the carefree look he knew she hated with every inch of her soul. "What can I say? Soyina's a big fan."

"Have you ever tortured anyone, Baroness?" Soyina asked, pulling Andi's attention back to her. "I can only imagine the things you could do with that darkness you harbor. The Xen Pterran queen would be wise to hire you on as a colleague of mine. Or a mercenary, perhaps."

"A colleague?" Andi raised a brow at Dex as she scooted back in her chair, clearly done with Soyina's closeness.

Dex took a sip of his drink and nodded. "Soyina practices the art of torture," he explained, smiling as Andi's eyes widened a bit at his explanation. "She works on Lunamere as one of Queen Nor's more *forward* ways of getting information out of the prisoners."

"A nasty job, most would think," Soyina said. She ran her fingers down her dark curls. "But it's not without its certain charms." She giggled, then folded her hands on the rickety table in front of her. Her tattoos swirled like a nebula across them, then trickled back toward her elbows. "Daggers and sparks of fire. Channels of electricity. The screams of the women are good and well, but the men…oh, they do *so* love to plead with me."

Dex sighed as she continued.

"Of course, it's not all bad," Soyina said, twisting a braid around her fingertip. "When they die, I don't always leave them dead."

Andi raised a pale brow, and Soyina smiled that same gorgeously chilling smile that had drawn Dex to her in the first place. He wondered what she looked like to those on the fringes of death, as they spouted information about whatever they knew of the Unified Systems. It was rumored that, though there was a peace treaty in place, Queen Nor still seethed with the desire for revenge and sought a way to destroy the other systems. They'd never be able to come back from the destruction The Cataclysm had caused for them, though. The damage was too much, the lives lost, too many.

"I'm also a Revivalist," Soyina said, drawing Dex's attention back again. "With every death comes the chance for a second life. The opportunity for more information. I bring them back, as long as I'm within the three-minute window, of course."

"With what?" Andi asked. "How can you bring a dead man back to life?"

Soyina chuckled arrogantly, clearly relishing Andi's ignorance. "With science, dear girl!"

This was the downside to working with someone like Soyina. She loved to talk and brag and talk some more. Dex's head was beginning to spin, wondering how he'd ever taken an interest in a woman who was so clearly off her axis.

He glanced sideways at Andi.

Two women, then.

"The map, Soyina," Dex reminded her. "You have it with you?"

She blinked, a crooked smile on her lips as she seemed to come back to the present. "Before we dive into the matter at hand, I hope you remembered the payment I requested?"

Dex took another healthy gulp of his drink, relaxing as the fire swam into his bones. "Half of your payment has already been anonymously wired to your account. Untraceable. When the mission is complete, you'll get the other portion. You're sure you can't go with us?"

Soyina lifted her wrist and rolled her eyes. "The great queen tracks her prison workers. I'm afraid I'd ruin your mission if I were to join you. Although, imagine all the time we'd be able to share together, if I went. Which reminds me, Dextro, of the other portion of my payment."

"I haven't forgotten…" Dex felt heat sliding into his cheeks as he glanced sideways at Andi, then back at Soyina. "The other part of your payment, you'll receive…"

*"Now,"* Soyina said, smiling like a predator. Her lips pressed together in a pout as she saw the look of horror on Dex's face. "A deal's a deal, bounty hunter. I'll be waiting." She stood up from the table, her chair scraping against the floor as she walked away.

Dex watched her slip into the bathroom, waggling a finger at him as she disappeared behind the closed door.

"You can't be serious," Andi said, her face aghast. "You're actually paying her with…"

"I'm not paying her. I'm simply offering her memories," Dex said. He stood up, mussing his hair with a hand as he backed away from the table. "You should know, Androma, how much fun five minutes with me can be."

"Three minutes," she said. "On a good day."

"Jealous, love?"

"Hardly."

He watched her reach across the table and down the rest of his mug in one swig. Then she pulled her hood over her head and settled back into her chair. "Good luck, *bounty hunter*. And this time, try not to lose your pants when you're done."

Dex froze midstep. "How did you…?"

Andi laughed from beneath her hood. "I have a reputation to uphold, Dextro. I made it a priority to learn every hidden detail about my partner's past."

With that, she dismissed him.

Dex turned on his heel and stalked toward the bathroom, cursing to himself as he left one devil behind and went to greet the next.

Lunamere was almost impenetrable.

They'd known it days ago, when not even Alfie's advanced hacking systems could get any information on the prison moon, let alone an actual blueprint of the building. There weren't any survivors to question—not because they couldn't find any, but because they didn't exist. Lunamere prisoners were there for life, or until death took them.

The moon on which the prison stood was a cold, barren wasteland. The prison itself, a towering fortress with no windows and only two doors.

One way in, for entering prisoners. "And one way out," Soyina said, as she explained the map to Andi and Dex, leaning close so they could see her strange eyes light up when she spoke. "For the corpses."

Andi looked up. "That's it? No other exits? Not even…"

"It's a prison, Dark Heart," Soyina said with a wave of her hand. "Once you go in, you're not meant to come back out. Fortunately for the two of you, I can take care of that part. You simply have to find your own ride inside, as we spoke of earlier, Dextro."

"Ten thousand Krevs for a one-way ticket," Dex said from Andi's left. His jaw clenched as he spoke, as if he were holding himself back from saying something he'd likely regret.

Soyina smiled with all of her teeth. "Not nearly enough to make this worth my while. And yet here I am, helping you. I may as well offer myself up on a platter for Nor to slit my throat."

*Money talks*, Andi thought. She looked back down at the map on the dimly lit screen Soyina produced, at the twisting and turning halls of Lunamere. It was seventeen levels, a building made of black obsidinite, mined from the moon itself. Impossible to shatter, scratch or dent, except with tools specially crafted to work the stone. And it was the only building on all of Lunamere that hadn't been completely annihilated during the Battle of Black Sky.

"The cells," Andi said. "What are they made of?"

"The same as the rest of the building. Don't think you'll be able to break out once you're in. Men have gone mad trying to dig themselves out of the darkness."

They went over the map for a while, Andi doing her best to memorize every inch of the layout. There were no elevators to reach the seventeen floors of the prison, and each stairwell would only allow them to descend one level. Andi and Dex would have to traverse the entirety of each hall—and dispatch any guards they encountered—in order to reach the next stairwell down.

Countless men and women—and children, if the rumors were true—had lived the remainder of their lives inside those prison walls. Andi felt sick as she looked down at the map.

In her mind, she saw herself four years ago, seated on a marble bench while hundreds of Arcardian soldiers stared back at her. Classmates, who now hissed her name like a curse. Teachers and trainers, whose bodies were rigid with hatred for her failure.

She saw a silver gavel gripped in an angry fist, the *boom* as it came down like a war hammer. The general's twisted expression as he stared down at her, and Kalee's mother with tears in her eyes, a sadness burning so deep that it scalded like the still-fresh lacerations on Andi's wrist.

*Guilty*, the judge had intoned. *Guilty of treason.*

"Andi?" Dex asked.

He waved his hand in front of her face, drawing her back to the present. She shook the memories away to find Dex and Soyina staring at her.

"You have our plans," Andi said. "Now I want to hear how you're going to uphold your side of the bargain. Once we get ourselves inside, how do you intend to get us out?"

"Once you're inside, I'll locate your cells. It's likely they'll have the two of you near each other, on one of the upper levels. We're reaching overflow levels this time of year." She spoke as if the prison were one of Mirabel's finest hotels, full of visiting tourists from all across the galaxy. "I'll have your cells unlocked by the time you wake."

"Wake?" Dex asked.

Soyina lifted a finger to her lips and smiled. "You have one hour to find your prisoner and free him before I myself will sound the alarms that you've escaped. What?" she asked, seeing Dex's clenched jaw and fists. "A girl has to save her own skin *somehow*."

"And how are we to track the time?" Dex asked.

Soyina considered this. "The guards rotate every half hour. That will be your marker." She focused back on the map, pointing to a large section of rooms on the second level that led to the only exit door.

The one for the corpses.

"This room here will be your goal."

"And that room is?" Andi asked.

"That, my dear friends, is my playground. My palace of pain. The prisoners come in, and I pick and choose the tools that will make them sing. And when they die? They go out that doorway on a transport ship. Up and away, out to float with the stars."

Dex nearly choked on his drink. Andi simply stared the strange woman down, wondering how much she could really trust a person who derived so much joy from others' pain. She killed to stay safe, to keep her crew alive when all the other options ran out. Afterward, she meditated and mourned the deaths. In sleep, the faces of the dead haunted her. But Soyina smiled about stealing lives, as if each death only upped her pride.

"What about weapons?" Andi asked. "Can you leave some in our cell?"

"My weapon is my mind," Soyina said with a crazed grin. "You would do well to learn to fight in the same way."

*If only she knew the things I could do with my fists*, Andi thought, remembering all the times she'd sparred with Lira in the storage bay of the *Marauder*. All the months she'd spent with Dex and his bounty-hunting guild, learning how to snap a man's neck as easily as if she were snapping a thin tree branch in two.

"My cuffs," Andi said, glancing down at them, "cannot be removed. You'll see to it that they stay intact."

Not a question. Rather, a demand.

Soyina nodded. "There are two guards stationed on each level at all times. They are armed with electric gauntlets and whips, programmed to paralytic levels, should you be hit too many times."

Dex gave a curt nod. "We'll take care of them. How will we get into Valen's cell?"

"I'll leave the key." She shrugged again. "Seems too simple, doesn't it? Lucky for you, Lunamere is age-old. It's worked for centuries without all that tech the Unified Systems are so prideful of."

"And what about Valen?" Andi asked. "Have you…?"

She wasn't sure how to ask the question, and yet Soyina seemed to read her thoughts.

"The prisoner," she said, leaning forward with her chin balanced on her hands, "is a strange one. Easily broken, and yet…" She trailed off, staring past Andi. For a moment, she almost looked haunted. "He's never died on me."

Andi wondered what information Soyina had pulled from Valen. He had always been silent, a boy of few words. She'd lived just down the hall from him for several years, and she could scarcely remember a conversation with him that was longer than a passing *hello* in the hallways. Andi knew that pain had a way of making people, silent or not, spit out the truth. If there wasn't any truth to be given, they made something up. People would do anything, say anything, to avoid pain.

She wondered what Valen had said.

She also wondered what he would say when he saw her.

"Any questions?" Soyina asked.

The silence hung between them, broken at times by the clink of glasses, the tap of heels, the barking laughter of nearby patrons.

This was too easy. Too simple. Andi stared at the woman across from them, searching her face for some sign of a betrayal, some other plan in the works. But sometimes asking was easier than trying to divine another's intentions. "Why are you helping us?"

For the first time since meeting her, Soyina's wild grin fell. In its place was a new expression, something deeper and darker. The woman beyond the mask.

She unbuttoned the top two buttons of her black prison worker's uniform. When the fabric fell away, Andi frowned.

Soyina's chest was a patchwork of scars and burn marks, just like the rest of the patrons scattered around them in the poorly lit pub. Her burns were similar to the ones on Andi's wrists.

*Mistakes*, they seemed to hiss, itching and squirming on her skin as the tattoos writhed around them, morphing as they passed over the scars.

"My marks," Soyina said, her voice low and steady, "prove that I am a survivor of The Cataclysm. One would assume that I was born and raised on Xen Ptera, suffering with the rest of them when the Unified Systems struck." She sighed and began to button her uniform back up, concealing the scars. "I am *not* of this system. I was here visiting with my family when the war hit, and my own planet refused to allow us reentry for fear that we had become spies."

Andi had heard stories like this, about the hundreds of refugees who were forced to stay behind in the Olen System when the fighting began. It was a stain on the history of the Unified Systems that many rallied to change. They had tried and failed and failed again. Others tried to sweep it under the mat, as if it had never happened at all.

"My parents and I were forced to fight. They died hating the Unified Systems for leaving us to this fate," Soyina said with a snarl. Her eyes met Andi's when she spoke again, flashing like a knife. "But I survived. Many would think my allegiance would still be to the Unified Systems, that I would hate the Olen System even more for forcing us to fight in a war against our own home planets. At first, I did hate Olen. But my allegiances changed when I saw what the Unified Systems put the people of Olen through for nearly a decade." She sighed. "Ah, well. I guess I'm considering this job a chance to leave Olen behind, head back to what was once my home and rally for change in my own ways."

"You'll have a hell of a time," Dex said.

Soyina smiled a soldier's smile. Dark, and full of secrets. "I'm prepared to do what I have to. Now, back to work."

She tapped the map again, drawing Andi's attention back to the rooms that held the exit door. "One hour to find and rescue the boy. I'll meet you at that door, no sooner and no later. My partner has mysteriously fallen quite ill, so I will be the only one on body duty. But if you're caught by any of the patrolling guards…" She laughed again, the mask returning. "Well, I guess we'll be seeing each other in that room either way. It's up to you what the circumstances will be."

Cold dread slithered its way up and down Andi's spine.

*Dead or alive.* Andi hoped for the latter.

Soyina glanced between the two of them, laughter tugging at her lips.

"Death is a simple thing. It's pirates I'll never understand." She stood from her chair, turning only once to glance back at the two of them still seated at the table. "One hour. If your plan goes south, you keep your mouths shut about me and I will do the same for you."

She winked at Dex. Before she left, she leaned down and whispered into Andi's ear.

"We *didn't*, by the way. Earlier, I mean. Your comrade wanted to whine like a baby about his *feelings* for you."

Andi's mouth parted in shock as Soyina backed away and winked once more. Then she turned and left, fading into the crowd, and the two of them were alone.

Dex stared at Andi for a moment. "What did she say?"

"Nothing," Andi said. Soyina must have been lying. Dex had about as many feelings as a hunk of varillium. "Nothing at all." Sitting in this pub, alone with Dex, was making her feel slow. The smoke burned in her lungs, and the taste of stale liquor was heavy on her tongue. She sighed and stood up, stretching out her limbs, cracking her knuckles as she readied herself to make a move.

Dex stood, as well, frowning for a moment as he looked at her.

"Do you trust me, Androma?" he asked, taking a step closer.

Long ago, she would have whispered, *yes*. Her pathetic, traitorous heart skipped a beat. Andi scolded it internally and barked out a laugh. "I'd never be so foolish again."

He stopped an arm's length away, close enough that she could see the stubble on his chin. The sleepless lines beneath his eyes. "Then this should be fun," he said with a sigh. "Play along with me."

He grinned like he was holding on to a secret.

Then he lurched forward and, in one sweeping movement, mashed his lips up against hers.

# CHAPTER 18
## NOR

NO MATTER HOW MUCH AIR FILLED HER LUNGS, she was still left gasping for breath.

A stone was crushing her. A single solitary stone, no larger than the palm of her hand, was leeching the life from her very soul. It felt as if the weight of a thousand boulders were all forced into it, seeking to torment her endlessly by giving her air but never actually allowing her to breathe.

A disembodied voice whispered sweet, terrible nothings in her ear.

"Pathetic."

"Unworthy."

"Weak."

In these moments of complete helplessness, when she couldn't move or think for herself, Nor felt like a pawn in someone else's game.

*She needed control and power, but those were oceans away from the cracked ground she seemed to become.*

*The weight of the stone increased to an unbearable pressure. No longer did it allow air into her quivering lungs. She was dying, being forced into a premature grave.*

*No matter how much she willed her invisible tormentors to stop, she kept on sinking, until even the ground could not take the pressure any longer.*

*A chasm opened up underneath her broken body and swallowed her whole.*

*Falling.*

*She was falling into the black abyss. She plummeted toward a fiery furnace that welcomed her with its jagged fangs.*

*All the while, the stone never left her chest. Not until the fire devoured her.*

*Even then, she still felt the pain of a thousand boulders.*


Nor jolted awake, grappling for something, anything, to anchor her to reality.

She was so cold. Her body, coated in sweat, was attracting the frigid recycled air that clung to her like a second skin.

Darkness surrounded her, compressed her. She was back in the nightmare, must be. Then, no more than a heartbeat later, she was grounded in this world by a sturdy hand she knew all too well.

Zahn.

"Nor?" His hand came around her shoulder, pulling her toward his bare chest. "I'm here. Everything is fine, I'm right here." He cooed into her ear, attempting to calm her erratic breathing.

"I had the dream again," she whispered. "It was…so dark."

His lips were on her skin, his breath warm as he spoke in a low, even tone. "I'm going to open the curtains."

His naked form slid from the bed, leaving it feeling unfamiliar and empty. An ache spread through her chest, reminding her of the dream.

Across the room, the curtains slid open. Nor shielded her eyes from the red haze of early morning as it drifted toward her. Zahn seemed to become one with the shadows of her bedroom as he stepped away from the window.

"Come back to me," she whispered.

He trotted back to bed then pulled her to him, chasing the monsters of her dream away.

The heat that radiated from him was so comforting, warming her shivering body, unlike the fiery hell she had fallen into during her dream.

By day, Zahn served as her personal bodyguard, protecting her from physical harm. By night, when she had the same nightmare over and over, he was here to perform this dance.

No one but Zahn was allowed to get this close to her. Not just physically, but emotionally, beneath the layers she'd surrounded herself with. No one, not even Darai, was allowed to see her so vulnerable.

"Tell me about it," he whispered. "Was it the same?"

She nodded. "I couldn't breathe. I couldn't think, Zahn." She lifted her prosthetic hand to her face to wipe away the tears, then dropped it, disgusted by the sight of the gold metal, of the scars marring her upper wrist. Disgusted with herself for feeling so weak.

But Zahn gently wrapped his warm fingers around her metal ones, then pressed his lips to her cheeks. Kissing away the tears.

"You're safe," he said with a sigh. "I will always protect you, Nor."

"I don't need protecting," she whispered.

His soft chuckle sent a shiver down her spine. "Everyone does, at one point or another. You don't fool me, Nor Solis. You never have, and you never will."

She leaned her head on his chest, listening to the sound of his heartbeat.

Strong. Steady. The only constant in her life, besides her desire for revenge.

To many people, Nor was the stone-cold ruler who haunted the nightmares of her foes. But to Zahn, she was just Nor. The love of his life, as he was hers.

It had been just the two of them since The Cataclysm took both of their families years ago. He'd seen her at her weakest, and without him she would have lost herself to grief. He was her only friend; the only person she loved. He'd broken through her walls when her father died, and then kept breaking through them until she no longer wished to shut him out.

Leaders, fearless and honest in all the ways that seemed to count, still had other dimensions to them. Other secrets.

Zahn was Nor's best kept one.

"Don't leave me," Nor said, looking up into his eyes. Seeing the passion mirrored there.

"I would never dream of it," he said.

Their lips touched, and his hands slid down her bare back, gentle at first. Then hungry for more as she let him lay her back down.

"I love you," Zahn said. "My *Nhatyla*."

The lingering fear from her nightmare trickled away as a very different sort of feeling took its place.

# CHAPTER 19
## DEX

DEX HAD FORGOTTEN HOW FAST ANDI'S RE-
flexes could be when she was mad.

*Furious, actually*, he thought, as he watched the shock on her
face melt into a mask of pure, boiling rage.

He had only the briefest of seconds to ponder his possible mistake as Andi pushed some sorry fool out of her way. Then Dex's
chair was in Andi's hands as she lifted it high over her head.

*"Dex!"* she screamed. And was that a *growl* he heard coming
from her lips?

He barely had time to lift his arms over his head before she
slammed the chair down on top of him. Dex crashed against

the table, toppling over three glass mugs that shattered against the metal floor.

*"What the hell?"* Andi yelled.

Dex groaned as he stood, swiping glass from his shirt. Without a doubt, that was going to leave a bruise or two. But at least his plan, painful as it may be, was working.

He turned back to smile at Andi. "That's all you've got, *Captain?"*

He just needed her to play along, make a big enough show to draw in the Lunamere warden. That would be their ticket inside.

Andi spat on the ground, then rubbed her lips with the back of her sleeve. For one moment, she looked purely *Andi*, angry as a wet feline and terrifyingly beautiful. Dex felt smug, like he could strut for hours with his head held high.

Then he saw the moment when Andi's face changed. She transformed into someone else entirely; an actress playing the perfect part.

"How *dare* you cheat on me!" she snarled.

Dex's hands fell to his sides. "Wait…*wha*t?"

Lira appeared, hands on her hips as she leveled a death glare on him. "So this is the other girl, Dextro?" She looked Andi up and down, then back to Dex. "I'm not very impressed."

What in the hell were they doing? *This* was not part of his plan.

All around them, people stopped talking. The music faded as yet *another* voice joined the mix, and Dex heard heavy footsteps approaching.

"You honestly thought you could screw around with two other girls," Breck said, stepping up between Lira and Andi, "and not get caught by us?"

Dex lowered his voice. "Ladies…"

"Girls talk, Dextro," Andi said, tossing her hair over her shoulder. She looked to Lira, then to Breck. "He deserves to be taught a lesson about relationships."

Her voice grew louder with every word, more bar patrons craning their necks to see what the ruckus was all about.

Rubbing his still-stinging forearms, Dex quickly whispered, "What exactly are you three doing?"

Andi ignored him. "Who wants the first shot?"

Breck cracked her knuckles, and people began to rise from their chairs, slowly surrounding them in a circle, ready for what looked to be a promising fight.

"You can have him," Lira said. "He's a waste of my time."

"Mine, as well," Breck agreed as men hooted and hollered, laughing at the cheater caught in a bind.

"Come on, ladies," Dex drawled, catching on to their plan. If they had to give the onlookers a show, well...they'd get one. "It was just one little kiss."

"Like hell it was!" Breck howled.

Before he could prepare himself, her foot slammed into his gut.

Dex went flying.

He landed with a sickening crash against a table, all air gone from his lungs. The table tipped, and more glass mugs shattered as cards and Krevs spiraled into the air, a flurry of black and red and gold.

Dex slid to a stop, his head slamming against the back wall.

*That* was going to leave a mark, too.

Silence swept through Dark Matter, and as Dex's vision began to clear, the only sounds were the crunch of boots on shattered glass and the constant dripping of wasted alcohol pooling over the table's edges as its previous occupants stood, surrounding Dex in a half circle.

The giantess had catapulted him right into the middle of a table full of Lunamere guards, every single one of them looking as furious as the last.

"Pardon me, boys," Dex said. "I seem to have fallen right into the middle of your little card game."

SASHA ALSBERG & LINDSAY CUMMINGS

The guard closest to him, a brute as tall as Breck, curled his upper lip and actually growled like a feral dog.

"You disrespected those ladies," the giant man said. "And you messed up my game. I had a winning hand."

"Easy, big guy." Dex held up his arms in surrender. "We can talk about this."

The guard reached out with a meaty hand and grabbed Dex by the collar, twisting his fingers into the fabric. Then he hoisted him up until their noses were nearly touching, Dex's legs dangling below him.

"No talking, then?" Dex asked.

Andi's chuckle from behind him was the only sound in the room.

Then the guard swung, and all hell broke loose.

Dex wasn't the tallest man by Mirabel standards, but what he lacked in height, he made up in speed and agility—and above all, the desire to *win*.

Besides, he'd never live it down if he couldn't take out a few dozen drunkards in a bar fight.

He was all grace and glory as he spun and whirled, taking out Lunamere guards as they rushed forward in hopes of sinking their knives into his gut. Two men lunged at him, and Dex swiped out with a knife from a nearby table, a *snick* sounding as he caught one of them in the cheek.

Blood splattered a one-eyed woman at a nearby table, who promptly howled about her ruined meal before rushing into the fight. Her companion dove in after her with a black club he'd pulled out from under the table. Dex leaped, narrowly avoiding a hit.

*One step, two steps, leap.*

Dex landed on the bar top, his boots skidding as glasses fell over and spilled the contents on their owners.

An entirely new group of pissed-off patrons screamed and rose to join the fight.

Ten men from the left.

Six from the right, all hefting weapons.

And Andi, sprinting from the back with…

Dex's eyes widened as he dodged a chair sailing past his head. Were those *meat cleavers* clutched in her fists?

Angry shouts filled the pub, music to Andi's ears as she joined the fight.

The world melted away, every patron turning into a single muddled shade, until all she could see was the swinging of too-slow fists, the swish of a dulled blade cartwheeling through the air to stick itself in another man's back.

Andi sprinted forward, plucked the blade from the man, then whirled around and drove it down into a Lunamere guard's thigh right as he rushed past her in pursuit of Dex.

He howled and dropped, and then she was off again, leaping over his fallen form, her hands itching to raise hell, draw blood and spread the glory of her name.

The Bloody Baroness was here.

She'd make sure every single one of them knew it.

Dex laughed as he swung a bottle at a guard's head. It shattered as he grabbed another and another, sending them both sailing across the pub to explode against the metal walls.

Everywhere was a symphony of sound, bats swinging against metal, men and women shouting at the top of their lungs as people too far under the influence swung at everything and nothing at once.

Chaos circled throughout the room, building like a wildfire.

*Speaking of fire…* Dex thought as he took on two men at once. Andi was by the bar, but where were Breck and Gilly and Lira with their Sparks? He ducked down just as the man in front of him swung. The man's fist connected with the person behind Dex instead. There was a crack and a shout, and the two sorry bastards went down fighting, hissing and spitting like cats thrown in water.

The plan was in place. Everything was glorious, beautiful, blessed disarray.

They just had to keep it going until the warden of Lunamere arrived.

Andi searched the bar for a clock, her eyes scanning past the swinging fists and people standing on tabletops to get a better view of the brawl. The holo on the wall above the bar said 13:23. Plenty of time to raise a little more hell.

Dex was cornered with his back against the bar, fresh green blood oozing from a cut on his brow. Three men had closed in on him, one hoisting a broken chair leg as a weapon, another snarling with thick red canines bared. The little table-waiting droid spun in circles nearby, one of its squeaky wheels missing. Beside it, the six-armed bartender was using the missing wheel to bludgeon another man's head.

Every part of Andi's soul told her to get the hell out of there before the Sparks went off. She could abandon the mission. Leave Valen Cortas in prison, with Dex beside him once the warden of Lunamere caught wind of this.

But as she stood back and watched the clock tick down, some tiny part of herself, some animal thing deep down, began to claw its way back up and out into the smoky pub light.

The Bloody Baroness never turned away from a fight.

With a sigh, she pushed herself forward, swinging her borrowed knives as if they were extensions of her body. Little pieces of heaven clutched in her hell-raising fists.

She hacked through the crowd and cleared the area in front of Dex just in time to pull him down behind the bar.

"Time already?" he asked.

She didn't even have a chance to nod before the Sparks went off.

Then the whole world exploded around them.

# CHAPTER 20
## KLAREN
## YEAR EIGHTEEN

*THE GIRL STOOD ATOP A HILLSIDE ON A DYING world, watching the sky drip acid rain.*

*The journey here had been long. Yet, like she'd always dreamed, the girl had survived.*

*Sickly green clouds blocked out the horizon, but through the shroud, she could just barely make out the top of the Solis Palace in the distance. Towering spires made of black glass stood at its highest point, shimmering panes of red woven into the black like trails of dripping blood.*

*Below the spires, deep in the belly of the palace, the King of Xen Ptera prepared himself for a long-awaited meeting.*

*The wind blew, tossing the rain about. The girl shivered and pulled her cloak tighter, the protective wrap around her face closer, to better save her skin.*

*Today, she'd make her first move.*

*"It is time, Klaren," a voice said from her right.*

*The girl turned. Her greatest ally, her trusted adviser, was not the kind of man many would wish to gaze upon.*

*Something had gone wrong in his Formation, leaving half of his face mutilated, as if it were made of melted, discolored wax. His eyes shimmered, their color nearly as black as the palace spires far below. Bits of metal held together his flesh.*

*A gruesome creature Darai was.*

*But the girl knew his soul, and she knew that it was pure.*

*He had, after all, given her the blade that ensured she would be the only Yielded standing when the Conduit chose.*

*"I'm ready," the girl said. She took his arm as he helped her into a stolen carriage.*

*"Remember what we spoke of," Darai said softly as a borrowed servant snapped the reins on a sleek, spidery Xentra, its many legs clicking as it crawled down the hillside. The wheels of the carriage slipped into motion, pulling them downward, where they joined in with the countless others heading toward the palace. "Remember what is at stake."*

*The girl nodded, then turned her gaze to the window. As they neared the palace, she felt for the thread of the dreams that she kept locked away in her mind, like a constant glowing trail of embers that never quite burned out.*

*She felt its warmth and tugged.*

*The future spilled into place, flooding her mind.*

*She could see a man's face, gentle and kind, but with sharp edges when the girl really looked. His green eyes, bright as emeralds, met hers as she stepped into the light and pulled her hood back to reveal her perfectly sculpted face. Her womanly curves. She could almost hear his heart beating, almost taste the desire spilling from him as he looked at her, took her hand in his and pressed it to his lips.*

*A hundred girls stood around her, and yet in that moment, they all paled in comparison. She was everything this king wanted. Everything he'd ever dreamed of in a wife.*

*"Are you certain you will succeed?" Darai asked now, pulling the girl from the thread of her dreams.*

*"I am certain," she said, without a hint of doubt in her voice. She lifted her chin proudly. "Just as I was certain years ago, during my Yielding, that I would be chosen." She smiled sideways at him. "I will do anything, Darai, to ensure that my dreams become a reality."*

*Darai inclined his head. "You are a worthy sacrifice."*

*The girl smiled. She had worked her entire life to claw her way here, fighting with her words and her wit and her smile to get noticed by the right eyes, to speak into whatever ears would listen. It had taken everything she had to make it here, to stay alive, to grow strong enough to secure a spot in the king's lineup of potential brides.*

*Today, it would all come to fruition when he laid eyes upon her, when she spoke the words she'd practiced, year after year.*

*The carriage rolled to a stop at the bottom of the hill. Acid rain pelted down from the skies, thunder booming as the carriage shook.*

*"May the light be your guide," Darai said, opening the door for her.*

*The girl lifted her hood and stepped out into the acid rain.*

*Soon, very soon, she would become queen.*

# CHAPTER 21
## LIRA

GLASS RAINED DOWN ON TOP OF THEM.

Lira opened her eyes to see Breck hunched over beside her, coughing smoke from her lungs, eyes watering and red.

*Mountains crumble*, Lira thought.

How strong had Gilly's homemade Sparks been? Perhaps they'd been a bit too generous with the amount of powder they'd poured into the orbed casings.

Lira rolled to her hands and knees and crawled past the scattered playing cards, bottles of broken liquid and moaning bodies on the floor. Somewhere across the room, the bartender howled out curses over the wasted liquor.

"My leg!" someone screamed. "My leg!"

An android, headless neck sparking, walked around in circles, bumping into overturned tables and blown-apart chairs.

*Definitely too strong*, Lira thought.

Beside her, Gilly appeared. Her nose was crooked and bleeding. "That...was awesome."

If the warden hadn't been drawn in by the fight...surely, after this, she would come to restore order. Any moment now.

Lira kept crawling forward, coughing as the fires from the Sparks flickered out. She scanned her surroundings, looking for Andi and Dex.

At first, she couldn't see her captain. For a moment, fear swallowed Lira whole.

They'd ruined this.

They'd blown up the entire plan along with the pub.

*That was quite a show, Lir.*

The com message flashed into her vision, and she knew Andi was safe.

She blinked it away, scanning the darkness again.

There. Motion to her left, near the bar as Andi stood, using a table to pull herself upright. Beside her Dex struggled to his feet. The poor fool looked like a baby fresh out of the womb, disoriented and confused. Lira knew a sympathetic person would help a teammate get his bearings.

Unfortunately for him, Andi was anything but. Lira smiled at that.

With so much smoke clouding the room, she found it hard to see anything farther than a few feet in front of her. But she could hear people moaning. Curses hissed out through clenched teeth.

"Her pub," the bartender was mumbling. "Her pub, *her beautiful pub*... The warden will *kill* me..."

A wail reverberated through the cavernous room. Lira craned her neck around toward the entrance to the pub as guards plowed in through the unhinged doors, guns held before them, emerald lasers cutting through the smoke as they angled about the room, searching for the cause of the attack.

Lira's stomach twisted.

This was it.

The final step in the plan.

From her vantage point, Andi's pale hair and metal cheeks, visible now as she stepped forward, were like beacons in the chaos. Smoke curled around her feet like dancing wraiths.

*You still have time to stop this plan*, Lira's mind hissed at her. *You can't trust Soyina. You can't trust Dex.*

But then Dex was speaking, his voice like a gunshot amid all the groans and moans.

"It's about time you showed up."

The guards lined up in front of him and Andi. Too many rifles aimed at their chests, their heads, their necks. Kill shots, all of them.

*Help your captain*, that little voice begged Lira. *You can't let this happen.*

A single figure stepped through the smoke, and the guards fanned out to make space. Lira watched, teeth clenched, as the warden of Lunamere surveyed the scene.

"Seeing as you're the only people left standing in this room right now, I'm going to ask you a question and you're going to answer it truthfully." She puffed herself up, the red-and-gold sash on her chest shining even in the smoky room. "Were you the perpetrators of this attack?"

Dex tilted his head and flashed her his best smile. "Guilty as charged."

The warden stepped forward.

And slammed her fist into Dex's face.

His head turned sideways, and he toppled against an overturned table with a sickening crash.

"You've just destroyed *thousands'* worth of assets for me," the warden growled. She looked to her guards. "Detain and scan them. I want to know who these bastards are and what the hell they're doing in my pub."

Lira watched it all with a sickness in her gut.

Dex rose and turned back around, his mouth spreading into a bloody smile. "Well, well, Warden. The rumors about your strength are true. I'd love to take you on a date sometime. Perhaps to the Unified Systems, where I can show you a planet truly worth your time."

The warden's fists clenched. "Gag him."

"Do you have any Griss on you? Not the cheap kind you serve here," Dex said, riling her up further. "I'm positively parched."

"What is the meaning of this?" the warden demanded, looking to Andi. "Explain yourselves."

Andi smiled at her like a predator. "Screw you. And screw Xen Ptera."

A guard marched toward Andi, gun outstretched. He was about to cuff her when Andi leaped to her feet, whirling so fast that she'd grabbed his gun and used it to shoot out his kneecap before the guard could even scream in surprise.

"*Detain them!*" the warden howled. "*Now!*"

The rest of the guards converged on her and Dex.

Through the chaos, a single word filtered into Lira's vision from Andi's channel.

*Run.*

Lira shook her head. This couldn't be the best plan…this couldn't be the only way. It was happening too fast.

*Run.*

"Come on," Gilly said. "It's time to go."

But Lira was frozen.

"Lira," Breck whispered. "We have the command."

Gilly's small hand wrapped around Lira's. She began to pull, gently at first, then insistently as Dex screamed curses and Andi began to shout about damning the queen of Xen Ptera. Once they had them on the ground, bound in cuffs, half of the guards began to move about the room. One of them uncovered the shell of a Spark.

"Right here, Warden. Looks homemade."

"I want every single person in this pub checked. Identified. Backgrounds. Do it now."

Unless they left now, the guards would soon discover the rest of the girls.

*Run.*

The message was there in bright red, hovering before Lira's eyes.

Lira hated herself for what she was about to do, hated the command Andi had given.

But she allowed Gilly to lead her into the shadows. She stood patiently as Breck silently disabled the single, unsuspecting guard by the hole they'd strategically blown in the back wall. A quick exit point.

Gilly slipped into the darkness. Breck squeezed in after her.

But Lira stopped and looked over her shoulder one last time, her gut begging her not to go. Never, in all of their missions, had they abandoned their captain.

Even now, the warden of Lunamere was standing over Andi like a predator ready to spring.

"You will rot in hell for this," she said.

*Not happening,* Lira's mind screamed. *This is* not *happening.*

It went against every fiber of her being.

But it was an order—all part of the plan—and Lira could not disobey.

It was with great pain that she left her captain behind, a prisoner, and went to secure sweet freedom back on the waiting ship.

# CHAPTER 22
## ANDROMA

THE MOONS ABOVE ARCARDIUS HUNG LIKE
*two glowing eyes, their mingling light creating a purple hue in the sky.*

*They stared down onto Averia, the floating green-and-purple mountain
that housed the Cortas estate. In daylight, Averia looked like an oil painting rendered by a master's hand. The rolling green hills, the blue streams
flocked on either side by flora in deep reds and yellows and oranges. Then
there was the estate itself, all angles and solid lines, like a sprawling white
bird with its wings spread across the grounds.*

*At night, however, all of Averia was bathed in blue.*

*The moonlight winked down onto the estate, peeking into the win-
dows on the fifth floor, illuminating two girls as they tiptoed their way
through the halls, careful not to wake the house.*

"It's just one little ride," Kalee whispered as Andi followed her best friend and charge past an open doorway that looked like a dark, gaping mouth. "We'll be back before he even knows we're gone."

"You're crazy, Kalls. It's not going to happen."

Over a year had passed since Andi had been sworn in as Kalee's Spectre. Until that moment, her life had been so confusing, utterly without direction. Andi was a soldier without a cause, living in the shadows of her mother's perfect Arcardian image, her father's constant urge to train harder. To swing faster. To be a better soldier.

Andi loved her planet, dearly, but she was too young to be drafted for anything. Too angry to make friends. She wouldn't graduate for another three years, and no matter how hard she trained to make her father proud, or danced to become the graceful daughter her mother wished her to be, it couldn't fill the void.

Andi loved fighting, and dancing. But she'd needed something to call her own.

Then, through a strange twist of fate, General Cortas had chosen her out of thousands. Now she was a Spectre, guarding the general's daughter. Living in the residential wing of his estate, attending family dinners, her face displayed across the screens of Arcardius as she stayed close by Kalee's side at balls and high-profile gatherings. She had purpose. She had a position of the highest honor. Her service made her family, and her planet, proud. The title was hers, earned by her.

But more than that…Andi now had a friend as close as a sister. She'd broken through Kalee's perfect outer image to discover the girl beneath, a girl who had wounds and hang-ups just like Andi. Kalee worked hard to please her father and her planet—she truly wished to lead Arcardius someday, with a military mind and gentle soul, and the general worked her hard. The pressure of it often became too much to bear.

Andi was always there to help pick up the pieces.

Andi had helped Kalee through the hard times, and in return, Kalee had helped Andi break through her own walls, to work through her anger and her feelings of unworthiness.

*Though Andi guarded Kalee, she often felt like Kalee guarded her, too. Together, they were a unit.*

*Now, as they tiptoed past a closed doorway, Kalee put a finger to her lips. A sliver of bright white light peeked out from the crack near the floor.*

*It was his room.*

*Valen Cortas, Kalee's strange, silent older brother who always seemed to appear at the most inconvenient times. She could imagine him in there right now, seated at his easel, bringing images to life on canvas. Rearranging his tubes of oil paint. Or perhaps organizing his clothing by color, much of which was splattered with paint.*

*"Come on," Kalee whispered.*

*Andi took care with each step, holding back a laugh as they slipped past Valen's room and made it into the main hall of Averia. A grand, sweeping staircase led down to the rounded entry of the estate, where a holo of Arcardius's symbol spun in midair far below.*

*Andi leaned on the marble railing beside Kalee and looked up.*

*One floor above them was the sitting room, tucked away in the far corner, with a picture window overlooking the gardens. It was Kalee's favorite place to sit and flip through the pages of an ancient paper book. Illustrations covered the pages, a fairy tale of the planets from long ago.*

*One floor past that was the docking bay, where Kalee's father kept his personal transport ship.*

*"You've never even considered taking it out for a ride?" Kalee asked.*

*"It's state-of-the-art," Andi said. "The engine alone is worth more than my life, Kalee. If your father caught us with it, I'd lose my position."*

*Kalee shook her head, pale ringlets spilling down her back. "It's my birthday. He won't mind."*

*Andi sighed, gripping the railing so tightly her Spectre gloves grew taut against her skin. "What if I told you it's never going to happen?"*

*Kalee smirked. "What if I told you it already has?"*

*Andi whirled to look at her, eyes widening to match the moons outside. "What did you do?"*

*Kalee reached into her pocket, then revealed the silver ignition card she'd swiped from her father's office earlier. Andi had thought she'd seen Kalee slip something from the desk, but Kalee had learned a few too many tricks from Andi.* "One little ride, Androma," *she whispered, a smile tugging at the corners of her lips.* "Do it for your best friend?"

"I could lose my job," *Andi said again.*

*Kalee frowned.* "My father will never know. He sleeps like the dead. And besides, you're practically part of the family, Andi. A slap on the wrist. Maybe a harsh talking-to from the general if he catches us. But other than that?" *She waved a hand.* "You took plenty of flight classes. We both know you'd have become a pilot if you hadn't been given this job." *Her blue eyes turned pleadingly large.* "Just one little flight around the mountain. Come on, you're the one who's always telling me to lighten up."

*Andi laughed as Kalee wiggled the card in her face.*

*A voice that sounded like her father's told her that no soldier, at any time, would disobey orders. But if she was keeping Kalee safe while she flew the transport…she wouldn't be disobeying at all.* "Fine. But if we get caught, I'm saying you kidnapped me and forced me into it."

*Kalee nodded, then grabbed Andi's hand and tugged her down the hall, toward the stairs.* "It's going to be the best night of your life, Androma Racella," *she said as they reached the steps.* "It's not like it's going to kill you."

Andi woke to darkness, the scent of sweat thick in her nostrils and the too-hot feeling of a metal floor just beneath her, a ship's engine rumbling close below it.

She cursed, then tried to lift her hands to wipe sweat from her brow.

They were stuck. Bound in chains that clinked as she tried to squeeze her wrists out of the manacles.

For a moment, panic swept through her, twisting itself into her skin, making her itch with the need to run. To get the hell out of here before it was too late.

But then another sound mixed in with the rumble of the engine.

Snores, coming from her left, like the growl of the *Marauder* when Lira punched it hard and heavy.

Andi knew that snore, had found comfort in it from the very first night she'd heard it, years ago, in the bunkhouse of some brutal bounty hunter on Tenebris. It had always meant she wasn't alone.

The snore belonged to Dex. And at the sound of it, despite all her anger at him, Andi relaxed as memories of their last moments in the Dark Matter Pub settled into place.

The fighting. The Sparks.

The *kiss* that left her feeling momentarily like putty as their lips met, like they had so many times before—until her fury took over.

Why was she thinking about that damned kiss? She *hated* that kiss. She hated Dex's stupid lips.

She needed to focus.

The plan had worked. They were on a small transport ship, both of them bound in chains, bathed in complete and total darkness. They were prisoners of Xen Ptera, heading to Lunamere, the most horrific prison in all of the Mirabel Galaxy.

They were exactly where they needed to be.

Andi loosed a breath, then leaned her head back against the hot metal wall of the transport ship.

The tranq still in her system called to her and, willing or not, she closed her eyes and sank back into the shadowy depths of sleep.

# CHAPTER 23
## VALEN

VALEN WAS A MAN MADE OF REGRETS.

Stuck in this endless turmoil—absent of light with only his memories to keep him company—his mind often wandered.

At first he tried to remember the positive memories from his past. His mother's warm smile, the adventures he'd shared with his sister, diving off the floating chunks of rock that littered Arcardius into the warm pools of water below with friends.

It gave him peace, a tiny glimmer of hope when he couldn't grasp on to anything else.

Then the darkness chased the good memories away.

Others took their place.

The void expression on his mother's face when Valen walked

past his parents' bedroom doorway, peering through the cracks as a single word floated out.

*Unfaithful.*

The shattered conversations at the dinner table. A glass thrown, Valen's father standing up as his chair fell backward. And not just a single word, but a phrase this time that broke him: *you could have stopped her.*

It was Valen's fault his sister was gone. Valen's fault that he was a weak, pathetic protector who couldn't do his damned job.

What were older brothers for, after all, if not to protect their younger siblings?

Kalee would still be alive if not for his cowardice—singing in the halls, chasing him through hidden water coves and underground tunnels. Sitting beside him in the dance hall as Androma Racella, Kalee's best friend from school, performed on stage in front of them.

As he drifted to sleep, he was haunted by one reality.

His sister was dead, and he was alive.

And somewhere out there, her killer ran free.

Thoughts like these were the worst of all.

*Valen sat in his room, staring at a portrait of his sister's protector turned killer.*

*A full moon ago, he'd been hard at work on it when Kalee had breezed past his closed door, thinking herself silent on bare feet. But Valen had always been one to pick up on the smallest changes in sound. And even more so, the changes in color.*

*He loved the way the paint on his brushes dried when he didn't wash them, deepening from a royal, cloudless sky blue to a nighttime, starless black. Sometimes he saw the way a star shone purple, then white again, as it winked at him from high in the sky. He loved getting his hands on samples of fabric, observing the changes in shade as he twisted them this way and that in his fingertips.*

*And he always noticed—despite Kalee's thoughts on the matter—the*

SASHA ALSBERG & LINDSAY CUMMINGS

*shifting of shadows slinking beneath his closed door. A dark, formless shape that was there one moment and gone the next.*

*It was how he'd come to be so good at following Kalee and her Spectre.*

*How he'd come to notice the grace with which Androma Racella walked. And her hair—a soft shade of pale blond to others that was much more to him. In sunlight, it shifted to a white so bright, it reminded him of freshly fallen snow. In darkness, it took on a silver sheen the color of the moon.*

*In the portrait before him, he'd painted her in two halves.*

*One bright white beneath the shining sun, almost blue at the points where it hung in shadow. The other half of her, he'd painted a muted gray, Androma's hair like liquid moonlight spilling across her shoulders, the perfect accent to her stormy eyes.*

*He'd thought it a masterpiece. One of the best he'd ever done. And on that night, he'd been on his way out of his room, pride and a bottle of his father's best Griss warming his chest, when he saw them leaving to take the transport for a joyride.*

Valen closed his eyes and breathed deep.

His chest ached, as if it were about to split down the middle.

*Tonight no shadows slipped by outside his doorway. No footsteps scampered along the cool marble floor, no hushed whispers or muted giggles bounded off the crisp white walls as the two girls rushed by, heading for Kalee's room.*

He should have stopped them.

He should have grabbed Kalee's wrist and begged her not to go. Fallen to his knees like a child, or simply scooped her up and hauled her away while she screamed obscenities in his ear.

The memories pulled him under again.

*"Valen."*

*His mother's voice, soft and broken, behind his closed door.*

*"She… She'd want you there. You're her brother, Valen." A deep sigh, followed by the unmistakable sound of her sniffing back tears.*

*He closed his eyes. He wouldn't cry.*

*If he cried, the chasm in his chest would open wide, and he'd fall, and he'd keep falling until he reached the end.*

*His mother had always been strong. But tonight, she was like fractured glass. If he pressed too hard, she'd break. And then who would be there to pick up the pieces? Certainly not his father. General Cortas was busy giving press conferences and formal statements, and beneath his facade of cool, diplomatic calm was a belly full of liquor, downed from the cabinet in the back of his closet.*

*The chasm in Valen's chest began to open, the heat in his eyes threatening to turn into flames. He blinked once. Twice. He could hear the moment his mother gave up and left, and the room seemed to take on a sudden chill in her absence.*

*So Valen sat and stared down at the portrait again, forcing himself to look, to see.*

*He'd done an excellent job, so real in his brushstrokes that it almost seemed as if Androma Racella was staring up at him now.*

*He didn't want to do it.*

*Gods, he didn't want to at all.*

*But tonight, Valen lifted his brush and uncapped a fresh set of colors ripe for creation.*

*His paintbrush, clutched in his hand, nearly snapped in two. But with each stroke, he let the sorrow slip away and something harder and stronger took its place. When he was done, he realized he'd been wrong before.*

*The old painting was child's play. Now he'd finally created a masterpiece.*

*He hung it up to dry and left the room, casting only one glance back over his shoulder.*

*Androma Racella stared at him from the wall.*

*Half of her, the moonlit side, he'd left untouched. But the other he'd taken his time with, her face coated in splatters of crimson, in shades of purple so dark they looked nearly black against her pale, smooth skin.*

*Wet red paint trickled down her cheeks and slipped from the canvas* onto the floor. A soft drip, drip, drip that reminded him not of tears, but of his sister's blood.

A masterpiece indeed, as if Andi had ripped off the mask she'd been wearing and revealed to the world her second self, the one she'd been hiding just beneath the surface for so long.

With effort, Valen tore his eyes from the painting and closed the door.

The hallway was empty, the sprawling estate whisper silent. Everyone had already gone, adorned in shades of muted Arcardian gray, to attend Kalee's funeral.

Androma Racella would not be in attendance. Instead, she was bound in chains, awaiting a trial she would not win. Thrown behind bars, stuck in some deep, impenetrable darkness that no color could thrive in—and no one, no matter how strong, could survive.

Until the injection finally stole her away.

Valen took equal amounts of pain and comfort in this as he walked.

They could throw Andromeda into the Pits of Tenebris for as long as they liked—even give her the death sentence—but it wouldn't bring Kalee back.

When he passed by his sister's room, he caught the slightest hint of her summertime scent.

It lingered like a distant breeze, quickly swept away when reality took its place.

The chasm in him broken, Valen Cortas fell to his knees in Kalee's doorway and wept.

# CHAPTER 24
## ANDROMA

ANDI WOKE TO PAIN LURCHING THROUGH her skull.

She was lying on her back, staring up into the darkness. Or she could have been staring *down*, for all she could tell. There was no end to it—no glimmer of moonlight shimmering on the walls, no smudged outline of her feet sprawled out in front of her as she slowly sat upright.

This wasn't like the transport.

There it had been black all around, but the too-hot heat of a ship's working engine beneath her—a feeling that reminded her just enough of the *Marauder*—kept her calm. Calm enough to focus on the plan. The prize at the end of the Lunamere tunnel.

This was something else entirely.

This darkness felt as if it held a thousand watching eyes, a pressing sort of black that seemed to seep into her very soul, settling deep inside the marrow in her bones.

She shivered, but she didn't think it was entirely due to the cold.

The ground beneath her was rough, made of stones that felt like blocks of ice. Andi ran her hands across it, pleased to discover that her shackles were gone. As she moved to push herself to her knees, however, her head seemed to wobble as if under the stupor of spiced Rigna.

*Or*, Andi thought, as she raised her hands to her temples, feeling a lump where some Xen Pterran guard had punched her with his electric gauntlets, *the stupor of whatever tranq they knocked me out with*.

This could have been her life—*should* have been her life. Locked away behind bars, awaiting the death penalty, the ghost of her best friend the only thing to keep her company.

That familiar wave of fear spiked through her, and Andi wanted to reach for her swords, to slash and slice and tear apart that piece of herself as she tore apart the bodies of others. Death after death, to cover up Kalee's. To give herself the kind of fate she deserved.

But then a groan sounded out from beside her.

*You're not alone*, Andi remembered.

"What the hell?" Dex rasped. "Andi?" Seconds passed, with the sound of his labored breathing seeming to echo against the cold stone walls. She could hear his hands as they groped against the floor, searching. She didn't even flinch away as his fingertips scraped hers and he froze. "Please tell me this is Andi, and not some love-hungry Xen Pterran carriage slug named Stubby."

Despite herself, Andi laughed. The massive slugs were gruesome, oily beasts that tried to bed anything with a heartbeat.

"It's me," Andi said. Then she pulled her hand away, immediately colder with the absence of his touch.

"How long have we been out for?" Dex asked.

"Hell if I know," Andi said.

Time seemed to have slipped away from them. Soyina had said they only had one hour.

Hardly enough time to make their way out of their cell and find Valen, especially with shadows as thick as the obsidinite walls surrounding them.

Andi reached down, feeling the varillium cuffs around her wrists with relief. For a moment, she feared they wouldn't be there, that somehow the Lunamere guards had managed to break the impenetrable varillium—impossible as that may be without the right tools—or that Soyina had taken Dex's Krevs and left them in here to rot together.

A terrible turns of events that would have been.

But there the cuffs were. Cold on her wrists, and with them, a surge of solid hope. Andi pressed the small button on the back of each cuff, and light flooded from them. A talisman to keep the shadows at bay.

"The best gift you've ever received, Andi," Dex said. "I wonder who gave them to you?"

She remembered the day he had gifted them to her, and how many Krevs he'd saved up to pay for the cuffs to be designed and installed by a surgeon he had connections with on a tiny rogue moon near the center of Mirabel. The installation had been painful, but once the cuffs were in place, Andi felt nearly whole again. On the outside, at least. They were a gift she'd always be grateful for.

Andi sighed. "One of these days, Dextro Arez, I'm going to help you pull your head out of your own ass."

Andi turned away, then slowly rose to her feet, ignoring the shouts of pain from her fight-sore muscles. The cell had one gate, with obsidinite bars so thick that Andi instantly knew they'd have been screwed without Soyina's help. The material was almost as strong as varillium. There was no way they would have been able to break out of here otherwise.

She pressed her face against the cool bars, staring out into the black abyss beyond.

No movement. No shadowed shapes milling about. Far off, she thought she could hear screams, or cackles of laughter. But the darkness had a way of playing tricks on one's senses.

"My head feels like it's been cracked in two," Dex whined.

Andi rolled her eyes. "If you're done complaining," she said, remembering how much of a baby Dex could be when he had an ailment of *any* sort, "we need to get moving. We don't know how much time has passed, and if we don't make it to Soyina with Valen in under an hour, we're not leaving this dump alive."

Dex rolled to his knees, cursing as he stretched out his muscles.

"Voluntarily letting myself get beat into submission," he said, "is *not* one of my prouder moments in life."

Andi raised a brow as she braided her hair back from her face, then flexed her muscles to test for any weak spots she hadn't noticed earlier. "I wasn't aware you had any moments to be proud of."

Dex hauled himself upright. "You're the worst partner I've ever had, Androma Racella."

Andi stuck out her tongue at him, then reached out to test the cell gate. The handle turned, but the gate was heavy. She leaned against it, digging into the bars with her shoulder.

The gate creaked and groaned in protest.

"I'd say I agree with you on that point," Andi whispered, stepping aside to make room for Dex as he joined her, "but I think Soyina takes the award on this one."

They pushed on the gate together. "Soyina has her charms," Dex said through gritted teeth. "You have to admit it."

Andi seriously doubted that, but focused her attention on their escape.

"This would be a good time to talk," Dex said.

Andi sighed. "We're in the middle of a prison with the clock literally ticking down on our lives, and you want to talk *now*?"

Their shoulders pressed up against each other as they worked at the gate. "I can't seem to get you alone," Dex said. "So, yes, while we're trapped inside of a prison cell, it seems like the best option."

"We don't owe each other a conversation," Andi said. "We just have to finish this job, and the deal is done."

"There are two sides to the story we share, Androma."

Andi grimaced. "I don't need to hear your excuses, Dextro. Now *push*."

"If we get out of here alive, promise me you'll just hear me out?" Dex whispered. "I won't ask again. We can talk about the past, and…end it for good."

"Things ended when you sold me out."

"Five minutes," Dex said. "Please, Androma. Don't make me beg."

She smiled then. That would be interesting.

"Five minutes," she said. "*If* we get this damned gate open and get Valen safely out of here."

With a final shove, the gate popped open. It swung outward with a horrible cry, then hung ajar, the light from Andi's cuffs casting crooked shadows against the black wall just beyond, no more than a few arm's lengths away. No guards came running. No prisoners shouted out from cells nearby.

The darkness was strange and still, just begging them to step out of their cell and explore.

Andi looked left, then right.

Nothing but bars, as far as the light from her cuffs allowed her to see.

For a moment, she and Dex simply stood there, staring out at the narrow hall, their boots frozen on the threshold of their cell.

"Looks like I'm halfway to earning my five minutes. What's

the matter, Baroness?" Dex finally whispered. Andi could feel the warmth of his breath on her cheek. "Scared?"

She feared a lot of things.

Loneliness. Losing the lives of her crew or damaging her ship beyond repair.

But not darkness. That was a part of her; the very thing that had allowed her to survive for this long.

Only one hour—or less, depending on how long they'd been out for—and the silence would be shattered by blaring alarms, the frenzied tap of guard boots on stone floors, the *click* of bullets sliding into rifle chambers held by guards who would shoot not to disarm, but to kill.

This is what she had trained her whole life for.

The thrill of the moment had arrived.

Without a word, Andi took a step forward, shedding the weakest parts of herself as she allowed the Bloody Baroness to take over.

Dex followed, and together, they left their empty cell behind.

# CHAPTER 25
## DEX

*NEVER AGAIN*, DEX THOUGHT.

Never again would he allow one of his clients to outsmart him and land him in a situation like the present one.

Rescue missions.

They were *not* his idea of fun.

After this Dex would go to one of the warm moons of Adhira. He'd lie by the golden water's edge with a beautiful, soft-skinned woman by his side, preferably one who spoke sweet nothings into his ears. One whose favorite type of makeup was rouged lips instead of blood-splattered cheeks. One who didn't separate limbs from bodies, or stomp through piles of corpses in the middle of some dark, dank prison moon in the most miserable system in Mirabel.

*That* woman stood beside Dex now in the darkness, brushing her purple-streaked hair back from her face. Splatters of red had mixed in with the other strands.

Dex hadn't even seen the guards appear from the black before Andi cursed and was on them, tackling the first so that his head slammed into the stones with a sickening crack.

"Help me finish him!" she'd ordered, and by the time Dex stole the electric short-whip from the guard and shocked him into unconsciousness, Andi had stolen a key ring off the other's belt loop. Her arm had coiled back like a spring, and then she'd stabbed the guard in the eye with the largest, longest key.

"Godstars, Andi," Dex said now as he leaned over to inspect the corpse.

The key looked strangely at home in his eye socket, perfectly positioned in the center, as if Andi had placed it there with an artist's flair. The river of blood was already slowing to a trickle, pooling in a small puddle on the stone floor beside his gaping mouth.

Dex shuddered, then looked back up at her. The light from her cuffs made her look like a ghost, pale and speckled with the proof of more deaths.

"If you haven't noticed," Andi said, leaning down and plucking the guard's whip from his belt, "we're short on weapons and time. I don't have a lot of options here, Dextro."

"You shoved a key through his eye," Dex said. He looked down at the corpse again, then back at Andi.

She ignored him, a skill she'd always possessed, and pressed a button on the whip. There was a crackle, and an arc of blue spiraled out, bathing the hall in flickering light. The drying blood on her face looked dark as oil as her eyes met his. "If I didn't take care of him, he would have sounded the alarm. Then we would have been facing fifty guards instead of two. Those aren't odds I'm willing to bet on today."

As Dex stared at her, he suddenly understood the bare truth.

There was no remorse in her eyes for the kills. Not even a flicker. There was nothing but the promise of the mission pulling her forward.

Once, Andi felt things to the point that they nearly broke her, and she'd allowed her feelings to control every action. She'd cared deeply for him, and he'd felt the same feelings resonating inside.

For years he'd wondered if the rumors about her weren't entirely correct. If maybe the Bloody Baroness was just a show, a persona Andi had created to keep herself and her crew safe. He figured that when the metal shields covered up the *Marauder*, she mourned with her crew for the lives lost, the dark things she'd had to do in order to get the job done.

Dex had been wrong.

The Bloody Baroness didn't feel remorse for these kills, nor had she mourned for the members of Dex's crew she'd taken out when he'd captured her.

"It's not just a reputation, is it?" Dex asked.

Andi raised a brow at him.

"The Bloody Baroness," he said, stepping past the fallen guards, wondering about who they were, what they would have done with their lives had they not ended up in this pile at his feet. The Bloody Baroness *was* Andi, through and through, and probably had been since the day she stole his ship. Now she turned to the darkness, standing tall and strong as she stared ahead, not a hint of fear on her beautiful face.

She dealt out death like a deck of cards. How many more would die before they got Valen Cortas out of here alive?

"Two," Andi said quietly, as she turned off the electric whip and doused them in shadow once more.

"Two?" Dex echoed.

"Two deaths. Two tallies on my swords." She looked down at

the dead guards, then back up at him. A flicker of pain flashed through her eyes. "I have a code, you know. Lines that I don't cross."

"And today?" Dex asked, as he looked down at the bodies. "Have you crossed a line?"

"I remember them, Dex," she said. "Every last one."

For a moment, he *did* see the Andi he'd once known. He saw the same haunted look in her eyes that she'd had as she stood above him, her knife in his chest. Her trust shattered because of him.

Maybe his original instincts had been correct. Maybe somewhere, hidden deep within…a fragment of her compassion remained.

"Cell 306," Andi said, reminding Dex of their mission. "We still have twelve levels to climb down, and the clock is ticking."

Dex nodded, then followed her into the darkness.

It wasn't until they reached the next set of guards, when they slipped into soundless action side by side, that Dex realized something frightening.

He loved this. Fighting beside her in perfect sync, as a fluid team.

For the first time in a long time, he felt fully alive.

# CHAPTER 26
## KLAREN
## YEAR NINETEEN

THE GIRL, NOW A QUEEN, SAT IN HER PALACE, *gazing down at her greatest mistake.*

*It was beautiful, this tiny mistake. A creature born from the queen's very body, woven together in her womb. Protected from the bitter, dying world outside the palace walls.*

*It wasn't part of her plan.*

*And the queen knew, from the moment she'd first birthed the babe, that she would be forever changed.*

*The infant was wrapped in her arms now, warm and soft and full of the power to change the fate of entire worlds.*

"Nor," the queen said, stroking the child's tiny cheek with her fingertip. "A strong name, fit for a child of the light."

Footsteps sounded outside the room.

The queen looked up as the king swept inside, followed by a trail of guards.

"You look lovely, my heart," he said, placing a kiss on her lips. A second later, he pressed one to Nor's tiny forehead.

Years the king and queen had shared together, and still his eyes held the glassy look of a man helplessly bewitched by love.

The queen smiled at him. "You love me," she whispered. "As much as the day you first laid eyes on me."

"I will always love you, Klaren." He said it as if it weren't even a question.

She'd hardly had to try to entice him. Perhaps, in some way, that meant he was her gift. A man who loved her despite what she was. Despite the past she'd kept hidden from him all these years.

"Rest, my girls," the king said, and then he was swept away by his entourage, worried looks on their faces as they bowed their heads respectfully, their voices full of strain, a single word ghosting onto their lips.

War.

Outside, the acid rain bit at the palace walls, stripping them away little by little, eating at the crumbling spires. Below, the ground rumbled with the warning of another quake soon to come.

Far beyond, on the city streets, a hundred thousand lives hungered for salvation.

The baby wailed, drawing the queen's attention. "Sleep now, my perfect little mistake," she whispered. "Sleep, and remember to dream of the light."

The baby calmed at the sound of her mother's voice.

In moments, her eyes closed.

Alone in her palace quarters, the queen of Xen Ptera rocked her daughter gently, a tear slipping down her cheek as she remembered her mission and thought of how little time they had left.

# CHAPTER 27
## VALEN

THE DARKNESS WAS OFTEN SILENT, THE SLOW, steady beating of Valen's heart serving as the only reminder that he was still alive. Still suffering the pains of Lunamere.

Sometimes he imagined he was back in his former bedroom, listening not to his heart, but to Kalee.

*You're strange, Valen*, she'd always told him. *But you're my favorite kind of strange.*

Tonight, he tried again to remember her.

She'd always had kind, curious eyes, and the sound of her laugh was like birds chirping on a spring morning as the sun rose up from beneath the floating gravarocks of Arcardius.

SASHA ALSBERG & LINDSAY CUMMINGS

And yet, when he tried to bring forth an image of her face, it slipped away.

Instead, a sleek, cruel smile took its place. A queen of darkness and shadow. A mistress of misery and salvation.

The image of her was swept from his mind, leaving him to rock back and forth in the darkness, trying to remind himself of his mantra. His hold on sanity, his reason to stay alive.

*Vengeance will be mine.*

Revenge. It would taste so, so sweet.

As he rocked, he imagined that he heard footsteps in the darkness.

But along with the footsteps, he saw a glimpse of softly glowing light. Not the cold, bitter kind that came from his torturers' electric whips or gauntlets, but instead, a light that danced and flickered as it moved and bounced off the walls outside of his cell.

Like the stars.

Valen gasped and held back a groan as he pulled himself forward on hands and knees. The fresh gashes in his back were still bleeding, his ragged shirt soaked through, parts of the fabric sticking to his shredded skin. He'd nearly died again tonight, beaten down until he'd slipped into that place of calm, warm light. He'd wanted to stay there, to feel the light on his skin.

But then he'd heard his sister's voice.

*Be strong, Valen*, she'd whispered. *Remember, we are stronger together.* He held on until the beatings ceased, refusing to give up. Refusing to break.

He crawled forward now in his cell, desperate to get a glimpse of the strange new light. Even if it was a part of his imagination, it had *color*. It had a softness he hadn't seen since being thrown into this hard place.

With effort, he made it to the door, where he knew a guard was always waiting, keys attached to his belt loop, fresh taunts on his lips when he knew Valen was awake and listening.

The sound of footsteps slowed.

The light in the hall winked out, and Valen was thrust back into darkness again.

"Who's out there? Joneska?" Valen's guard called out into the black. "We aren't supposed to switch out for another half hour."

With trembling limbs, Valen reached up and gripped the bars on his cell door, then pulled himself up so he could peer out through them.

There was a flash of light, a familiar crackle that made Valen's guts roil as another guard, standing just down the hall, turned their short-whip on. The man holding it wasn't one Valen had seen before.

Though he couldn't remember the faces from his past, he knew the ones of his tormentors well—every cold gaze, every wrinkle in their haunting faces.

In the crackling light, this new man looked like he had stars trailing down his tan arms. Constellations that almost flickered with light, as if he were a painting, a work of art.

"Your shift is over," the star-covered man said, smirking.

"Who the hell are you?" Valen's guard barked out.

Another crackle of light as a second short-whip crackled on. Valen gasped, and pain raced through him as his broken ribs screamed in response to the movement.

But he couldn't hold back the cry that escaped from his lips.

Couldn't believe the sight of the pale-haired woman standing in the darkness, two glowing cuffs on her wrists, illuminating the dark scars on her arms and the blood splatters on her face that looked like paint.

She took a step forward, graceful and lithe as a predator— and so *real*, despite the fact that she couldn't be. "What you should be asking instead," she said with a menacing grin, "is why you're still alive."

The guard lifted his wrist, where Valen knew a com was attached.

But before he could speak, the woman reacted. She was a

blur of color—pale starlight hair, red splatters on her face, soft glowing light around her wrists and the sharp, electric blue whip sparking as she brought it down in a sharp, solid arc.

There was a *hiss*.

A small puff of smoke.

And the man's hand fell to the stone floor with a thump.

The guard was too shocked to even scream. He simply opened his mouth, staring down at his dismembered hand, his smoking stump of a wrist, then back up to look at the woman in the darkness.

"You're going to do exactly as I say," she said, but it came out like the purr of a demon, the croon of a devil's pet. "You're going to release the prisoner in Cell 306, and if you object, I will cut you into pieces, little by little, until you do."

The tattooed man beside her smirked. "What piece will you start with?"

"I'm not entirely sure." She smiled, but it was all wrong, as if she should have had fangs instead of teeth. Her pale eyes flicked back to the guard, who still stood frozen in front of Valen's cell. "You have ten seconds to unlock the door. Do it now, before I change my mind."

The guard turned, fumbling with his remaining hand. He dropped the keys, then cried out as he sank to his knees and tried to grab them. His fingers scraped his dismembered hand, and with a gasp of pain, he slumped to one side, unconscious.

"Disturbing," the tattooed man said with a chuckle. "Did you really have to cut off his hand?"

The young woman didn't answer. She stepped forward, silent and light as a ghost, and scooped the keys up off the stones.

Valen stumbled backward, suddenly unwilling to leave this place.

Unwilling to believe this was reality. That she was really, truly here, bringing light to him in the darkness of Lunamere.

The lock clicked open.

The door swung forward silently, its hinges well-used from his frequent visits to the torture chambers.

The tattooed man stayed in the hallway, holding the door. But the young woman stepped into the cell, those strange, glowing blue cuffs illuminating her face. Valen had painted that face many times in years past. He'd thought her beautiful once; an angel with fair hair and even fairer features who'd given his sister joy. A girl he'd been desperate to understand.

But when the accident happened, he knew he'd been wrong.

Androma Racella wasn't an angel.

She was death incarnate.

"Hello, Valen," she said now. She held a steady hand out to him, but he scuttled backward like a bug. "We're here to rescue you."

He hadn't used his voice for weeks, and not for anything more than to scream through the pain. He opened his cracked, bleeding lips, was ready to tell her the words he'd imagined saying, after all these years.

Then a blaring screech exploded from the walls.

# CHAPTER 28
## ANDROMA

THE ALARM SPLIT THE SILENCE LIKE A KNIFE.

"Damn it all!" Dex shouted, though Andi could barely hear his voice above the alarm. "We're too late!"

She turned back to face Valen, her mind racing.

One more floor down, and they'd find Soyina waiting for them, along with the promise of escape. They had to go. *Now*.

"Valen," Andi said, rushing to his side. "Come on. We're getting you out of here."

Valen's eyes slammed shut. He fell to his knees, shaking his head, murmuring, "No, no, no," as he scrambled away, leaving a trail of blood in his wake.

How in the *hell* were they supposed to get him out of here like this? He was a bleeding, shattered mess, hardly able to stand, let alone run down a flight of stairs while being chased by guards.

"Help me get him up!" Andi shouted to Dex.

Valen howled and skittered back even farther, leaving another fresh smear of blood on the stones. He tried to stand, but his legs shook with the effort. His arms were covered in bruises and lashes, and they were far too thin.

It was a wonder he was still alive. Andi tried to tamp down the wave of horror she felt at seeing him in this state. They didn't have time for this. Somewhere in the distance, shouts rang out, and blue lights danced on the walls outside Valen's open cell door as guards came closer.

She peered out the cell door. In the mouth of the stairwell, a guard appeared. Then another behind him, followed by two more.

She hadn't expected things to go this way. But she knew this was the only part of the mission that counted, the part that would earn her and Dex and her crew their pardoned names and a shipload of Krevs.

Andi looked down at Valen and frowned.

He was a shadow of the person she'd once known, but he was still a Cortas—a living fragment of Kalee. Andi hadn't been able to keep her friend alive, but she'd be damned if anything happened to Valen under her watch.

"I'm sorry about this," she said.

Then she brought the solid base of a short-whip down over Valen's head.

He crumpled in a heap.

Dex stared, openmouthed, from behind him. "That's your plan?"

"Take an arm," Andi commanded.

Soon the two of them stood in the mouth of the cell, Valen's unconscious body hanging between them.

"You remember all those sword-fighting lessons you gave me

on Tenebris?" Andi asked. "The ones where we fought single-handed?"

"Oh, love." Dex lifted a dark brow. "How could I ever forget?"

Valen's head lolled against her cheek, and she nearly gagged at his rotten scent.

"One more thing, Dex?" Andi asked, shoving Valen's head the other way. Dex met her eyes as she doused the light on her cuffs. "Don't call me 'love.'"

She gripped her short-whip tight, imagining it was one of her swords, already seeing the way she'd slice it through tendons like a blade carving through raw meat. In her mind, she was a Spectre again. She imagined Kalee in Valen's place.

*No one* would harm her charge.

"Steady," Dex whispered. "Silent."

They waited for a breath of a second, allowing the guards to get closer, the light from their weapons brightening with each stomp of their boots.

"Now," Andi said.

Together, she and Dex stepped out of the cell, carrying Valen Cortas between them.

Six guards stood just around the corner, weapons raised, looking ready for a fight.

They sprang, their two bodies moving in one single motion, Valen still between them.

Dex on the left, Andi on the right. They moved so fast the world around them seemed to pause.

Andi's whip flashed in a glorious arc, striking the guard closest to her just as he moved to action. The end of her whip curled around his, snaking like electric fingertips intertwining, and Andi yanked backward. The guard's whip soared past them, then exploded with a shower of sparks against the cell door beyond.

"Cover me," Andi growled.

Dex attacked as Andi rose, using the counterweight of both

boys, and swung her foot into the weaponless guard's jaw. A crack sounded as bones shattered beneath her boot.

"Down!" Dex shouted.

A short-whip soared past the space where Valen's head had just been. It severed the end of Andi's braid, the scent of burned hair wafting into her nostrils.

She rose, snarling, as a lock of her hair tumbled to the floor.

These Lunamere bastards were going to die.

The world moved in flashes as darkness and light fought and intertwined. The guards before them were like ghosts that appeared and then flickered out as the whips and gauntlets cracked from blue to black and back again.

With each patch of darkness, Dex and Andi moved forward. Valen's body was like dead weight against their shoulders.

"Take them out!" a guard screamed.

Passing Valen to Andi, Dex dropped to the floor, leg extended as it rammed into the guard's legs and sent him sprawling.

"Come on!" Andi yelled from behind him, moving toward the stairs.

Dex looped an arm around Valen, pulling the three of them into the stairwell. He slammed the door behind them, quickly fusing the lock with the electric heat from his short-whip.

Fists pounded the metal behind them.

"One more level, and we'll be out. Soyina will be waiting at the door, if we're lucky," Andi said, already pulling the three of them down the eerie staircase.

Something whizzed past his face.

Andi yelped as a knife sank into her shoulder.

In a blink, she yanked it out and held it before her.

"Hold Valen," she growled.

Before Dex could stop her, she rushed down the stairs, swinging the knife.

There were too many guards. Even as Andi fought her way down, more poured up the steps toward him and Valen.

He was out of weapons. Out of options.

"Sorry about this, friend," Dex said.

With one grand shove, he pushed Valen down the remaining stairs.

The guards toppled in Valen's path.

The guy was unconscious. No harm done unless he died on the descent—it was only one flight of stairs, not twenty.

Dex leaped over the railing to the floor below, scooped up a whip from a fallen guard, and swung his way to Valen's sprawled form.

Andi was already there, wrestling a final living guard away. The guard swung with his gauntlets, electricity spitting blue. Andi ducked, then came up swiftly enough to knock his head backward against the wall.

A final grunt, as she kicked him into silence.

Then, nothing. The alarm cut off.

Silence swept over them as a door creaked open behind Dex.

On the other side was a sight for sore eyes. Soyina, holding a key and standing beside a rolling cart. Her mismatched eyes flashed as she looked at the aftermath of the fight.

"Looky looky," Soyina said. "The gang got out."

"You threw him down the stairs?" Andi asked.

Dex helped her lift Valen onto Soyina's waiting cart. "I had to get creative."

Beside him, Andi's breath came out in ragged huffs. "We need to go," she said. "Finish the job, Soyina, and get us the hell out of here."

Soyina stared at them, a sickening, sideways smile on her lips. With a strange cackle, she said, "Alright then. This may hurt a bit."

She reached behind her, pulled out a gun and, with a single shot, sent Dex reeling into darkness.

The last thing he saw was Andi's head hitting the ground beside him, her pale eyes wide as moons. Then white light enveloped him, and all semblance of the world melted away.

# CHAPTER 29
## NOR

THE QUEEN'S LAB WAS A SPACE BORN OF DESperation.

A pathetic echo of the grandeur that was long ago destroyed in The Cataclysm. The remnants were mere scraps of her father's once glorious dream—a place meant to heal the planet of Xen Ptera, to bring back abundant life before it was too late.

That dream had died with her father. Now his old lab had morphed into the birthplace of death.

Nor was a queen, bred from the purest of blood, and she couldn't bear stepping foot inside the lab unless absolutely necessary. It had taken Darai ages to convince her to come down here herself, ages more for Nor to actually do it.

Now, as she walked down the crumbling spiral staircase beneath the planet's surface, she could almost feel the walls caving in on her, threatening to crush her once again.

She froze as an image of her father ghosted into her mind. She could see his eyes bulging from their sockets, his skull caving in under the foot of a broken stone statue, blood staining the crumbling toes. It was as if Arcardius, and the rest of the Unified Systems, had stomped the life right out of her father when they dropped their final bombs.

"*Nhatyla?*" Zahn asked, stopping beside Nor to place a warm hand on her elbow. "What is it?"

She'd almost forgotten he was there beside her in the darkness. "I'm fine," she said, swallowing the lump in her throat as she shoved the memories away. She breathed deep, despite the tightness in her chest, and silently recited the words Darai had raised her on: *Fear Is Only an Illusion*. Nothing would crush her or stop her until the fates had had their way. And they'd decided, long ago, that Nor would be the one to bring about Xen Ptera's revenge.

"Should we turn back?" Zahn asked. His fingertips spun gentle circles across her skin.

Nor looked over her shoulder, where the faint light of day waited, beckoning her to turn back. To give in to her weakness.

The claustrophobia was one of her best-kept secrets. Only Darai and Zahn knew the truth about the trauma she'd faced the day of the attack, and the physical and mental scars it had tainted her with.

There hadn't been many places within the vicinity of Nivia where they could put the lab, so when Darai found the ancient bomb shelter, still holding strong despite the crippling quakes, they started fortifying its boundaries to last.

"I am a queen who seeks to be a conqueror," Nor said as the image of her father, and the sharp spike of fear, still begged entrance to her mind. She closed her eyes and focused on Zahn's hand, soft and warm. "There will be battles far worse than this one."

"And rewards for winning them," he whispered, "should my queen wish it."

Despite herself, Nor smiled. Silently, she walked past him, deeper into the torch-lit tunnel where Darai waited ahead.

The structure was run-down, and it didn't improve the farther one went below. Nor's metal heels clacked on the crumbling stones. Dark, putrid water ran beneath her soles as she hurried to keep up with her uncle, Zahn trailing behind her like a moving wall.

At the base of the steps, Darai turned right into a narrow hallway. The rafters creaked above them as subtle shockwaves shuddered their way through the ground. Nor pulled the hood of her cloak lower, shielding herself from the falling pebbles raining down from above, the edges of the hood like blinders to keep her at ease. One could easily get lost in these tunnels, so deeply carved that none would hear their call.

A few more steps, and they turned left at the end of the hall.

Straight ahead was a silver door, at such odds with the scenery around them it was almost laughable.

"They are expecting you," Darai said. "I think you will be pleased at what you find inside."

He held out a hand, ushering Nor toward the retinal scanner on the door. Faint green light illuminated the space as it beeped her in, and the door swung open with a heavy groan.

As she stepped inside, the pungent fumes of preserved bodies and toxins immediately overloaded Nor's senses. She quickly covered her nose and mouth with a scented handkerchief.

It smelled like fire callas. They were her mother's favorite flower, grown by gentle hands in the courtyard of the old palace. Now their scent brought a fresh wave of memories that only fueled Nor's urge to seek revenge.

Zahn and Darai guided her deeper into the lit space, a cavernous bunker with heavy rock walls and ceilings that made her feel small.

Lab techs in red Xen Pterran coats stood before stone tables, their hands deftly working, tapping away at dimly lit screens, stirring milky vials full of bubbling substances. Long ago, Nor had stood in this very room, watching her father move down the aisles. She'd marveled at the glowing substances, the cherished seeds that her father's scientists had so carefully tended to in hopes of making food grow.

The mission had changed, but the feeling in the room was the same. It was a place of order. A tangible bit of progress that set Nor at ease.

"They have been working around the clock, Majesty," Darai murmured as he led her down the aisle.

The scientists bowed their heads as she passed, Zahn behind her like a living shadow.

Another metal door stood at the back of the room. Zahn entered in the code to unlock the private lab of her lead scientist, Aclisia, and the door opened instantly.

The two-headed scientist alone understood Nor's passion for destruction, and her equal desire to make it a true work of art. Together they would give the galaxy a show, and every eye would be watching.

Aclisia stood behind a lab table with her back to Nor. In front of her, rows and rows of glowing silver vials lined up like tiny soldiers awaiting their orders. Zahn didn't follow as Darai and Nor stepped forward, remaining back to guard the door.

Nor approached the table slowly, appraising the view. Half of her life had passed since the idea for Zenith had bloomed in her mind, and only now, after years of dreaming, was her weapon finally coming to life.

"Ahh, my queen," Aclisia's two voices said at once.

Nor looked up as her head scientist shuffled over.

To anyone else, Aclisia was a shocking sight. But Nor had

spent years in her presence, watching the two-headed woman work. Two brains should have meant two separate people, but Aclisia's heads worked together, as if they were one. The right head held her rational side and could converse for hours without skipping a beat. The left head was more off-kilter, but it was the part of Aclisia that Nor perhaps admired the most. It allowed her to dream, endlessly, until even the most irrational ideas became possible.

"Are you in the final stages of finishing the weapon yet?" Nor asked.

Aclisia's two heads swung around to look at the lab table, both hands grappling for a single silver vial. The glass clinked as the scientist produced one, lifting it out of its case and holding it up to the light.

"Slowly, you dolt!" the right head screeched to the left.

The left head huffed in annoyance. "I'm merely trying to give our queen a glimpse of her new toy."

"It's a wonder I've been able to put up with you all these years," the right head retorted.

"You haven't a choice, my dear," the left said back.

Both heads glared at each other, the right with short reddish brown hair sticking out like flames, the left with pale blond curls coiled tight against her skull.

Nor cleared her throat. "My patience is running low."

Aclisia nodded her heads, then held out the vial. "Steady now, my queen," the right head said.

Nor cradled the vial in her hands like a newly polished gem. It sparkled in the dim light of the lab, and it was warm to the touch, rather than cool, like she'd assumed it would be.

"Each vial holds thousands of doses," the right head told Nor.

"Now we just need someone to play with," the left head added.

"A test subject," the right corrected.

Aclisia looked expectantly at Nor.

"That has been taken care of," Nor said. She raised her gloved hand to signal Zahn's attention. "Order the guards to bring forth the subject."

Behind her, Zahn pressed a button on his wrist com, then whispered a command into it. Less than a minute later, a knock sounded at the door, and he strode forward to open it.

In the doorway stood a ragged-looking woman, struggling against her bonds as two guards hauled her inside.

"Queen Nor! Please, grant me your mercy." The warden of Lunamere fell to her knees before Nor, her bound wrists held out before her as if in prayer.

Nor peered down her nose at the traitor. "You had one of the Unified System's most wanted fugitives in *my* prison. And instead of keeping her there, where she could have been persuaded to join the right side of the galaxy...you lost her. Not only that, but an entire squadron of guards is dead, the prisoner from Arcardius is missing and my best Revivalist is mysteriously absent from her post. And you dare ask me for mercy?"

The warden sobbed at Nor's feet. *"Please."*

"Aclisia," Nor said, not taking her eyes from the pathetic woman before her. The scientist hurried to stand by Nor's side. "Here is your first living trial. And for the sake of this traitor here, let us all hope that it works."

The warden screamed as the guards hauled her to her feet. The sound intensified as they strapped her to a chair in the corner of the room.

The screams turned to furious moans as they gagged her. Then a vial of silver liquid was produced, almost glowing beneath the overhead lamps. Aclisia looked to Nor with four bright, hungry eyes.

"Would you like to do the honors, Majesty?"

Nor looked upon the scene with a sudden warmth in her heart, as she listened to the warden's unrelenting moans.

"I came for a show," Nor said. "Give me one to remember."

"With pleasure," Aclisia's two heads said at once.

Darai and Zahn appeared at Nor's sides, flanking her like soldiers.

As Aclisia unstoppered the vial, Zahn took Nor's hand in his.

They held on to each other, their heartbeats pulsing in time as they watched Nor's greatest dream come to fruition.

# CHAPTER 30
## KLAREN
### YEAR TWENTY-FOUR

*THE GIRL WAS BORN TO DIE.*

*She'd always known it; had been preparing for it since the day she was created.*

*Since her Yielding, and throughout all the years spent working to get to where she was, the girl had remembered the dream. For how could she ever forget? In her mind, she saw it now.*

*A burning black-and-red palace.*

*A crumbling planet, starved for life, nearly ready to explode in the midst of a battle. A king, trying desperately to save his people.*

*A starship heading across the skies, delivering one chance at a change of fate.*

"Klaren? It's time."

She opened her eyes. The king of Xen Ptera knelt before her, his eyes reddened and full of tears. His forehead creased with worry. He'd aged so much since the war began. But he was still handsome, still the man who had given her and Nor a wonderful life.

"Time?" she asked.

He nodded and held a hand out to her. "The threat to the palace was true. The soldiers are closing in, and half of my troops are off-planet." He inhaled a trembling, defeated breath. "I fear that they will win, Klaren. The Unified Systems will destroy us soon."

"There's still hope," she whispered.

He shook his head. "No, my heart. Hope is as dead as our planet. I'm going to continue this war, but…time is fleeting. We must hide, now, before they breach the palace gates."

She let her husband sweep the blankets back and help her from their bed.

The queen had fallen ill over the past several months, her body worn from breathing the tainted, war-torn air on the planet. Even with the iron shutters closed, she could still make out the hint of greenish light slipping through the edges of the window. Could still feel the rattle in her lungs with each breath she took.

Now she could hear the whine of ships outside. The shouts of soldiers, as yet another battle waged. How many more would there be? She could hear the screech of ammunition seeking out living targets. She could nearly taste the hot, metallic tang of all the blood that had been spilled already, all the lives lost in the endless fighting. Women. Men. Children. No one on Xen Ptera was safe.

So many years the planet had held on to life.

And today the queen had a choice.

She already knew, as she'd dreamed years ago, which one she would make.

Her body was racked with trembles as she lifted her hands to her husband's face. She wasn't supposed to feel this way for him, for the life they had made together. For the daughter they shared.

*Just thinking of Nor, so young, so unprepared for what was to come…*

Tears slipped down the queen's cheeks.

She wished she could go back. She wished she could change that passionate night they had shared, the careless days after and the tonic she'd forgotten to take…

"Go to the bunker," she whispered. She looked into his eyes, leveled her voice to a calm state of solid steel. "Take Nor with you. Go now."

He parted his lips to speak, but she kissed him with all the fierceness in her heart, all the fire of the battle raging beyond. Behind her, Darai slipped from the shadows, his ruined face grim as he watched the queen draw herself away from her king.

"I will care for them as I have cared for you," Darai said, placing a hand on the queen's elbow to steady her. "Remember the mission, Klaren."

Together, they watched the king leave the room without looking back. She kept her eyes on him as she spoke.

"I fear I am not strong enough. That all these years have made me weak. That…love…has made me weak."

"We do not have room for love, my queen. Just as we do not have room for you to remain here, wasting away where there is no hope." Darai squeezed her elbow and forced her to pull her gaze from the retreating king. "You will go and create it for us. You will carry on toward our goal. You are the strongest Yielded I have ever known."

"And my child?" the queen asked. "What of her?"

"Where you go, she cannot follow."

The queen's heart twisted in her chest.

Darai smiled sadly at her, even though she knew it pained him because of his scars. "The light will guide her. Just as it continues to guide you."

The queen placed a kiss on his cheek, committing his face to memory. Somewhere outside the palace, screams rang out. There was an explosion. A rattling that shook the walls.

The soldiers were here.

Klaren gripped Darai's hands in hers.

"*You will train her in the truth. You will see to it that she is strong.*"

His eyes were like fire. "*I swear it upon the Light. I swear it upon the Conduit.*"

The queen smiled, thinking of how fiercely her daughter always held on to things. How stubborn she was. How devilishly determined. "*She will be a great queen, Darai. Teach her, just as I would have taught her, that she should always choose her duty over her heart.*"

Even now she could feel her own shattering in her chest.

"*Go. Into the next world, my Yielded,*" Darai said, placing a finger beneath her chin. Lifting her gaze to his. "*Do not look back.*"

The queen swept from the room.

She did not pause, even as smoke began to curl through the hallways. Even as footsteps pounded up the spiral stairs and the dark forms of her soldiers swam into view, fighting back the intruders who dared enter her crumbling palace.

No bullets touched her skin as she walked gracefully to the doors.

No one stopped her as she unlocked them and slipped out into the battle raging beyond.

Enemy soldiers swarmed her at once.

Outside the palace walls sat a starship coated in deepest blue, the symbol of an exploding star on its side. The ramp was already open as a figure marched down it, guards flanking his sides.

He marched slowly to greet her, that devil from her dreams with eyes like the sky.

"*What's this?*" he asked. "*A Xen Pterran rat, caught wandering outside her cage?*"

"*General Cortas,*" the queen said. She smiled at him, a practiced thing that had yet to fail her, and was pleased to feel the familiar, warm spark ignite in her chest when their eyes met. When, through his war-honed hatred, he noticed her beauty and hungered for more.

"*Take the fool queen aboard,*" General Cyprian Cortas commanded. "*As my personal prisoner.*"

She did not fight the soldiers as they escorted her onto the ship, as *her feet crunched across Xen Pterran soil one last time. She did not look back at the palace, not even once.*

*Her husband was wrong.*

*Hope was not dead.*

*Hope, in the form of the queen's sacrifice, had only just flickered to life.*

# CHAPTER 31
## ANDROMA

*"WHAT ARE YOU DOING?"*

*Andi whirled around.*

*Valen stood at the bottom of the staircase with his arms crossed over his chest, his hair rumpled as if he'd just woken from a long sleep. Or finally resurfaced from hours of painting abstract images on the canvases littered about his room.*

*He'd never spoken to Andi much before she was a Spectre. And now, even with her living in his home, their rooms a short walk away from each other's, he'd spoken to her even less. But he always seemed to be listening when she and Kalee were giggling about the latest drama to spill across the streets of Arcardius. During meals, when Andi and the other Spectres stood guard, she'd watch him curiously. Valen usually sat*

in the farthest seat from his father, hunched forward as if he were battling some deep, silent pain. Sometimes she'd catch him staring at her
with his strange, unblinking hazel eyes, his paint-stained fingers gripping his golden fork like a weapon he didn't want to use.

And several times over the years, Andi had caught Valen following
her and Kalee through the twisting halls of the estate, quickly ducking
into open doorways with heat flaming on his cheeks when she'd whirled
around to catch him, worried it was an intruder come to harm Kalee.

Valen Cortas was silent and strange—a mystery Andi really had no
interest in cracking. And yet, despite his oddities, the older students at
the Arcardian Academy always talked about him, whispered his name
in the halls in between classes when he shuffled past, his shoelaces undone, splatters of paint on his rumpled uniform.

General Cortas hadn't even assigned a full-time Spectre for Valen.
Kalee said it was because he wasn't the heir, but Andi had always wondered. The tension between father and son was palpable. It made for
awkward meetings when the whole family and their Spectres were present.

"I asked you a question," Valen said now from the bottom of the
stairs.

"And I don't have to answer." Kalee tossed her pale hair over her
shoulder, the polar opposite to Valen's dark brown.

Valen frowned. "I was asking Androma."

Andi's mouth opened. Valen never tried to speak to her directly.
And now…he was angry, looking at her like she was trying to steal
his best friend.

"We're going to have some fun, Valen," Andi said. "Maybe you
should join us. Put down the paintbrushes for a little while and see the
real world."

She hadn't meant it rudely, but his mouth twisted at her words. And
then his eyes fell on the silver ignition card clutched in Kalee's hand.
"You're not going anywhere. Not with that."

He started up the stairs, his bare feet soundless with each step.

"That's enough, Valen." Kalee whined like a caged dog as she nudged Andi farther up the staircase. "Come on, Andi. He's not going to stop us."

"I'll wake up Father," Valen threatened.

Kalee laughed. "You wouldn't dare."

Andi stared down at Valen, who, before tonight, had always seemed so quiet, so focused on things inside of himself rather than the world around him.

"There isn't room for three in the ship," Kalee said.

He continued upward anyway.

"You can't come."

"Kalls." Valen said her nickname with a heavy sigh. He looked to Andi, frowning again. "You aren't going to stop this?"

"Of course she's not," Kalee said. "Come on, Valen. It's my birthday."

Valen frowned. "You're not yourself when you're with her, Kalls. Don't do this. It's not a good idea. Just…come down. I'll walk you back to your room."

Kalee circled her arm through Andi's. "I'm better when I'm with Andi, Valen. You're just jealous because no one is interested in getting on a ship alone with you."

Andi blinked in surprise as Valen froze. He stared up at Kalee like she'd just shattered his heart.

And maybe she had.

"Don't come crying to me when Father catches you," he whispered. Then his face warped with a sad smile. "Happy Birthday, Kalee. I hope it's everything you want it to be."

He turned, slinking back down the stairs.

For a moment, Andi wondered if maybe he was right. Maybe they shouldn't go. Again, that little voice whispered, This is a mistake. This isn't in your orders. Your orders are to keep her safe, Androma, not keep her happy.

But as Andi stared down at the card in her charge's hand, the thrill of the night swept over her. A promise that adventure was waiting, and a ship with engines larger than any she'd ever had in her control at the Academy.

"Let's go, Kalee."

She tugged her friend along with her, up the stairs and out the door to the docking pad. The transport sat waiting for them, a silver beast crouching in the moonlight. Andi screeched with laughter as Kalee chased her across the platform, the wind in their hair, the kiss of the night on their skin.

Tonight, they would be more than just a Spectre and her charge. They'd be partners in crime. Girls on a mission, out to tear apart the silent skies.

# CHAPTER 32
## LIRA

IT HAD BEEN 86,400 SECONDS SINCE THE TIMER started on their mission, and not for a moment had Lira allowed herself to stop moving.

She paced back and forth on the *Marauder*, her steps whisper silent as she worried her way past Andi's empty captain's chair.

So many nights she'd found her captain here, scratching tallies into her swords, neck bent as if pressed down by the weight of her sins.

The first part of the mission had gone as planned. Andi and Dex had gone in, the latter assuming they'd stick to *his* plan. Little did Dextro Arez know that the Marauders weren't up for following his lead.

They'd executed Plan B with the ultimate amount of finesse. Lira would never forget the moment Breck sent Dex flying across the pub with a single kick to his gut. The snarl on the Lunamere guards' faces as Dex destroyed their card game, Krevs scattered across the pub for anyone to claim.

After the Sparks had gone off and the Lunamere warden had arrived, Lira and the crew had hightailed their way out of that putrid pub as fast as their legs would allow.

The last she saw of Andi was when she turned to face the warden, and her inevitable transport to Lunamere.

They'd locked eyes across the pub, and as Xen Pterran guards surrounded Andi, she'd sent one desperate message to Lira.

*Run.*

It wasn't a suggestion born out of fear. It was an order.

Despite everything in her, Lira had obeyed.

But with every step, she'd felt like a traitor.

*Your captain is in chains*, a voice whispered in the back of her mind. *You should be by her side. Instead, you're running.*

*All you ever do is run.*

*Run from your duties.*

*Run from your family.*

The voice, as always, had sounded like Lon's. Chest deep, full of knowing and love all at once.

Lira had shoved it away. Forced herself onto the *Marauder*, her hands clutching the throttle as she reversed away from the old, crumbling satellite's docking bay.

This was all part of the plan. And yet, Lira couldn't help but feel as if she'd just repeated an act she'd done four years ago.

*Running from what you love most*, Lon's voice ghosted into her mind again.

As she'd flown the *Marauder* away from Dark Matter, Lira could only hope, and pray to the Godstars, that Andi and Dex would make it back out alive and with Valen Cortas in tow.

Hopefully Andi and Valen would be uninjured. Dextro, she didn't care a single star about.

She knew enough about the damage he'd once caused Andi to wish the worst upon him. It took a lot to break a woman like Andi, and yet somehow, he had managed to do it.

"I'm bored," Gilly said, interrupting Lira's thoughts. "I wish Dex was here."

The pilot looked up from the dark dash before her. *"What?"*

Gilly shrugged. "He's funny. I like him."

"He's not funny," Lira said. "He's Andi's enemy, and therefore, he is *our* enemy. And he's *late*."

A full twenty-four hours after leaving Dark Matter, the *Marauder*, powered down into survival mode to avoid detection, sat like a dark shadow in the Junkyard. The irony of pretending to be dead in the air when only days ago, Dex's men had literally killed the ship in order to board it and start this entire mission process in the first place, was not lost on Lira.

Lira's scales sizzled as another wave of newly formed hatred swept into her.

"You're going to melt the dash," Breck said.

Lira sighed and shook out her palms.

*Remove the anger,* she told herself. *Remove it, because you're strong enough. Find the control.*

It had been far too long. Andi and Dex were supposed to be out of Lunamere by now, safely back on board the ship. They should have already left this ship graveyard behind, a mere speck in the distance.

But now?

They were thirty minutes late.

Thirty minutes *far* too late.

Lira twiddled her thumbs, not knowing what to do with her hands otherwise. A tight knot had formed in her chest, one that refused to relinquish its grip no matter how deeply she breathed. What was the cause of the delay? Had something gone wrong in

ZENITH

the dark halls of Lunamere? She couldn't simply patch into her captain's channel—the distance between them was too great.

"I can't wait any longer," Lira said to the girls, gaining their attention.

Gilly, who was flipped upside down on her chair, sat upright. "Andi ordered us to stay put. Do *you* want to disobey her?"

"Not entirely," Lira said, shaking her head.

"What are you going to do then? We aren't just going to leave them behind, right?" she asked, eyes wide with anxiety.

"Of course not, Gilly," Breck answered for Lira. "She's just… concerned." Breck narrowed her eyes at Lira in warning. A private message from the gunner flashed across her feed. *Keep it together. Don't scare the kid.*

Sometimes Lira forgot how young Gilly was. Her youth had been pulled out from under her by the awful things done to her in the past, and her innocence certainly hadn't been restored by the road she now followed with the girls.

But she didn't know the truth, and neither did Breck. Lira frowned as she thought about what Andi had commanded just before they entered Dark Matter.

If they didn't return by the designated time, the girls were to save themselves. They were to hide in the darkest hole they could find until they were long forgotten by General Cortas and his lackeys.

Lira's scales lit up again.

She'd followed Andi's other orders. But this was not one she could obey.

How could they even trust Soyina? She'd checked out, by their snooping…and yet, Lira didn't truly trust anyone in this galaxy. No one could, with its twisted history.

Another minor problem was the fact that, for the second time this week, Lira had been forced to assume her role of Second-in-Command. She hated the title, and wished she could discard it as easily as Breck and Gilly discarded used bullet casings.

If it was just Lira alone on this ship, without Breck and Gilly, she would storm Lunamere herself until she found Andi, dead or alive.

It was the very least she could do for the sake of their long friendship. For the chance at a real life, without the heart-clenching, back-breaking responsibility that waited for her back on Adhira.

But when the other two girls' lives were on the line? Lira forced her emotions aside, as Adhirans should, and told herself they had to stay put.

"I'll be back," Lira said, turning on her heel.

"Where are you going?" Breck asked. When Lira didn't answer, she added, "Lir?"

"You know she never tells us," Gilly whispered back, though Lira heard it as she left the room. "Play me in a game of Fleet while we wait?"

Breck sighed. "Why, so you can slaughter me again? And where is Alfie, anyhow?"

"I'll tell you if you play me in Fleet," Gilly offered.

Their voices trailed off as Lira exited the bridge, stomped down the hallway and deftly climbed down the ladder hatch onto the deck below. The cool metal felt like heaven on her bare feet. Another ladder, a few quick, graceful strides across the catwalk and she found herself storming through the door at the end of the hall into her quarters.

Her room was clean, organized and mostly empty, save for the single welded bookshelf, which held her entire collection of romance novels on handheld pads, each with stories of pilots who stole their lovers away on adventures across the skies. Andi herself had gifted the entire collection to Lira on her Aging Day last year.

Lira had requested a room alone. Breck and Gilly shared the one across from her, which was stacked with soft, overflowing bunks, while Andi took the captain's quarters above.

But Lira?

She enjoyed time to get lost in her thoughts. And she enjoyed the domed window wall that looked out into endless, swirling outer space. No matter where the *Marauder* traveled, it was always a glorious view. Ever-changing through the varillium walls. Today, Lira gazed out upon the hull of a broken warship, battered and melted into a mere hunk of waste. The Xen Pterran insignia was half missing on one side.

What size of bomb, Lira wondered, had been used on that ship?

The Cataclysm was more of a mystery to her than to the others, having come from a planet that was hell-bent on peace. Lira chose not to study it. She was too afraid to discover what a leader would have to do when faced with the horrific prospect of war.

She sighed and turned her back on the window wall. A small metal cot was pressed up against it. She sank onto the firm metal slab, relishing the cold on her back.

It was here that she could find a few moments of peace during their busiest days. Here that she could work out the constant barrage of questions and thoughts that peppered her mind day in and day out.

She'd made a lot of choices since leaving Adhira.

All of them had involved Andi and the girls. They worked together as a unit. A single organism with many arms and legs—some smaller than others, some with more scars or markings. But still one and the same once all was said and done.

Some might say that the girls were soulless.

But they *were* Lira's soul. And if she had to bet on it, she'd say that she was a part of theirs, too.

For years, Lira had dedicated her life to this crew. She had come here as a girl dreaming of freedom. Now, she had it in her grasp.

Only General Cortas was in the way of that.

And if anything happened to Andi, after all she'd been

through…especially on this mission, Lira would never forgive herself for letting Andi go in alone.

She hated to think it, but if anything happened to Andi, Lira would be in charge. What would she do then?

*You'd run*, Lon's voice echoed again. *Because power and responsibility are too much for you, little bug.*

But that wasn't entirely true. Lira piloted the *Marauder*. She held the lives of Andi and the girls in her hands each time they set out onto a new mission.

She sighed, closing her eyes. Chasing away the demons. They weren't as large or as horrifying as those of the other girls, Lira knew…and yet they still plagued her.

When Lira's father died from Wexen Pox, a great sweeping disease that took out many on Adhira, her mother had shut down. Then she'd drowned herself in bottles of Griss, refusing help when the need for the drink became too strong. Eventually, she left in the night without a word, leaving Lira and her twin brother, Lon, behind. The last Lira had heard, her mother was still living on Adhira, near the Endless Sea, shacking it up with a gilled man who drank more than the sea creatures he made his living catching.

Without their mother's sister, Lira and Lon would have been alone as children. But their aunt had swept into their lives, welcoming them into her home. They were well cared for, well loved. But each year they grew. And with growth came *responsibility*.

The family career. Their aunt had no children to take up the job when she died, and so the offer had gone to Lira. She'd refused it, time and time again.

She'd spent her days training and studying how to pilot a ship instead of attending lessons with her aunt.

Lon had encouraged her all along, knowing it gave her joy, but hoping it would not be what determined her future.

And so when Lira had packed her bags and left… She'd never

forget the look on her twin's face. As if she'd just betrayed him. As if she'd reopened the wound their mother gave them both years before. It was the very same look Lira *thought* she saw in Andi's eyes when Lira left her in chains, surrounded by guards in Dark Matter.

It was just her mind playing tricks. Pulling at her weakness. Andi had planned for that capture to happen, step by step. But seeing it play out was an entirely different thing.

Again, Lira's scales heated.

Again, she forced them to cool.

It was why she slept on metal, and with no sheets. Because the dreams became too real, and by the time she'd awoken, any bedclothes would have burned to cinders anyway.

A knock on the door pulled Lira from her thoughts.

It swung open, revealing Breck and Gilly again.

"I'm just resting," Lira blurted out. A stupid, unbelievable lie.

Breck frowned, her hands on her hips. She had to duck to keep her head from hitting the doorway as she entered. "You're sulking, Lira. And Marauders don't sulk alone."

Gilly tossed a deck of cards onto Lira's lap. An expensive edition of Fleet, a game widely played across Mirabel.

"I just beat Breck," she said, twirling one of her red braids around her finger. "And I think I would also like to beat you."

Lira sighed. She couldn't be beaten. Gilly knew it.

But she also knew how to make Lira feel better when it felt as if the galaxy was pressing in around her.

"Come on, then," Lira said, waving the girls inside. Gilly giggled and settled cross-legged on Lira's metal cot, smiling as she dealt out the glowing cards.

Lira looked down at her hand. A good set of armor, a solid few soldiers, but her weapon? Of course—a Godstars-damned sword. It was as if fate was laughing at Lira, reminding her constantly of Andi's absence on the ship.

SASHA ALSBERG & LINDSAY CUMMINGS

"What if they don't make it out?" Gilly asked, laying down her first card.

An Explorer ship, quickly followed up by a fully trained pilot. Plenty of attack power.

Lira cleared her throat, staring out the window at the floating pieces of twisted metal as she laid down a card to cancel Gilly's attack ability for the turn. "They'll make it out," Lira said, even though she herself didn't quite believe it. "Trust me. And if you can't trust me, then trust Andi."

"We trust you," Breck said. She frowned as Lira dug into her pocket and popped a chunk of Moon Chew into her mouth. "If you keep chewing that stuff, you're going to make me vomit."

Moon Chew was her stress reliever. The sickly sweet substance wasn't to everybody's liking, but to Lira, it was one of her favorite things.

Lira spat a wad of it into the cup she kept by her cot. "Your turn, Gil."

"I'll draw a card instead."

Lira nodded her permission.

"Andi is only mortal," Breck said to both girls. "We don't know who the Xen Pterrans are anymore, or what they're capable of. If they've really got the capability to kidnap Valen Cortas and cart him across the galaxy without being seen or heard... it makes me wonder what they've been up to all these years." She was staring out Lira's window, ignoring the game of Fleet, as if she were able to see Andi from this distance. "It makes me wonder what else they could do, or have done, without the rest of Mirabel knowing."

"We just have to hope," Lira said, "that Andi and Dex have thought of that. And that Soyina can truly be trusted. Because right now..." She sighed as she remembered her aunt saying these very words, years ago, when the Wexen Pox swept across Adhira. "Hope is all we have."

"Hope is a raging asshole," Gilly said.

"Explain to me, Gilly," Breck said with a sigh, "how exactly can an asshole *rage*?"

Lira choked on a sudden, unexpected laugh. "I swear, the two of you. You were both born with my brother's sarcastic soul."

"You're dead," Gilly said suddenly, slamming down three rare red-glowing cards.

Lira absentmindedly set down three more, the stats already having formed in her mind, the win instantaneous. "Apologies, Gil."

Gilly howled a round of fresh curses, and Breck silently shook her head, finally giving up on censoring the young gunner's language.

They played three more rounds, and soon Lira lost herself in the laughter of her friends, the swift dealing of cards from her fingertips, the revel in each and every win.

It wasn't until she heard the knock on the door and turned to see Alfie walk in that the terrified ache returned to her chest. And a sudden smell came along with it, pungent and horrid enough to make her eyes water.

Gilly jumped up off the cot, her cards scattering to the floor, their light winking out. "How did you escape?"

Breck's head whipped to her. "What are you talking about, Gil?"

Alfie glided over silently, his head tilted to the side. The smell arrived in full force with him. "With help from the *Marauder*'s Artificial Intelligence system, I was able to unscrew the bolts on the waste bay's door to remove myself from the room. It would be most appreciated if you would remove further attacks on me from your in-flight agenda. It is in the best interest of your mission."

Lira sat there, trying to make sense of what had just happened. Then a large bark sounded from across the room as Breck doubled over laughing. "Gilly, you beautiful little demon. You actually did it! You locked him in the waste bay!"

Gilly smiled smugly and crossed her arms.

Then a thought came to Lira. "Alfie, did you rebolt the door to the waste bay?"

Alfie cocked his oval head. Lira could see the gears moving in his body, as if he was deeply pondering her question.

"No, I did not reassemble the door. The mechanic bots should be reassembling it now."

The three girls let out an exasperated moan.

"Alfie, you *idiot*," Gilly groaned. "We don't *have* mechanic bots on this ship."

Lira bent over and nearly gagged from the smell.

Before they could let all hell loose on Alfie, the ship's cool female voice spoke over their heads.

*"Incoming message for Lira Mette."* After a moment, Memory added, *"Hello, Alfie."*

Alfie glanced up. "Memory's voice is very enticing to my inner programming. I should like to converse with her when you are done, Lira Mette."

"Oh, Godstars," Breck said. "Do *not* tell me our ship is about to hook up with the general's AI."

Lira raced to the opposite wall, tapping a holoscreen embedded into the metal. Seconds passed before the screen lit up and a message blinked into view.

She could practically feel the tension unwind from her muscles as she turned toward the waiting crew.

"It's from Soyina," Lira said, smiling as she swept past Alfie and out into the hall, where she raced toward the bridge, her fingers already itching to grab the *Marauder*'s wheel. "Time to go get our girl."

# CHAPTER 33
## ANDROMA

*"ANDROMA! OH, GODSTARS, WAKE UP!"*

*She was lying in the darkness beside a burning ship. Her father's voice called to her, muffled as if he were underwater.*

*His hands gripped her face, and they were warm against the frigid night.*

*She wanted to keep sleeping, but the voice was desperate. A pleading, almost ruthless thing that begged her to wake.*

Andi opened her eyes and gasped.

Cold. It was *so* cold.

Dex hovered over her, his hands on either side of her face. "You're alive," he choked out. His breath slipped away from him in a thick cloud. His eyes were wide. Terrified, as if he'd been staring at her corpse. "I didn't know if... I couldn't live if you were..."

Shock overwhelmed her, and she struggled to keep the panic at bay. Her chest ached as if she'd been shot, each breath threatening to snap her apart. She tried to gasp in air, but there was a weight on her chest.

"Can you breathe?" Dex asked. "Stay with me, Androma!"

He began to pull something heavy off her. It felt as if he'd pulled a boulder from her chest.

She gasped in a breath and realized, with horror, what had been on top of her.

A corpse.

Now when she breathed, she felt the cold press of something *beneath* her, like an uneven carpet. Slowly, with the rational side of her mind—the part that had been honed by years in military school and then, later, life on the *Marauder* with the girls—she gained control of her thoughts.

*Assess the situation. Remember to breathe.*

But Godstars...the *smell*. Andi choked on it. She looked left and right. Corpses, all around her.

She gasped in another breath. The weight of death and the pressing odor of decay were everywhere, filling the small transport ship they were in. Stiff, frozen fingertips pressed in between her shoulder blades. She felt the sharp prod of a bare foot leaning up against her knees. And finally, a woman's hairless head, her four eyes wide and unblinking as Andi turned her face to get a closer look at her surroundings.

"Get me out." Andi gasped again. In her mind, all she could see was Kalee, dead beside her in the transport ship, eyes closed, blood everywhere. "Get me out!"

Dex pulled and shoved and finally, finally, she was free.

He wrapped his arms around her and they practically tumbled backward. Together, Dex's arms still around her, they sank back against a metal wall, the corpses near their toes looking as if they were trying to pull them back into the pile with dead, frigid fingers.

"What the hell happened?" Andi asked through her teeth.

"Soyina shot us," Dex said. "She actually *shot us*."

He was still holding her. Andi knew she should pull away, but he was so warm and the transport was *so damned cold*.

Finally, after she stopped shivering, Andi removed herself from Dex's grasp and turned to look at their surroundings.

Low, rounded metal ceilings seemed to press in on her from overhead, the walls equally claustrophobic. There was a single door across the small space, and as Andi breathed in again and quivered from the putrid stench, she felt a rumble beneath her.

It was the unmistakable feeling of a ship's engine roaring as a pilot, likely behind that closed door, accelerated. Her body swayed with the motion, which meant the ship was small.

The memories clicked into place. Soyina, that sneaky fiend.

Andi could still see the way the Revivalist had leveled a gun at them in their final moments inside Lunamere, still feel the *pain* that had bloomed across her body. Then darkness. A space as empty and unknown as a black hole. Soyina had made good on her promise to get them out of Lunamere, that much was true. But Andi had never imagined it like this, on a transport ship designed to cart dead bodies from Lunamere to the Junkyard, out past Dark Matter, where dead ships and even deader people swam endlessly through the starless sky.

Andi lurched to the right, and a wave of nausea hit her along with the scent.

She wouldn't vomit.

The Bloody Baroness did *not* vomit.

Andi took another gasping breath, forced her body upright and promptly loosed the contents of her stomach.

Into Dex's lap.

His mouth opened and closed as he stared at the mess.

Then, incredibly, he laughed. For a moment, she thought he'd lost his mind. But then the chaos of the past job and the realization that they had escaped Lunamere and *lived* to tell the tale swept over Andi.

She laughed with him. When she could laugh no more, she got a good look at him for the first time in the dim emergency exit light above their heads.

Beneath her sick mess, he was covered in dried blood that stained his black suit. A green-and-yellow bruise had spread across his forehead, as if he'd been smacked with a hammer the size of a fist.

She'd seen bruises like this before, from Gilly's double-triggered gun. A stunner bullet, meant to incapacitate, but not kill.

*Soyina*, Andi thought again. She was devilishly smart, capable of completing their mission while saving herself at the same time. But this certainly hadn't been part of the plan. And what if Soyina's bullets hadn't been stunners?

Black holes ablaze.

Death had never felt so close.

"We actually did it," Andi said. "We actually made it out."

Then her heart lurched against her chest.

*Valen*.

Andi turned, staring across the lumpy space, wide enough to fit thirty dead in a row.

"Help me find him," she demanded. "Help me find Valen!" When Dex didn't move, Andi cursed and began to dig through the cold dead on her own, swearing to the stars that if she'd screwed this up after all they'd gone through, after all the lives she'd stolen…

*There*. Across the pile at the opposite end of the transport, lying facedown, his shredded back open and bare. Andi crawled toward him, ignoring the disgust roiling in her gut, the feeling of wrongness spreading through her as her hands pressed down against frozen, scarred skin.

He was cold when she reached him, but his pulse was there. A delicate flutter. Dex finally joined her, and together they heaved him over onto his side, careful not to touch the lacerations on his back. The wounds looked like sharp claws had shredded his skin, allowed it to heal and shredded it all over again.

Andi's gaze traveled to Valen's face.

It was the first time she'd truly been able to stop and look at him, to study the way his features had changed in some places and stayed the same in others.

His hair was shorn near the scalp, but she recognized the dark mahogany color he'd had years ago. His cheeks were shallow, the bones protruding at sharp angles. And his lips, once full, were colorless and empty.

"It's a wonder he's not dead," Dex said.

Andi found herself unable to respond. Staring at him was like staring at her past. But saving Valen—her one chance at redemption—hadn't changed the emptiness she still felt inside.

The void was still there.

Seeing Valen had simply opened it up, and now it threatened to suck her back in.

"How long have we been out?" Andi asked.

Dex shrugged. "Not sure. I woke up and then I saw you and..."

She couldn't forget the haunted look in his eyes when he woke her.

Soyina's voice echoed in her mind. *We didn't, you know. Your comrade wanted to whine like a baby about his feelings for you.*

But Dex wasn't allowed to have feelings. He wasn't allowed to look at Andi the way he had a few moments ago, wasn't allowed to hold her face as if he were cradling the world in his hands.

Andi dismissed those thoughts. He'd been shocked. He'd thought his partner was dead. Of course he'd been concerned.

"Lira's probably wearing a hole in the floorboards of my ship with her pacing."

Dex raised a single brow. "*My* ship."

She didn't argue this time, knowing in her heart that she'd already won the fight long ago. With effort, Andi tore her eyes away from Valen. The job wasn't done. She wouldn't relax until they were back on her ship, reunited with her crew and had Valen taken to the med bay, where Alfie could get to work on healing him.

Plus, the smell was starting to get worse.

Asking for Dex's help wasn't one of her favorite things, especially after he'd just seen her lose control upon waking. But she knew he was the only way they'd be getting out of this damned transport before it emptied them out into the Junkyard.

"Dex." She said his name like a sigh, hating the way it felt so familiar on her tongue.

They were too close together. Too alone, despite the corpses and Valen's unconscious form beside them.

"Androma," Dex replied, inclining his head.

"Do you remember the night you bypassed the locks on my door in your old Junker ship?"

"How could I ever forget?" Dex's eyes glittered like stardust. "Your nightgown was—"

"Not a point of discussion right now," Andi hissed, cutting him off. *There* was the old familiar annoyance. She sighed. "Can you do it again? To that door?"

He glanced past her shoulder, his eyes sparkling with a different sort of mischief as he nodded.

"Good," Andi said. She looked down at her boots and began to remove their laces. They were strong and sturdy, luckily not frayed from the fight in Lunamere. "Then do it now." She coiled the bootlaces around her fists, then pulled them taut. The strands sang with a satisfying *twang*.

"Are you going to kill me with your shoelaces, Baroness?" Dex asked.

Andi looked at Valen's sleeping form, begging the Godstars

to keep him breathing until they got him to the safety of the *Marauder*.

"No," she said as she began to crawl back across the bodies. "But I am going to take care of the pilot once you get us through that door. And then *you* are going to fly us back to my ship."

"Not you?" He raised a brow at her. "After all the fear you've instilled in others, you're still too afraid to fly a—"

"You don't know what you're talking about," Andi spat out.

"Does your crew know?"

Andi was silent, and he smiled like he knew her secret.

Like he'd very much enjoy keeping it for himself.

Five minutes later, Andi sat in the copilot's seat, a fresh corpse tossed in the pile behind the open door. Another tally, another face to haunt her. Dex took the throttle and angled the transport toward home—the glass starship that sat waiting like a gem in the starlit sky.

# CHAPTER 34
## DEX

DEX'S SENSES WERE BEING WRONGFULLY AS-saulted.

The mystery of the missing AI had finally been solved, leaving an unhinged waste bay door in its place, and now the scent of unmentionable things had begun to swim its way through every deck of the ship, rivaling the smell of the corpses. To add insult to injury, Andi's crew of she-devils hadn't stopped following her around since they'd nearly crash-landed in the *Marauder*'s small docking tunnel.

Their voices were like gunshots to his head.

The little fire-haired gunner had wanted to know if the blood on Andi belonged to her or some "now-ball-less bastard," to which the giantess had responded, *Of course it's not hers, Gil. And don't say* bastard. *Say* prick. *Are you hungry, Andi?* All of which was followed by the Adhiran pilot circling Andi like a bird of prey, pecking at her cuts and bruises, then throwing icy glares in Dex's direction, as if he had been the one to give them to her.

"This," Dex said as he sat in the med bay, letting the AI fawn over his own cuts and bruises, "is my own personal version of hell."

"You may experience some pain," Alfie said, tugging a little too hard on a fresh line of stitches on Dex's brow, only adding to the already planets-wide list of things he wanted to drink himself into forgetting tonight.

Andi glowered at him from the table next to his, then resumed whispering to her crew. She'd refused Alfie's help and given Dex a dismissive wave of her hand as thanks for helping her haul Valen's body into the med bay.

And hadn't said a word to him since.

It was so purely Androma to be as cold as a Soleran day, and that ounce of normalcy took a bit of the tension from Dex's shoulders as he quickly thanked Alfie for his stitches, then slid down from the table.

"I'm going to check in with the general," Dex announced.

Alfie turned back to Valen, who still lay unconscious on the table in the center of the med bay, eyes closed and bruises deepening in the bright white light. The crew didn't even lift their heads to acknowledge Dex, save for the littlest one, who quickly lifted two fingers in his direction, a Tenebran signal for him to go screw himself.

He sighed, working his sore jaw back and forth as he headed for the exit. The cool metal doors slid open, then closed shut behind him.

Silence. It was so immediate, Dex almost wept with relief. For years, he'd been on his own, doing things *his* way. Keeping every reward for himself. Working with a crew, especially *Androma's*, was almost more than Dex could take sometimes.

"Krevs, Dex," he told himself. "So many Krevs you could drown in them, and the glory of becoming reinstated as a Guardian." He enjoyed being a rogue bounty hunter. It made quick money, but his whole life leading up to the moment he met Andi had been devoted to Guardianship over Mirabel. Now he had a chance to get the status he'd lost back, and he'd taken it. He had his last bounty in hand, and both the Krevs and his title were so close, he could hardly contain his triumph.

He actually smiled as he made his way through the narrow hallway, then hauled himself up the ladder and onto the level above. His muscles cursed him for the effort.

Dex passed through another narrow hallway, heading toward the meeting room. There were drawings tacked to the walls, mostly stick figures with heads blown apart, little red dots in the background that he assumed were splatters of blood.

He'd have to keep an eye on the smallest Marauder. And sleep with his pistol in his hand. And booby-trap his door with a paralytic fog. And not wander into dark corners where she might be waiting.

Dex entered the meeting room and slumped into the chair at the head of the table, trying not to grimace as he realized his old prized seat no longer conformed to his body the way it used to. How he felt out of place in what had once been his home.

He scooped up the Com Box and, with a sigh and a hell of a lot of reluctance, hit Send on the call.

General Cortas picked up immediately.

"It's the middle of the night, bounty hunter." His face, projected on the wall across from Dex, seemed to have produced more wrinkles since the last time they'd spoken. Why he didn't take advantage of Arcardius's facial rejuvenation procedures, Dex didn't know. "This had better be urgent."

Dex leaned back in his seat and crossed his tattooed arms

over his chest. The white constellation of The Foxling seemed to peer up at him. "Hello, General. I'm alive and well. Thank you for asking."

General Cortas was lying in a plush golden bed. Beside him, Dex could just make out the shadowy form of his wife. "My son," the general said without skipping a beat. His graying hair was mussed from sleep. "Do you have him?"

Offscreen, his wife asked, "Is Valen safe? Is he coming home?"

Dex took his time responding, relishing in the fact that, if only for a moment, the tables had turned. Now the general was at *his* mercy.

"Speak, bounty hunter," General Cortas said, "or I'll make sure I cut your funds in half."

*Not quite turned, then*, Dex thought. "We have him," he said. He picked at a fleck of dried blood on his forearm. "He's alive but not well."

His wife burst into tears. Dex waited a moment while the general calmed her.

"Details," General Cortas said when he turned back to the camera. He glanced sideways at his weeping wife. "Keep them delicate."

Dex nodded. "It seems they had…less than pleasant ways of garnering information from him, all this time in Lunamere." The general's face twitched, but Dex went on. "He's under Alfie's watch right now. The AI has assured me, *many times*, that Valen's health is of the highest priority."

"Good," the general said. Already, he was raising a hand, snapping his fingers at some hidden attendant just offscreen. The red-and-blue lights of a servant droid flashed as General Cortas addressed it. "Send a message to my office. Let them know that my team has rescued Valen. Begin preparations for his return at once."

"We lost several hours in Lunamere," Dex interrupted. "A

few unforeseen problems, but we're estimating no less than a day's delay in returning him to you."

"Make up the time," General Cortas said, his pale eyebrows knitting closer together, "and I'll add to your pay."

Dex nodded. "I'll do my best. If you'd hired me alone…"

"If I'd hired you alone, your head would be stuck on a spike in the darkest corner of Lunamere. I was right to bring in the Bloody Baroness." The general's voice turned acidic when he spoke of Andi. "Keep an eye on my son, bounty hunter. Don't leave him alone with that girl for a second. His safety is of the utmost importance."

Dex nodded again. "As you wish, General."

"I don't need to remind you," the general added, leaning closer to the camera, "of your fate, should you fail to deliver him safely back to me?"

"I remember quite well."

"Very good." General Cortas lifted a hand to hover near the screen. "Don't signal me again on this line. I don't want Xen Ptera picking up on any transmissions."

"Don't you want to see him before you go?" Dex offered.

The general froze, his eyes taking on a strange haze. "I'll see him when he's safely home. Remember who you are, Arez. Remember that you're nothing without me."

With that, he tapped the screen. It faded to darkness.

Dex took a moment to gather himself.

Then he rose, remembering Androma's promise to him back in Lunamere.

His heart in his throat, he slipped back out into the halls of the *Marauder*, walked the familiar path to his old quarters and stopped before the closed door.

Classical music spilled out from inside.

He sighed as he imagined her in there, alone, facing the ghosts of every man and woman she'd killed over the past several days.

He knocked. He knew she wouldn't answer, even if the music hadn't drowned out the sound.

But it was now or never, he supposed.

With a deep breath, Dex opened the door of the captain's quarters and slipped inside.

# CHAPTER 35
## ANDROMA

THE DEAD WERE WATCHING HER DANCE.

Andi closed her eyes tighter, willing them away. Though she sat in the darkness of her captain's quarters on the *Marauder*, classical music blaring over the loudspeakers, her mind and her body were light-years away.

Arcardius. A planet adorned with glass that she had once called home.

She spun on the stage of the Academy, the domed ceiling overhead speckled with lights in the shape of Arcardian bursting stars. The seats that overlooked the stage were filled, though not with the living.

They were filled with the dead.

Her victims watched as Andi took the stage. As the music began, gentle at first, the tinkle of bells. Then a great swell of cymbals, and she took flight. Her body was a vessel, a conduit through which she allowed the music to move.

Her arms extended. Her toes rose to a point, and she spun, round and round, a planet in orbit.

When she opened her eyes, she saw the first man rise from his seat.

Blood pooled from a slit across his throat, red like a smile. Staining the Arcardian Patrolmen badge on his chest.

"I'm sorry," Andi said. "I'm so sorry."

He didn't speak. The dead never did, and so she extended her hand to him. He took it in his featherlight grip, and together, they danced.

Round and round, they spun, gliding across the stage as weightless as two ghosts in the night. As they danced, Andi forced herself to look at him. Through the blood, through the mask of horror that he'd held in his final moments as he died by her swords, she saw the man she'd murdered.

He was a human being. A man who had lived and breathed and loved and hated, a man she'd killed in cold blood. She'd done it because he would have done the same to her. Because if she hadn't, she would have died.

As they danced, she forced herself to look at every detail of his face. The wrinkles at the corners of his eyes, the way his skin was tanned, as if he'd recently spent time outdoors beneath the blazing sun. A soldier training for a mission he knew was soon to come.

He couldn't have known he would die by the hand of the Bloody Baroness on board the *Marauder* as his borrowed commander, a bounty hunter with eyes that pierced, urged him to take his enemy down.

Tears streaked down Andi's cheeks, pulling her from the vision she'd created so clearly in her mind. The music grew louder, silencing her tears. She closed her eyes and forced herself back into her mind. She owed this to the dead. This pain, this dance, this time where she gave herself fully to their memory.

The next corpse stepped onto the stage.

This one was a woman, a guard she'd silenced in Lunamere. As they joined hands and spun in time with the sorrowful strings, Andi saw that the woman was young. She had tired eyes in a thin face. As if she hadn't slept, hadn't had a full meal, in days.

"I'm so sorry," Andi said to her.

The woman simply danced, on and on, until her form faded like mist.

Another of the dead took her place.

They danced, cold palms pressed to Andi's warm ones. Bodies intertwining like vines that twisted together and then came apart.

Andi danced until she'd remembered them all. Every last person she'd killed, every beating heart she'd stopped too soon. It didn't matter that they were her enemies. It didn't matter that in those final moments, Andi had allowed herself to make a choice.

To cross the line she'd drawn for herself. Deal out death to another, or die.

She danced in her mind until her tears had run dry. She danced until the audience was nearly empty. Until the lights of the stage had begun to grow dim, as if the stars overhead were falling into a restful sleep.

Only a single form remained in the audience now. Andi turned to face her as the figure stood. She was dressed in a shimmering blue gown that swirled around her ankles like fragments of cloud. It had always been her favorite, had made her smile and feel, for a time, like a queen.

Her pale hair, matted to her skull on one side, had turned red from fresh blood. Her eyes were closed as she stood at the base of the stage, unmoving.

Every time, no matter the dance, no matter how many deaths Andi had to remember, this girl appeared.

"Kalee," Andi said. "Wake up."

The girl did not move, did not open her eyes.

Andi tried to reach her, but the stage had morphed into something smaller, the space tightening, the walls closing in until she was seated in the captain's chair of a transport ship, fire blazing, smoke clouding her lungs.

"WAKE UP!" Andi screamed.

The transport creaked. Groaned, as the fire licked closer and closer.

Heat had begun to bloom across Andi's wrists. Pain that throbbed and screamed and begged for her attention, but she could not give it.

Because Kalee was dead.

Tears pooled in Andi's vision, and she reached out a final time, desperate to save her charge.

Something touched her from behind.

She slipped from the vision like water through fingertips, and turned around to see him standing there, bathed in the starlight that glowed through the glass wall of Andi's quarters.

"You promised me a conversation," Dex said. She could scarcely hear him over the music still playing. Over the echo of her own screams, still haunting her from her vision.

Wet tears still streaming down her cheeks, Andi nodded.

Dex sat beside her on the floor of her quarters. "Whenever you're ready," he said. He knew her routine. She had done it since the very first night they'd shared together. Different places, different times, but the motions were always the same.

Wrapped up in the music, they sat until the song ended. Silence swept over them, thick and uncomfortable and still, but familiar. Like a long-unseen friend returning home.

"Go ahead, Dex," Andi said.

# CHAPTER 36
## ANDROMA

"DANCING WITH THE DEAD AGAIN?" DEX ASKED.

"Some habits aren't meant to change," Andi said.

She turned to face him. Alone in her private quarters, his presence felt too large. Too real, after all they'd just shared in Lunamere. Old memories of the two of them, once lovers who had shared this very room, began to take shape.

*I love you, Androma*, Dex had said. He'd picked her up, carried her to the small cot in the corner of the room. In between kisses, he'd looked at her like she was sunlight in the darkness.

Three days later, he'd sold her to the Patrolmen for her crimes.

Andi silenced her mind. She would not allow the memories in. Not now, when she already felt so weak.

Dex had showered, finally, the dried blood and vomit washed away, the collar of his shirt open to reveal the scar she'd once given him. The bruise from Soyina's stun shot had darkened on his forehead. Even now, the one on her chest throbbed.

"I still can't believe she shot us," Dex said, noticing Andi's stare. He placed a hand to his bruise and winced. He swallowed and looked at her directly. "When…when I saw you in that pile of bodies, Andi…"

"I promised you five minutes," Andi said, cutting him off. "You said you wanted to talk about the past. Let's talk about it."

His lips parted slightly. Then he closed them and looked away, hesitating before he spoke.

"I've run through this conversation in my mind a million times. And now that we're actually together, I'm not sure where to begin."

"How about this?" Andi asked. The weakness from her dancing visions, the pain of facing her ghosts, suddenly faded. Acid took its place. "You betrayed me," she said. She got to her feet, suddenly unable to sit still. "You knew I was facing a death sentence back on Arcardius. You left me in the hands of those who would give me that death, all for a few Krevs!"

The words were out.

She'd told the girls about the horrific fate Dex had left her to, but never, in the years they'd spent apart, had she imagined seeing him alive and saying it to his face.

It was so absurd, and he was so silent that she threw her head back and laughed. He flinched as if she'd hit him. "Oh, Dextro," Andi said, stepping closer to him as he got to his feet. "Don't tell me you thought, just because we managed to do a job together without killing each other, that I'd forgiven you? Let me remind you that this job wasn't my choice. I took it only because you forced me to, by teaming up with that devil of a man!"

"If you only knew the full story—" Dex began, but Andi didn't want to listen. She was so angry, but hidden behind that rage was pure pain. It was so raw it made her want to burst. Had he ever thought about the pain he'd caused her? Had he ever imagined himself in her place, betrayed by the one who'd sworn her his love and facing the death she'd spent so many years running from?

"I loved you!" she yelled. Her voice cracked on those horrid words, but she kept going, unable to stop. "I loved you, and you threw me away like some common whore!"

Her heart beat so fast she thought it would explode.

He took a step backward, as if he'd been shoved.

"You have to listen to me, Andi," Dex begged. His dark eyes were wide, his tattooed arms held out, hands pressed pleadingly together before him.

She hated how handsome he was. Hated the curve of his jaw, the brown of his eyes, the way the starlight spilled across him like a lover's caress.

She could scarcely stand to look at him.

"I don't have to do anything," Andi growled.

She didn't feel the cool trickle of tears trailing from her eyes, didn't know there were any tears left to cry until she tasted the saltiness on her lips. She sucked a breath through her gritted teeth. She felt her fists clench, felt the weight of her cuffs begging to swing. To give in to the anger. To sink into that darkness she'd been swallowed by years ago. But as much as she wanted to swing at him, she knew her fists weren't in control of this fight.

Her words were.

She wanted him to hurt. To feel the soul-deep pain, just as she did.

Physical wounds would heal, but the internal scars never would.

"Do you not understand?" Andi cried out. He looked broken, his constellation tattoos like cracks across his skin. She wanted to shatter him from the inside out. "You were my whole world. You showed me that I could still be loved. When everyone else—an entire *planet* full of people—hated me so much they wished me dead, even *my own parents*...I found you. I started to live again. I started to trust. Then I lost you, too, just like all the others. You turned away, just like they did."

She didn't care that the tears were now flowing freely, spilling across her metal cheekbones to splatter at her feet. They had been pent up for too long. They needed to be released. "You were a coward. A pathetic, Krev-hungry coward. You failed me when you were the only person I thought never would."

Her words echoed in the space.

For a second she thought he would turn and leave, too cowardly to listen.

Then Dex crossed the room in three strides, so close to her that she could feel his breath on her face. "I turned you in because you were running from the law! You lied to me about your past, Andi. I did nothing that wasn't expected of me! My duty as a Guardian was to the welfare of the galaxy, not to some runaway Spectre who'd failed her entire planet! You made the choice to fly that transport ship. It was *your* hands that crashed it. *Your* failure that killed Kalee! You ran, Androma." He laughed, then, a short bark that exploded from his chest. "And now look what you've become! The Bloody Baroness!"

"You made me this way," Andi snarled. "I became a monster of your creation. I killed, and I liked it. And you liked it, too. All those deaths across the galaxy have your name on them, just as much as mine."

"You're blaming me for the murders you've committed?" He laughed in her face.

"'You're amazing when you fight, Androma,'" she said, throwing his past words back at him. "'You're unstoppable.' Every time you saw me take someone down, every job I helped you with, you looked at me with pride. With love."

They circled each other like predators, blood boiling, bodies shaking with rage as the stars looked on.

"Did you ever think about my side in all of this, Androma?" Dex's voice cracked suddenly as he ran his fingers through his dark hair. "You may think you know the whole story, but you are so consumed by hate that you only see yourself."

She ran her palm over her face, feeling the chill of her metal cheekbones as she wiped away the tears. "You are such a hypocrite! Did you ever ask for my side of the story?"

He paused, then said, "Your side of the story doesn't matter. You sunk a knife into my chest. You stole my ship and left me to die."

"And I'd do it again, a thousand times," Andi growled, stepping closer until they were practically touching, until their furious hearts beat as one.

She saw tears in his eyes now, as well. Felt his chest rise and fall as sobs overcame him.

"You are the only woman I have ever loved," he whispered.

He stepped away, and the space between them felt as distant as the black sky outside.

"If you loved me, why did you betray me?" Andi asked in a whisper.

Dex released a breath. His voice was softer now when he spoke. "There is more to the story than what you think, if you would just listen to me."

She shook her head. "Not tonight, Dex."

"If not tonight, then when?"

He was so stubborn it made Andi want to scream.

"I've heard enough."

He rushed toward her again, grabbed her hands in his and squeezed them tight. Forced her to look up at him.

"I didn't have a choice. When I found out you were a wanted fugitive, I felt like a fool for not realizing it earlier. The way you could fight, the burns on your wrists. How could I not have seen it after the general had blasted your name across the feeds? Godstars, Andi, only a few days had passed when I discovered who you really were, and you'd already wiggled your way into my heart. I was in shock. I knew I had to turn you in, but...I let time go by. I let myself love you, protect you, help you rediscover the strength I always knew you had."

"And yet you still turned me in," she said.

"They had my father!"

He barked out the words in one breath. His eyes were wide, like he couldn't believe he'd actually said them.

Dex had never spoken about his family before, and she'd never pushed the subject. Just as he'd never pushed her for details about her own past.

"The Arcardian Patrolmen took him hostage. The general... all who were loyal to him...they were so furious when you escaped Arcardius before your death sentence could be carried out. I was approached by some of his men. They said that if I didn't lead them to you, my father would be killed. He was just a mechanic. An innocent man! He hadn't killed like you had, he hadn't..." Dex took a deep breath. "They gave me a choice, Andi. I could turn in the woman I loved, whom I'd only spent a year of my life with...or I could watch the man who raised me die at their hands."

Andi didn't know what to think, what to believe.

Dex wiped tears from his cheeks as he sunk to his knees before her.

Broken.

Dextro Arez was finally, *finally* broken. She saw it as plain as day before her, a victory she'd imagined in her heart for years.

So why didn't it feel good?

"When they told me exactly what you had done to Kalee—not only allowing your charge to die on your watch, but the fact that you'd *caused* it? A part of me—the Guardian part—wanted to turn you in so you could face the traitor's punishment you deserved." He looked down at his hands. "But the other part... my heart, Androma, told me that you were only a girl when it happened. A soldier, yes. But so young, with so much responsibility. It was a mistake. No matter how strong the person, everyone makes mistakes.

"I tried to warn you, so you would at least have a head start. When I left that morning, Andi… Don't you remember my words?"

She racked her brain, searching.

And there it was.

*Dex, leaning against the door frame. He'd been ill all morning, puking up his guts in the sick bay.*

*He got dressed slowly and came to sit beside her on the cot, watching her with sadness in his eyes.*

*"You know you always have to be on the lookout when I'm gone,"* he said. *"You know you're never truly safe in this galaxy."*

*"The* Marauder *is my home, Dex,"* Andi said. *"I'm perfectly safe when I'm here."*

*He sighed. "I'd feel better if you kept a weapon on you at all times." He glanced beneath the cot. "Your stash of knives is freshly sharpened."*

She'd laughed then and told him he was worrying for no reason. Told him she'd be fine until he came back. That she knew how to take care of herself.

She'd thought he was just talking nonsense. That he was exhausted and worried for her, because the job he was embarking on would be a longer one than usual.

"I pleaded with them," Dex said now. "I begged them to understand that you had made a mistake. You could never return to your home and wasn't that enough of a punishment? But they wouldn't listen. They just wanted you, Androma. They wanted General Cortas to have justice. They offered me money and a position as a leading Guardian for Arcardius. They also said they would let my father go. If you had been there, Andi…" He looked down at his boots. "If you had seen the fear on my father's face in the video they showed me of him, captive and bound in chains…if it were one of your Marauders, and if it were my life or theirs on the line…you would know why I did it."

He looked up at her now, his eyes pleading, the emotion so raw on his handsome face.

"I'm so sorry, Androma," Dex whispered. "I will never forgive myself for what I did to you."

His shoulders slumped.

In her mind, she saw that final, fleeting moment on the fire moon. The knife in his chest, his shirt blossoming green with his blood.

She felt the pain of her heart breaking in her chest. The feeling that she could hardly breathe.

"Andi," Dex whispered. "Please. Look at me. Tell me we can move past this. We both made mistakes. We both made our choices, and we've had to live with them."

She turned away from him, unable to look at his face.

"We can't ever go back to how it was before," Dex said. "But…if you're willing…we could make something new."

She didn't look at him as she said, "Just go, Dex." Her voice cracked on his name.

He slipped past her silently and left her room without another word.

She settled down on the floor again.

There, alone in her quarters, she picked up her swords and added more tallies, the blades turning slick with the flow of her tears.

# CHAPTER 37
## KLAREN
## YEAR TWENTY-FIVE

*"LET ME GO," THE QUEEN WHISPERED. "CYPRIAN ...please."*

*In the darkness of her private chambers, lit only by the moonlight, all she could see was the general's ghostly outline as he stood before her, pressing her up against the wall. His ruffled shirt was half undone. His blue eyes looked like flames trying desperately not to flicker out.*

*His hands, curled into fists, were tangled in her hair.*

*Wrapped around her throat, as he pressed her harder against the wall.*

*"I will kill you," he growled. "You have...done something...to me..."*

*His grip grew tighter. She could hardly breathe. Her vision grew dim. For a moment, panic called her name.*

"*Let me go.*" *She choked out the words, fighting for air.*

*Even in her hatred, she made herself reach out and touch him. With trembling hands, she ran her fingers down his back. Felt the shudder race up and down his spine. She dug her fingertips in, pressing so hard she drew blood.*

"*Let me go.*"

"*Damn it, Klaren!*" *His entire body shook as he finally released her.* "*Damn you!*"

*He stumbled backward.*

*She slipped down the wall, gasping for air. Tears streamed down her cheeks. Cyprian was strong. Stronger than she'd ever anticipated. She hated this fight. Hated the lack of control. The queen looked up, meeting his gaze as he stood across from her, hunched over.*

"*What are you doing to me?*" *he asked, his hands outspread before him, as if he were afraid of them. Afraid of himself.* "*Every night, I find myself here. You plague my dreams. You come to me in visions. Your name forces itself to my lips when I wake.*" *He ran a hand across his creased face.* "*When I am with my wife…I think of you.*"

*Two years she'd waited for this. A queen away from her planet, a prisoner deep in the belly of the Cortas lair.*

*Two years she'd endured questions from his men, allowed herself to be removed from her quarters and forced to sit in front of a camera. To record videos that were sent across the galaxy to her husband.*

"*Tell him to surrender, Klaren,*" *Cyprian had said.* "*Tell him to surrender, and you can go free.*"

"*Do not surrender,*" *she'd responded into the camera, using her eyes and her voice as she'd been taught. Knowing her husband would obey her demands.* "*Do not give in. You can still win this war, my love.*"

*The Unified Systems continued to blast Xen Ptera with bombs, spreading more death.*

*And so the war had carried on.*

"*Tell me!*" *Cyprian screamed now, in her room. He ran his hands through his thinning hair. The war had changed him, turned him into something fractured.* "*Tell me what you've done to me!*"

*The obsession had spread. She could sense it in him, like a disease that festered.*

*Even now, as he sank to his knees before her, tears welling in his eyes...*

*He couldn't look away.*

*She may have been his prisoner, but he was her toy. A wad of putty to mold and shape to her own liking.*

*It was time.*

*Time to make her next move.*

*All her life, she'd waited for this moment. And so it was with a smile that Klaren looked up, stared into his eyes, and whispered, "It is because you love me."*

*He froze.*

*He glared at her, still three steps away, as he got to his feet. "What did you just say to me?"*

*The queen swallowed and gathered strength from deep within. She was born to do this. Born to sacrifice herself. Her heart, to the king of Xen Ptera. Her daughter, unplanned, had been sacrificed, too.*

*Now, she would willingly give up her body to the cause.*

*"You love me, Cyprian," the queen said, stronger now, as something powerful surged through her. She rose to her feet, using the wall for support, and stepped closer to him. "All these years, you have watched me. You have longed to touch me. To taste me. To make me yours."*

*Her words were poison.*

*She, the tipped arrow, aimed for the kill.*

*"You will take me as your lover," the queen whispered. "And you will come to me, night after night. Until you can no longer look upon your wife without wishing to replace her."*

*Her captor glared at her, trembling with a rage that he had been so desperately trying to hide these past two years.*

*Tonight, she would win.*

*"I...love...you?" he said, through gritted teeth.*

*A question, still.*

*She must try harder.*

"You love me, Cyprian Cortas," she whispered, putting everything she had into her words. Stepping forward until her breath was on his lips. Until her chest pressed against his, and she grasped his hands, guiding them around to the lowest part of her back. "You love me, and you will make me yours tonight."

"I...love you," he whispered.

"Again," she said. "Say it again."

His eyes met hers. "I love you, Klaren."

She took his hands, lifted them to the front ties of her thin gown.

"Then show me."

A growl rumbled from his lips as pressed himself against her.

"I love you," he said again.

This time, she knew it had worked.

He meant it.

They spent the rest of the night together, tangled in the sheets.

Tangled in her lies.

# CHAPTER 38
## ANDROMA

"IT'S A MASTERPIECE, REALLY," GILLY SAID AS she sat with her chin resting on her folded hands, examining Valen's lacerated back.

"A masterpiece if you're someone like Soyina," Lira said. "We'll likely never see *her* again, especially if Nor catches wind of her helping us."

"Soyina enjoys delivering pain," Gilly commented from across the med table. "Right, Andi?"

"What?" Andi looked up to see the two girls watching her.

"Still considering whether or not to kill Dextro?" Lira asked.

The girls, apparently, had heard the entire explosive fight go down. Andi's and Dex's screams could be heard echoing through the halls of the ship. They had found Andi afterward, when she'd emerged from her quarters. The tears had dried, and the girls spent time sitting with her in silence.

No music, no laughter. Just a few moments of quiet that allowed her mind to reset.

Now, a few hours later, her mood had improved. Her thoughts were still muddled, her emotions were still raw, but her body felt strangely lighter. As if hearing the truth from Dex, whether she had wanted to or not, had lifted a weight from her shoulders that she'd carried for years.

"I don't want to talk about it," Andi said with a heavy sigh.

Lira watched her closely. "Later," she said. "Otherwise, it will consume you."

Andi nodded, knowing Lira—as always—was right. She leaned back in her chair, wincing as the pain in her chest flared up. "That damned stunner."

Lira practically growled beside her. "The next job you go on will be with us watching your back." She sighed and ran a hand across her hairless head. "If I ever see that *Revivalist* again, I will personally deliver my own special dose of pain, and we'll see how she enjoys it."

Andi smiled, despite the ache still pulsing in her chest. "I don't doubt that you will."

"Did she really shoot you?" Gilly asked. "Dex, too?" Andi nodded, and the gunner's eyes widened. "I can't believe I didn't get to meet her. Can she really bring people back to life?"

Andi shrugged. "She claims she's capable of that."

The med bay door slid open with a cool hiss, and Breck stomped in. "Ladies," she said impatiently, tucking her hair behind her ears. "I'm not interested in dining alone with Dextro tonight. We have a ship stocked with actual *edible food* since taking on this job. Come enjoy it with us."

Gilly and Lira stood from their places on either side of Valen, but Andi stayed put, unwilling to move.

She'd helped Alfie clean his wounds, the blood-soaked rags now piled high in the corner of the small white room. Vials of his blood, freshly drawn by Alfie, were sitting in a testing box beside the rags. The AI wanted to ensure Valen hadn't picked up any diseases or been injected with any strange pathogens during his time in Lunamere.

Valen's back looked cleaner, but by no means was it in better shape. It made her ache just to look at it, imagining the lash of the electric whips that caused it, ripping and shredding and burning.

"Andi?" Lira's voice drew Andi's attention back to her crew.

She looked away from Valen to smile softly at the three of them. Gilly was standing on tiptoe, still trying her best to get a good look at Valen's wounds. Andi waved a hand, which, she noted, was still covered in remnants of the battle waged in Lunamere. "Go on without me. I'm going to stay. Someone should be here with him when he wakes."

Breck shrugged and pulled Gilly along with her, but Lira stopped for a moment.

"There's a fissure in you. I can sense it even from here." Lira loosed a gentle sigh before explaining her words. But when she did, they sunk like a rock into Andi's gut. "Sooner or later, you're going to have to choose between forgiveness or hate. And you and I both know which one is harder to live with."

She didn't wait for Andi to answer. She simply turned, graceful as a bird, and left the room.

Andi waited by Valen's side all night, unsure of why she stayed.

Unsure of why she couldn't look away from the lashes on his back that crisscrossed his skin like ribbons, or the bruises blooming across his pale skin like paint.

Valen Cortas had never been Andi's favorite person. She'd hardly known him in her old life. He'd been strange and silent and always seemed to be watching with eyes a little too interested in keeping track of her.

But he was a Cortas.

He was a piece of Kalee.

And seeing him here reminded Andi of what *could* have been. Not if she'd stayed and faced the punishment of her trial, but before all of that. Before the night that changed everything. If she hadn't taken the throttle of the transport ship in her hands, or gunned the engine a little too hard, or looked away for too long to laugh at what Kalee had said…

She could still remember the exact moment of impact. The horrible, mind-melting screech of metal against rock.

She could still remember those few strange, weightless seconds in between the stolen ship's engine cutting off and the transport wing clipping the side of a floating mountain. The crash as the ship hit the ground. The hot flames of the burning engine, and the sound of Kalee gasping for life, sticky wet blood dripping onto Andi's hands as she pressed and pressed and tried like hell to staunch the flow.

"It hurts," Kalee had whispered, but the words came out all wrong. The voice wasn't hers, and the rattling cough that followed made her lips too red, as blood trickled from them and her eyes closed…

Andi stood up.

This was a mission, like any other. Even if it was Valen Cortas. She owed him nothing—not her life or her emotions or the time she could have been spending now, sharing a meal and stories of Lunamere with her crew.

She paced, focusing instead on the pain in her muscles, the screaming knife wound in her shoulder that she still hadn't allowed Alfie to patch up.

Pain was her anchor.

It was the only true thing in life that never lied or cheated.

Best of all, if she tried hard enough, she could usually overcome it.

She wanted to believe Lira was wrong. But Andi knew there were fissures in her soul. She had always thought herself to be a wall as solid as the glass that made up the *Marauder*. She was the captain. She would not bend, and she sure as hell would never break.

But today, she *had* broken. And now she had to find a way to put the pieces back together.

She was just preparing to leave, to force herself away from Valen's sleeping form, when a flicker of movement caught her eye.

His steady breathing had quickened, the burns and scars on his back seeming to squirm with each fast breath. His head was turned to face her, and his cracked lips fluttered like he was trying to form words.

Andi stepped back to his side, wondering whether she should call on Alfie. But the AI was currently charging back up, plugged in to the ship's dash a floor above.

"Valen?" Andi asked. Her voice was a weak whisper.

She hated the sound of it.

She almost reached out to touch him when a beep sounded out from the testing box behind her. Andi turned, brow knitting. The small screen on the silver box flashed with an update.

Abnormal Reading. Seek further tests.

Alfie had been right. She wasn't entirely surprised, judging by the conditions inside Lunamere. She turned back to look at Valen, wondering what lurked beneath the surface of his skin.

His breathing had quickened again. His hands, which had been lying still at his sides, began to curl into fists.

"Valen. You're safe," Andi said, feeling like a fool with each word she spoke, unsure of whether he could even hear her.

"You're not in Lunamere anymore. We're taking you back to your father, back to…"

His eyes flew open and locked on hers.

"Valen?" Andi asked.

One moment he was stone still. The next, Valen's hand shot out, ice-cold fingertips gripping the stained fabric of Andi's bodysuit.

She backed away, but he pulled with a strength he hadn't possessed before, keeping her in place.

He tugged her closer, hazel eyes wide and haunted. His voice was raw and ragged as a demon's when he choked out two harsh words.

"Kill…me."

# CHAPTER 39
## ANDROMA

"SO YOU'RE SAYING OUR CARGO IS A MUTANT."

A shirtless Dex lounged like a lazy cat on the floor of the main deck of the *Marauder*, his lithe muscles out on display. His legs were draped over the edge of the couch Andi was sitting on, and beside him, Gilly sat cross-legged, focused intently on painting his fingernails red.

"Stop moving," Gilly commanded. "You'll smudge it."

Dex chuckled and promptly stilled his hands. Seeming pleased, Gilly hefted the tiny nail brush like a weapon, whistling softly as she painted away.

The soles of Dex's filthy boots grazed Andi's thigh as he shifted.

She swatted them away and threw him an icy glare.

Apparently, her youngest gunner had fully succumbed to Dex's charms, but Andi wasn't ready to let go of the past just yet. Everyone, in fact, was acting far too normal around him as they enjoyed this rare time of relaxation while the ship was on autopilot toward Arcardius.

"Valen is no different than us," Andi said to Dex, "and he's not a mutant. And put on a damned shirt. This is a spaceship, *not* a pleasure palace."

"It *used* to be both." He waggled his eyebrows at her, then winced as Andi ripped off one of his boots and launched it at his face. Gilly cursed as Dex smudged her handiwork yet again.

When Andi first got her hands on the ship, the main deck could only have been described as a *man cave*. Sagging, stolen couches with empty Griss bottles, dirty boots and socks strewn about, a scattered game of Fleet cards from whomever Dex had invited onto his ship and screwed over in days past.

Since then, it had been transformed.

It was comfortable and classy, almost all of the furniture Dex had owned had been thrown out and replaced by genuine Adhiran cowhide couches, purchased after the girls took on their first few well-paying jobs. Gone were Dex's old messes, and in their place was a bright, airy room that was the most well-used part of the *Marauder*, save for the bridge.

Classical music played softly on the ship's overhead speakers, the deep swell of stringed instruments serenading the crew as they sat together. It was Andi's favorite music, the kind that didn't need words to speak to a person's soul. It was one of the only things she'd brought with her from her past.

The ship was *much* better now that she and the girls had placed their mark on it.

"Looks beautiful," Dex said, as he looked at his freshly painted nails. "This is definitely my color, kid."

Gilly grinned proudly.

But Andi seethed. He'd stolen her youngest gunner's heart. Now he'd stolen her trademark red polish, too?

"I disagree," Andi said, as she leaned forward and swiped the bottle from Gilly's hands. "I think black, like his soul, is the better shade. Wouldn't you agree, Gilly?"

The girl only shrugged, then leaped up from the couch and joined Breck and Lira at the varillium table nearby.

The table was shaped like a large oval, and was currently stocked with Gilly's and Breck's tools for creating their own Sparks. They sat there now, mulling over their latest creation. Beside them, a metal cabinet was fastened to the wall, which held all of the girls' playthings, and Lira's stash of Chew, which Andi not-so-secretly wanted to blast out the airlock.

Across from the lounge area was the small kitchen, no more than two burners, a rusted sink that needed replacing, a few lockable metal cabinets for food stores and a cooling box for fresh ingredients. Alfie stood over the latter now, digging through its contents, wearing a Kiss the Cook apron that somehow looked strangely fitting on his metallic frame.

For the past hour, he'd been cataloguing their food stores as they waited for Memory to finish her own secondary diagnostic on Valen's blood. Every so often, he'd glide over to the crew to spout out the exact nutritional value of each item, then proceed to define each word he'd just said as he dodged the various things Breck threw at him in response.

"So," Dex said, nudging Andi with his bare foot. "Who's in favor of calling the cargo a mutant?"

"Dex?" Andi glowered at him. "Would you do me the favor of removing your head from your neck?"

From the chair opposite them, Breck cleared her throat. "I don't want to get in the middle of this little...battle?" She said it like a question, waving her hand as if swatting away a blood bug. "But unfortunately, I agree with the bounty hunter on this one."

"Traitor," Andi muttered.

"Apologies," Breck said back. "But you saw the test results! Abnormal blood, Andi. After spending how many years inside of Lunamere? They probably royally screwed with him in there and caused the abnormality…" She paused, cocking her head and seeming to reconsider her answer. "Actually, that seems more likely than his just being a mutant."

Dex groaned as the single person who had been in agreement with him switched sides.

Lira and Gilly, seated beside Breck, were busy looking over a new set of exploding Sparks Gilly had manufactured herself. The kid had talent, Andi had to admit, though sometimes Gilly's passion for destruction unnerved her.

She reminded Andi a little too much of herself.

"What do you two think?" Andi asked.

Lira turned one of the Sparks over in her blue hands, scrutinizing it. "I think we should wait for Memory's further test results to come in before we jump to any illogical conclusions."

"Ah-hah!" Alfie's head emerged from the cooling unit, frost covering the tip of his oval chin. "I have discovered the source of the smell." He held up a dripping hunk of green meat, then proceeded to march over to the small ejection site and blast it out into space. "The full diagnostic results from Memory will be complete at any moment, Lira Mette. Until then, can I comfort you with a mind-numbing beverage of your choice?"

Lira ignored Alfie, tapping a space inside the small metal orb and inclining her head to Gilly. "Right here, little one. It needs to have more of a reaction. Add more powder."

Gilly twisted her mouth to the side in thought. "My opinion on Valen is that he's a mutant," she said, flashing Andi a grin before she turned back to the Spark in progress. "*Definitely* a mutant."

"Ha!" Dex clapped his hands triumphantly.

Andi sighed and kicked her feet up on the table. "My crew are losing their minds."

"We're not losing anything, just gaining imagination," Breck said. "It makes life a little more interesting."

"As if we need any more of that," Andi responded under her breath just as Alfie walked over to the table in front of her, swiftly removed her feet from it and tapped on the screen embedded in the top. Once it lit up, he typed in a number of codes.

"So?" Dex asked, wiggling the toes on his exposed foot. Andi was so close to making him lose a toe or two. Or ten. "What do we have, Alfie?"

"The tests are providing inconclusive results. I am not certain what to make of this outcome," Alfie said.

Well, that wasn't something you heard every day from a highly advanced AI, especially with Memory's programming to supplement Alfie's systems and knowledge base.

"I will arrange for the great General Cortas's personal medical team to run more extensive tests on him. We do not have what we need aboard the *Marauder*." He glanced up. "That is not to say, my beautiful Memory, that you have not done well."

"Did he just call our ship's system *beautiful*?" Breck asked.

Alfie continued on with his explanation. "All I can determine is that Mr. Valen Cortas's DNA seems to have…changed."

"What, like he changed blood type or something?" Andi asked.

Alfie continued to scroll through a series of coded numbers and symbols. "It is not possible to switch blood types, Androma Racella. I believe that a pathogen is the source of the DNA alteration, though it is not one currently listed in any Mirabel records." He tapped the screen again. "An anomaly, perhaps. I will continue to screen for further results. Until then, I must alert General Cortas."

Andi nodded her head, wishing they had more answers. Wondering what the Xen Pterrans had done to Valen in Lunamere, and to all the other prisoners locked behind bars. Her skin crawled just thinking of it.

It seemed to be a good enough explanation for Gilly. She jumped to her feet, nearly knocking a Spark over and letting out a devilish cackle.

"*Mutant!* I was right." Her freckled face was so full of excitement, truly showing her young, vivid spirit. It made Andi's heart warm, seeing the proof that Gilly, contrary to popular belief, still had a soul, tainted as it may be.

"Maybe you are. Only time will tell, Gil," Breck said from her chair, a smile softening her face.

"I will excuse myself now," Alfie said, removing the apron and hanging it back up on the hook by the kitchen sink. "I have further things to attend to."

As he left the main deck, Andi looked around at her team.

It was still shocking that the lot of them had accomplished a mission where the odds were so stacked against them. The worst was behind them, left to rot in Lunamere. Just another memory to lock inside her head so that she could move forward with the next job, the next payday. That was, of course, if General Cortas kept his word and didn't choose to damn them to the Pits of Tenebris instead, which were supposed to rival the horrific conditions of Lunamere.

Even with questions about Valen still floating in her head, and the truth of Dex's story still sinking in, Andi was somehow able to relax back into the couch. The music had changed to one of her favorite songs, "The Song of the Snow," an almost mournful piece by a Soleran composer who'd been inspired by the bleak, unceasing winters on the ice planet. As Andi closed her eyes and listened, she finally felt at peace again in the presence of her crew, on the ship she loved so dearly.

Sleep began to whisper her name.

"Who wants to play Shadow Chase?" Gilly asked.

So much for closing her eyes for a moment. Andi sat forward, yawning.

Breck groaned, but Lira leaped up, excited to join in another one of Gilly's favorite games.

"I'll play," Dex said. "If you're prepared to lose horribly."

"Gilly doesn't lose this one," Breck said. "Ever."

"It's true," Andi said. "She'll poison your drink with laxatives the moment you take the lead."

Breck muttered something about bad experiences in the background.

Dex howled with laughter. Andi smiled back, the response instinctive and easy.

Before she could consider how she felt about that, the ship rumbled beneath her feet.

Once. Twice.

Then a horrible lurch threw her from the couch.

The lights winked off, quickly replaced by the deep bloodred of the emergency systems kicking on.

"What the hell?" Dex yelped as he scrambled to his feet.

The room felt like it was falling sideways, as if the *Marauder* was tipping.

Memory's voice came on overhead.

*"Alert. Systems crashing. Alert."*

# CHAPTER 40
## NOR

ALL HER LIFE, NOR HAD KNOWN THE PAIN OF The Cataclysm.

She was only an infant when it began, only eleven years old when it ended.

A child, turned into an orphan queen overnight.

She'd seen things no one should ever have to see. Burning bodies falling from the sky as her family's palace was struck by the debris from hundreds of destroyed ships. Screams rising from the smoke as soldiers from the Unified Systems tore through the streets of Nivia, razing it apart until they broke through the doors of the Solis Palace.

Nor had been only five years old when she heard her mother's scream ring out through the palace in the dead of night. The night she was taken from them, stolen by General Cyprian Cortas of Arcardius.

For six years, she'd felt the emptiness of her mother's absence. The depression, when her father, a king with a lost queen, tried in vain to rule in the midst of losing a war.

On the darkest, coldest nights after her mother was kidnapped, Nor used to lie in the bunker of the palace and imagine the face of the Arcardian general. She would imagine the pain she'd someday inflict on him, the deep chasm she'd rip through his heart when she stole everything he'd ever loved.

It was with great pleasure that she allowed her torturers to harm his son, Valen. For a while, she'd felt that desire for revenge slowly ease. But since the general's son had escaped, Nor felt empty all over again.

Alone, just as she'd felt after the Battle of Black Sky, when Nor's father left her, too, crushed to death in the rubble.

It was Zahn who had pulled Nor from the ashes of the palace. He'd taken her to Darai, who had raised her to take up her throne and become a mighty, relentless queen.

He filled her brain with the desire to lead. Not just with her head, but with her entire heart. Body and blood, a head raised high, an iron fist intent on crushing their enemies.

But now, fifteen years after the fighting had ceased, despite everything she had done, Nor was out of options.

*Or, rather,* she thought, as her eyes adjusted to the dim hallways of the Lunamere prison, *the best option has only just been revealed.*

The click of her heels and the steps of Zahn beside her were the only source of noise in the corridor. Darai, who was following them, had a way of slinking silently in the shadows. Not even a whisper of his cloak brushing the ground was noticeable.

Sometimes Nor thought of him as a shadow himself, quiet and hidden.

They passed a series of closed doors before walking into the observation room. A glass window separated the three of them from the five prisoners cuffed to chairs inside.

"Queen Nor, it is a pleasure to see you again," Aclisia said. Her two heads each grinned at Nor, bowing slightly as the queen stopped and pulled her cloak tighter around her shoulders against the chill of the prison.

"We are very pleased with the latest batch of Zenith," her lead scientist continued. "The test subject's death was actually quite fortuitous. It showed us an unstable property in the weapon that was previously undetectable."

"How did she die?" Nor asked.

Aclisia's left head smiled. "Painfully."

"Quite a mess," the right head agreed. "But we are happy to say that we think we have finally perfected the solution."

Nor, stone-faced, nodded once.

The right head continued. "We have handpicked these prisoners to be the first participants in this study. It will be interesting to see if there are any further side effects."

The left head nodded in earnest. "We are very confident that this new sample will meet your expectations. If all goes well... this will be the final batch."

Aclisia rubbed her hands together, both heads in agreement.

This was reassuring to Nor, as Aclisia's two heads were often at odds with each other. As she opened her mouth to order the testing to begin, however, a wad of discolored spit landed on the window in front of her.

*"Scnav!"* one of the prisoners growled at her. Nor ignored the slight; she had been called worse names before. Such insults stopped bothering her a long time ago.

Zahn, however, took a step toward the door that led to the adjoining room, a deadly look on his face. Nor held up a hand to stop him.

"Enough."

Zahn froze, but his eyes were molten with rage. "He has no

right to call you such a name," he said under his breath, but a sharp look from Nor silenced any further commentary.

She turned to the window, her gaze falling on the prisoner who'd forgotten the meaning of fealty.

"Aclisia, begin the testing with that one." She paused, a thought occurring to her. "Can the weapon be activated on any part of the body?"

"Yes, it can be," the right head said.

The left smiled. "As long as it makes contact with living flesh, and can enter the bloodstream, the fun can begin."

Nor tilted her head, pinning the prisoner with her gaze.

"Then we should have a little fun, Aclisia. Let's see how painful it is when placed in the eyes."

She watched as the prisoner's mutinous expression transformed to one of fear, his body trembling as Aclisia and two guards moved into the room where he sat.

"Stop. No, stop!" His voice was frantic, and his hatred toward her morphed into a plea for mercy. "Please, I'll do anything!" He kept yelling as the guards held his squirming body still and a metal instrument was placed on his eyes to hold them open.

"The lively ones truly are the most captivating," Aclisia's left head said.

Nor watched with equal amounts of amusement and fascination as the glowing silver liquid dripped from the vial, slowly inching its way toward the prisoner's eyes. The silver liquid was an art form of its own, one that had the ability to enthrall a person or terrify them, depending on how strong their will was.

As it made contact with his right eye, Aclisia stepped back, the guards still restraining the man. Nor watched with curiosity as the silver bled into his iris like paint dropped into water. The prisoner, pleading forgotten, was back to yelling profanities at her, pain lacing his voice each time he spoke.

Suddenly, his screams cut off.

He fell blessedly silent.

The other four prisoners looked at their fellow inmate, then at Nor, bowing their heads to her. She wasn't a fool. Their sudden respect was just a facade to save themselves, but it was thrilling to see the power she now held over the people who had spent their entire lives despising her.

Nor turned to Darai, and he gave her an approving nod.

"Go on, my queen," Aclisia's two heads spoke together. "Test him."

Zahn held open the door, his hand lightly brushing Nor's as she walked past. He and Darai followed her inside, the guards behind them ready with hands on their guns.

She stepped up to the prisoner. His gaze, once full of hate, was now awed.

She stopped over him, glancing down her nose the way Darai had taught her, chin still held high.

"Who do you follow?" she asked him.

"You, my queen."

He lowered his head in an attempt to bow, even with his hands tied. Nor watched as the other prisoners received their own doses of the liquid on their forearms. She saw again, the way it slipped through their skin, leaving no trace of evidence behind.

Nor waited a moment before asking all of them her most vital questions.

"Will you fight for me? Die for me? Bow down to me?"

"Yes, my queen," the five responded in unison.

Nor let out a breath.

Her dream, her mission in life, was on its way to becoming a reality. The weapon was complete, a success fully capable of changing the future of her planet, and that of the entire galaxy.

She turned to Darai and Zahn with a grin as solid as steel. "My soldiers, it's time to darken the stars."

# CHAPTER 41

## ANDROMA

"CAN YOU TURN THAT CURSED SIREN OFF?"
Andi yelled over the ear-splitting noise, running to her captain's
seat on the bridge. Lira was already punching in the override
code, blue hands a blur.

The alarm turned off, leaving the room eerily silent as Lira
righted the ship.

Andi's stomach swayed as the *Marauder* leveled out.

"What the hell's going on?" Andi asked finally, breaking the
silence. She activated her com and signaled to Breck, request-
ing permission to view her gunner's feed. She granted the request, and Andi blinked, suddenly seeing through Breck's eyes.

Breck was down below, in the med bay. Her large hands and

Alfie's metallic ones were frantically working to strap Valen's again unconscious form to a table. Gilly and Dex slipped in and out of view as they tried to help.

"Memory!" Andi barked. "Run a ship-wide diagnostic, now!"

Silence for a few moments, and then Memory's mechanical voice filled the bridge.

*"According to assessment, the engine is in meltdown. Please proceed to the nearest landing bay and prepare for engine failure."*

"Meltdown?" Andi barked. "How in the hell is that even possible? We just got her repaired a few days ago!"

Lira popped a wad of Chew into her mouth. The scales on her arms began to light up. "It's possible the fools who repaired her missed something. She's overheating." Lira pressed a few more buttons, yanked on a lever and tapped on the screen again. "If we can cool her down, we should be able to make a safe landing. But according to the numbers, with the velocity we're going at right now—plus our weight—the situation seems rather dire."

"Breck," Andi spoke into the ship's main com system. "Get down to the engine room and see if you can cool it down."

Breck's voice echoed back in Andi's ear. "On it!"

Andi's stomach swayed again, and Lira gobbled up another wad of Chew. When the Chew came out, it meant the situation needed her full attention.

Moments later, Breck's voice came back, nearly hysterical. "Oh, Godstars. Andi. The cooling system is totally blasted. I *knew* I should have demanded to oversee the repairs."

Andi blinked, slipping into Breck's open feed, viewing the scene through her eyes.

Smoke billowed through the open hatch. Breck's hand waved in front of her face, trying to clear a path through the haze. She pointed, leveling her gaze onto the cooling system. All the wires were melted, along with the outer shell.

"It's bad, Andi," Breck said. "Like…'kill us all' bad."

Andi blinked again, pulling herself out of Breck's view and

back into her own. She cast a glance sideways at Lira, and could tell from her stricken expression that she'd seen Breck's feed, as well. "How in the hell could that even happen?" Andi asked.

"Fool mechanics who don't know how to work on a classic," Breck growled.

Lira hissed out a breath. "We have to make an emergency landing. If we leave hyperspace now, the closest system to us is…" She cursed. "Stuna."

"Which means we'll have to land on Adhira," Andi said.

Lira nodded, her scales flashing.

Her past on Adhira, her home planet, was something Lira did not speak of often. But Andi knew—especially judging by her pilot's rapidly heating scales and the way her fingers gripped the throttle tighter than ever before—that going back home was something Lira definitely didn't want to do. She'd avoided jobs there for years. But if Lira was openly *suggesting* they land on Adhira…then the *Marauder* really must be beyond helping right now.

"Are you sure about this?" Andi asked, pulling her long hair into a braid.

Lira's skin began to smoke, but her voice was calm and even. "I can tap into my connections there. We will have help."

"Good help?" Andi asked. "Or bad help?"

Lira bit her lip. "I am undecided at present. The queen and I have…a bit of a muddled past."

Andi groaned. "I guess we'll find out soon, then." She reached up and tapped her com. "Ladies…"

Dex's voice echoed back into her ear. "And handsome gentleman."

The ship rattled, a reminder of how little time they had. She'd *kill* those pathetic mechanics for this.

Andi grimaced. "We're making an emergency landing on Adhira."

Gilly's voice chirped into the com. "But Lira doesn't want to go there!"

"This is my order, Gilly!" Andi commanded. "Get to the bridge, *now*. Alfie, com the general. Tell him to let the queen know we'll need a quick repair if we're going to finish this stars-forsaken mission."

"Already on it," Dex said.

After all they'd gone through to get Valen, things just *had* to go wrong now. *The life of a space pirate*, Andi thought to herself.

She tightened her harness, then sat back and watched as they exited hyperspace in a wounded ship, soaring straight for Adhira, the planet full of color and life.

Beside her, Lira looked like she would rather die.

# CHAPTER 42
## ANDROMA

THE SIGHT OF ADHIRA SPREADING BEFORE HER should've taken Andi's breath away.

Instead, she was just hoping she would still be breathing once they landed. The crew's fate was in Lira's hands, and Andi could only hope her pilot could keep them from exploding into bits of metal and flesh.

As they neared the planet, Lira sent a message to the landing dock she'd managed to secure moments ago in the capital of Rhymore. This would be their first time landing on Adhira as a crew, and Andi didn't think it would bode well for any future visits they might make to the planet if they crashed.

Especially for Lira, whose scales had already begun to glow to the point of smoking.

"Those complete airheads," Lira mumbled as she turned off the com. "They think we have enough power to make it to the landing base, but at this point, the engines are so bad I'm surprised we haven't lost the oxygen pump yet."

"Don't listen to them—land where you can, and they will come to us," Andi said, trying to calm her Second. This was the first time Andi had ever seen Lira so close to losing complete control of her emotions, and she knew that it was the impending return to her home planet that was unnerving her so.

As they entered the atmosphere of Adhira, the ship gave a lurch. Andi definitely did not like the screeching groan the ship made—or the fact that they weren't slowing down as they should.

This definitely wasn't a normal atmospheric entry.

"Come on, baby," Andi said, patting the *Marauder*'s dash as if it would actually listen to her plea.

"Coming!" an unwelcome voice came from behind her.

Andi let out an audible groan.

"Get in a seat, Dextro. *Now!*"

"I'm trying to lighten the mood, Androma. We all know Lira is fully capable of handling this situation."

"Thanks," Lira muttered as Dex plopped into one of the chairs behind her, legs sprawled out in front of him like he was about to watch a film. Breck and Gilly rushed in after him, strapping into seats, as well.

"Where's Alfie?" Andi asked.

"Down making sure Valen doesn't fall off the table," Gilly said. "Which wouldn't matter, anyway, since he said there is a 93 percent chance of immediate death or dismemberment upon impact."

"Damned artificial lifeforms," Breck growled.

Andi turned back around, eyes wide as she took in the on-coming view.

Below, the Endless Sea appeared, the single ocean on Adhira that made way for the large central land mass, which was scattered with veiny rivers, monstrous trees, red deserts and the central Rhymore mountain.

Lira's hands were steady on the controls as she eased the ship the best she could toward the quickly approaching ground. Andi watched as her pilot maneuvered around the massive trees that dotted Adhira's landscape. They were so tall that they peaked above the clouds, and some even towered higher than the mountain.

Dex hooted from behind her, as if this was a joy ride instead of a highly dangerous emergency landing that could kill them all.

Godstars, he was a fool.

Blocking Dex out, Andi gripped the armrests of her chair and looked out the viewport again, which was now full of trees and utterly devoid of any glimpse of the sky.

"This had better not scratch my ship!" she yelled, thinking of its already damaged hull.

"Scratch?" Gilly yelped. "I think we're in for more than that, Cap!"

"You want the good news or the bad new first?" Lira asked Andi, teeth gritted, eyes wild as she wove around the worst obstacles in their path.

"The good news," Andi said, hoping it outweighed the bad.

"The good news is that the trees should lessen the impact, and when we come out of the forest, we should be only a few meters from ground level. There is a field up ahead, according to the radar, and at this angle, I'll be able to manipulate a semi-controlled landing."

Andi was momentarily relieved, but tensed again at the ominous expression on Lira's face.

"And the bad news?" she asked.

Her pilot grimaced. "We'll be landing in one of the clearings that has a major village surrounding it. Even with the trees slowing us down, we're still gaining too much velocity, meaning we'll likely plow right into the village." Her voice caught in her throat, as if she were holding back equal parts terror and nausea. Her hands flew over the controls. "The field isn't large enough to land in without potential casualties."

Andi's head spun, racing for any idea to grab a hold of. "If the ship was lighter, would we be able to stop in time?"

There was a pause before Lira responded. Andi could almost see her making the calculations in her head.

"Yes. But we'd need to lose at least one ton if we want to make a dent in the velocity."

A sudden lurch threw Andi forward against her harness as they hit a wicked bout of turbulence. By the time she looked back up, rubbing the back of her now-tender neck, her view was no longer of the catastrophe happening outside, but of a rear end.

*Dex's* rear end.

"Do you have a death wish, Arez?" Andi yelled, trying to reach the band of his cargo pants to pull him back.

"No, I'm not hell-bent on destruction like you are, Racella. If you would pull your head out of whatever dark hole you have it in, you would notice that I'm helping you."

Before Andi could stop him, he'd slammed his palm against a big, red button and a whooshing sound echoed throughout the ship.

"Did he just hit the red button?" Gilly screamed.

"You're welcome, ladies," Dex said. "You can thank me later. I just released the escape pods and lessened our load enough for us to stop before we completely annihilate that village with my ship."

"*My* ship!" Andi barked at him.

"Would the two of you just *stop fighting*?" Breck howled.

Lira cursed as the harness strapped across her chest began to melt away beneath the heat of her scales. Already, the suit she wore was turning to cinders. If she didn't regain control of her emotions, Andi knew she'd lose consciousness.

"Lira." Andi tried to sound calm. "You have to breathe. You have to keep yourself present."

Her pilot's brow wrinkled, scales flashing ever brighter. "I will breathe when I see us safely on the ground, Androma."

An enormous tree loomed in front of them, and the ship screamed as Lira tilted them sideways to avoid it. Dex toppled into Andi's lap.

"Lira!" Andi yelled, shoving Dex away. "Steady us!"

But the ship was careening even farther, tilting so far to the left that Andi felt as if she'd been turned onto her head.

With horror, she looked back at Lira, just in time to see her pilot slump forward in her seat, her head lolling against her chest, her scales so bright it was like staring into a purple sun.

"She's out!" Andi yelled.

And they were out of time.

Every muscle in her body clenched as she saw the rapidly approaching field and village in the distance.

Memory's voice spoke, loud and clear, through it all.

*"Prepare for impact in 3, 2, 1…"*

# CHAPTER 43
## DEX

DEX DETESTED THE WEIGHTLESS, STOMACH-dropping sensation of falling from the skies. There was no control, no stopping it.

The feeling of impact, though, he hated even more. He had just one second to enable the ship's metal outer shields before they hit the ground.

As they crashed into the planet, it felt like the *Marauder* was a giant bullet gouging through hard, solid rock.

Dex's skull rattled as he was knocked off his feet and back into his seat. His bones felt like they were going to snap beneath his skin as he clung to the armrests of his chair, trying to avoid being flung into the air. The wounds he'd sustained on Luna-mere screamed in protest.

There was a horrible, jarring jerk as the ship bounced once. Twice.

*Oh, hell*, Dex thought.

The ship soared across the Adhiran landscape as if it had sprouted claws and was tearing apart the ground.

*"Emergency,"* Memory's cool voice spoke, barely audible over the screeching and rumbling as the ship mercifully slowed its forward movement. *"Emergency."*

Her voice flickered out, and the entire system went dark as a last final screech and groan exploded from beneath them.

Another lurch, like the ship was teetering on the edge of a cliff, followed by the sound of something cracking.

Then it all stopped, as quickly as it had begun.

Silence, pure and simple, so sudden that Dex wondered if maybe he was dead. He groaned, and tried to stand, but his legs wouldn't hold him. His teeth were still vibrating, and his head, *holy hell of all hells*, felt like it was going to explode.

"Not exactly my idea of fun," Dex said, stifling another groan.

No one answered.

Maybe he'd survived, and *they* were all dead.

Then, somewhere in front of him, a whimper, a rustle, the pop of a harness coming loose. Andi's disembodied voice came from the captain's chair. Dex's heart leaped at the sound. "Is everyone okay?"

Gilly and Breck answered in a soft chorus as the *Marauder* settled to stillness around them.

"Help me with Lira," Andi commanded. The pilot was still hunched over in her harness, the scales on her skin finally dimmed but still smoking. As if she'd been aflame moments before.

A horrible pop sounded, and then a flash of light blinded

them as part of the *Marauder*'s metal shielding actually fell away from the viewport.

Like a piece of flaking skin.

Dex stared through the new opening. They'd stopped a mere wing's length from a row of stone houses. People flocked outside, all of them wide-eyed, *most* of them looking furious as hell.

Adhira, like most capital planets, had a melting pot of citizens. But despite their dizzying array of appearances, the villagers all had the same look of hatred plastered on their faces as they glowered at the *Marauder*.

Dex was a little impressed. Anger and hatred were incredibly rare emotions on this peaceful planet.

He loosed a sharp exhalation as the ground trembled beneath the ship.

In the distance, beyond the row of homes, the edge of the rainforest loomed. Already, he could see the cause of the shaking earth.

A set of two monstrous, black-tusked creatures emerged from the tree line. They were ugly as sin, with scaled, rough hides and curling tusks that stretched up toward the rainforest canopy. The beasts pulled a two-story wagon double the size of the *Marauder* behind them. Its wooden wheels were as tall as most of the village homes, and painted on their axles was a golden spiral with a horizontal line jutting through the middle, the symbol of Adhira.

*Sentinels.* The queen's personal, private guard.

The waiting crowd split like a river to allow the wagon to pass through as it headed straight for the wreckage.

Dex took it upon himself to break the silence.

"I hate to break it to you, loves," he said, finally managing to stand up from his chair on unsteady legs.

"Then don't," Andi told him as she and the girls gently unstrapped the unconscious, still-steaming pilot. "Please don't."

Dex spoke up anyway. "We are *so* dead."

Andi sighed as she looked out at the oncoming wagon. "For once, Dextro, you have no idea how right you are."

# CHAPTER 44
## ANDROMA

THE LAST TIME ANDI SAW HER HOME PLANET, she'd been a fourteen-year-old girl with tears in her eyes and her best friend's blood on her hands.

By sheer mercy, she'd been able to escape her death sentence. After that, she'd made her way out into the galaxy and traveled through worlds she'd never known, unsure of who she was, where she was going or who she would have to become to survive.

The only thing certain was the whisper of death, a monster made of fear and fury that followed her no matter how far she tried to go. Many nights, Andi stayed awake, looking over her shoulder, terrified that General Cortas would send men from her planet to come and lock her away.

They'd never found her.

Instead, *she'd* found a bounty hunter with a lust for life and a bag full of Krevs, and he'd helped her rediscover her strength. He gave her a reason to keep going, and later, replaced that with a broken heart.

In return, she'd stolen his ship, filled it with the fiercest females in the galaxy, and together, the girls had made it their own.

The *Marauder* was Andi's true home, a spear that was capable of tearing apart the skies.

Now it was a junker. Her pilot, who had succumbed to the exhaustion of her emotions, was still unconscious. The medics had injected her with adrenaline when they disembarked from the ship, but Lira had yet to wake.

And Andi was pissed.

She sat on the upper deck of an Adhiran transport wagon, the strange, tumbling roll of the massive wheels below her churning her stomach into a state of unease. The animals stank like dung, to no one's surprise, what with the person-size piles of it they left behind.

And Andi's ship, her blessed, beautiful *Marauder*, was currently being dragged behind the wagon, balancing precariously on a wooden sled of sorts.

One of the beasts dropped another pile of steaming, stinking dung.

The *Marauder*'s sled slipped right over it with a *squelch* that splattered green on a ruined viewport.

Andi had to look away.

"Is it dead forever?" Gilly asked, wide eyed. She sat across from Andi on the wooden floorboards of the wagon, waving her hand as winged bugs the size of her fists fluttered around her, flashing different colors each time they dodged her swings.

"Not entirely," Breck said, staring past Gilly at the *Marauder*'s sad, corpse-like form. "It just needs a little love."

Valen, still unconscious, was with Alfie, wrapped in a clean moss blanket on the lower deck of the wagon. Dex, blessedly, was up at the front, chatting happily to the Sentinels as if he hadn't a care in the world. Andi had a feeling that if she heard him speak right now, she'd rip his throat out with her nails. She still hadn't sorted through her feelings since their fight in her quarters. But right now, allowing her anger to overwhelm her was easier. To even consider forgiveness, to consider *anything* when her ship was so destroyed…Andi couldn't fathom it.

"We can fix the ship," Lira said in a weary voice.

Andi turned to her, surprised, and glad to see that their pilot had finally awoken.

"Are you alright?" Andi asked.

"I feel terrible, but I'll survive," Lira replied, sitting up and glancing back at the *Marauder*. "The repairs will set us back a few days, but Adhiran ship workers are capable of getting us back in the air." She sighed. "And connections, of course. I'm in for a world of trouble."

"That you are, Lira," Breck spoke up. "But don't worry. We'll be there to pick up the pieces."

Andi knew she should be more concerned about Lira's issues. Her pilot's past with Adhira was muddled and painful, a constant struggle for Lira to overcome. But Andi's mind was ragged, stripped free of the pieces that made her mortal. In this moment, she felt as if the veil of the Bloody Baroness was still stuck to her eyes.

"*General Cortas* will fix the ship, as he should have before," Andi said with a heated growl. The eyes of her crew went wide at the sudden rage in her voice. "If he doesn't, I'm going to tear the sagging skin from his face."

This whole mission was the general's fault. If he hadn't allowed Xen Pterran spies to come in and steal *his* son, the old man would never have sent Dex after Andi and her crew. Then they wouldn't be in this mess in the first place, and the *Marauder* would still be up there in the sky, doing what it did best.

Smuggling. Thieving.

*Not* rescuing a privileged, somehow-still-unconscious general's son with a mysterious, unknown pathogen in his blood, nor with Dex, sharing all his terrible truths about the past.

Andi couldn't help remembering that smile they'd shared just before the *Marauder* crashed… What did it mean, that she was still able to share such a moment with him?

*What is happening to my life?* she wondered. It was out of control. *She* was out of control.

There were a million questions in Andi's mind, none of which could be answered.

"There's nothing we can do right now," Lira said. She reached out, and Andi felt the warm flutter of Lira's fingertips on her shoulder. She stiffened at the touch, and Lira pulled away. "A calm mind is a decent one."

"Not now, Lira," Andi growled. "Save your Adhiran proverbs for another time."

Lira sighed and turned to look at the others. "Your home may be the ship, Androma. It's all of ours, too. But Adhira is the planet that gave me life. I just lost control of myself before I could stop our ship from crashing into one of its most profitable crop fields. When Queen Alara finds out…"

Andi didn't answer.

Lira's eyes narrowed. "You are not the only one suffering today, Captain." She scooted over to sit with Breck and Gilly.

Andi slumped back into her seat, hating the action as soon as she'd done it.

She was tired. She was also hungry, and—for some hellish reason unbeknownst to her or her crew or that ridiculous AI the general had sent with them on this death mission—she may have just lost her damned ship.

She needed to be a leader. She needed to talk to her crew and devise a plan. She needed to apologize to Lira. She needed to sort out how she felt about her conversation with Dex.

But right now, she simply wanted to sit and not be bothered.

So she did.

With her mind reeling, her hands balled into fists at her side, Androma Racella, the Bloody Baroness of Mirabel, stared out the back of the wagon as her ship slid over another pile of fresh green dung and allowed herself to pout like a child.

# CHAPTER 45
## NOR

LEAVING HER TOWER FOR THE CITY WAS LIKE entering a completely different world. The one she came from was that of privilege and wealth, while the one she walked into was born from death and chaos, left to rot under the clouded sun.

Queen Nor Solis lifted the train of her burgundy gown as she, Darai and Zahn mounted the steps to the waiting hover carriage that would carry them to the former palace grounds just outside the city. Today her people would answer her call to action. Today was the day her plan would be set in motion, all the pieces finally sliding into place.

"Where to, Majesty?" a servant asked from the driver's seat just beyond the curtained barrier.

"The palace ruins," Nor said with a casual wave of her prosthetic hand. Her scars ached today, as they did every day. But something about returning to the place where it all happened made the throbbing worse. A constant tick in the back of her mind that whispered, *Death, death, death.* "Make it slow. I want every eye to see us pass."

"Just be sure they don't get too close," Zahn added to the driver. "Hover just above their reach."

The moment Nor settled into the plush cushions, the hover started moving. Darai sat on the seat across from her and inclined his head toward her. His scars and the bits of metal holding his flesh in place practically squirmed as he smiled.

"You are a vision today, my queen. Your people will be blessed to look upon you."

She slid the curtains open, the better to see her city and its citizens below. The better to remind herself of what she was striving so hard to save.

So close to her tower, the only residents around were the few remaining wealthy citizens of Nivia, the last habitable city on Xen Ptera. Old crumbling buildings stood like skeletons, stretching their ragged arms into the sky. The hover carriage glided through a plume of smoke, bathing the windows in sooty gray.

"I trust you are prepared?" Darai asked. "I haven't heard your speech yet. Are you sure you've…"

"Be silent, Uncle." Nor did not bother to even glance his way as she continued her admonishment. "If you really trust me as you say you do, you would not have to ask."

His silence was a welcome gift as the smoke cleared and the carriage continued on, its engine wheezing in the background.

"Nor," Zahn whispered, leaning close enough that his breath tickled her ear. "You're too tense. The people will see it, and it may cause them to doubt." His hand grazed her thigh. "I know it was a late night. Perhaps we should try this tomorrow."

Warmth shot through her at his touch, quickly followed by a spike of frustration from his words.

"They will see what I wish them to see," she said. She gently moved his hand away. "In this time of darkness, they will find a queen able to guide them into the light."

Darai chuckled silently across from them. "Someday, boy, you will learn that she does what she pleases, when she pleases. And she does it with flair." His smile stretched as he added, "A gift inherited from her late mother, no doubt."

"I thought I asked for silence," Nor snapped at him, her frustration barreling toward fury. "Your bravery lately is verging on foolery, Uncle. I'm growing tired of it."

Darai's eyes flitted to hers. "A wise queen does not speak down to others."

Nor sighed. "But a niece, desperate for silence from her talkative uncle, does."

Darai shook his head, a smirk on his face, but he remained mercifully silent.

Zahn's hand found Nor's thigh again. This time, she allowed it to stay.

Outside the carriage below, the streets transformed from sturdy, fortified houses made to withstand the unstable planet's constant trembling to rickety pieces of rubble thrown together by shaky hands. For most people, having a roof over their heads to protect them from the poisonous fumes and acidic rain was a luxury. Others were not so blessed.

As they passed, beggars reached their dirty hands up in hopes of touching their queen, starvation and illness etched on their faces. Nor glanced down at them, the fissure in her heart widening.

The Unified Systems had done this. She would make sure that they paid for such a heinous crime.

"Start distributing the rations and med kits," Zahn said to the driver and the guard seated beside him. "Make sure the citizens follow us to the grounds."

The guard nodded, then motioned for his soldiers to drop the silver boxes down to the citizens as he exited the carriage. One by one, the boxes fell, like angels descending to the needy. The citizens crowded around them like bugs, ripping and tearing at the contents inside.

"Greet them, Darai," Nor commanded.

Her adviser opened the window and leaned his balding head out. "Come, Xen Pterrans!" Gasps rose from the now-massive crowd of onlookers. Darai's voice was soft, but it carried like a wave. Faces covered in filth and grime angled toward the carriage in the sky. "Your queen will feed you. She will heal your afflictions, if you will only come and listen to her words."

Below, the citizens trailed after them in hordes.

Darai leaned back into the hover and smiled at Nor, the bones in his cheeks standing out. The scars on his face had never faded, though his, unlike hers, had not come from the war. And yet he wore them with a survivor's pride.

"Why feed them, my dear, when you know how low our resources are running? We have soldiers to feed, scientists to…"

"I do not wish to hear any more of your opinions on this matter," Nor said. They'd been arguing about it for weeks. "This is your last warning, Uncle."

Darai crossed his arms over his chest. "Someday, I will grow old, and I will be gone. Then you'll miss my commentary, and my advice."

Nor huffed out a breath.

Many times, Zahn had asked Nor about her short temper when it came to the old man. He'd raised her, protected her, and yet she was often so cold with Darai that he could have been an unwelcome stranger. But Nor knew Darai didn't truly mind it.

He respected her coldness, her short temper, the way she spoke to him—because it made her stronger.

Darai believed that love was a weakness.

He never wished for her to show him her softer side. The few times she had growing up, he'd punished her for it. And so she gave him exactly what he desired. The cold queen, rather than the tormented, injured child she'd once been.

After several long minutes, Nor asked, "Do you remember that insipid little creature my father gave me as a gift on my seventh birthday?"

Darai nodded with a small smile. "The feathered Indriga. It followed you around the palace as if it were starved for attention. Your constant shadow."

"It was loyal to me from the start," Nor said. "And do you know why, Darai?"

His silence was answer enough.

"I fed it," she explained. "Give a pet food, Darai, and it will do anything to stay by your side. Starve it or beat it, and it will begin to fear your very existence, only coming out of hiding in the moments when you have something to give and it to take."

"I'm afraid I don't understand."

Nor closed her eyes and pinched the space between her brows, a headache brewing from the exposure to the polluted air outside her tower. Her uncle was growing dim in his old age. Lately, she had begun to outgrow him, seeking his guidance less and less. "The people of Xen Ptera are my responsibility now. But more than that, they are my soldiers, and I wish for them to follow me always. No matter how dark the path I choose to walk upon."

"Wise words, my queen," Darai said with a bow of his head. "A ruler is only as strong as her army. Your father used to say the very same thing."

"His army was weak," Zahn said, rejoining the conversation. He looked at Nor as if she were a goddess. "Hers will be the strongest this planet has ever seen."

She took his words to heart and reminded herself to reward

him later, in her private quarters. Together, they looked down upon the crowd of people still following below.

Nor slid the curtain closed as the hover moved on.

She knew her people were struggling to survive, but she couldn't allow herself to think about their pain when there were bigger plans in the making. Her people were resilient, capable of surviving the very worst betrayals from the other cursed systems in Mirabel.

She had to fortify herself against the past in order to bring about the future. Today was the mark of a new start. Today, she would call her Xen Pterrans to arms.

When her plan came to fruition, they would cheer her name in these desolate streets, knowing they would soon be free.


Nor's carriage slid to a stop at the base of a mountain of rubble. Years ago, a glistening, pristine black-and-red spired palace stood in its place. As she took in the sight of the destruction, memories flooded her senses.

*Rubble crushing her arm. Blood dripping into the dust. Nor's father beside her, his screams dying out as the weight of the palace stole his last breaths.*

*Somewhere in the sky, an explosion rocked the world.*

*A voice from the past called out to her, keeping her conscious.*

*"Nor, my sweet Nor. You were meant for so much more than this…"*

"Are you ready, Nor?" Darai asked now, his voice pulling her back into the present as he motioned her toward the door. Outside the curtain, she could see her people—thousands of them crowding in to stand amid the wide expanse of debris.

This very place used to be the palace courtyard, so vibrant with life that on the sunnier days, her eyes had ached to look upon it. She remembered running through the gardens here. Laughing as her father chased her, the ever-blooming *Nhatyla* flowers changing colors with each season. They were the only flower that never died with the cold. In winter, when all else faded, they grew the brightest, a purple so deep it rivaled a nebula.

Such colors no longer existed on Xen Ptera. Nor's personal guard, dressed in bold red uniforms, were scattered amid the crowd, the only bright shade aside from her gown. It reminded her of the blood that once pooled in these crumbling streets, the fires that burned after the bombs were dropped on thousands of innocents.

"Majesty?" Darai stood before her, holding out his veined hand. "It is time."

She pulled the skirts of her gown away from her ankles and stepped out of the carriage under her own strength onto the slab of rock that would act as a stage while she addressed her people. A silver microphone stood ready to amplify her words.

Nor stopped before it. Her breath carried out across the crowd. Thousands of bodies were packed in around the ruins of the palace. Voices hummed throughout the crowd, pleading with her to feed them, clothe them. Mothers lifted their infants overhead, begging their queen for salvation.

There was a reason Nor rarely left her tower. Standing here, so close to the chaos and destruction, her silk shoes standing atop the bones of her past… A weaker woman would have bent and broken. Xen Ptera was her home, and the citizens were living, breathing pieces of the whole—and each of them was falling apart little by little.

Soon there would be no life left in this desolate place.

The screams got louder as she stood there, looking out at the throngs of people below. This was the future of Xen Ptera. This was her army.

Weak.

Ruined.

She needed to give them strength, and strength was nothing without hope.

She took another deep breath. In, out; steady and true.

*Sway them. Make them join you.*

She smiled.

This was what she was made for.

Nor raised her arms, her golden fist gleaming in the dying light. As if on command, the crowd hushed.

"My fellow Xen Pterrans," Nor said in a voice that radiated power. "Our planet is dying—this we have known for the past century. For far too long we have sat in silence, waiting for our planet's end. When we tried to take action, our galaxy betrayed us. And so began the war."

The crowd shouted in agreement as she continued. "My mother was taken captive during The Cataclysm. For years, she was a prisoner of Arcardius. Alone, my father tried to help our planet, but instead he was crushed beneath the weight of the Unified Systems, like so many others in the final battle." Nor paused, taking a breath. "I come to you today, standing upon his grave. Standing in the exact spot where my own body was marred."

Silence, marked by a few scattered coughs. A wailing child.

They were without hope. They had no desire to fight; could not be lifted up by their queen's words.

For a moment, fear gripped Nor like an icy fist. She would fail. She would not become the leader she had always hoped to be. She would end up just like her father, a ruler who died with no honor. No victory. Only shame.

She looked to the edge of the crowd, searching for a way out. But Zahn caught her eye and nodded encouragingly. Beside him, Darai stood watching. She remembered his words to her after her father's funeral, as the two of them stood atop her tower, acid rain trickling from the sky.

*You will become what he could never be, Nor. I will stay by your side until I see that become truth.*

She breathed deeply, her lungs aching from the tainted air as she looked down at her golden prosthetic.

It was a shield. One she could no longer hide behind. Not if she wished to be seen, *truly seen*, by her people.

One by one, Nor undid the latches that held the prosthetic in place, each pop like a gunshot in the microphone.

*One shot. Two shots. Three.*

The golden hand fell away, and the outside air washed across her skin, causing her to flinch. Where her true hand used to be, only an angry stump covered in swollen red welts and scars remained.

She lifted her arm high, ignoring the impulse to bury it within the folds of her gown.

"I stand before you, Xen Pterrans, not as your queen…but as your equal." The lie slipped like a delicious poison from her lips. If this was what they needed to hear, she would speak it. "I was broken here as a child, born in the trenches of the war that left us all shattered. For years, I have battled with the wounds of my past. Just as you have."

Thousands of eyes stared back. Scars and burns and limbs healed wrong—some limbs missing altogether.

But they were listening. She could see it in the widening of their eyes. *Feel* it, in the palpable anger and pain that seemed to sweep across the crowd among the whispers.

Her ruined arm still in the air, Nor continued. "I stand before you, marked by the destructive ways of our enemies, and tell you…no longer will I bow to pain and fear. No longer will I allow myself to cower when I hear my enemy's name. You deserve a leader who will rise above. You deserve a queen of blood and rage."

Shouts of agreement began to spread throughout the crowd.

"The Unified Systems think themselves strong, and us weak. For many years we have allowed this to be true. But now is the time to strike, to send a message that we still remain. That we are stronger than they believe."

Rage flowed through her, hot and furious.

"I ask you now, Xen Pterrans...will you join me?"

She lifted her arm higher, and allowed her voice to soar, rising above the cries of her citizens. "The Unified Systems think we are defeated, but we have only just entered the fight. I am calling upon you now to rise up with me against an evil that has been waiting too long for our vengeance. They deserve to share our pain. They deserve to share our desolation, to see their streets flow like a river with their betraying blood!"

The crowd roared, continuing to grow in size as others joined Nor's audience.

"This is the turning point in a war that never ended. For fifteen years we have sat in silence, but soon the galaxy will hear our cry." The citizens began to shout for revenge, for salvation, for blood.

She turned to Darai, lifting her chin in a proud nod as the people roared.

He shuffled over, a small silver box cradled in his palms. He bowed before kneeling, the box held before Nor. The lid flipped open with an audible *pop*. Inside, nestled on a plush cushion, was a small vial of softly glowing silver liquid.

Nor took it in her remaining hand, lifting it up for the crowd to see.

She waited until their voices fell to a hush.

"The fruits of our labor have been harvested," Nor said. "The contents of this vial will bring the Unified Systems to its knees. This is the final piece in a plan that has been in the works for years, and finally it is time to unleash its power upon our foes. Xen Ptera is the shoreline of a new ocean ripe for the taking. This galaxy—every planet in every system outside of Olen—is about to be swept up by *our* revenge." Nor paused, looking out at the thousands gathered before her. They looked at her with wide eyes full of hope, something that had once been lost beneath the weight of years of struggling.

With pride in her heart, Nor belted one last line. "Remember, Xen Pterrans, and never forget, that even the stars can bleed!"

The roar of the crowd was deafening as she placed the vial back into its box, lifted her train and strode back to the carriage.

Their cries followed her as she gracefully climbed inside.

They remained as Zahn and Darai joined her and the carriage took to the skies.

"A true show, my dear," Darai said as they left the rubble of the palace behind. Tears glistened in his black eyes. "What next?"

"We will proceed with Zenith," Nor replied. She glanced out the curtained window, smiling as her people pushed and shoved in the streets below, desperate to be close to her as she soared toward her tower. "And have a crown forged for me," she added.

"A crown?" Darai asked.

"Every queen needs one," Nor said, sliding her hand along Zahn's thigh as she watched her people celebrate in the streets. "I want to wear it while we feast on the galaxy's bones."

# CHAPTER 46
## LIRA

LIRA HAD ALWAYS BEEN ONE WITH THE SKIES.

Adhira, a planet terraformed into extremes, had taught her to love living a life without having her feet on the ground.

The ground was a confusing place, with limits and laws.

The skies offered nothing but endless freedom.

They had everything to give, and demanded nothing in return.

And yet, being back on Adhira…

*Home,* Lira thought as she stood in the rock temple atop the mountain fortress of Rhymore, the centermost point of the terraformed world.

It had taken the transport wagon two hours to drag the ruined *Marauder* here from the crash site, another hour of explaining to Queen Alara's Sentinels what had happened and another after that to finally find a moment to escape from the girls once they'd settled into a guest wing deep inside the mountain.

Their questions and the concerned looks they cast Lira's way were too much for her already fragile emotional state to handle.

She needed a moment to settle herself again.

To rediscover her peace.

She'd slipped away from her crew while they ate lunch, walking past Dextro and Alfie as they patched in a call to General Cortas. She'd been surprised when Dex had looked up and asked her how she was feeling—she wouldn't have believed him capable of such courtesy. She'd given him a small, stunned smile in return before slipping away.

Finally, after remembering her way through the winding tunnels of the mountain and climbing a set of stairs so tall Lira thought her legs might combust from the strain of her burning muscles, she'd made it to her destination.

Now here she stood, at the very top of Rhymore. Catching her breath, drinking sweet water from a polished red rock basin in the center of the towering temple and admiring the early afternoon view that she'd missed the most since leaving this planet four years ago.

Though the temple was small, with only room enough for a few bodies at a time, Lira found it the most spacious place in the world. Nothing but the four rock columns and the waist-high ledge stood between her and the sky, and Lira's view was endless.

From here, she could see *all* of Adhira, as far as her eyes could carry her.

It was here, atop the mountain itself, that Lira had come countless times as a child.

She'd come when her father passed on to the next life. She'd come when she had her Efflorescence Ceremony, and when she simply wanted to escape from the weight of the world on her shoulders. Here, the mountain had always offered to bear her burden instead.

It was here, year after year, that a much younger Lira used to sit with a heavy woolen shawl around her shoulders, the cold wind combing across her face, and allow herself to dream.

A single, massive eyeglass stood empty and waiting in the center of the mountaintop temple. It was made from the very same varillium as the *Marauder*, acquired long ago in a trade with Xen Ptera.

Though the varillium was unbreakable, Lira still took care as she pressed her eye to the cold eyepiece.

A little adjusting, a few swivels and flashes of light, and Lira felt a smile spread across her face.

Her chest lightened. Her heart raced.

Although she'd seen this view a hundred times, it still took her breath away. Through the eyeglass, all of Adhira unfurled before her like a perfect, tiny map.

Heavens above, she'd missed this planet.

To the north, she could see the emerald expanse that made up Aramaeia, the terraformed rainforest full of monstrous trees, which spread all the way into the clouds and beyond. Inside those trees, entire cities buzzed with life. At Aramaeia's edge, tucked into the trees, sat the Falls of Amorga. They boomed so loudly that it was impossible to hear anything else once you got within half a mile of their location.

She'd been to those falls. She'd swum in their depths, and explored the Sunken City beyond.

The wind blew, tickling Lira's senses. She swiveled the eyeglass to the west, where endless green faded into deep reds and browns. The Sands of Bailet were pocked with giamounds, desert rocks that stood miles tall. The city of Lavada thrived inside the monstrous pillars, where the cityfolk milled about in a series of twisting tunnels. They weren't the only inhabitants within those pillars. They shared it with vergs, gentle sand-colored creatures whose many eyes helped them see in the depths of the giamounds. They had almost as many legs as eyes, which helped them crawl through the deepest tunnels below ground, not yet inhabited by other Lavadian residents.

Lira shivered. She'd never been a fan of giant, wriggling bugs.

She shifted the eyeglass again, fighting against a fresh gust of wind. She adjusted the view until a vision of deep, beautiful blue appeared. The Endless Sea, a world of water that was as deep as it was wide, its people gifted with gills, webbed fingers and toes, able to live beneath the crashing waves.

And here Lira stood, far away in the sky.

In the center of it all.

She loved this place. It was here, standing alone on this very balcony, that Lira first met the greatest loves of her life.

The sky.

The stars.

And the ships that soared through them.

"Admiring the view?"

Lira looked up so fast she nearly fell over.

That voice. How much she'd missed it.

"You sneaky bastard," Lira hissed.

Then she sidestepped the eyeglass and crossed to the other side of the temple in three quick strides, where she threw herself into her twin brother's arms.

Lon was older than her by just a few minutes, but he'd never let her forget it. He was the loud, brute strength to Lira's calm, calculated silence. The one who'd always laughed at her for having her nose buried in the pages of books—and yet, he'd frequently spent his wages on the very best ones he could find to give to her.

"I have to admit, little sister," Lon said, holding her out at arm's length, "you've outdone yourself with your entrance this time. Destroying an entire field of hrevan crops *and* your ship in the process?" He grinned, his purple eyes flashing. "You've certainly changed."

He always knew how to press her buttons. But Lira still smiled as she looked at her brother.

Godstars, how he'd grown.

He was at least a head taller than her now, his pale blue arms rippling with muscle, spreading up into a thick neck and strong shoulders. He wore the traditional loose, sleeveless green shirt of the Sentinels. A shiny golden Adhiran emblem was pinned on the fabric right above his heart.

"You've been promoted!" Lira gasped.

"Queen Alara isn't easy to work for, as you can well imagine." Lon grinned like a forest cat, earning another smile from Lira. He rapped his knuckles on the Adhiran emblem, the endless spiral that signified life. "A lot has happened since you've been away, little bug."

She wrinkled her nose. "I thought I'd grown out of that horrendous nickname."

He laughed, a booming thing that rivaled the mountain wind. "You can leave your planet behind, Lira. But it doesn't change who you are inside."

Silence swept over them, sudden and piercing.

A single scaled patch on Lon's right cheek warmed, glowing the slightest blue. He closed his eyes and clenched his jaw, willing the emotions away.

He had always been better at controlling them than she was.

"Lon," Lira whispered. "I've missed you. I think of you every day. I've wanted to visit, truly. It's just that…"

*That I became a criminal*, she thought. *That I was afraid of what you would think of me, of the person I have become.*

"You stopped sending me updates," he said. "You disappeared, Lira. All I had to keep up-to-date with you were the—" he swallowed hard, the scale flashing again on his cheek "—the updates about a certain crew of wanted girls, halfway across Mirabel. The crimes I won't even begin to discuss."

She closed her eyes. Looked away from the pained expression on his face, so much like her own. "Things changed out there. Situations got out of control. I…reacted."

"There have been *deaths*," Lon hissed. His voice was so low it was nearly lost in the wind.

"Not at my hand," Lira promised. "I swear it, Lon. I swear it in this holy place."

His jaw flexed as he gritted his teeth. "I know you aren't a killer, Lira."

Her heart relaxed, just slightly.

"But you left. You left *me*, and you chose to forget about home."

"No." Lira held up her hands. "I chose to protect you from who I have become, Lon."

Silence fell between them. Somewhere down below, a bell clanged. The sound, deep and full, swept up the mountainside, trickled past Lira's ears. It meant that Queen Alara was accepting petitions from the Adhiran people, young and old, rich and poor.

Alara was a wise leader, loving and attentive. She cared whole-heartedly for Adhira, giving her all to the care of her people.

It was something Lira could never do, could never even *dream* of doing.

So she'd fled. She'd made herself into someone unworthy.

She'd created demons to chase her, the kind she could never outrun.

"We don't have much time alone together, so I'll make this brief," Lon said, drawing her attention back to him. "What-ever you think you've become…" He sighed, turning to face her. "You are still my sister. And I will always have room in my heart for you. The old you. The new you. The you that you have yet to become." He pressed two fingers to her forehead. "I

don't have to agree with it all, Lira. But my loyalty is yours…
until the mountain falls."

*Until the mountain falls.*

They were the last words he'd said to her—before she ran
away on a starship and took to life in the skies.

Her heart clenched again.

"It's not all bad, what the girls and I do," Lira said, trying to
lighten the tone in her voice. She moved back toward the eyeglass and ran her fingertips across it. "You can't even begin to
imagine what's happened in the past few days."

"I can guess it's quite a tale," Lon said. "Seeing as you and
your friends aren't rotting in a cell in the belly of Rhymore
right now for that crash landing. And just before Revalia, too."

Lira winced. She'd forgotten all about the peace festival. It
was a yearly occurrence on Adhira, a celebration of the end of
the war against Xen Ptera.

"Let me tell you my side of the story, then," Lira said. "Let
me explain to you what's gone on, so you can try to see it in a
different light."

Lon shook his head. "Lira…I can't."

"Just the good things?" Lira asked, her voice settling into that
little pleading tone she'd used on him when they were younger.
When she desperately wanted the last bite of his moss meringue,
or to play with one of his toys. "I'm a starship pilot, Lon. Just
like I always dreamed I'd be." She placed her hand on his warm
arm. "I've even taken up that nasty little habit you try to hide
from the queen."

His eyes flashed.

"You have your secrets, too," she teased.

"Moon Chew, little bug?" He clicked his tongue and shook
his head. But then he smiled, the warmth slowly spreading back
into his features as he took the bait. "What in the Godstars led
you to that?"

"You can't even imagine," Lira said, and turned to look up at the sky. "The things we see up there, Lon. It's…"

"Not something the queen would approve of," Lon finished for her. He held up a finger as Lira frowned. "But she tends to be a little uptight. Which is exactly why…if you hold back the things she doesn't need to know…I will not tell her a single detail of what you're about to tell me."

She opened her mouth to share, but he stopped her with a raised brow.

"Only the good things. If it has anything to do with Adhira, anything that might threaten this planet, I cannot hear it."

"I swear it," Lira said. "You know I'd never do anything to harm this place, Lon."

He bowed his head. "Then go ahead, little bug." When he looked back up, his eyes were eager. "Just…go ahead."

And so they stood there, brother and sister, two halves of one whole, the Adhiran wind whipping through the temple as Lira told her tales.

He shook his head in amusement when she described Gilly and her fiery spirit. He smiled when she spoke of Andi's dancing and her red polished nails and the way her music spilled through the halls of the ship. He grumbled something about cocky Guardians as Lira talked about Dex and hummed in appreciation when she described Breck's exquisitely cooked meals. He laughed when Lira told him some of the New Vedan's jokes and the banter Breck shared with Gilly.

He gripped Lira's arms when she spoke of their high-speed chases. The way she could fly a ship like a tireless bird. The planets they'd visited, the amazing atmospheres they'd entered, the glorious worlds beyond this one. Planets made of ice. Planets made of diamond. Planets that never saw the light of day, so cold that the air nearly froze the engines on their ship before they could soar away.

All along, he listened, occasionally biting his lower lip in thought.

Lon always knew that Lira harbored a darkness in her soul. A little *tug*, a tiny *whisper* at the back of her mind, that led her to go above and beyond the pranks that Lon had always pulled while they were growing up here.

She'd fallen, not for a lover, but for the skies. For adventure.

She'd found a ship full of girls with their own affinity for darkness to mirror her own.

When she was done, Lon stared at her for a time.

"You were never meant to stay here," he said. "I've known it since the moment you tried to leap from this very temple with wings made of leaves tied to your arms."

Lira laughed.

He put an arm around her and pulled her close.

"Welcome home, little bug." She felt him inhale beside her. Exhale, deeply. "I hate to ruin your strange homecoming... but..."

"What is it?" Lira pulled away.

Lon shrugged, a lopsided smile on his face. "The queen has requested a private meeting with you. And, seeing as I'm to be your personal Sentinel for the time being...I'm here to escort you to her. And ensure that you don't escape while she delivers whatever punishment she sees fit for the damage your ship did to the hrevan fields."

"Of course you are," Lira said with a groan. "And my crew? Will they be there, too?"

Lon shook his head. "No. Just you. She has no desire to speak to the crew." He lifted his hands. "Her words. Not mine."

"Fine then," Lira said. "If you're such a big, terrifying Sentinel now..." She pinched his cheek, forcing the scaled patch to illuminate with a flash of anger. "You'll have to chase me down there."

"Lira, I don't have time to play childhood games."

But she was already on the move.

"You're already losing!" She yelled as she dashed past him, deftly slipping through the hole in the ground where the temple ladder led down into the mountain tunnels below, pretending it was a ladder back on the *Marauder*.

"*Lira!*"

Lon's booming growl echoed after her as he tried in vain to catch up.

He didn't stand a chance.

# CHAPTER 47
## VALEN

THE FIRST THING HE NOTICED WAS THE LIGHT.

Even with his eyes closed, Valen could sense it shimmering just on the surface of his memories. It reminded him of the short springtime season on Arcardius, his favorite time of the year. On those mornings, he used to love to sleep with his windows open, a soft breeze fluttering in through the curtains.

If he tried hard enough, he could imagine he was lying in his bed, the distant trill of birdsong nudging him awake. The sound of leaves dancing on branches, the gentle patter of feet just outside his door. Likely a servant, coming in to start their workday.

But that was the past. Soon he would wake, and the harshness of reality would take its place.

Lunamere had a way of digging its claws into one's back and refusing to ever let go.

Valen sighed and rolled over onto his side, wincing as he anticipated the harsh chill of the stones beneath his cheek, the spasm of pain that would slice through his aching body.

But instead of stone, he felt the plushness of a pillow. Instead of pain, he eased into a soft mountain of blankets. The shivering cold of Lunamere was gone, replaced instead by warmth he hadn't felt in years.

Valen coaxed his eyes, coated with the sticky residue of sleep, open.

He *was* lying in a bed, his body covered by plush green blankets spun from the softest silk. At the end of the bed, Valen noted with a raised brow, was a ball of orange fur. An animal of some sort, curled up so tightly that he couldn't tell where its head was, only that its back rose and fell with long, lazy breaths. He hadn't seen an animal of any kind in years. His gaze swept past the slumbering creature to study the room.

It was a place straight from the storybooks he'd read as a child, and for a moment he wondered if this was his own version of the afterlife. Perhaps he'd finally died, and this was where he'd traveled to. A soul set out among the stars, finally settling on the safest place his subconscious could remember.

The walls were curved and made of rock with vines that snaked their way across its rough surface. His eyes trailed along the vines, following them to where they twisted and curled through a large, elegant window carved from the rock.

Valen's eyes widened as he glimpsed the world beyond.

Afternoon sunlight winked in through the open window. Far below, an endless, sprawling forest spread for miles, trees so tall they pierced through the clouds in the sky.

Valen could just barely see a massive white waterfall tumbling in the distance, and when the wind blew, he could almost imagine the taste of the water on his lips.

He wished his sister was with him in this moment to drink in such beauty—fresh and cool and so full of life.

This room, these blankets, this view. It was like a painting rendered by an artist far more skilled than he. Valen shifted slightly, wincing as the all too-real pain of his ruined body finally hit him. If this were a dream, he'd have imagined that pain away. He waited for the darkness to sweep back in and steal him away.

"Marvelous view, isn't it? There's nothing like an Adhiran afternoon."

Valen turned his head at the sound of a woman's voice.

Behind him, the side of the rock room had seemingly opened up, revealing a hidden doorway he hadn't seen before. Standing in its opening was a beautiful woman who reminded him of a palette of paints.

Her body was a patchwork of colors all melting together, some an orange as bright as the ball of fur still sleeping at Valen's feet, others a pink that reminded him of the sunsets that swept across the Arcardian sky. She wore a thin gown of green fabric, the color such a stark contrast to the sunset shades of her skin that Valen nearly sobbed at the beauty of it all.

She was incredible. His fingers twitched with the need to paint her.

But strangest of all…Valen *knew* this woman.

It all came rushing back to him now. Memories of her face on holos with his father, speaking about trade. Photographs of her in books as he studied the leaders of the other capital planets.

"Your Royal Highness," Valen said, somehow finding his voice. His throat felt ragged, like he hadn't used it in weeks. "But…you're Adhiran. How?"

He'd never been to the terraformed planet of Adhira—strange, that he'd dream it up in his afterlife.

The woman inclined her head, a small smile on her lips like she was holding back a laugh. "I prefer simply Queen Alara, young Mr. Cortas. And to answer your question as to how I am Adhiran…well, I'd imagine that would be akin to me asking you how you're Arcadian. We simply are who we are. Wouldn't you agree?"

Valen nodded his head, wincing as he felt a stab of pain.

A strange dream, indeed.

"I meant," he said, focusing more closely on his words now, "why am I here?"

"You must be confused," Alara said, smiling gently. She smoothed out a wrinkle on her dress with delicate fingertips. "You've been through quite a traumatic experience, Mr. Cortas. It's lucky your father sent along a medically programmed AI with your rescue crew. Otherwise…" Her hairless brow furrowed. "You and I would not be here having this conversation."

"My father?" Valen's stomach turned.

He tried to push himself up from the pillows, but it was as if something tore in his spine. The pain in his back blossomed. Valen closed his eyes and breathed deep, trying to imagine it away. But it didn't leave.

With each breath, it got worse, and suddenly he found himself groaning, gritting his teeth so he wouldn't scream.

Alara swept silently across the room and stopped at his bedside. "Oh, dear. It seems you're overdue for another dose of JemArii. The lacerations on your back were quite deep. The sedative is likely why you slept through the entire crash."

"What crash?"

"The details don't matter right now, Valen. What I'd like to know is…what is the last thing you remember?" She stepped closer to him, that cool smile still on her lips. "You were in Lunamere for a very long time." He felt her cool fingertips on his skin, and suddenly an image of another person flashed into his mind.

A queen of darkness.

A demon wearing a woman's skin.

He flinched away, gasping again as his mutilated body throbbed with pain.

*"Nor,"* he breathed. He slammed his eyes shut, and there she was, standing over him, hands outstretched.

"She's not here, Valen," the queen said.

But he wasn't listening anymore.

"Open your eyes, child," she said. "Open your eyes and see that you are safe."

He couldn't. He *wouldn't* open them, because he knew that when he did, he'd be back in his cell again.

"I am Valen," he whispered to himself.

He could still feel the soft bed beneath him, but in his mind, he knew it wasn't real.

"I am Valen. I am Valen. I am…"

The door swung open with a shuddering boom. Then there were hands on his wrists, voices saying his name, telling him to remain calm, that he was safe, that he was no longer in Lunamere.

"Not now," he said. "Not now, not now…" He thrashed against his captors. He couldn't get free.

He would never be free.

"Put him back under," Alara's voice said. "We're going too fast."

Valen felt a sharp pinch as something sunk beneath his skin. Warmth enveloped him, and with it came a lurching wave of dizziness, as if he were standing on a crashing starship.

He slumped back against the pillows, and as he did, his eyelids fluttered open.

The last thing he saw was Androma Racella leaning forward from the shadows across the room, half of her face aglow as sunlight spilled across her skin like paint.

# CHAPTER 48
## LIRA

LIRA HAD FORGOTTEN HOW STRANGE IT WAS to be planetside.

She hated the feeling of extra weight on her shoulders. Like there was baggage she couldn't shake, clinging to her bones.

But she'd made it here alone. She'd lost Lon far back in the tunnels, remembering an old hiding place she'd used as a child. She'd wedged herself between the tunnel wall and the old, hand-carved bust of the original ruler of Adhira, King Rodemere Ankara, the man who'd so strongly influenced the Adhiran creed of living harmoniously with others.

Lira stood up now and made her way through the final tunnel that led to the queen's private quarters, doing her best to catch her breath and smooth out the wrinkled folds of her dress as she walked.

The rock floor was cool on her bare toes, the flickering blue torches lighting her way like old, familiar friends waving hello. But it didn't feel like a homecoming anymore.

It felt like a death march.

Lira passed others from her past as she walked: a horned woman who was the Rhymore seamstress. A retired Guardian who'd moved from Tenebris to become one of Lira's tutors. Some looked surprised that she had returned. Others—not fully given over to the idea of harmony—stared or glared or asked why she'd come back after all these years.

At long last, Queen Alara's private quarters came into view. The massive oak doors, at least two stories tall and handmade by crafters from Aramaeia, stood closed at the end of the tunnelway.

Two Sentinels, both with the same golden emblems that Lon bore on his chest, stood waiting, stone staffs clutched in their fists.

The doors swung open as Lira approached, creaking and groaning beneath their own weight.

And there the queen was, waiting inside, her attention focused on a glowing screen in her lap.

Alara was beautiful in every sense of the word, inside and out. She had a lithe frame, perfectly proportioned, and no scales on her skin. Her posture was elegant, one she always seemed to hold without effort.

Lira had always admired Alara's beauty, but it paled in comparison to the woman's intelligence.

She was seated on a moss-covered bench beside a small window carved out of the mountainside. Wind trickled in through diamond-shaped holes, letting in just enough light to make it seem as if Alara were glowing.

The queen who feared none, but loved all.

"You asked to see me?"

Lira's voice shook a little as she entered the large space, stepping past the old woven tapestries hanging on the walls and the twisting vines that curled all around, covering even the domed rock ceiling far overhead.

"Lirana," the queen said without looking up. "Please, do come in." She continued scrolling through the holoscreen on her lap, tapping away in a cadence that reminded Lira of a small, pecking bird.

Lira swallowed, then steeled herself.

She was the pilot of the *Marauder,* and despite the fact that her ship went down unexpectedly—*not her fault*—and despite the fact that she'd damned an entire field of crops to ashen waste—*partially her fault*—and despite the fact that she absolutely did not want to be here…she would accept the consequences.

She swept farther into the room with her shoulders rolled back, stopping just before the queen of Adhira.

She knew how this would go. So before Alara could speak, Lira opened her mouth to explain.

But the queen held up a palm.

Silence hung between them.

Frustration wiggled at Lira's senses, like a worm trying to sneak its way into her skull. She gritted her teeth. Clenched her fists.

Then, finally, Alara looked up to meet her eyes. "I've just had a rather unfortunate conversation with Valen Cortas, the poor, tortured soul, so spare me whatever dramatic greeting you must have prepared."

Lira's mouth dropped open as Alara stood. "Valen is awake?"

The queen nodded. "It's always interesting when you're around. Welcome back, my young niece. It's been a very, very long time."

# CHAPTER 49
## LIRA

LIRA'S KNEES SHOOK.

How, after all the things she'd seen in this galaxy, after all the things she had done and the enemies she had faced, did her loving, beautiful, stars-forsaken aunt manage to make her feel fear?

"You left," Alara said, "without a word to me. You tricked my Sentinels. You boarded a ship with an outsider crew full of men and women I did not know, from a rogue planet I have not visited, and decided to take up a life where the only updates I had on you were the wanted posters appearing in my bi-moonly feeds."

Somehow, though Alara was still seated, her voice soft and calm and even, Lira felt as if she were being screamed at while she cowered against a wall.

"It wounded my heart, Lirana," her aunt continued, all the while keeping her emerald eyes on Lira. "But what wounded me more was to watch your brother walking through the halls here as if he were searching for a ghost. After all the two of you had suffered through together, you chose to leave him here alone."

That was it, then.

Each word was worse than a stab to Lira's gut.

But she'd known this was coming. She prepared herself for this speech, year after year. It was why she had not returned home since leaving to seek out a life piloting starships. It was why Andi had agreed not to take any jobs on Adhira.

Because she understood the pain of facing the past.

Andi and Dex had had their conversation. Now it was Lira's turn.

"I have offered you my title, many times over," Alara said. Still staring, still speaking with that calm, even, queenly tone. Lira looked at her toes. "I have offered you a life of safety and comfort inside this very mountain, where you could have had everything you ever wanted. And what is more, Lirana, you could have all of Adhira at your fingertips. An entire planet full of people for you to call your own. To protect. To rule."

"But that's the point!" Lira hissed, then blinked in surprise, shocked that her voice had simply slipped out. But now that the dam had broken, she couldn't stop it. "I don't want your stupid title. I don't want to rule. I don't want to look after an entire planet full of people." She took a deep breath, and finally looked her aunt in the eyes. "I love you, but I don't want to *be* you."

And there they were.

The words Lira had held in her chest for so long, ever since her aunt had begun grooming her for the position. Alara had never been able to have children of her own, but when her sister had stopped caring for Lira and Lon, Alara had become their sole guardian.

And Alara thought she'd found her heir.

She'd wanted to share her world with Lira, every animal, plant and person living and breathing throughout it.

But it was too damned much.

*I don't want the title. I don't want the job. I don't want the responsibility.*

*I want to soar through the stars. I want to navigate through nebulas. I want to fly my ship so close to a black hole that the fear nearly shakes the bones from my body. And then I want to overcome it.*

All of those things, Lira had already said.

But this?

This, she had never had the guts to share with her aunt.

Alara nodded slowly, as if she were mulling over Lira's words.

She stood, pressing a button on the small silver band wrapped around her thin wrist. Moments later, the double doors to her chambers opened, and a Sentinel walked in.

Lira's heart sank.

Lon.

He smiled apologetically at Lira as he walked past, his eyes downcast as he took up his place beside their aunt.

"I have loved you as if you were my own daughter," Alara finally said. "After all these years, Lirana, and even with the pain your brother and I have endured from your absence...I still consider you a piece of my heart. A vital part of this planet." She looked sideways at Lon. "Show her."

"Show me what?" Lira asked.

With a deep sigh, Lon held up a glowing screen.

On it was a photograph of Lira, smiling as if she hadn't a care in the world. She knew that photograph. It was from her Efflorescence Ceremony. Her gown was beautiful, the fabric like an elegant flowing stream, in every shade of blue she could imagine. Lira stood before a sunset, her face aglow with both a smile and the evening light. Lon stood beside her in the image, his arm draped over her shoulders. His own smile matching hers.

SASHA ALSBERG & LINDSAY CUMMINGS

"This is a photograph of a girl who once loved her home and her family," Alara said. "This is the daughter I raised." She stared at the image, smiling sadly.

"I still love you!" Lira yelped. She could feel her scales heating again, and she willed the emotions away. "I have never stopped loving you. But I'm not the same girl anymore," she pleaded. "I never have been, Alara. It's as if during my entire life here, I was…playing a part. For you. Not for me."

Alara nodded, and Lon chewed on his bottom lip, worrying away at the skin until Lira feared it would bleed.

"You have always been a dreamer," Alara said. "I have known it since you were born. I don't know what sort of web you've gotten yourself tangled up in, but I know that with General Cortas involved, I fear for your safety."

At the mention of his name, Lira raised a brow.

"He's a good leader, but his honesty, and his methods, are questionable at best. Nevertheless, he has been in constant communication with me, and I with him, since the very first time your wanted posters appeared on the feeds."

"I'm sorry," Lira said.

She truly was. For the shame it brought upon her aunt. For the worry she must have caused both Alara and Lon.

"I know of the plans he has for you, and the rest of the—" she took a deep, shuddering breath "—the crew you have aligned yourself with. If you succeed in your mission to return Valen Cortas home, General Cortas has promised you a full pardon of your crimes. Has he not?"

Lira nodded.

"I would like to offer you something else, as well." Her aunt turned to Lon, who tapped something onto his screen and turned it back around so Lira could see it.

Her eyes nearly bugged out of her skull.

"For years now, I have been in talks with the other planetary leaders about their own starfleets. It's something I should have acted on long ago. And ever since Valen Cortas was stolen by a Xen Pterran rogue force, I realized that Adhira needs a stronger presence in the sky, stars forbid they strike again, on this planet—or if anything should ever happen to return us to that black pit of war." She tapped two fingertips to her forehead and whispered a silent prayer to the Godstars. "I love you, Lirana. I always have. You have wounded me. You have betrayed my trust. But we are family, by blood, bound to this planet by duty, whether you see it that way or not."

Lira nodded again, still staring at what was on the screen.

"And so, through many negotiations with General Cortas, I am able to offer you this."

She pointed at the screen.

On it was an official document stating that Lirana Mette would become the pilot of a new Adhiran Skyback Explorer.

It was the fastest model in the Mirabel Galaxy. The most advanced. Plenty of cargo space, plenty of room to gather and collect and return home with whatever she pleased. Plenty of room for weapons, something Alara had never, in all her years ruling Adhira, truly condoned.

The ship, sleek and beautiful, was the most desired by anyone who knew anything about ships. It wasn't even available on the public market yet.

"You would reside in Rhymore alongside your brother and me," Alara said. "You would, of course, have to work without wages for a year to pay for the ruined crops from your recent crash landing. And I would ensure that you enter pilot's mechanical training, with the very best in the field, so that you do not repeat your mistakes again. You will also work to control your energy output when faced with strong emotions, as I have always insisted. It's clear you have not maintained that practice on your journeys. After you agree to my terms, you are free to pilot this ship. We trade with several of the planets across Mirabel. You would be the one traveling there, with Lon at your side, and a handful of others, to collect and deliver goods. And in case the need should ever arise…you would help train other pilots to protect this planet."

Lon stepped up beside Lira and spoke. "It will be yours, Lir. Your ship. You'd pilot it for good. For Adhira. For us. And I would be with you on your adventures! It's everything you've ever wanted, Lira."

Lira felt herself spiraling into a deep, dark space.

There were so many memories here. Of her childhood, the pain of her mother leaving her, the feeling that there would be no one to care for her and Lon. Then the rescue, when their aunt brought them into her mountain fortress. Into her heart and her waiting arms.

This was a chance to set things right with Alara and Lon. This was a chance to come home, and still do what she loved most.

No leading the planet. No title other than pilot.

Hell, she didn't even have to captain the ship if she didn't want to. Someone else could make those choices, and she'd simply keep her hands on the wheel, her eyes on the sky.

Everything inside of her begged her to accept.

But then her aunt's words filtered back through. Lira glanced up at the two standing before her. "You said General Cortas was involved. That you were…negotiating with him?"

Lon bit his lip again. This time, the blood broke through. A tiny bead of delicate, springtime sky blue.

"The offer only stands this once," Alara said. She seemed to stand taller. "On the stipulation that you remove yourself from the current mission at hand. Say the word, Lirana, and you will be free of General Cortas's job and all of the dangers and frustrations that come with it. Your crew can remain here, of course, until their ship is fixed. But when they leave, you would remain on Adhira. I have already set aside the funds to begin building your ship."

Lon stepped forward, close enough that Lira could feel his

ZENITH

body heat. He took her cold hands in his warm ones. "Just say yes, Lir. You've had your fun. You've had your adventures, and they wouldn't be over. They'd just be...safer. Something the Godstars would approve of."

Lira's heart rocketed into her throat.

She felt thrust into a battle, the two sides of her heart waging war.

Smoke filtered up from the heat on her scales. And yet, Lon did not let go, even though she knew she was burning him.

"I..."

Two sets of eyes upon her.

Two dreams.

"You have until your crew leaves this planet to decide," Alara said.

"And the girls?" Lira asked. "What if I wished for them to be my crew, here?"

Lon pushed the screen into Lira's hands, the sketch of the ship—and Lira's name above it—still in full view.

"We love you, little bug," Lon said. "And we want the best for your future."

"And we feel that future should not include them," Alara said softly.

Lira stared at them both for a moment, then looked back at the screen in her hands. She felt her scales betraying her emotional state, so Lira simply nodded curtly before turning to leave the room.

Walking out into the halls.

Seeing the past and the future colliding. The faces of her crew. Dead bodies lying at her feet. The pain of leaving her family behind, and the joy of finding a new one beyond the Adhiran borders.

After wandering for some time, Lira finally found Dex in the living area of their borrowed quarters. Alfie sat beside him on the couch. The AI was oiling his gears while Dex oiled his insides with a bottle of Griss.

"They're in the Well," Dex said, waving a hand.

Lira raised a brow. "Doing what?"

"They are attacking each other, quite voraciously, with a series of defensive and offensive moves," Alfie said without looking up from his task.

"It's called training," Dex explained. He caught Lira's eye. "Gilly said there were no boys allowed."

"She's correct," Lira said. She watched Dex for a moment as he talked with Alfie, smiling as the AI asked further questions. "Dextro?"

Dex glanced up.

"The story that you told Andi, back on the ship," Lira said. "Was there truly no other way to save them both?"

His smile fell as he said, "If there had been another way, Lira…" He shook his head, his brow creasing as he took a long gulp of Griss. "I would have torn apart the galaxy in order to take it."

Lira nodded in understanding. Dex lifted his bottle of Griss to her in a gesture of farewell as she left the room, heading for the Well, a freshwater lake deep inside the mountain where her crew would be waiting.

Her heart twisted with the weight of the offer she'd just received.

# CHAPTER 50
## ANDROMA

"YOU'RE SULKING AGAIN," BRECK SAID TO ANDI as they circled each other like two hungry sharks.

"I'm not sulking," Andi said. "I'm simply regretting my decisions. Deeply."

Breck lifted a dark brow. "You're too much in your head. It's time you got out of it." She lunged forward, and before Andi knew it, Breck's giant foot was in her gut.

Andi went flying.

She landed, with a great splash, in the massive lake that made up most of the Well. It was twice as deep as it was wide, and colorful, flashing fish swam beneath its depths, sucking the algae away so that the lake remained a glittering, almost crystal shade of blue.

Andi came up sputtering for air and shivering to find Breck, Lira and Gilly laughing by the water's edge. Their laughs echoed throughout the massive cavern, slipped across the surface of the blue lake. Workers nearby looked up from their posts on the bridge that spanned the lake, their tubes that pulled water from the Well momentarily forgotten.

The Well of Rhymore was not exactly a prime location for training. The space surrounding the giant lake was slick, solid rock, and the only source of light came from the random flashes of the fish beneath the surface of the water. It was hard to see and difficult to move, plus they had a captive audience of Queen Alara's workers watching.

All of which, to Andi, made it the perfect place for her and her crew to practice their fighting skills, something they hadn't been able to do on solid land in quite some time.

"She just owned you," Gilly said as Andi hauled her dripping self from the lake. A suckerfish, with its almost humanoid mouth, just barely missed a chance to latch on to her leg.

"Not funny," Andi said as she slung the water off and shook out her hair. She never should have allowed that kick to make contact. She felt slow, as if her mind were weighing her down.

"It was actually quite humorous," Lira replied with a grin.

"As humorous as this?" Andi asked.

With a growl, she sprang.

Lira deftly sidestepped her, bare feet moving with ease across the rocky shores of the inner-mountain lake.

Andi's punch nearly clipped Gilly instead, but the young gunner ducked, then came back up with a punch of her own. Andi blocked it with her cuffs, and Gilly howled like a creature of the night.

"You're going to pay for that!"

She lunged at Andi, but Breck stepped in front of her, and Gilly's swings missed their intended mark.

"Lira, on my side," Andi commanded. "Breck and Gilly, face off."

Her pilot joined her, and together, they turned to face Breck and Gilly.

"The first to draw blood wins," Andi said. "No weapons. Only fists and feet."

Gilly flashed her teeth and glanced up at Breck, who stood with her hands raised, fists already in place to protect her face. "You're so going down, ladies."

In a flash, the girls all sprang into action. It was a flurry of fists, Andi's wet clothing helping her to slip between Breck's fingers, Lira's graceful leaps keeping her out of Gilly's range.

As they moved, Andi's distracting thoughts tried to worm their way into the fight. Another opponent for her to face, and no matter how hard she swung her fists, no matter how effortlessly she landed each jab and punch or made a successful dodge, the thoughts attacked harder.

Fiercer than Breck and Gilly's hits could ever be.

As Breck leveled a kick to Andi's thigh, Andi swiftly returned it with a kick of her own. The giantess chuckled as Andi dropped to the floor, rolling away from another attack. Lira was there to back her up, swiftly dealing blows to Breck's left arm. Gilly retorted with a flurry of curses and a rock thrown at Lira's face.

As the girls moved and spun, Andi thought of what she had yet to face.

Valen, upon waking, had looked at her like he knew that her soul was black. Andi supposed it was. A soul that had taken so many lives must be tainted.

Breck's fist clipped her jaw.

*"Yes!"* Gilly howled.

Pain screamed at Andi, but she willed it away. She would not go down that easily.

And yet, as she and Lira backed up, taking a few paces away to regain their composure, thoughts of Valen came back stronger.

*Of course he wouldn't want to see you, Andi. Why would he ever, in a million years, want to see his sister's murderer?*

In more ways than one, Andi blamed herself for his pain and his capture. Everyone—reporters and gossips galaxy-wide—had spoken of how the young general's son wasn't the same after Kalee died. If Andi hadn't crashed that ship…then maybe Valen wouldn't have been out in the night, walking alone in Kalee's memorial garden.

He wouldn't have been captured by Xen Pterran forces. And then all of this—Adhira, the crash landing, the tidal wave of emotions Lira was suffering through…

None of it would have ever happened.

Andi knew she was the beginning of the spiral that bent Valen's life—and many others—out of control.

"Your left!" Lira yelped.

Andi narrowly dodged another rock thrown by Gilly. The young gunner would always find ammunition, even in the belly of Rhymore.

Gilly twirled past, hissing taunts and laughing as Breck and Lira went head-to-head.

"Come on, Cap," Gilly said, waggling a finger at Andi.

With a quick bend, Andi splashed frigid water into Gilly's face.

They tumbled back into the fight.

Andi's thoughts followed right behind.

After the transport wagon had dropped them off, and the remains of the *Marauder* were carted deeper into the mountain, Andi and Dex had patched in a call to General Cortas.

That had gone *very* poorly. Andi still had a headache from the conversation, in which the general had been so upset that Alfie had suggested he "consume a bottle of his calming tonics and resume the conversation at a later time."

At one point, General Cortas had called Andi and her crew a waste of his time. Dex had vehemently disagreed with him, to which Andi promptly reminded Dex that she could stand up for herself, and a flurry of bitter retorts had gone back and forth between them at once.

The general had then chewed them both out and ended the call.

"It could have gone worse," Dex had said before they parted ways. Things had gone as well as they probably could have with the general, at least.

It was Queen Alara whom Andi had yet to have a full conversation with.

She knew a reprimand was coming—likely more marks on her record—but she guessed that Lira would get the brunt of the scolding from the Adhiran queen.

And speaking of Lira…

She was currently fighting off Breck at the center of the bridge. The glowing blue water below lit up Lira's face, making her eyes stand out boldly as she tracked Breck's motions and mirrored them when it was Breck's turn to go on the defensive.

Workers scattered, gasping as the two girls moved so swiftly, and with such ease.

"Come on!" Gilly yelled.

She grabbed Andi's hand, abandoning the attack for a moment as captain and gunner headed to join the other two members of their crew.

As they ran, more thoughts poured in.

*Complete this job, and you'll be pardoned from your death sentence. Arcardius will be open to you again. What will you do, then, with your crew?*

Opening herself up to each of the girls had been difficult. A captain needed a crew, loyal and true, but a crew had to trust their captain in return. It had been an uphill battle to let the girls enter her heart, especially after the pain of losing Kalee and then Dex. Andi was wary of becoming emotionally attached to anyone.

But her crew had won her over, and Andi couldn't beg the Godstars enough to keep them safe.

"I'm going back in," Gilly said.

She sprinted across the bridge and leaped onto Breck's back, where she placed her tiny hands over Breck's eyes to block out her vision.

"*Gilly!*" Breck yelled, and Lira stopped fighting long enough to give in to laughter again.

Andi stopped walking. She stood at the base of the bridge, watching them. Realizing, suddenly, that her heart physically *ached*.

She loved these girls. They were the strongest women she'd ever known, and all she had in this galaxy now. If anything ever happened to them… If she were ever faced with a decision like the one Dex had had to make, to trade a single *one* of them in exchange for the life of another…

Andi's vision blurred as she watched the girls laugh, all of them doubling over as if they hadn't a care in the world.

She could hardly see them now as she stood a few paces away on the bridge, and though she was still wet from her fall in the lake, she realized, as she felt warmth spill onto her cheeks, that she was *crying*.

Godstars.

What in the hell was happening to her?

Andi tried to swallow them away. But the tears, almost as if they were spurred on by her noticing them, began to fall harder. Faster, until she thought they would never run dry.

Until Andi realized that the girls had fallen silent.

"Andi?" Lira asked.

They all turned to face her on the bridge.

Andi heard footsteps, and then the girls were suddenly surrounding her, taking her by the arms and herding her away. Back down the bridge, past the edge of the great lake, into the shadows of the cavern. They settled down beneath an overhang of sharp rock.

The girls closed in tighter around her, waiting in silence until Andi's tears finally ceased.

The workers, now no longer disturbed by the queen's niece and her fighting friends, went back to what they were doing. A calmness washed over the cavern.

Finally Lira spoke. "You're afraid."

It wasn't a question, and Andi was grateful that she didn't actually have to answer. Gilly and Breck had always looked at her and assumed she was fearless, completely beyond the struggle of having to face such a petty, frail feeling.

To them, she was a captain. A breeder of fear.

But Lira saw the truth as plainly as they saw the view of the mountain lake stretching out before them.

"I want to apologize," Andi said. "To all of you, for getting us into this job." She turned to Lira. "And to you, for earlier, on the transport wagon. I know being here isn't exactly easy for you."

Lira shook her head. "I don't need an apology, Captain. I need you to speak your mind about what's bothering you."

"Do you want to hear about Dex or Valen first?"

None of the girls answered, as if they were all gently nudging Andi to make up her own mind.

"What Dex told me…" Andi started, unsure of where her words were leading. "I'm not sure if I can handle it."

"In what way?" Breck asked.

Andi's heart cringed as she considered what she was about to say. "All these years, thinking he was dead…it was easier that way. Easier to believe that he'd truly betrayed me because money was more important to him than love. But now that I know the truth? If it were any of you three held captive…if it were Kalee, and I had to offer up Dex to an enemy in exchange?" She realized, suddenly, that she was afraid of her own thoughts. "I'm not sure that I would have decided any differently than Dex did."

"The choice he had to make was unfair," Gilly said.

So simply put. And she was right.

Lira nodded and pulled her knees to her chest, wrapping her arms around them. "The pain he put you through was unfair, too. But life, I'm quite sure, never considers our feelings when it decides to take us down an unsteady road."

Andi stared at the lake, her eyes burning from the recent tears.

"I tried to kill him. What if I'd succeeded?"

"You didn't," Breck said. Her dark eyes met Andi's pale ones as she spoke. "And now you know his side of the story, and he knows yours. You both did terrible things, broke promises, ruined a mutual trust. You can hold on to your anger, if you think that makes you strong." She smiled a little then. "But brute strength isn't everything, Andi. Trust me, I would know."

"Breck is right," Lira agreed. "Anger and hatred have never given any man or woman lasting peace."

"So I just forgive him?" Andi asked. "Move on?"

"That is for your heart to decide," Lira said.

They all stopped talking for a while, lost in their individual thoughts. Gilly settled beside Andi and started combing her fingers through the drying strands of Andi's long hair. "Now we should probably talk about Valen," Gilly said, twisting Andi's hair into an elaborate braid. "Because we all know that's an entirely different issue than Dex."

Breck chuckled. "Yeah. It definitely is, Gil."

The girls turned their gazes to Andi.

She sighed. She was already spouting plenty of truths. She guessed it was time to unleash a little more, before her courage ran out.

"Valen will wake up again. When he sees me…if he tries to kill me…" Andi paused, swallowing hard. "I'm afraid I won't try to stop him."

Lira was silent as she pondered this. "Revenge is a powerful creature."

"So is guilt," Breck said.

"And shame," Lira added, looking down over the railing. "Shame is a monster I know all too well."

These things were a part of Andi now, as much as her blood, as much as her bones. Companions as constant as the crew that surrounded her now.

"You have many demons upon your back, Androma," Lira said. She reached out and placed a warm, soft hand on Andi's cheek. Andi relaxed beneath her touch, knowing that Lira had never, and would never, judge the things that any of the girls did. She saw beyond what they were, uncovered the motives beneath each and every one of the moves they made.

"I have never known someone, in all of my travels, who carries them with such persistence, who refuses to put them down when the burden grows too heavy to bear."

"Breck could probably carry a heavy burden," Gilly suggested suddenly.

Lira and Breck both laughed softly.

"Yes, she could. Which leads me to my point." Lira dropped her hand from Andi's cheek. But her eyes held Andi's knowingly. "You have a...loyal crew, Andi." She seemed to choke a bit on the word, as if it pained her. Then she shook her head slightly and carried on. "While we are here, together, in one piece...allow us to help you carry some of the weight."

"What if I can't?" Andi asked.

She stared out at the lake. She imagined that, outside, the sun was probably about to set, signaling the start of the Revalia Festival, a celebration that signified the end of The Cataclysm. The girls needed to go and get ready.

"That is a choice you must make yourself," Lira said. "We all have them. Some of us simply take a little longer deciding what to do."

"And you, Lira?" Andi asked. "Do you have a choice to make?"

"I have many," Lira said with a sigh.

"Do you want to talk about them?" Breck asked. "There's already a world of drama pressing in on us all right now. Why not add some more?"

Lira chuckled. "I'm afraid of what you all may have to say about it."

"Don't be," Gilly said. "We just saw Andi cry. We're definitely *not* going to judge you."

Andi laughed, then gently pulled away from Gilly as the little girl finished up her braid.

"You're my Second, Lir. I'll help you with whatever choice it is you have to make. And I know the gunners will, too."

All the girls nodded.

Lira closed her eyes.

For a moment, her scales glowed a gentle blue. A shade Andi had seen only a few times, when Lira thought no one was looking.

Sadness.

Deep, bone-touching sadness.

"Lir?" Andi asked softly. "You can tell us."

Across the cave, a heavy door burst open. Alfie suddenly appeared, his oval head swiveling back and forth as he searched the cave for the girls.

"We could hide," Gilly suggested. "We could stay in this cave forever."

Breck chuckled. "We'd miss out on Revalia, then, little one. We can't miss such a perfect chance to get dressed up."

With a nod of agreement, Gilly leaped to her feet and waved Alfie over.

The AI marched across the arching bridge over the lake to join the girls.

Though he couldn't show emotion, Andi felt as if his words were tense as he spoke.

"Apologies for interrupting you, Captain Racella," Alfie said. "But Mr. Valen Cortas is awake."

Andi's stomach sank to her toes.

"Dextro Arez went to greet him and escort him to our temporary living quarters upstairs."

The girls all stood, ready to follow Alfie back to their borrowed space.

"You should say a prayer to the Godstars, Cap," Gilly said as she skipped along beside Andi, heading back across the bridge and to the exit of the Well.

"A prayer for what?" Andi asked.

"That the two of you don't start The Second Cataclysm."

"Gilly!" Lira chided.

But Gilly was already gone, running ahead to catch up with Breck as they exited the giant stone doorway and turned into the narrow hall beyond.

Andi glanced once over her shoulder, back at the lake. Wondering if she really could find a place to hide away and forget about the world.

But she knew that was never an option. Captains—leaders—did not hide. They faced their problems head-on, accepting their fears and attacking them anyway.

"Fly true?" Lira suggested.

"Not the best statement right now, Lir," Andi said. She sighed. "What you were going to say before Alfie interrupted us?"

"Never mind that, Androma." Lira draped her arm across Andi's shoulders and guided her out into the hall. "It's not important."

Despite Lira's words, Andi still felt the warmth of her Second's scales, heating slowly into sadness as they joined the rest of the crew.

# CHAPTER 51
## ANDROMA

"WOULD YOU *STOP* PACING, BEFORE YOU WEAR a hole in this mountain?" Breck asked.

"I'm sorry," Andi said. "But we're on Adhira, on the eve of a peace festival. Of all the planets and times to have this conversation with Valen. It's like the Godstars are laughing at me."

This planet was a tranquil place. Queen Alara had her Sentinels, but no army. And certainly not trained soldiers-turned-killers like Andi.

Adhira had no weapons, no major issues with violence. During The Cataclysm, they were the last planet in the Unified Systems to join the fight, and perhaps only because Alara hoped to save her people from a fate similar to Xen Ptera's.

Andi's skin prickled at the thought of being here. She didn't belong on this planet, and never could.

She felt as if she was tainting the ground of this beautiful planet with every step she took.

This would be the first time Valen had really seen her in four years. The day he was rescued didn't count—she doubted he'd truly registered who she was before blacking out, much like earlier today.

It wasn't just Valen seeing her that unsettled Andi, but her seeing him. This time around, he wouldn't be bloody with scraps of clothing falling off his thin frame. He would be coherent, cleaned up so that he resembled the boy she'd shared an estate with, and she had no idea what to expect. A man who had been driven mad by his years of imprisonment? Or the brother of Kalee, finally facing his sister's killer?

She'd seen many Arcadians since her escape, but none who personally knew her past. Not only was Valen the first person she had seen who truly knew the *old* Andi—excluding General Cortas, of course—but he was also one of the people she'd hurt the most.

This was not going to be a happy reunion. Of that she was sure.

The guilt she felt toward the general wasn't the same as it was toward Valen. It was hard to explain; a feeling she couldn't quite pinpoint, almost as if she were a ship without a mapping system. Barreling endlessly toward some place she didn't truly know the route to. Perhaps it was because Valen had always been so pure and good, while General Cortas had a way of manipulating her guilt for his own gain.

She focused instead on the fact that tonight was supposed to be a celebration. Revalia would soon begin. It had been fifteen years since The Cataclysm came to an end, and today was a time for the Unified Systems to celebrate their victory.

Each individual planet celebrated in their own way. Adhira's

Revalia Festival was full of dancing and drinking, blissful oblivion and starry skies. Something Andi would have loved and longed for once. The Arcardian festivities weren't as lively—the militant planet chose to celebrate with banquets and strictly orchestrated parades rather than with a carefree nature.

Celebrating on Adhira should've excited her, but today, the idea of *celebrating* seemed false. To add to that, a few days from now, when they landed on Arcardius, the Intergalactic Summit would take place. The leaders from each of the four systems would be present to symbolize that peace still existed in the galaxy, and would continue to exist between the planets that made up the Unified Systems.

Andi hadn't taken part in the celebrations in years. If they hadn't landed here at such a time, she imagined she probably would have let another year go by unnoticed.

"Hey, Cap," Gilly said, drawing Andi back to the present.

She was sitting cross-legged on the floor, playing with a fuzzy orange ball. At first Andi thought it was some sort of strange fruit she'd picked up outside, but as she slowed her pacing, Andi saw that it had two large eyes and what seemed to be three horns protruding from its head.

"Gilly, what the hell is that?" Andi yelped.

"Not sure. I found it upstairs and thought it was cute," Gilly mused, eyes never leaving the thing in front of her. It batted at her with a paw nearly as large as its smushed face. Gilly giggled and scratched it on the head behind its protruding horns. "I like him."

"What if it's poisonous?"

"It's not."

"How do you know that?"

"Because the little bastard bit me," Breck interjected from her seat. She held up a finger wrapped in gauze. "And I'm not dead yet. I am, however, planning tens of thousands of ways to kill it."

"Don't listen to her, Havoc." Gilly scooped the fuzzball up and held it close.

"For the love of the stars, she's named the beast!" Breck howled.

"I find the name quite fitting, Breck," Lira added. "Every beast deserves a strong name."

"Allow me to assist," Alfie added, walking over on silent feet. "*Havoc* is defined, in the *Great Universal Dictionary*, as 'great destruction or devastation. Ruinous damage.'"

Breck held up her bandaged finger again as further evidence. *"See?"*

The furry beast snarled and pounced from Gilly's arms toward Breck's feet. Breck leaped across the table onto Lira, who turned on her with an array of curses, her scales flashing bright purple.

"Oh, dear," Alfie said, with a whirr of his gears that sounded like a sigh.

This was something Andi could deal with.

It was familiar, the soothing sound of their argument like music to her ears. She'd never been more thankful for a distraction.

Her relief didn't last long. A moment later, the door opened and in walked Dex and Valen. Two men from completely different parts of her life, neither of the relationships ending in the way she'd envisioned.

They were polar opposites—one from a life of privilege, strange but pure at heart, and the other from a world that demanded a warrior's determination. Seeing them side by side seemed so wrong.

Andi couldn't look Valen in the eyes. It was too personal. She worried that if she did, he would see the rot she harbored within. He had seen her at her best and watched her fall. She couldn't possibly fathom what he would think of her now.

The two men went to the plush chairs across from the couch.

Mustering up her courage, she followed them to the sitting area.

She allowed herself a glance at Valen. Beneath his green tunic she could see he was frail; a mere shell of what he'd once been. Instead of paint-stained fingers, she saw bruises. Instead of eyes alight with curiosity, she saw dark circles that swallowed them whole. He looked as if he wanted to curl into himself the way he had when she and Dex had found him in his cell in Lunamere.

What horrors had he lived through?

"Valen Cortas." Alfie shuffled over, stopping before Valen to bow deeply. "I am Alfie, personal Artificial Lifeform Intelligence Emissary to General Cyprian Cortas. It is my command to assist your father in returning his son home."

Valen inclined his head at Alfie. "My deepest apologies that you're programmed to work for my father."

Alfie's unblinking eyes stared at Valen. "I am detecting strong levels of distaste toward…"

"That'll be enough, Alfie," Dex interjected. "Why don't you go check on the ship repairs? Memory could probably use some company."

At the sound of Memory's name, Alfie's posture straightened. "I find my gears are warming at an alarming rate. Excuse me." He turned, seeming all too eager to spend some time alone with the ruined ship. His footsteps hastened as he left the living quarters. Andi wondered briefly if all AIs could feel emotion like Alfie did, or if it was purely some quirk of his programming.

"Alfie helped stabilize you when we got you out of Lunamere," Dex said, breaking the silence as he propped his boots up on the table. "Now that he's gone…how about we have a completely calm, completely adult conversation?"

He raised his dark brows at Andi.

It was an effort to force herself to speak.

Andi knew she didn't have a choice. Whether she liked it or not, she was the captain of this hellish mission. She'd allowed her pilot to fly her ship to the Olen System. And even if they weren't on the *Marauder*, it was still her game to play. Her move to make.

Valen had always been a gentle soul, but things could have changed. He'd been a prisoner to Lunamere, on enemy ground, tortured to the point of death. Now that he was awake, she had to make sure her crew was safe in his presence.

She couldn't believe she was about to do this. But they had to get him to talk.

She took a deep breath. "Hello, Valen."

# CHAPTER 52
## VALEN

AT THE SOUND OF HER VOICE, VALEN FROZE.

Everyone did, as if they were watching the single moment in time before an explosion rocked the world. He could feel more than hear the sound get sucked from the room, and suddenly the silence was more than he could bear.

Her eyes were locked on him. Burning a hole into his skin.

She was just as he remembered…and yet somehow different, all at once, and it wasn't just the metallic plates that shone from her cheekbones. It was something deeper. Her pale hair was braided back from her face, instead of the loose way she used to wear it. She'd added streaks of purple, a color that somehow brought out her eyes. Her skin was covered in cuts and bruises, but beneath it all, there was still that horrible, destructive beauty she'd always had.

She had been lethal then, and was something entirely more dangerous now.

While everyone else lounged on the plush seats, Androma stood. They all wore colorful, loose clothing, but she remained in a fitted bodysuit, reinforced in places with what looked like hardened armor.

She was the ice to her crew's warm demeanor.

And she was staring right at him, unafraid.

He stared back.

"Ten seconds," Dex said suddenly from Valen's left.

Every head swung to look at the bounty hounter.

"It gives me hope," Dex said, smiling sideways in a way that Valen took to be his trademark grin, "that Valen may not try to murder Androma as I had previously expected." He held a hand out to the giantess sitting across from him. "Pay up."

Andi's jaw dropped, and she swiveled to glare at the New Vedan. "You made a bet on this, Breck?"

The young woman, who Valen assumed was Breck, looked down at her toes and grinned sheepishly. "Sorry, Andi. You know I can't resist a good wager." She reached into her pocket, pulled out a few golden Krevs and slapped them into Dex's waiting hand.

"I'm beginning to think you two are becoming friends," Andi said.

Breck's cheeks reddened.

Dex chuckled as he pocketed his new Krevs.

A moment passed in awkward silence before Dex turned back to Valen.

He guessed it was his turn to be the show now.

"So, my newly freed friend," Dex said, "it's time for you to talk. What did they do to you in there?"

"Dex!" Andi hissed. She turned to Valen, her jaw working slightly back and forth. "What Dextro means is…"

"Why are *you* here?" Valen blurted out.

She paused midsentence, her mouth half open, her gray eyes suddenly wide.

For a strange moment, Valen almost thought she'd turn and run.

But that didn't seem like the Androma he once knew, a Spectre who'd guarded his sister without fear, and certainly not like the young woman who'd rescued him from Lunamere. He still didn't know how many guards she and Dex had dispatched in order to set him free or how they'd even made it inside in the first place.

"Your father hired me and my crew," Andi explained matter-of-factly.

"I know that. Dex told me on the way over here," Valen said, closing his eyes and shaking his head, still shocked that he'd opened up a line of communication with this…murderess. "What I want to know, Androma, is why *you*?"

She stared at him.

Her crew stared at them both.

The little girl's strange creature purred from her lap, the only rescue from the world's most uncomfortable silence. But Valen refused to break it until Andi answered him.

She owed him this much, even if she had already saved his life.

"It's been a long time since we've seen each other," Andi finally said. She spoke to him gently, as if he were a child who might burst into an angry fit. It made his insides roil. "Things have changed since then." She took another deep breath. "*I* have changed."

Back when Valen had known her, she hadn't just been a trained shadow who was meant to protect Kalee and failed. She'd also been a dancer who moved like the music was part of her soul. She'd laughed so hard her voice could be heard throughout the halls of Averia. She'd been alive. Now she was a young woman with scars on her arms and fire burning in her eyes. She looked like she hadn't stopped running since she'd escaped Arcardius.

"You're a killer, Andi," Valen said. He had to say it. For himself. For Kalee. "As far as I can tell, you haven't changed a bit."

He expected her to cringe, but she took it like someone who was used to taking hits.

"What happened was a mistake," Andi said. This time her voice was raw. "What happened was..."

"Why did my father choose you to rescue me? With all the decorated soldiers in the galaxy..." Valen inclined his head toward Dex, who bore the marks of a Tenebran Guardian. "He picked a traitor. A runaway. With all the other options he has available to him on Arcardius, why would he choose his daughter's murderer to be his son's savior?"

There it was. Out in the open like a bleeding wound.

"Because," Andi said, her voice bordering on cold, calculating fury, "I'm the best one for the job. And because your father, as I fully expected him to do, threatened to throw me and my crew into prison if I didn't agree to the mission. We are the expendable ones in this galaxy—a part of it, but not. He could risk us getting caught."

That was the truth, Valen knew without question.

"As you should have been in the first place," he snapped. "And worse."

Dex's jaw tensed. The young Adhiran woman placed a hand on the Tenebran's arm, as if holding him back. Or maybe, judging by the expression on her face, she was holding herself back, too.

Valen glanced away in disbelief.

He remembered the results of Andi's trial. Death. She'd been in holding for several days, ready for her sentence to be delivered. And then somehow, against all odds, she'd escaped, fading into the night like smoke on the wind.

"It was a mistake," Andi said again. "If I could take it back—"

Valen gritted his teeth. "Murder isn't a mistake."

"If I recall, you were the one who allowed your little sister and her friend to sneak out for a joyride on your father's brand-new transport," Andi replied. Her words were soft and casual, but her eyes were on fire.

"Spectre," Valen said. "Spectre first, and always. You failed her as that."

"Again," Andi said, "it was a mistake. I've had to live with the cost of it."

"Kalee didn't!" Valen screamed. "She didn't get to live, Androma!"

The world spun around him. He sucked in a breath, intent on staying in control. He would not lose this fight.

She crossed her arms over her chest. Her face was impassive. Infuriating. "What I want to know, Valen, is how the hell you were taken from Arcardius in the first place. The boundary is well protected. Your father's Spectres work around the clock, and then some. Yet he said you disappeared without a trace."

"Are you accusing me of something, Androma?"

She simply stared at him, fierce as a lioness.

"I was out walking in the gardens. After Kalee was killed, things were a little tense at the estate, as I'm sure you can imagine."

She flinched at his words.

"What happened next?" Dex asked, leaning forward, hands resting on his knees. Drawing Valen's attention away from Andi. "It's important for us to know, Valen, so we can prevent it from happening again. So we can keep the families of the other system leaders safe."

Valen swallowed hard, recalling the events of that night.

"A group of masked men came from the trees. I tried to run, but they surrounded me. I called out for help, but nobody was around to listen. And then they shot me with something," he said, pulling down his tunic to reveal a circular scar just above his collarbone. "The next thing I knew, I was lying in a transport ship, bound in chains."

He could still remember the fear that had spiked through him in that waking moment. The questions that had no answers until far later.

"We landed on Lunamere sometime later. I got one glimpse of the outside before they took us in. Then I was knocked out again. I woke up with my head shaved, my clothes gone and my cheek pressed to the stones in my cell."

*Frozen to the stones*, he thought to himself, *by tears I didn't remember crying.*

"I was no longer a name," Valen continued. The anger had suddenly left his voice, replaced instead by a solemn whisper that made his throat ache. "I was a number. Cell 306. I don't know if minutes or hours or days passed before they came into my cell. And...then it all started."

He realized he'd sunk back down onto the couch beside Dex. That he was shivering, despite the warmth of the room. That he was feeling the threat of darkness looming over him, despite the bright beam of moonlight pouring in through the open curtains.

"What started?" Dex asked. "You're safe here, Valen. You can talk to us."

But he wasn't. Not with Andi here.

She was looking at him like she used to. Like he was a question she couldn't answer.

He looked down at his hands as they clutched his knees. He'd grown so thin. He hadn't fully realized it until he looked at himself in the mirror today. He'd barely recognized the ghost staring back.

"The beatings," Valen said. The wounds on his back seemed to squirm in response to his words. "They started slow at first. For every question I didn't answer, I got a single lash of the whip across my back."

"What kind of questions?" Dex asked.

Valen sighed. "About my father, mostly. What he did each day, what his schedule was like. Who he spoke to, who came and went from our estate. At first I didn't answer. I was afraid what they'd do if I did."

"But eventually…" Dex helped guide him along.

"You have to understand," Valen said, now looking up. "They knew when I was lying. Maybe they had some sort of system, or perhaps it was just from years of torturing people for answers. They've turned pain into an art form. I had to tell them."

"About what?" Dex pressed.

"I…" Valen paused, growing frustrated as he remembered the interrogations. "None of it made any sense."

"Can you elaborate? Can you give us any information you may have come across about Queen Nor?"

Valen felt the change in his chest.

Like something suddenly broke, or slipped loose.

He felt the *rage* unlock inside him. And this time, he didn't try to control it.

He simply got up and left the group behind as quickly as he could.

# CHAPTER 53
## ANDROMA

AFTER VALEN'S ABRUPT DEPARTURE FROM THEIR quarters, Andi left her crew to prepare for Revalia while she tracked him down. She knew that being alone with him might not be the best idea, but she had to find him. Make sure he was safe.

He wasn't in his room. She'd scoured Alara's fortress, determined to find him. Everywhere she looked, from the many scattered balconies to the mountaintop temple to the steaming, fragrant kitchens deep in the bedrock, she was met with wide-eyed workers with no recollection of seeing Valen.

Even a little rusting sweeper droid, its arms replaced with dusty brooms, had simply turned away when she'd asked it about Valen, wheels squeaking as it disappeared around a corner.

"Thanks for the help," Andi muttered.

Valen was gone, disappeared without a trace.

Andi's worries intensified.

It wasn't that she cared about *him*, specifically. Clearly, he didn't care a bit for the likes of her. It was that she knew, beyond a shadow of a doubt, that if the general got word she'd lost his son, he'd have her head.

And every member of her crew's, as well.

Valen was a prize worth thousands of Krevs, a lifetime of freedom from the law and all the mistakes she'd made as a Spectre.

Fuming, Andi stomped her way down the twisting, narrow halls in the carved-out mountain, heading downward to the ground-level exit.

She quickly patched in a message to the girls' channels.

*Going outside. Still haven't found him. Might need your help looking.*

Gilly's response was instantaneous.

*Havoc + Me. On it.*

"She's not bringing that damned fuzzball on my ship," Andi muttered under her breath as she blinked the message away and slipped outside, walking past two Sentinels stationed by the massive wooden exit doors.

Adhira had taken on an entirely new shape in the darkness.

She walked down the hillside, her boots leaving rocky mountain terrain behind, suddenly landing on the lush edges of Aramaeia.

The terraformed quadrant was so odd. So beautiful. Massive tree trunks as large as buildings stood like sentries around her. The farther she walked, the more the undergrowth began to take over the ground—strange, fernlike plants with jagged leaves, green melding into purple ends that gently swept across her calves.

Andi looked up, craning her neck to see into the canopy. It was magnificent tonight, the sky like a painted ceiling, the wink of distant planets and moons glowing in otherworldly shades through the darkness. Every so often, a blazing ball of fire shot past overhead—a meteor, falling through the sky. The air was comfortably cool, enough to fill her chest with a spark of life, and when the wind blew, the leaves on the trees seemed to whisper overhead, then tumbled down like a colorful rain, twisting and dancing as they neared the ground.

Andi felt herself relaxing as another meteor shimmered past and faded behind the treetops.

It was the perfect view for a painter, were it not blocked by leaves the size of her head. At that thought, a hunch tugged at Andi's mind.

Valen would be somewhere with a full, unobstructed view of this. Somewhere that made him feel closer to who he used to be. Somewhere that made him feel closer to Kalee.

At the thought of her old friend and charge, a little pang snipped at Andi's gut.

Footsteps sounded behind her, and Andi whirled, reaching for her swords.

Lira's twin brother stood there, bare chested and beautiful. His blue eyes locked on hers.

"Exploring?" Lon asked. "The rainforest is dangerous after the sun goes down."

Andi lowered her arms and crossed them over her chest, her cuffs cool on her skin. "I'm not worried."

Lon looked so much like Lira that Andi felt herself staring. "You may be a skilled fighter in the skies, but this is Adhira."

Andi sighed. "So you're here to escort me back to the mountain?"

Lon shifted on his bare feet. Another thing he shared with Lira—a hatred for the confinement of boots. "I'm actually here to help you. I saw where he went."

"Yeah?" Andi ran her fingertips across a fern leaf. It shivered and curled inward, away from her touch, as if it were sentient. "Nobody else saw him pass by. It's like no one pays attention around here. They go about their lives, gliding about, smiling like everything is always okay."

"Maybe you should spend a little more time on Adhira," Lon said. Then he chuckled when Andi scowled at him. "I see where Lira learned that expression."

"She's learned a lot of things on my ship."

"Like how to lose control of her emotions and nearly die while crash-landing a glass starship?" Lon asked. His words weren't acidic. They simply...were.

"It's varillium," Andi said. "Something you would know if you took any interest in Lira's passions." She sighed. "I don't have time to argue about Lira. If you would excuse me, I have a general's lost son to recover."

She turned, heading into the sea of ferns without a word, happy to leave him behind.

But Lon was soon at her side again, silent on his feet as he said, "Not that way. Follow me."

He headed off into the darkness, and Andi followed reluctantly, yet she was also grateful to have a guide—even if he did seem to have a grudge against Andi and the girls.

"There's something strange about him," Lon said as he held aside a massive, spiked plant so Andi could pass unscathed. Behind it, a trampled path led deeper into the trees. "Something I don't quite like. Especially since he's been on a ship with my sister."

"Lira is capable of defending herself," Andi said. "She loves what she does, you know. And we love her, too. We're a family, all of us on the *Marauder.*"

"*Family?*" Lon asked, a bit of heat creeping into his voice. "Has she spoken to you about what her *real* family...what my aunt...has planned for her?"

"No one plans anything for Lira," Andi said. "You and Alara shouldn't, either."

Lon sighed. "So she hasn't told you, then."

For an Adhiran, he sure was making a valiant effort at getting under her skin. "She'll speak to me about it when she's ready."

"And if you don't like what she has to tell you?" He pointed a long finger ahead. "Take a left here."

They followed a fork in the path, heading deeper into the rainforest.

Andi mulled this over in her mind. "What is that supposed to mean?"

"I'm not here to anger you, Androma." Lon said, stepping over a small stream that ran through the path. "I'm simply making sure that when my sister speaks to you about her conversation with my aunt, you'll help Lira see what is best for her."

Andi stiffened. Whatever Lira had debated sharing with the girls earlier, it was deep. Enough to make her pilot sad in a way Andi had never seen. Enough to make her hide her words, when Andi had offered her a chance to share them openly.

Was she going to leave the crew?

*No.*

Andi refused to think it. Lira would never leave the Marauders. Especially not now.

"Whatever it is that you're getting at, Lon," Andi said, stopping to face him, "I hope you know that I love Lira as if she were my sister. Whatever she has to tell me, I will listen with an open mind and heart."

"And you will not try to sway her decision?"

Andi laughed at that. "No one sways Lirana Mette."

He smiled at that, a look that again reminded Andi so much of her Second.

"She's a great pilot," Andi said. "She loves her life, up there in the stars."

Lon nodded. "That's what I'm afraid of." He stared ahead at the path as it curved again. "Go a bit farther. Valen is up ahead, at the stream."

"Thank you."

"I will be here waiting, should you need assistance." He lifted a shoulder in a half shrug. "Lira's orders."

"Of course."

Andi walked down the path that soon opened wide, revealing a clearing with a stream running through it, moonflowers blooming in the darkness, some of them glowing as if made of strands of sunlight.

In the distance, Andi could hear the faint string music of a *sumdrel* floating in the wind from a nearby village. Revalia was already beginning, the start of a wild, carefree night.

Andi scanned the clearing, eyes finally settling on a figure who sat alone on a large rock by the water. She practically slumped to the ground with relief.

From here, he looked peaceful, as if he hadn't a care in all the world.

He sat with his head bowed, his skin aglow from the flowers and a steady beam of moonlight that lit the water nearby. He was drawing something in the wet mud on the bank of the stream, his hands moving effortlessly as if the stick were a paintbrush, the mud a fresh canvas. Andi approached slowly, hoping for a glimpse of his art. But she didn't get to see what it was before he turned at the sound of her footsteps. His face was unreadable.

"Andi," he said softly. "How did you find me?"

She took another step forward, approaching him slowly. Half of her wanted him to keep spouting painful words, tearing at the scabs on her heart until they ripped open, and the truth of the past bled out.

The other half was relieved that he now seemed so much calmer in her presence.

"A Sentinel saw you leave," she said. "Thought I'd check in to see if you were alright." She paused, waiting for a response he didn't give. "We need to head back to Rhymore."

She started to turn, but he stopped her.

"No, wait." His voice sounded pained, but then he swallowed

and nodded. "I...need a few more minutes. It's been a while since I've seen the outside."

In all the years they'd known each other, this was perhaps the only time they'd ever been alone. Andi was acutely aware of that as she slowly walked forward and settled down next to him, a full arm's length away.

They sat in silence. The stream burbled cheerfully. Every few seconds, Andi heard the telltale *swish* of a tail flicking out of the water.

She remembered, with a sad smile, the times she'd tried to catch fish with her bare hands on Uulveca. How hopeless she'd felt, ten times larger and stronger than any animal beneath the surface, yet still incapable of catching one to feed herself with.

If Dex hadn't given her a meal, she might not be alive today.

Valen shifted beside her, his clothing rustling, and she got a whiff of his scent. Not *fresh paint*, like she remembered, but not the rotten smell he'd had on Lunamere, either.

It was fresh and cool, like the air around them, like the strangely comfortable silence they shared.

Who was going to speak first? She couldn't imagine it would be her, because what would she say?

*I'm sorry I killed your sister.*

She noticed in her peripheral vision that Valen was drawing in the mud again. Peering over, she finally got a good look at what he was sketching. It was a woman, a crown atop her head and hair swaying in the phantom wind.

"Who is she?" Andi asked.

"No one."

His voice was bored as he said it. And yet his eyes, so much more haunted than the eyes Andi remembered, did not look away from the image in the mud.

The silence swept over them again. Andi tried to find a middle ground between the two of them. A safe topic to discuss. She knew he must hate her, but found herself desperately wanting to mend this bridge between them—and hoping he wouldn't try to jab that stick in her heart.

"I remember your paintings," she offered. "Your mother used to hang them up all over the estate. My favorite was the one you painted of the waterfall falling off the gravarocks." She could still picture the unique hues of green, blue and yellow he'd used. The gravarocks were Arcardius's most unique feature—large mounds of earth floating in thin air, as if they'd been magicked to stay aloft. Valen had managed to capture their beauty in a whole new way, making them even more captivating than they already were. "You were always so talented with art."

"When I was locked up, I almost forgot what colors looked like," he said, lazily brushing the stick back and forth against the mud. "Did you know that black is more than just a single shade?"

He turned and raised a brow at her, his eyes full of a meaning that Andi couldn't interpret.

She shrugged. "It all looks the same to me."

Valen leaned back onto his elbows, peering up at the night sky. "There's a million colors up there. A million shades all mixed together. When you look at the world in more than just black-and-white, you begin to notice them." He sighed and shook his head. "In Lunamere…I lost even that ability."

She didn't know what to say, worried she might set him off if she dug too deep.

"I hated you for a very long time," he said.

There it was.

That pang of guilt again in her gut, and with it, the sick satisfaction that she was finally getting what she deserved. She'd heard these words from General Cortas and his wife, but never from Valen.

After the accident, he'd never shown himself to her again.

"You took away the most beautiful thing in my life," Valen whispered. "Kalee was the only person in my life who was *true*." He swallowed hard, as if he had bits of broken glass in his throat. "I know that we have a bad past, Androma. There are things you did, choices you made, that I'm not sure I can ever forgive you for."

"I don't expect you to," she said.

He closed his eyes and breathed deep. "But I can never forgive myself, either, for being a part of those choices."

Andi kept her face calm, her body motionless, too afraid to reveal the shock she felt racing through her at his words. Her earlier accusation must have struck him deeply for Valen to say such things.

She wanted to look into his eyes, to see her own pain mirrored there. Instead, she stared up at the starlit sky, waiting for him to continue.

Valen shifted beside her again. "I could have stopped you that night. I *should* have stopped you. But instead, I stood there frozen, watching the two of you walk up that staircase without me. I blamed you, for the longest time, for killing her."

Another stab of pain in Andi's heart.

Stupid, foolish, feeling thing. She wanted to tear it from her chest.

"In Lunamere, I had nothing to keep me company but my pain and my thoughts. I had lots of time to think about that night, and everything leading up to it. Time to realize that we were raised in a society where perfection is the only option. But that doesn't mean it's always possible. We all made bad choices that night, not just you. *She* got on that transport herself. And I chose to stay behind."

Andi wanted to speak, but she feared it would shatter this strange, heart-wrenching moment they had somehow found themselves in.

"What I'm trying to say is, I've held on to my hatred of you for too long. And while I can't ever truly forget what you did...I know that you didn't do it alone. We all had a hand in

SASHA ALSBERG & LINDSAY CUMMINGS

that night." His shoulders bowed as he said the next words. "Even Kalee."

She had never been sure if the Godstars were truly real. But right now, in this moment, she could almost feel their presence. A soft, calming sense that replaced the dread that had weighed her down since they'd rescued Valen.

"I'm sorry," Andi whispered. That horrible, hellish pain in her chest returned, bubbling up into her throat. She swallowed it down, forced herself to stay in control. "I knew I shouldn't take her. Several times I felt this little whisper telling me not to do it. But she was so insistent. I just wanted to make her *happy* on her birthday. Did you know your father hardly spoke to her that entire day?"

Valen huffed out a breath. "My father," he said bitterly.

"But that night? Everything was perfect. We were having so much fun, and Kalee was laughing, and it was the most beautiful evening, Valen. The stars were practically alive. And then the wind picked up and I just...lost control."

She could still remember the empty sky before her.

Then the lurching of the transport. The crash as the wing clipped the mountainside. The tumble down to the ground.

"I wish I had died with her," Andi confessed.

"I wish I had died, too," Valen said.

She nodded, staring out at the moonflowers, marveling at how they looked like little delicate flames, dancing in the wind.

"Without Kalee..." Andi began, finally voicing the realization she'd come to terms with these past few days. "Without Kalee, there wouldn't have been a sentence for me to run from. And without that running, I never would have found Dex. And without him..."

"You wouldn't be the Bloody Baroness," Valen finished for her. "My father would not have hired you."

It was a vicious cycle, one that Andi wished she could have undone before it had ever started. But it was her story. Her life.

And it was her burden to bear.

"I'm sorry," she said again. "Truly sorry, Valen."

*For everything*, she thought. *Even me.*

He didn't respond. But the expression on his face was a little lighter, the tension in his shoulders a little less.

"We'll leave as soon as the ship is repaired," Andi said. "Then you'll be home."

"Home?" He said it like a question. He must have felt like this was a dream, that the two of them had been stuck in a nightmare for the past four years.

A breeze drifted through the trees, and with it, the faint sound of music.

"Do you want to go to the festival?" Andi asked hesitantly.

Valen, after a moment, nodded his head. "I think I'd like that."

They stood and walked a few paces apart toward the rainforest's edge.

Andi peered back up at the night sky.

The darkness seemed a little lighter now. As if it wasn't entirely black after all.

# CHAPTER 54
## LIRA

LIRA STOOD AT THE BASE OF RHYMORE, THE cool kiss of the night air slowly dancing around her.

She'd always loved Adhiran nights, the peace that came with each flicker of the stars far beyond the mountaintop. She closed her eyes and leaned her head back against the mountainside, relieved as Andi sent her and the girls a com.

*Found him. See you at Revalia.*

Lon had helped her find him, then. Good. The two Arcardians could talk more, wade through their tangled webs and hopefully enjoy the festival tonight.

*Revalia,* Lira thought, still in awe that they were here on

Adhira at the same time as the festival. Though it looked as if she was going to be late to the festivities.

Even on board the *Marauder*, with its limited supplies, Breck and Gilly took ages to prepare for social events. But here, with an entire planet full of beauty supplies they could get their hands on?

*Your silent pacing will be our demise,* Gilly had hissed at Lira back in the girls' temporary quarters, right after she'd thrown a moss pillow at Lira's face. *You heard the kid,* Breck had said as she winked apologetically, slapped Lira's behind and shoved her out of the room.

Lira herself had left the mountain fortress in a simple sand-shaded dress and with a pair of twisting sandals on her feet. Now she was fairly certain that she'd be waiting here for her friends forever.

But that was fine with her.

She couldn't help but smile as she watched the continuous flow of people exiting Rhymore. Each year, Revalia took place in a different quadrant of the planet, the attire changing to suit the location.

Tonight, it would be in the Sands of Bailet. Already, massive cargo wagons, pulled by Albatusks with their many curling and hissing tongues, were carting citizens from Rhymore toward Bailet.

In the moonlight overhead, Lira could see the winged outlines of creatures from the rainforest taking their riders toward the desert. She could hear the distant, tolling whine of Sky Whales, soaring from the Endless Sea with hundreds on their backs.

"I thought you weren't one for parties."

Lira glanced sideways as a warm arm sidled up against hers, and with it a familiar musky scent that reminded her of the mountain tunnels.

"And I thought you were supposed to be guarding Andi," Lira said to her brother.

SASHA ALSBERG & LINDSAY CUMMINGS

"She's fine out there. I have a feeling whatever creatures may come her way would be afraid of her." Lon grinned and crossed his arms. Though he wore a pair of loose black pants, the rest of him was bare. Muscles and a sculpted chest were out in full view of the people who passed by in their festival attire, some whispering or giggling to each other as they tried to catch Lon's eye. "And besides, every princess needs an escort to the ball. I figured, who better than your trustworthy, protective brother?"

Lira gave him a glare worthy of Andi. "I'm not a princess."

"Technically, you are," Lon said.

Lira rolled her eyes. "And this isn't a ball." She shoved away from the mountainside as two familiar forms finally came through the exit doors. Breck and Gilly, at last ready to take on the night, and fully decked out in Adhira's best gowns. Lira turned back to her twin. "And even if it were a ball, who says I'd want to attend on my brother's arm?"

"Come on, little bug," Lon said in a wheedling tone. "I know you're desperate to perform the dance we learned for our Efflorescence Ceremony. If I remember correctly, those feet of yours could stomp for days."

She laughed, recalling the countless hours of lessons. The horror of having to stand in public, before hundreds of eyes, and perform. With her brother, of all people. How Andi used to dance for *fun*, Lira would never understand.

It was the torture of all tortures.

A roar sounded in the night, followed by a series of hisses, as another transport wagon arrived, massive, towering wooden wheels squeaking as the Albatusk came to a stop.

"That's our ride," Lon said. "Magnificent night, isn't it?"

Lira wasn't listening.

She had turned back to watch Breck and Gilly emerge from the mountainside, looking so *alive*. Their faces were luminous with smiles and laughter. Gilly's hair was elegantly braided on top of her head. Breck's handiwork, no doubt. And Breck's eyes, the lids painted to look like a desert sunset, were completely mesmerizing.

Revalia was a night for celebration. A time to lose oneself in the joy that came from being on a planet dedicated to harmonious peace.

Lira was home. Her brother was at her side. Her aunt had forgiven her, more or less, for the crash landing. She should feel as light as the wind that tickled her cheeks and tugged at her loose tan gown.

She should feel as jubilant as everyone else around her.

But as Lira looked at Breck and Gilly racing toward her and thought of Andi finally facing her demons when she'd confronted Valen and when spilled her thoughts to the girls about Dex...

Her heart fractured a little more.

All she could think of was the image of the starship with her name above it, the promise that she could stay here and live a life where she was always meant to be.

"Lir?" Lon asked. He pointed toward the transport, which was nearly full as everyone piled on. "Time to go."

Lira nodded.

She tucked her arm into her brother's, then reached out the other to take Breck's hand as she and Gilly finally made it to them.

"Ladies," Lon said, smiling at Breck and Gilly. "The desert awaits us."

Together, the four of them walked to the transport, joining the crowd. Lon talked to Breck and Gilly, explaining how the festival would go, telling them how lucky they were to be here on Adhira's most exuberant night.

All the while, even as they climbed onto the transport, even as the wheels began to move, as the pathway toward the Sands of Bailet opened wide and Lira could see, far down the hillside,

SASHA ALSBERG & LINDSAY CUMMINGS

the expanse of glittering red sand pocked with dancers already twirling in the firelight…

All the while, her heart whispered, *You can't have two families.* Her mind hissed, *You can't have two lives.*

She didn't know which she should choose.

Her own flesh and blood or the heart-deep bonds she'd formed with these girls over the past three years.

The clock was ticking, moving toward a decision. If she rejected Alara's offer…it would never come again.

"It's time to let loose," Breck said. "Lir, you look like you've just puked up a pound of Moon Chew."

"Lira doesn't puke," Gilly said.

"That's ridiculous. Everyone pukes," Breck added.

"I've never seen her do it. And I spy on her, like, *all* the time."

Lon chuckled beside Lira. "I see it," he whispered. "What draws you to this crew." He lowered his voice even more. "Whatever you decide, Lira…I will still love you."

An explosion rocked the night. A trail of fire spread into the sky, illuminating it bright pink. Sparkling like a falling star.

"I do so love explosives," Gilly sighed, staring up as the rest of the show began.

Lira smiled, rolled back her shoulders and shoved the choice she had to make down deep.

She wouldn't decide tonight.

Tomorrow, perhaps. She'd sit down with Andi and the girls, tell them what she'd been hiding.

For now, she settled into the warmth of her brother on one side, Breck and Gilly on the other, and let the glittering sky call her forth into the promise of a perfect, thoughtless night.

# CHAPTER 55
## DEX

IF EVER THERE WAS A TIME FOR DEXTRO AREZ to drink his way into blissful oblivion, it was now.

As he climbed down from the transport wagon, his boots landed on soft desert sand. He felt his face break into a grin that stretched from ear to ear.

The Sands of Bailet.

Dex had been here before, shortly after he'd first met Andi. It was one of the first places they had traveled together. She'd helped him track down a target for Raiseth, his former boss and leader of the Bounty Hunters' branch. They'd marveled at this planet's beauty and, later that night, celebrated their victory by drinking and dancing in a small village bar until morning.

Spread across the Sands of Bailet were towering, spiral mounds of red rock, each large enough to house hundreds of citizens.

Tonight, the giamounds had been transformed. Glowing Adhiran spirals were painted on their sides, and some had flags staked to the rock, waving in the wind.

Hundreds of people twirled beneath them on the sand, their loose clothing dancing in the wind as their bodies moved in time with the music. The beat was alive in the firelight, hundreds of hands clapping at once whenever the stringed instruments rose to a sweet, piercing high note.

On the edges of the festival, booths had been set up, and shopkeepers called out their wares to passersby. Colorful garb hung from the booths, fluttering in the wind. A flock of pure white birds soared from a cage, exploding into the sky as the crowd cheered below.

Dex almost tripped over his boots as a pillar of orange flame suddenly spiraled high into the sky before him, then arced back down, where it disappeared into the waiting mouth of a fire-breather from the Endless Sea, the green gills on her neck glowing as the fire shot out of the slits.

*She must have a hell of a time fire-breathing underwater*, Dex thought sarcastically.

Beside her a little round droid rolled around on the sand, collecting Krevs from outstretched hands, depositing them into a waiting seashell the size of Dex's head.

Dex passed a star-reader, her stand draped in holographic sheets and wind chimes, their music mingling with the sounds of the festival.

As he got closer to the center of the crowd, Dex could smell the mouthwatering scent of freshly cooked meat, likely coming from a booth where orange smoke trailed high into the sky. The shopkeeper, an Uulvecan man with four arms, quickly flipped slabs of meat into the air and slapped them back down onto a fiery table. A long line of patrons stood waiting, some with thick mugs of the sweet Jurum that swept its drinkers up into a warm, bubbling embrace.

*That*, Dex thought, *is exactly what I'm after.*

He looked back over his shoulder to where Andi's crew was making their way down from the top of the hill. Breck looked like a wonder in her gown. Gilly walked beside her in a dress of glittering purple that made her red braids shine bright as moon lava. She was already twirling in time with the music.

Thank the Godstars she'd left her furry horned demon behind in the mountain fortress with Alfie.

Then there was the pilot. Her face was alight with a serene smile as she led the pack, walking as if she hadn't a care in the world. Lira's twin brother glided along beside her, his muscular chest bared to the desert.

For a moment, as Dex looked at them, he caught himself thinking, *There's my crew.*

Though he hadn't set out to, he'd bonded with the Marauders. Their personalities were magnetic. They each shone brightly in their own ways, and the thought of leaving them behind once this was all over suddenly saddened him.

He looked back up the hillside just in time to see two figures crest the horizon.

Dex actually stopped walking at the sight of them.

Valen didn't look quite so off-putting as he had before. He was still atrophied and greasy, Dex noted, but there was a smile on his face. He looked more alive, transformed since Dex had last seen him shattering Andi's heart back in their living quarters.

He was too moody. Too strange. Dex reminded himself to keep a closer eye on him.

But it was Andi who really caught Dex's attention.

For one moment he saw her as the girl she used to be, standing on a hillside, staring out at the world below—not as if she wanted to burn it to a pile of ashes, but rather run down into it and celebrate everything life had to offer.

Gone was her scowl, and with it the tight braid that made her look like she didn't have room to smile even if she'd wanted to. Instead, her hair fluttered in the wind like silvery-purple ribbons, and though she still had on her tight black clothing, it showed off her curves in the moonlight.

Dex couldn't help it. His body warmed, and suddenly he was imagining all the times they'd danced together in the past, the feel of her smooth skin beneath his hands, the heated words she'd whispered that sent shocks of electricity running through his every nerve. The press of her lips to his…

"Godstars," Dex said to himself.

These were thoughts that he had to shove deep down until they withered and died, just like his feelings for her. He had no right even *thinking* such things.

Dex allowed himself one last glance at Andi and Valen, wondering about the moments they might have shared together in the darkness. He'd assumed, as everyone had, that the chasm between them could never close.

But not for the first time since the start of the mission…Dex was surprised to find that he'd been wrong.

He sighed and turned on his heel, his mouth watering for a taste of sweet, liquid freedom that would whisk him away.

Revalia had finally started.

Now it was time for Dex to have a little bit of fun.

# CHAPTER 56
## ANDROMA

SOMETHING ABOUT THE NIGHT HAD CHANGED.

Andi's feet felt lighter as she and Valen made their way toward the festival. It had been so long since she had last danced. *Actually danced*, not just imagined dancing with the dead during her times of remembrance. With the apology between her and Valen set free, it was time to allow herself some freedom. To let go and not be the Bloody Baroness for one night—just a girl who stared up at the stars instead of captaining a pirate ship through them.

Andi knew it was impossible to change things, to shed who she had become in the years past. But for right now, she didn't mind pretending she was someone she could never be.

Tonight she would drink and dance to her heart's content, toss herself into a blissful oblivion and sink back into reality once Revalia was over. After all, it was the festival of victory against the Xen Pterran forces, and in a way, the crew deserved to celebrate their successful mission of freeing Valen from Queen Nor's clutches.

Valen was safe, they were all alive and relatively well, and Alfie was probably still pining over Memory, deep in the belly of Rhymore. It was an added gift, seemingly from the Godstars above, that he wasn't present.

As Andi reached the bottom of the hill, the crowd before her undulated, then parted like a tossing sea. She spotted her crew disappearing into the wave of vendors and music. At the back was Gilly, dancing on her toes as she followed Breck. Lira led them, a smile lighting her features as she spoke to her twin brother, Lon.

Where was Dex?

Andi found herself searching for him, hoping she'd catch a glimpse of him in the crowd. They'd danced together on Adhira once before, in a drunken night that had left them both with plenty of hazy memories the next morning. She smiled, thinking of the memory. The laughter. The way their bodies had so perfectly intertwined…

*Stop*, she told herself. A part of her wanted to find Dex. To speak to him, and be near him. But she knew she shouldn't be searching for Dex, and she certainly shouldn't be thinking about him. He only complicated things. The two of them together were like Griss and Rigna. They just didn't mix well.

Tonight was about forgetting Dex, and everything else from her past.

And besides…Andi couldn't remember the last time she and her crew had had an outing this alive. The Marauders always worked under cover of darkness, hiding in the deepest parts of shadows so as not to be seen. Today, they'd be a part of the world, and celebrate beneath the stars.

She turned to Valen. "Ready?"

For a moment, she wondered if he'd be able to handle the crowds, the noise, the press of bodies against each other on all sides. His eyes were darting over the scene with stunned excitement, as if he couldn't take it all in and wasn't sure if he really wanted to.

"I'm not sure how to—" he nodded slowly, as if walking himself through his own words "—how to do this."

Andi stepped aside as a group of children sprinted between them, laughing and chasing a creature that looked similar to Gilly's bloodthirsty little beast. "Well…we've attended plenty of military balls before," she said. "It's just like that. Only better, because this time, neither of us are bound to any duties. We can simply live."

"And how does one live?" Valen replied with an anxious glance at her. "I seem to have forgotten."

Andi shrugged. "I guess we'll figure it out together."

She led them into the bustling crowd.

The smells of food, drinks and perfumes assaulted her instantly, wrapping around her senses like a warm blanket. Seated on the red sand were shops selling patriotic flags of the Unified Systems, four lines running vertically under the galaxy's emblem, a spiral with a star sprouting from its center.

"I haven't seen one of these in forever," Valen said.

He stopped and ran his hands across one of the flags, the purple and white colors a striking resemblance to Andi's hair.

"Oh, they're all over the galaxy now," Andi said. "Especially in the last couple years, as people are growing more optimistic that Xen Ptera won't ever retaliate again. The peace treaty holds that hope in place, but their silence has also had a part in it. You must have missed the trend while you were…" She trailed off, frowning.

"It's alright," Valen said with a shrug. "You can talk about my time away. It's as much a part of me as my scars are."

His eyes fell on Andi's wrists, where her sleeve had ridden up to reveal the marks left over from her accident with Kalee. Even with her cuffs, they were still obvious. She reached to tug her sleeves down, wishing she could take the marks from her skin and hide any evidence that might break the strange peace she and Valen had found.

Mercifully, he looked back to the flags hanging from the booth.

"*They* deserved to be removed from this flag," he said suddenly, his voice acidic, and Andi assumed he was talking about Xen Ptera. "*Millions* of people died in that war."

The altered flag was a universal *screw you* to the entire Olen System, displayed on dashboards of starships, hung in windows, tattooed on the backs of old, wrinkled soldiers who had long since retired.

The design on the flag had always been more or less the same, but when the Unified Systems won the war, what had once been five lines became four, signaling Olen's split from the Unified Systems.

Andi was very young during the last year of the war, the worst of the fear having passed her by in her youth, and the sparkling, wealthy haze that Arcardius gave off. She didn't live in constant fear the way that many of the other planets had during the last days of the war.

But she'd never forget the day the official removal of the Olen System was broadcasted across the galactic feeds, never forget the sound of her parents cheering instead of mourning when Olen was cast out. She'd never known life without Olen being a dark mark on the edges of Mirabel, an entire system that had exploded into acts of terror when the Unified Systems couldn't help them save their dying planet fast enough.

Survival of the fittest had been a saying passed on since the time of the Ancients, and there was so much truth behind those words. Olen wasn't fit, so they didn't survive. Andi believed Olen's act of war was a last, desperate attempt to get what they wanted. Sadly, it didn't turn out well for them. Even before The Cataclysm, Xen Ptera had been a weak planet, long bereft of resources.

Now it was shattered, hanging on to life support as it faded away.

"Let's go," Valen said.

He turned away, casting a final scowl over his shoulder at the flags waving in the wind.

As they walked on, Andi let her mind sink into a calm state of observance. There was no goal here, no mission to accomplish, no reward on the line. For once, she could simply *be*.

She stepped over two kids playing a board game in the dirt. One of them had scales like Lira, which lit up brightly in a summertime yellow. Her friend, a muscular girl who looked a bit like Breck, giggled as they threw the dice at each other instead of playing the game. Such pure innocence made her smile, until she heard their voices a little more clearly.

"You're the Xen Pterran. I'm the Arcardian fleetmaster."

"I don't *want* to be the Xen Pterran! That means I'll lose!"

A woman appeared from the tent behind the kids, telling them both not to speak of such an awful place on such a celebratory day.

As the crowd swept forward, she allowed it to swallow them up, carrying the bad memories away.

Before joining the dancers, Andi bought each of them a mug of Jurum. It was a famous drink on Adhira that was said to make its drinker forget their troubles. It sounded too good to be true, but Andi had had plenty of experience with Jurum.

"You sure about this?" Valen asked her, sniffing the glittering, bubbling liquid in his mug.

Andi nodded. "Yes. But don't drink as much as Lira does. She's a bit of a pro when it comes to Jurum, actually."

She took a gulp. When the drink touched her tongue, the sickly sweet taste turned smooth, like liquid heaven.

The instant effects were blissful, and Andi welcomed them with open arms. Her vision was enhanced, everything more vibrant and alive than it had been seconds before, making the whole festival pop with color, as if she were looking through a kaleidoscope.

The world became beautiful around her, all darkness swept away.

Valen took another sip from his mug. "It's so..."

"Lovely," Andi whispered. Her voice echoed and rippled like a droplet falling into water, and she laughed as she downed the rest of her mug.

She thought she could feel the ground breathe beneath her feet, hear the distant towering trees laugh with happiness, feel the spiral rock mounds sigh from high above the desert sand. The world was *alive*.

"Come on," Valen said. He faded into the crowd of dancers twirling in time, and as they moved, Andi had to question if her feet were even touching the ground anymore.

She felt weightless.

Like a starship made of glass.

# CHAPTER 57
## DEX

DEX SAT ON THE EDGES OF THE CROWD, WATCHing the dancers and enjoying the feel of two mugs of Jurum thrumming through his bloodstream.

This was the type of place he lived for. Dancing women, so beautiful and full of life that he should have been desperate to join the crowd. He'd been asked several times to dance, once even by a woman who'd even offered to buy *him* a mug of Jurum as she approached him on the edge of the crowd.

She could have been the woman of his dreams. But tonight... Dex didn't care.

In truth, all he cared about was catching a glimpse of Andi in the crowd.

Andi, with her "stab you in the balls and laugh at you as you scream" eyes.

Andi, who flung insults as sharp as her electric swords.

Andi, who'd stolen his heart and later his ship.

Andi, whom he'd betrayed.

*Andi, Andi, Andi.* Her name echoed through his mind like a flock of Adhiran siren birds.

"Crap," Dex muttered.

Something was truly wrong with him. Maybe he'd fallen ill. Maybe Alfie had given him too strong of a painkiller when the AI had patched him up on the ship a few days before.

*Or maybe,* an obnoxious voice in the back of Dex's mind whispered, *being back here, on the planet where you once had the luxury of being Androma's, is screwing with your brain.*

Dex shook his head. He'd been on land for far too long. Once he was back on board *his* ship, locked in close quarters with Androma Racella, he'd come to his senses again and realize she had absolutely no interest in a future with him.

He had hoped that telling her the truth about what happened years ago would help mend the break between them. That they could start over—maybe they'd never again share the intimacy they once had, but perhaps they could have become friends.

But since their conversation, Andi had done her best to avoid him. He hadn't pushed her. He knew she needed time to process the truth, and perhaps she'd never forgive him.

Perhaps true forgiveness—a resurrection of their past—would never come.

Dex shook his head and turned his attention to his third mug of Jurum for the first time since he'd bought it. He'd been too busy with his stupid, traitorous thoughts to pay attention to what was really important to him.

Getting star-blindingly drunk.

Right as he lifted it to his lips, the liquid having long since stopped bubbling, his gaze drifted to the dance floor that was slowly expanding into a circle. Dancers swayed left and right, clapping and stomping their feet to the steadily growing beat.

As they twirled and parted into halves, Dex caught a flash of white and purple hair. A woman with her arms raised to the sky, her hips swaying like they were rocking in time with a hidden current.

His heart eased a bit at knowing where Andi was.

As if that mattered. He didn't care. He *knew* he didn't care, and yet his mind—which he was *absolutely certain* was malfunctioning now—was tricking him into thinking that he did.

"Idiot," Dex murmured into his mug before downing the contents in a single chug. He knew he'd regret it tomorrow when he woke up.

*Androma.*

Her name whispered into his mind. Past the Jurum, past the wall he'd tried to build up.

He saw for the first time that she was the main spectacle the circle had been formed for. This Andi was so unlike the one he knew. She glided across the sand as if it were a polished dance floor. She spun in circles and twirled through the air, landing lightly as a feather. Her arms and legs performed dances of their own, flowing with the wind that fluttered through the desert.

She was sound and wind and movement. The elements that made up the world were hers to command.

And in this moment, he could see only her.

The rest was background noise.

Dex watched as she swayed forward and grabbed a hand in the crowd, bringing the observer into her dancing spell. Though his mind felt stuffed with cotton, Dex could still register the annoyance he felt upon seeing that the person was Valen.

The pretty little package all tied up like a bow, ready to be delivered to General Cortas.

Valen seemed cast in a shroud of undulating shadows as she

danced around him. He stood there in a trance of his own, eyes glazed over, body barely rocking to the music.

The crew joined them, Breck and Gilly and Lira laughing as they danced around Andi.

She laughed with them.

The sound of it made Dex's blood sing, but the laugh hadn't been for him, and at the thought of that, fury raced through him, shocking him like a spark of fire.

Damn it all to hell and back.

Even with his head muddled by Jurum, Dex couldn't blame the intoxicating brew for what he knew he was about to do.

Tonight, he was going to be an idiot.

He would deal with the repercussions tomorrow.

He moved forward on instinct, breaking through the crowd, their cheers roaring against him.

"Andi." His voice was a low, purring whisper. Smooth as the Jurum running through his veins.

She wasn't his—never truly had been, and never would be.

That was what undid him.

She didn't see him approach at first, but when she spun around, she stopped, gaze transfixed on him. Valen's eyes widened, and he took a step back, then another, until he faded away into the crowd.

"Dex," Andi said.

At first Dex thought she was going to punch him for interrupting her show.

He braced himself for the impact, readied himself for a fight, despite the warmth running through him, the ground undulating beneath his feet like rocking waves. But instead of curling her fists, Andi did the complete opposite.

She ran to him, leaping the last few steps into his waiting arms.

"Dance with me," she whispered, her breath tickling his lips.

Her words were full of such passion, Dex almost fell.

Her lips were so close as she pressed her body against his.

"Andi," Dex breathed her name like a sigh. "We shouldn't do this."

And yet as he held her in his arms, pressing her tightly to his chest, he didn't want to let go. There wasn't any space between them, and he reveled in their closeness, in the familiarity of it, the strong sense of balance between the two of them that had always made them so great.

"We should," she said.

So long, he'd wanted this without even knowing.

His mind screamed at him to stop, that she wasn't thinking straight, but his body hungered for more. She was looking at him like she used to, long ago. Her fingers were digging into his back.

The world around them fell away. The past disappeared, swept away in an instant.

Just before their lips touched, the desert exploded in a blast of fire and light.

# CHAPTER 58
## ANDROMA

SCREAMS, WROUGHT WITH TERROR, RANG out across the Sands of Bailet.

Time seemed to snap back together, a band of rubber popping into place.

Bodies began dropping around her, people fleeing from the crowd as masked figures appeared, rifles firing. They bore a strange symbol painted on their weapons, their red helmets and battered armor.

Something Andi had seen before.

Something she *knew* she should know, but there was a thickness still blocking her mind, like water drowning her brain.

Someone screamed and fell to the ground beside her.

It was a young Adhiran man with eyes as blue as the End-less Sea. A scaled patch shimmered weakly on his cheek as he gasped, pressing his hands to his chest.

"Lon?" Andi heard her Second say.

Lira fell on top of her brother, shouting his name, begging him to stay with her, pressing her hands against his chest.

Dex yanked Andi to the sand, covering her body with his as the crowd erupted into ear-shattering screams.

It was enough to clear Andi's head, rip the veil away, as she looked up, suddenly remembering the origin of the symbol on the rifles.

After fifteen years of peace, the Xen Pterrans had come to take their revenge.

# CHAPTER 59
## VALEN

VALEN DROPPED TO THE GROUND AND crawled blindly, feeling as if the world had sprouted claws and the sand around him had begun to turn into stone.

He had to get back to Arcardius.

He couldn't go back to Lunamere.

The festival began to fade from his sight. An image of cell doors took its place, stained with the black burn marks of electric whips.

The sky disappeared, replaced by the image of a cold, unbreakable stone ceiling.

Every gunshot was like a whip lashing down on Valen's back.

There were a thousand feet running past him, flashes of bodies sprinting past, tangled up in explosive screams as bullets ricocheted through the crowd.

He couldn't see the Marauders. He couldn't see Dex.

A soldier sprinted up to him, clad in armor, the Xen Pterran crest splayed on his chest.

The soldier lifted his rifle. Time slowed. Valen saw the soldier's gloved fingertip stretching toward the trigger, and in Valen's mind, he saw it all as if he were lying on cold, frozen stones, darkness closing in around him like a dense fog, the flash of a blue whip about to rip into his skin.

Valen lifted his head, forced his lips to stop quivering as he looked to where he thought the man's eyes were, beyond his mask, as his finger reached the trigger.

*"No!"* Valen shouted. "No! Not *me!"*

He closed his eyes and waited for the shot. But instead, a body brushed past his.

Valen opened his eyes, and the soldier was gone.

*You have to move, Valen,* his mind begged him.

He crawled forward in the sand, closing his eyes when his hands felt the sticky wetness of blood, ignoring the press of his skin against someone else's, clammier and colder than it should have been.

He begged himself to stay focused, to stay present, but the world was spinning, a planet cast free from its axis, and he couldn't keep himself in control.

He found a booth empty of its keeper, a severed tentacle arm splayed on the dirt floor. A smear of blood pooled across the suction cups. Beside it a golden droid lay motionless, torso blasted open and silver liquid oozing out.

Valen was about to crawl inside and hide himself in the darkness when a scream rang out with his name.

*"Valen!"*

He turned to see her.

Androma Racella, cutting through the chaos like the sharp

edge of a knife, her blades swinging as they took down soldiers. Her crew followed behind her, Dex's white constellation tattoos seeming to squirm across his skin as he ran, Breck hoisting an Adhiran man over her shoulder. The pilot, Lira, screamed and sobbed as she followed, her skin illuminated by bright purple scales, smoking in the night. In front of them, the smallest crew member held a stolen rifle in her arms.

One shot. The blast of a light bullet soaring from the chamber.

A Xen Pterran dropped in front of them, and Gilly leaped over his fallen form, dropped to a knee and aimed again.

Another shot, a second bullet set free, a whistle that soared just past Valen's head.

Behind him, a body dropped.

All Valen could hear was the hiss and crackle of Andi's blades. With each soldier who fell in their way as Andi came to get him, Valen winced.

"I am Valen," he whispered. "I am Valen, I am Valen."

Again, he saw the world flash from bleeding stone walls to the terrorized Adhiran desert and back. He shut his eyes and rocked back and forth, back and forth, until a hand gripped his shoulder, trying to shake him from his trance.

"Valen!"

Andi's voice, but behind that the sound of explosions, gun-shots, more screams. Her crackling swords like Lunamere whips that wanted a taste of his burned skin.

Hands ripped him from the ground, forced him to his feet. He opened his eyes to see Andi staring at him, blood splat-ters staining her face, her hair. Her mouth was moving, but he couldn't make out her words.

Instead it was the pounding of his heart, the echo of his labored breathing, that he heard.

Andi smacked him across the head. Sound flooded into his ears.

"We have to run!"

A fleet of ships was closing in overhead. Each ship was like a living corpse, born from the ashes of Xen Ptera's past, visible by the light of the moon and the raging fires.

Some of them were mostly old scattered parts of ancient warships. Burn marks and dents and patched-up holes littered the black metal.

But on the side of each one, a single golden symbol stared at Valen like a watching eye.

The Solis family crest. A sharp, dagger-like triangle.

They accompanied the face smiling at Valen from his mind.

*A queen of death and darkness, seated upon a throne of the galaxy's bones.*

# CHAPTER 60
## ANDROMA

THE GROUND TREMBLED. SAND SPRAYED AS the fleet landed at the desert's edge. Steam billowed in clouds as the loading ramps opened and uniformed figures poured out like bugs.

Dex growled. "Reinforcements."

"What the hell is this?" Breck shouted.

"Does it matter?" Andi yelped. "We're in the middle of a war zone."

On the sand beside them, Lon's bare chest was a mess of blood.

"We have to get him to the medics!" Lira cried, sobbing as she ripped off the bottom of her gown, pressing the fabric against her brother's chest. He was unconscious, looking near dead already.

"You have to get your emotions under control," Breck said. "Lira. You have to, or we'll lose you. Lon needs you to stay with us."

Lira pressed her scales to his wound, trying to cauterize it, but each time she tried, the light winked out. As if she couldn't control herself when she needed to the most.

"Gilly, left!" Andi commanded.

The girl swung to the left and shot off another round. Light spiraled from the barrel. A nearby soldier screamed as he was blasted off his feet, crashing into the stand that held the Unified Systems flags. Gilly dropped the empty rifle and scooped up another one from a fallen soldier, this one with two barrels. "Where to, Cap? The *Marauder*'s not ready to fly!"

"Hide in Rhymore?" Breck suggested. She leaped to her feet as another soldier appeared and shot. The bullets pinged off her skin. Gilly shot back. The soldier fell, paralyzed by a stunner.

"Not going to work," Gilly said. She racked the gun twice, switching to the upper barrel. "We just lost our ride."

In the distance, Andi could see the Albatusks' carriages in flames.

Breck cursed. "If someone doesn't come up with a plan soon, Lon will die. And then we'll all go down right after he does!"

Lira began to sob again.

The girls were falling apart before Andi's eyes.

She took it all in, her heart racing in her throat. Her mind screaming that this was *her* fault for drawing the Xen Pterrans here. She glanced to Valen as he knelt in the sand nearby, his eyes closed, his hands clamped to his ears as if he could block out the chaos.

Had the Xen Pterrans tracked him somehow?

"We're not going to Rhymore," Dex said suddenly.

Breck spun around to block a spray of bullets. She groaned, sinking to a knee, breathless. Bullets couldn't pierce her skin, but ammo this large packed a nasty punch. Soon, she'd tire out.

"We're not going to Rhymore," Dex said again, eyeing the group around him. "We won't make it far enough before they catch us. They must be here for Valen. They want him back. They won't leave until they have him."

"We won't let them take him," Andi said.

"No." Dex peered past her shoulder, to the distant edge of the desert. "No one is taking him back to Lunamere. Because I'm going to fly us out of here right now, and finish this mission before it kills us all."

"That's a good plan," Andi said. "But where the hell are we supposed to find a ship right now?"

"You're space pirates," Dex said. "I'm sure you can take your pick."

Grinning, he pointed into the distance, where the fleet of Xen Pterran starships sat ready and waiting.

"And your plan to get there?" Breck asked breathlessly.

They fell silent as a group of soldiers marched by, their masks and red armor like beacons in the smoke. Flames crackled and licked up the wood just two stalls away, the heat sparking a memory in Andi's mind.

"Remember the job on Sora?" Andi asked. She looked to Breck and Gilly, whose eyes lit up as Andi's plan suddenly became clear to them. "Find soldiers close in size to each of us. Kill them clean and quick. We need their bodies."

"What the hell for?" Dex yelped.

A grim smile spread across Andi's features. "For once in your life, Dex, just do what I say."

He nodded.

"Hurry," Andi said.

The three of them faded into the smoke, leaving Andi behind to protect Lon and Lira.

As a soldier appeared out of the smoke, the Bloody Baroness hefted her blades and swung, thinking of another tally soon to be added to them.

# CHAPTER 61
## DEX

THE XEN PTERRAN MASK STUNK LIKE ROTTING blood.

With each step Dex took, the stolen boots crushed his toes together and the dead soldier's armor rubbed in all the wrong places.

Dex's Tenebran blood boiled.

The...man who'd worn this suit before him had murdered innocents. He'd approached Revalia as if it were a war zone, shooting at anyone that moved. Man, woman, child.

"Hurry," Dex said as he helped haul a shocked Valen across the sand.

In front of them, Andi took point, her pace steady. Not too

fast, not too slow. Her Xen Pterran armor was too loose, but she looked the part nonetheless.

Other soldiers sprinted past them, and Dex's heart leaped into his throat.

*They'll know*, he thought. *They'll see right through our stolen masks.*

In his mind, he saw a lifetime behind bars, stuck in that horrible darkness they'd just freed Valen from. He readied himself for a fight, body like a coiled spring about to come loose.

But the soldiers only ran past, clicking freshly loaded clips into their rifles as they disappeared into the smoke beyond.

He hoped they, too, burned with the bodies he and the Marauders had left behind.


It took everything Andi had not to swing her swords at the soldiers as they ran past. But she held herself in check, continuing up the hillside as they got closer and closer to the desert's edge.

The line of ships was half a mile ahead, ramps still lowered, dark interiors waiting to swallow them whole.

Each step, each breath, they made it closer.

"Which one?" Andi asked. Beside her, Breck had Lon held over her shoulder, his body limp as if he were already dead. "*Lira*. You have to tell us which one."

She couldn't see her pilot's face behind the Xen Pterran mask. But she guessed it was blank as Lira ran, robotic and silent.

Andi looked to Dex instead. He knew starships better than she did, could look at them as if he saw their insides turned out. "Which one?"

"There. Middle of the fleet. It's the smallest, so it'll be harder to track."

The ship of choice was outdated. The wings were dented, the hull looked to be made of several different models, and yet…it had made it here in one piece, all the way from Xen Ptera, and unless this attack was planned as a one-way trip, she guessed the ship had enough fuel inside for a flight back to the Olen System.

Andi swallowed, glancing back only once at the distant destruction.

Soldiers were gathering together, knocking over the remains of booths.

They had droids lined up on the sand for questioning. People huddled together on the ground nearby, some screaming and begging for mercy. Others looked stoically out at the desert, as if resigned to the same shock that was swarming through Lira and Valen now.

"We can't leave them here to die," Andi said. Adhira had taken them in. Alara had allowed them to stay in Rhymore after they'd crash-landed. She knew the general had a hand in it…but this planet had opened its arms to her and her crew.

Now it was bathed in blood.

A victim to Xen Ptera's terrors.

Breck hefted Lon farther onto her shoulder. Her muffled voice came from inside the mask. "We don't have a choice. If we go back down there, we'll all die, too, Andi." She angled her head toward Valen. "*He* is our mission."

Andi turned away.

She would make this choice now and allow herself to consider the consequences later. More faces, more dead for her to call to a dance.

They continued until the sand beneath their stolen boots turned to metal.

Until they were marching up the ramp of the chosen ship, Dex whispering, *"Go, go, go."* Gilly ran inside, swinging her rifle left and right, searching for any remaining soldiers on board.

"Clear," she mouthed.

It was strangely hollow inside. Enough space to pack a hundred soldiers into the empty cargo bay. Overhead, a single catwalk spread left and right. Darkness waited beyond.

Breck set Lon down on the cold metal floor. Lira nestled beside him, shifting his head gently to rest on her lap. Valen knelt before them, speaking in hushed tones to Lira. His own hands shook, but it seemed he was in better control of himself for now.

*Go with Gilly,* Andi silently commanded Breck.

The giantess nodded and slipped past Andi to follow Gilly and Dex farther into the ship.

She watched them climb the ladder to the catwalk, no words shared between them as they split up, Breck and Gilly to the left, Dex to the right.

Andi waited, catching her breath and praying to the Godstars that the ship was clear.

Only a few seconds passed before a gunshot exploded above.

*The crew.*

Leaving the loading door open, Andi turned and sprinted into the heart of the ship.

# CHAPTER 62
## DEX

BLOOD POOLED IN DEX'S VISION.

He toppled and fell backward to the floor, his head ringing.

Of all the people to find waiting on the bridge, it *had* to be a soldier with New Vedan blood, didn't it? And one easily double the size of Breck.

After he'd entered and found the giant waiting to spring, Dex had only had time to fire off a single shot, useless against the bulletproof man. He'd probably been one of the many visitors stuck on Xen Ptera during his childhood, eyes opened to the neglect of the Unified Systems. Now he was fighting for Queen Nor.

"Tiny little Tenebran fool," the pilot's voice boomed as he

stalked forward. He ripped Dex's gun from his grasp as easily as taking a toy from a child.

Then he *bent it in half* over his massive thigh. The metal squealed as a similar sound slipped from Dex's throat.

"Easy there, big guy," Dex said, lifting his hands before him. He tried to stand, but his vision was spotty. His two hands, spread before him, suddenly looked like seven. "We can talk."

The giant laughed menacingly, advancing toward him.

Then the door to the bridge hissed as it slid open, and Breck and Gilly were standing in the entryway, their eyes wide.

"Oh, for the love of the stars," Breck said.

Gilly fired off ten rounds. Each one of them slammed against the man's chest, then dropped to the metal floor.

*Ping, ping, ping.*

The giant looked up at Gilly. A low grumble rolled from his chest as he took a lurching step forward and swung.

*"No!"* Breck shouted.

She leaped in front of Gilly. A sickening crack sounded as the man's fist connected with the side of Breck's face.

She landed beside Dex in a heap, limbs splayed across the floor.

Gilly screamed just as Andi rushed onto the bridge, her eyes wide, her swords already out and crackling.

Her face, bathed in the electric light, was the last thing Dex saw before darkness pulled him away.

# CHAPTER 63
## ANDROMA

THE GIANT SWUNG.

Andi ducked, and his fist whizzed past her head, punching into the metal wall instead.

It dented outward with a screeching whine.

"Come on, you bastard," Andi growled.

She moved backward, easing out of the bridge, her too-large Xen Pterran suit hampering her movements slightly.

The giant followed. Andi could see Breck's splayed form behind him, Gilly kneeling over her and Dex on the floor.

"You think you can steal my ship?" the giant growled as he stalked toward Andi.

She shrugged as she stopped in the center of the catwalk. "I've done it before."

The giant loosed a chuckle. "Not today, little girl."

Then he was at her again, bounding forward in two heavy strides that shook the metal beneath her feet.

Andi whirled her swords, then thrust forward with *one jab, two jabs, three*. The blades crackled and sang with each thrust. But each time, the swords rebounded off the giant's wrists as he blocked her, his bulletproof skin proving strong enough to ward off even a scratch.

*Damned New Vedans.* Andi's mind seethed as she dropped to her knee, allowing another swinging fist to soar past her before rising again.

He was strong, but he was slow.

And if she could just figure out *how* to disable him, perhaps make him lose his balance and topple over...

The giant gripped the catwalk railing and tore a piece away, the metal screaming in protest.

"I like sword fights," he growled.

Then he swung.

Andi lifted her swords in an X. Sparks flew as her blades met his makeshift weapon. She managed to shove him back, barely giving herself enough space to adjust her swords, take a half step back and swing again.

The giant blocked her and advanced.

On and on they swung. Andi's body took over, on autopilot.

*Left sword, right sword. Block.*

*Thrust.*

*Drop to a knee, avoid a hit.*

*Rise back up, advance.*

All the while, the giant's bulletproof skin warded off her attacks.

Andi's arms began to tremble as the giant pressed her backward, closer and closer to the end of the catwalk.

"Let us take the damned ship!" she yelled over the clash of metal.

"My soldiers will come back soon," the giant growled. "Then you will die."

He thrust the piece of railing at her.

It sang as it cracked against the wall just beside Andi's head.

She was running out of steam, running out of options. Guns didn't work, her best fighters were unconscious or helpless or, in the case of Lon, *actually dying* in the cargo bay below.

A hit made contact.

Andi screamed as one of her swords fell from her hand. It tumbled over the railing, where it landed beside Valen, the electricity fizzling out.

"Run, Andi!" Valen cried.

She hefted her remaining sword with both hands and swung.

The giant lifted his palms and gripped the blade. The electric currents made his body seize and shake, but he remained standing.

Slowly, eyes boring into Andi's, he pulled the sword from her grip.

He tossed it over the railing to join its mate.

*"Run!"* Valen screamed again.

Andi's breath hitched in her throat. She'd never lost a fight, not like this, not like...

*BOOM!*

Andi looked up just in time to see an explosion of red light barreling toward her from the still-open entry door. It rocketed through the air, a red swarm of death.

Blood sprayed against her face as the New Vedan warrior erupted into vapor. She blinked, hot blood dripping down her cheeks as she tried to figure out what had just happened.

Where the giant once stood, only his torn bit of metal railing remained.

Andi gasped and dropped to her knees.

Gilly appeared from the bridge, her mouth hanging open. "What in the actual hell just happened?"

Andi pointed over the catwalk railing. Down below, a whine of gears sounded as the entry door shut.

Standing before the door, with a giant, still-smoking launcher resting on his shoulder, was Alfie. He set down a wriggling sack. With a loud yowl, a fuzzy, horned creature emerged.

*"Havoc!"* Gilly shrieked happily.

Andi still stood motionless, staring down at the AI.

"Hello, Androma Racella," Alfie said. "It seems we found you right on time. How can I further assist you in this mission?"

"Program this ship to get us the hell out of here."

Moments later, the ship's engines blazed as it shot through the planet's atmosphere en route to Arcardius.

# CHAPTER 64
## LIRA

THERE WASN'T ENOUGH GRISS IN THE GALAXY
to drown out Lira Mette's thoughts.

She sat alone in the storage room of the stolen Xen Pterran
warship, slumped against a wooden crate she'd burned her way
through with her scaled palms. Smoke still lingered in the small
space, wafting among the stacked bags of food stores, the flag-
ons of water, the metal shelf across from her that held extra Xen
Pterran soldiers' masks.

"Damn it," Lira cursed. She looked at the bottle of amber
liquid that sat beside her on the metal floor, the final few drops
calling her name.

Ever since the ship had lifted off the ground, every horrific moment of the past few hours had begun to melt together until it formed one massive monster full of memories.

Now the monster whispered her name, begging Lira to lose herself in its siren song.

She wouldn't give in.

Instead, Lira scooped up the bottle of Griss and tipped it onto her tongue, quickly swallowing every last blessed drop.

With each sip she took, she remembered a little less. But still, despite the pile of four empty bottles to which she added the newly emptied one, it didn't drown out the *sounds*.

The feelings.

The pain.

She would never forget the screams that followed the first bullet, the first death. The squelch of hot blood hitting the sand as the Xen Pterrans came out of nowhere and attacked.

She would never be able to erase the image of her brother's body dropping beside her. How it felt to flee for their lives through the smoke, chests heaving, hearts racing. Lon's blood on her hands, wet tears on her face, scales blazing like purple torches in the midst of the firefight as they ran through the desert, desperate for escape.

Lira groaned, her head spinning and throbbing as she grabbed another bottle of Griss and tried to uncork it with her bare hands.

But looking at her hands brought back the memory of Lon lying in the sand and Lira pressing her palms against his chest, trying in vain to stop the bleeding.

She gasped and threw the bottle.

It exploded against the far side of the room, glass raining down like little shards of broken stars.

"Now, that was a waste."

Lira turned, feeling like her head might wobble off her neck.

Andi stood in the doorway of the small storage room, her arms crossed over her chest, her lips pulled back in a small smirk.

"I asked to be alone," Lira said.

The words came out jumbled, as if her tongue, too, were drunk on Griss.

"That's the problem with your being my Second," Andi answered with a sigh as she entered the storage room and joined Lira on the floor, legs crisscrossed beneath her. "I'm the captain, and I've denied your request."

Lira glared at her.

"Lira, you've been sitting in here for hours," Andi said. She reached out to place a hand on Lira's arm, but Lira shoved her away. "Lon is stable, thanks to Alfie, but if you don't go and check on him soon, he might wake up and find Gilly at his side. Or worse, Havoc."

Her voice sounded completely matter-of-fact, as if they were just carrying out a normal mission.

"What the hell is your problem?" Lira asked suddenly.

Andi looked like she'd been slapped.

"My problem?"

Lira reached behind her and grabbed another bottle of Griss. This time, she ripped the cork out with her teeth. A satisfying *pop* sounded as the liquid inside bubbled up and spilled onto Lira's lap. She downed half the bottle in one sip.

When she looked up, Andi was still staring at her.

"You're just waltzing around," Lira said accusingly, waving a hand. "As if *nothing* happened." She took another sip, glaring at Andi over the bottle. "But it happened, *Captain*."

"It was an act of terror," Andi said, spreading her arms out to either side. "Xen Ptera couldn't have been stopped, not when we weren't prepared. What happened was—"

"Your fault!" Lira barked out. The Xen Pterran armor she wore grew hot against her skin as her scales flared to life. "*You* got us into this mess, accepting that stars-forsaken mission from General Cortas! And now the *Marauder* is gone, my brother's chest is blasted open, Alara is gods know where and my planet is bathed in blood."

"Lira…" Andi tried again, but Lira was done listening.

*"Enough!"* she shouted. Lira could feel her anger writhing now, like a living, breathing thing ready to burn. To hurt. To destroy. "This entire mission has been a fool's journey. I should have taken Alara's offer when she gave me the chance."

The words fell from her lips like a welcome poison.

When she glanced up, Andi's face was stone.

"What offer?" she whispered.

Lira lifted the Griss bottle, disappointed to find it empty. She let it tumble from her grip and it rolled away across the metal floor. She was just reaching for another when suddenly Andi's fingers were around her wrist, gripping it tight.

"Lira," Andi rasped. Her eyes were like the surface of a smoldering moon. "What offer?"

Lira tried to shove her away, but Andi's grip held.

She met her captain's eyes, blurry as her vision was.

"My aunt asked me to leave the crew," Lira said, letting each word wound like a knife. "She said she'd give me my own ship. A state-of-the-art one that could never be disabled."

Lira loved the *Marauder*, knew she was wounding herself, too, by speaking ill of it, but she didn't care.

"I should have stayed on Adhira," she said. All menace had left her voice. Now the hot, choking feeling of tears replaced it. She could feel them spilling across her cheeks. "Oh, Godstars, Andi," Lira moaned. "I did this. All those people, *dead*, because I piloted a Xen Pterran prisoner onto their peaceful planet. If I hadn't flown Valen there, they wouldn't have come."

Andi was silent, her face pained as she let go of Lira's wrist.

A burn mark, red and angry, marred her palm.

"Lira," she whispered.

But Lira shook her head, then dropped it to lean against her knees.

"I have never wanted to kill," she said, tears still falling. She didn't try to stop them as a realization swam through her. "But

I'm afraid I've just brought about the murder of thousands of innocent people on Adhira."

"No," Andi said. "Lira, you can't think that."

Lira kept her eyes closed, blocking out the room as it spun in time with her head.

She wanted her brother to wake up, to be safe and sound and back on Adhira where he belonged. She wanted to scream and race up the stairs of Rhymore and hide herself in the mountain temple, away from prying eyes, where she could cast her feelings out to the sky and forget about pain and fear and unanswered questions.

Most of all, she wanted to drink another damned bottle of Griss.

"We did this job *together*," Andi said. "All of us."

Lira looked up, surprised to hear Andi's voice crack.

That didn't fit with the Andi she knew, the hardened captain who pretended she didn't give a damn about the world, who acted as if she would gladly burn it all to ashes in an instant if she could.

But here, in this storage room, with empty bottles of Griss scattered between them, Lira saw the true Androma Racella.

It cleared her mind for a moment, allowed her to watch and listen and understand. A distraction from the monster still lurking in her mind.

"*We* brought Valen to Adhira," Andi said. "*We* made the choice to go to Revalia, and have him out there in the open, without even considering the consequences." She took a deep breath. "Those are choices *we* made as a crew, and I, as the captain, oversaw them. They are *my* mistakes. Not yours."

"But the attack—" Lira began.

"The attack was horrific, and I will never forgive myself for leaving that planet and all those people behind," Andi said. "And for what? The freedom that the general promised, if we deliver Valen back to him?" She barked out a single laugh. "I just chose to save my own skin and my own future by running away. Running, Lir. It's what I always do."

"It's what I do, too," Lira said.

Silence hung between them.

Lira lifted an arm, making sure her scales had cooled before she gently reached out and draped it across Andi's shoulders, pulling her close.

Their heads touched as Lira leaned against Andi.

"Maybe we could stop," Lira whispered.

Andi sighed. "It isn't possible, Lir."

"But what if it could be? What if…after all of this, after Valen is home…we go back to Adhira? We help them recover. We fly my aunt's starship. We find the bastards who came from Xen Ptera, and we escort them to the doors of hell."

She could feel Andi's deep sigh against her as she considered this.

"You're talking about war, Lira," Andi said.

"No." Lira closed her eyes and saw all the smoke, the pain and the destruction. In one day, it had changed her, twisted her insides until she no longer sought peace. Rather, she desired something far different. "I'm talking about revenge."

"Revenge," Andi said. "Not something I thought I'd ever hear Lirana Mette speak of."

"They killed innocent people. They burned *my* planet. They shot my brother. I have no idea where my aunt is, or if she's even still alive." Lira sniffed back a remaining tear, thinking of Lon down below in the cargo bay, still unconscious as Dex piloted the ship toward Arcardius. They would arrive tomorrow. Lira didn't know if they even had enough time left to save him. "Alfie says that Lon may not wake up. And if he does, we don't know what the extent of the damage may be."

"He's strong," Andi said. "Just like you."

"I'm not strong," Lira said. "If I was, I wouldn't have fallen apart when they attacked. I would have picked up a weapon and fought back."

"You would have died. We all would have."

"And now?" Lira asked. "How do we live with the guilt?"

*The pain*, she wanted to say, *that is clawing at my insides, refusing to go away.*

"I know a thing or two about guilt," Andi said, reaching past Lira to where a single bottle of Griss remained. She uncorked it with ease and took a sip, then angled it toward Lira. "You're not going to make me drink alone, are you?"

Lira sighed and took the bottle.

They shared it, the captain and the pilot, in the darkness of the stolen Xen Pterran warship.

All the while, Lira hoped and prayed and begged the God-stars that her aunt was safe back on Adhira. And that her twin brother, asleep on the deck below, would somehow survive.

# CHAPTER 65
## ANDROMA

IN THE YEARS SINCE SHE'D ESCAPED ARCARDIUS, Andi had never returned to the Phelexos System. Not once. She'd feared that if she did, she would finally get caught and face the sentence she'd been running from all this time.

The bottle of Griss she'd shared with Lira last night had helped her forget about that fear—for a short while at least. But then sleep had stolen her away, and with it, the nightmares came lurking.

This time, they had been of Valen.

*You killed her*, he'd whispered into her ear as he hovered over her with a blade poised above her heart. *Now you will suffer her fate.*

His eyes bored down into hers, and as she screamed and begged him to release her, blood poured from his lips.

Even now, as Andi sat on the bridge beside Dex, she couldn't shake the feeling of cold dread that swept over her at the thought of the dream.

That, and the pressing nausea that came along with a wicked hangover—not only from the Griss, but from the Jurum she'd so foolishly guzzled at Revalia.

After everything that had happened on Adhira, she was grateful they'd found a way out. As soon as Alfie had dispatched the New Vedan guard, they'd fired up the engines and gotten the hell out of the desert, blasting through the atmosphere, then immediately soaring into hyperspace. The escape had been a quick one, the other Xen Pterran ships unable to track them, thanks to Alfie's scrambling the tracking systems on board.

After Andi's initial shock over his unexpected role as rescuer had passed, she'd questioned the AI until she'd nearly run out of breath.

"My mission is to ensure Mr. Valen Cortas returns home," Alfie had said as Dex piloted them out of Adhira, wide awake from an adrenaline pill they'd been fortunate to find in a med kit on board. "When the Rhymore guards heard of the attack in the desert, I had no choice but to embark on a journey to find you."

"But how did you find us?" Gilly had asked.

Alfie's shrug had been almost sentient. "Fellibrags have a heightened sense of smell. So I used Havoc to determine your precise location. I also determined that Gilly would be most displeased if I forgot him."

Gilly had squeaked happily and snuggled the orange creature. "What a good little fellibrag you are!"

"And Alara?" Andi had asked. "Do you know what happened to her?"

The AI's white face had tilted sideways. "Alara is not my mission, Androma Racella. Therefore, I am unaware of her current whereabouts."

Alfie had then gotten straight to work on Lon's injury, stabilizing him with the med kit. The wound from the rifle shot was deep, the bullet thick and ugly, as if it were made from salvaged scrap steel. If infection hadn't set in yet, it likely would soon.

"He will need immediate care upon our arrival on Arcardius," Alfie had said, his gears whirring as he stood and pressed the med kit into Andi's hands.

Dex had been right about the stolen ship. It shot through the galaxy, rocketing toward Arcardius. Despite that, time had seemed to slow, as if every second was counting against them. Knowing the journey would be a long one, Andi had joined Lira in the storage room.

Now, *finally*, as flashes of starlight streaked past the viewport, Dex pulled back on the hyperdrive and the ship was flung out of hyperspace just at the edge of the Phelexos System.

"Home sweet home," Dex said, glancing sideways at Andi.

Green blood had dried on his forehead, and a nasty bruise had spread across the entirety of his left cheek. His usual grin was missing.

"What's the matter, Baroness?" he asked.

Andi was too tired—and too ill—to deal with him right now. They hadn't talked about the almost-kiss they'd shared during Revalia. Andi wanted to pass it off as a side effect of Jurum, and yet…as she looked at him, heat flooded to her cheeks.

She turned away, pressing her fingertips to her temples.

The murmur of a faraway voice on the com sounded behind her, where Alfie was busy communicating with the transportation command center on Arcardius, warning them they were in a stolen Xen Pterran ship.

"Sir, I am on direct orders from General Cortas," Alfie's calm voice said. "I am detecting tonal suggestions of annoyance. Shall I inform the general that my mission cannot be completed because of your interference?"

More murmurs, then Alfie glanced at Dex and said, "I have

secured clearance to approach Arcardius. He also offered to polish my metal platings free of charge, should I ever need it."

"You know something, AI?" Dex asked, smiling through his split lip. "You're beginning to grow on me."

"I cannot grow," Alfie said. "It is not within my capability to do so."

Andi let the sound of their voices fade as she stared out the viewport.

They passed the swirling colors of the gas giant, Pegasi, and weaved around New Veda before flying between the two moons of Arcardius.

On the other side of the moons, Andi could just make out the lush blue and green hues of her home world. A line of sleek Explorer ships waited for them—their escort down to the planet's surface. She tapped her foot anxiously as they approached their destination. Coming from a mission in a system that was supposed to be her enemy, she couldn't help but question if she was about to enter another territory more dangerous than Olen. They had escaped from the atrocities on Adhira, but who knew what horrors might still lie ahead?

Andi felt selfish thinking these thoughts when she'd just come from a peaceful planet that was now immersed in a bloody battle. She felt even more selfish for wishing the news would distract General Cortas from any attempt to alter the deal he'd made with them. She just wanted to drop Valen off and be on her way back to Adhira to get her ship.

*If* there was still a ship to retrieve.

Dex angled them toward Arcardius, and Andi allowed herself a moment to stare out at the inky black beyond. Before this hellish journey began, she'd thought the stars were mocking her. But now, for the first time in a long while, she felt as if she'd surprised the stars.

As if, despite what had happened worlds away, they shone a

little brighter, encouraging her to be strong in the face of the unknown.

It was that thought that slightly eased the tension in her shoulders and loosened the tightness in her chest.

"Well, this is an inviting welcome," Dex said sarcastically as the Explorers surrounded them, two on each side and one in the back. They then proceeded to herd them down to the planet.

Andi never thought this day would come, had fully believed that the last time she would see Arcardius was through the rearcam of the ship she'd escaped on. But there it was before her now, a ball of swirling blues, purples, pinks and greens, not a single scar of white clouds obscuring the colors. The purple salt lakes glimmered like gemstones from afar, dwarfed by bright blue oceans that surrounded the lush green land.

There was the massive, half-moon–shaped island on the southern tip of the main continent, where she'd vacationed with her mother and father as a child. The sea from afar looked just as blue as it had when she'd splashed her feet in the cool water, running up and down the diamond-littered shores in search of the largest, shiniest one.

Above it, the main continent of Ae'ri showed itself off in shades of deepest emerald, scattered with shadows from the mountains and the floating gravarocks hanging in the air as if held by strings.

The largest of them, a rugged snow-capped mountain, held countless memories for Andi.

She had flown below it with her father on a day trip years ago. Andi could remember how she'd pressed her face to the glass of the tour ship, her breath fogging up the view, and dreamed of one day soaring her own ship to that very mountain. A soldier on leave, exploring the most hard-to-reach places of Arcardius and the worlds beyond.

Now she was the captain of a starship she was too scared to

fly. She was doing more than she'd ever dreamed of doing, but not quite in the way she'd planned.

A voice suddenly buzzed into the overhead com, drawing Andi's attention from the planet back to the dash.

*"This is Patrol 73 paging the Marauders. Do you copy?"*

She tapped the rear-cam and saw the telltale form of an Explorer Patrol ship looming not far behind.

"Marauders to Patrol 73. Do we have clearance to enter?"

Static crackled on the line. For a moment, her gut screamed at her to beg Dex to turn the ship around, soar back out into the skies and hide herself and her crew in the shadows of the nearest moon.

Before she could do anything rash, the voice on the com spoke.

*"Patrol 73 to the Marauders. Initiate hover mode."*

Dex pressed a button next to the throttle. "Hover control activated," he responded. Soon the prox alarm went off, signaling that the Patrol ships had latched on to theirs. They escorted the Marauders to the planet's surface, looking like monsters dropping from the night sky.

"Welcome home, Androma," Andi whispered to herself.

# CHAPTER 66
## DEX

DEX FANCIED HIMSELF A RUGGED MAN, PLENTY capable of surviving the harsher conditions that some planets in Mirabel had to offer. He'd survived a bone-shattering winter on Solera, sweated through half of his hard-earned wardrobe on the desert moon Kaniv, and spent countless hours forcing himself to stay awake in the midst of pointless meetings during his days training to become a Guardian.

But as much as he disliked the pompous, wealthy citizens of the military planet Arcardius, he relished the beauty of it as a whole. It was a shiny, glittering type of place and, rugged bounty hunter or not, Dex was not ashamed to be a fan of things that sparkled.

As the Patrol ships escorted them through the atmosphere and into the Arcardian skies, Dex could practically taste the fine bubbling liquor he'd drink—endless amounts of it, due to the planet-load of Krevs the general was about to deliver into his account, plus the badge of honor that would be reattached to his chest.

No longer would he bow in shame when he passed other Guardians. He'd be one of them again, after all this time.

He blew out a breath of air, focusing on the view as they dropped closer to the ground. There were plenty of other, smaller ships in the sky, all of which parted before them as their escorts cleared the way.

The main continent of Arcardius came into view, a glorious green scattered with waterside cities. *There* was Dex's sparkle. Spiraling towers of glass that soared high into the sky, razor sharp and yet soft all at once, rendered by a master architect's hand. Their reflections seemed to dance on the water's surface, doubling the beauty of it all.

The Arcardian flag, blue with a silver bursting star icon in the center, was on display everywhere. The largest one covered the entire edge of a domed building—the renowned military Academy Andi had attended before becoming a Spectre.

In between the buildings were personal transport ships of the finest kind. Racers and Thrusters and Dex's personal favorite, Sky Blades—black single-passenger carbon ships that were as light as a feather, capable of soaring faster than anything else on Arcardius.

From the number of transports in the city, it was clear that the crowds had begun to arrive for the Summit. Citizens traveled from all across Mirabel to meet each year and witness the system leaders renew their bonds of friendship and lasting peace.

No wonder General Cortas had been so insistent on their returning Valen on schedule—he no doubt wanted to publicly announce his son's rescue and Mirabel's triumph over Xen Ptera once more.

After the attack on Adhira, however, Dex didn't feel as if they'd truly achieved any kind of victory in bringing Valen home.

Across the city, set apart from the splendor, a cluster of natural gravarocks hovered in the sky. Large, floating bits of land—some mountainous, others not—where the wealthiest of Arcardius chose to take up residence.

Dex could pinpoint the general's with a single glance.

It was easily the largest of them all, save for the great floating mountain they'd passed on their way in. On its top, visible even from here, was the Cortas estate, Averia. It was made up of several sprawling white buildings so pristine and bright that just looking at the complex hurt Dex's eyes.

He glanced sideways at Andi and noticed the way her hands were curled tightly on her armrests. Almost as if she were flying into battle, rather than soaring toward the biggest payout of her life. Toward the place she'd once called home, which could soon be hers again, if she wished it.

"It's just a building, Baroness," Dex said, his voice light.

But he knew what the Arcardians had done to her.

He knew how broken she had been when he'd found her in that market so long ago.

A strange feeling came over him in that moment as he watched her looking upon her old home. He wanted to reach out and touch her hand. He wanted to kiss her—not in the way he almost had on Adhira.

Something gentler. Sweeter.

The kind of kiss Dex knew he didn't deserve to give her.

When this job was done, the best gift Dex could offer Andi was leaving. She'd never have to see him again after this.

It was almost too much, looking at her now and knowing it wasn't him she needed anymore. Perhaps she never truly had.

His voice hushed, Dex sent a com to Andi's crew to join them on the bridge.

When they arrived, he stood silently from his chair and headed for the door.

He stopped before he stepped into the hall and cast a quick glance over his shoulder.

The crew had formed a half circle behind Andi.

The giantess, with all her strength. The small gunner, with the yowling horned furball in her arms. And then there was the pilot, her expression sickly, whose gentle support was felt nonetheless.

It was then that Dex realized they weren't standing in a circle. Instead, they had formed a wall around Andi, protecting her with their presence.

Some things were far more powerful than weapons or words.

Dex left the four of them alone together, savoring the silence as the Patrol ships carted them toward the Cortas estate.

# CHAPTER 67
## ANDROMA

ANDI FELT AS IF SHE WERE TRAVELING INTO the past. Back to the only place in the galaxy that thought of her not as the fearsome Bloody Baroness, but as the soldier who'd failed her sworn duty.

The girl who had betrayed them all.

Andi took a deep breath, pulling herself up to her full height as the loading ramp of the stolen warship hit the ground with a soft *thunk*.

The massive dock spread before her and her crew, pristine white walls and marble flooring with gray veins running through it. Ships of all shapes and sizes lined the space like a waiting crowd. But despite the splendor of the space, it still smelled like grease stains and recycled air and hundreds of gallons' worth of fuel.

It was exactly as Andi remembered.

The last time she'd been in this room, Kalee was still alive.

Andi thought of her best friend's laughter, bright with the warmth of excitement. Her voice bubbling over with a palpable joy as she tossed Andi the ignition card to her father's ship and said, *Take us to the skies.*

A hand touched Andi's wrist, just above her cuff.

She glanced to the right, where Valen stood watching her closely, as if he knew and understood.

"I can feel her, too," he whispered. His eyes were haunted.

It was as if Kalee's ghost was here now, watching and waiting for Andi to bolt. To run away like she'd always done, one foot in front of the other, until she'd left the things she couldn't face behind.

She wanted to pave the way for her crew, to take the first step off the ship, but she was frozen in place.

If she felt this way now, what feelings would await her when she passed through this docking bay, into the halls of the Cortas estate? There were too many memories. Too many feelings she didn't want to uncover. Worst of all, there were people from her past waiting inside. People whose names and faces brought forth a terrible sense of longing and dread.

For a moment, Andi wished so desperately that the veil of the Bloody Baroness would fall across her eyes. That she could march fearlessly into the unknown.

"Well," Dex said suddenly, stepping up beside her. "Time to go collect our payment." He cast a sideways glance at Andi, a determined look in his eyes as he nodded curtly at her. "Ladies first, Androma."

She felt him nudge her, gently, with his boot.

With a deep breath, she stepped forward, each motion of her

leaden feet propelling her farther down the gangway until she was finally on solid ground.

They were halfway across the room when the exit doors burst open.

Lines of servants and guards appeared through them, all sporting Arcardian blue. A massive silver med droid rolled over, prong-like arms outspread for Breck to hand Lon over.

"Go," Andi said to Lira. "Make sure they take care of him."

Her pilot nodded gratefully and followed the med droid toward the infirmary.

As the crowd began to thicken, every estate worker greeting Valen like an old friend, a gasp suddenly rang out.

"Valen!"

The crowd parted to reveal a woman Andi hadn't seen since her trial.

Valen's mother, Merella Cortas.

She had aged dramatically over the past four years. Wrinkles surrounded her eyes and mouth, and her blond curls were liberally streaked with silver. Andi glanced at Valen, whose face was devoid of emotion, not even a twitch of his facial muscles to betray what he was thinking. His nervous energy was washed away, as if he had been drenched with cold water.

All eyes were on them as Valen's mother ran to him, heels clacking on the marble floor, her blue gown rippling like waves of water.

She swept Valen into a bone-crushing hug.

"It's you. It's really you, my boy," Merella sobbed into Valen's clenched shoulders. His arms cautiously slipped around her, as if he were afraid to touch her. "My boy, my precious little boy. You're home."

"Home," Valen echoed the word.

Andi turned away, knowing she didn't deserve to be here.

Feeling as if she had already tainted Averia with her presence, like a murderer returning to the scene of their very first crime.

# CHAPTER 68
## ANDROMA

AVERIA WAS EXACTLY AS SHE REMEMBERED.

Andi would never forget the first time she'd come here, following Kalee into the entry hall as she gave Andi a tour of her home.

*It's a bit much,* Kalee had said. *But it's home. And someday, I'll be the one running this place.*

*You?* Andi had asked. *Not your brother?*

*Oh, Androma.* Kalee had laughed then, tossing her head back in that glorious, carefree way that made everyone around her want to come closer. *You and I both know that a woman can rule better than any man ever could. And I'll look twice as good doing it, too.*

Those memories tugged at Andi's heart, colliding with the

present as Alfie guided her and Dex through the winding halls toward the general's private office.

Andi knew the route as well as she knew the halls of the *Marauder.* So many times, she'd walked this very path, always ensuring she'd arrive right on time for her debriefings with the head Spectre of Averia. Sometimes, even, with the general himself.

He hadn't even come to greet Valen as they'd landed. A sign that, no matter the circumstances, he would always put his position ahead of his family. That, Andi had always known, was something Kalee would never have done.

If only she'd grown up here the way she should have.

If only she'd become the general's successor, carrying the Phelexos System to heights that her father would never be able to attain, despite all his scheming.

Arcardius was built upon honor and glory. Andi had often wondered if General Cortas had discarded honor entirely. And yet he'd been determined to destroy Andi for the same mistake.

"Damn," Dex said with a whistle as they walked past family portraits and extravagant Arcardian landscapes rich with color, some of which Andi recognized as Valen's work. "Valen grew up in style." He glanced at Andi. "I can see why you befriended his sister in the first place."

"No one *befriended* Kalee Cortas," Andi said as they passed by a painted portrait of the entire Cortas family. Andi dropped her gaze as they walked on, not wanting to see her old friend's smile. Not wanting to look into Kalee's eyes and remember the last moment she'd seen them alight with life. "Kalee chose the people she wished to let into her life. I was honored that she allowed me to be assigned to her."

"Honored?" Dex asked, raising a bruised brow. "Or damned?"

"I'll let you know after we talk to the general," Andi said.

Light streamed in through windows that stretched from floor to ceiling and were draped with elegant satin the color of honey.

Even though she knew this place, had spent countless nights wandering these halls, Andi felt *wrong* here, as out of place as her work boots, coated in the evidence of the past as she tracked invisible stains across the ornate rugs that lined the hallway.

They passed several servants at work, dusting and shining the bright orb-lights on the walls and washing the windows.

The servants openly stared at Andi as they passed, not bothering to be discreet. If Andi was in their position, she would probably be doing the same thing. Who wouldn't, when the traitorous Spectre they'd thought long gone had returned, still alive and well.

*Let them stare*, Andi thought. *Let them look.*

She glared at them, pleased to find their attention suddenly move elsewhere as Alfie rounded a corner and they left the workers behind.

They passed many closed doors and vacant hallways, Dex whistling, Alfie's gears whirring with each step.

"You remember it all, don't you?" Dex asked.

"Every little bit," Andi said. "Even the hidden escape tunnels that the general installed. He loved to put them in closets, bathrooms, under the bars…"

She trailed off as they stopped before the sweeping grand staircase in the center of the estate.

This was where she'd last seen Valen. Before everything changed. Where he'd tried to stop her and Kalee, knowing how foolish their plans were.

They'd gone on anyway, leaving him behind.

"Andi," Dex said. She glanced back up to where he and Alfie stood waiting a few steps ahead.

"I'm coming," she replied, feeling like a ghost of her old self as she followed them upward, thinking of another time, a different person heading up the stairs in Dex's place.

The stairway stopped on the next landing, where they took

SASHA ALSBERG & LINDSAY CUMMINGS

a left, walked down a red-carpeted hallway and finally stopped before a locked oak door.

"General Cortas is just inside," Alfie said, waving his hand at the door. "His head Spectre will be out in just a moment to retrieve you. When you finish the job, General Cortas will send over your Krevs."

"We already finished the job," Dex said.

"General Cortas will decide that upon his inspection of Valen," Alfie answered.

There was something strange in his normally overpleasant voice that Andi couldn't quite place.

She nearly asked him if he was alright, knowing Alfie was capable of far more complex thinking than she'd originally guessed. He'd saved the crew's life, after all, with his launcher. And he'd even remembered to bring Gilly's hellish creature, a sign that Alfie had some understanding of feelings and attachments.

"Alfie, are you sure everything's—"

The click of the door opening behind her made her stop.

"I'm sorry for the delay," a man's voice said. It was kind, but in more of a diplomatic way than truly sincere.

It was also disconcertingly familiar.

She turned slowly, as if in a dream.

Andi knew the man standing before her—better than most. She remembered the pale white-blond of his hair, the moongray of his eyes and the way he stood tall and strong—the very same habit he'd imprinted upon his daughter from a young age.

For a moment, her heart leaped with joy.

Then it seized when she saw the deep blue uniform he was wearing. The gloves with the Arcardius symbol that Andi had once worn, too, and then Alfie's words came back to her. *His head Spectre will be out in just a moment.*

It took everything in her to speak as the truth struck her.

"Dad?"

# CHAPTER 69
## ANDROMA

ANDI WAS A SURVIVOR, AND ALWAYS HAD BEEN.

She'd survived the crash and the death of Kalee, the trial that had branded her with a traitor's fate. The weeks spent on the run across the galaxy afterward, the months beyond that when Dex had found her. She'd lived through twelve hours a day of training with Dex to hone the skills her father and the Academy had given her, gradually turning into the killer that she was now. She'd sustained cuts and lashes and muscles so sore she'd worried they had snapped, that she would never be able to raise a hand or stand on her own again.

Twelve months later, she'd endured the shattering aftermath of a broken heart from Dex.

And in the past week alone, she'd made it inside Lunamere and escaped with her life, then survived the attack on Adhira. She'd stolen a Xen Pterran warship, battled with a New Vedan giant and lived to tell the tale.

*And you almost kissed the man you thought you hated*, a voice chided in her head.

But this…her *father*, as General Cortas's head Spectre?

*This* might actually kill her.

He stood behind the general's chair now, his face impassive as he stared ahead, hands folded before him.

She knew those hands nearly as well as her own. They were the hands that had held her when she'd cried. The hands that had been placed over her own, warm and strong, and taught her how to steer a starship. To block a punch and deliver plenty of her own. Those hands had once pointed into the swirling sky as her father whispered, *Someday, Androma, you'll be up there, following your dreams.*

They were also the hands that had never been raised to support her at Kalee's trial—they had never even flexed a finger when the opportunity came.

Andi wanted to tear those hands from his wrists—almost as much as she wanted to feel them cradling her face now, the way they always had when she was a child.

*Before.*

Everything was always *before*.

Andi wanted to scream. She wanted to yank her father into the corner of the room, throw him to his knees in front of her and demand that he explain himself.

And yet she couldn't. Because she knew—*Godstars*, she could feel it—that if she made any wrong move in front of the general's watching, demon eyes, he'd destroy her and her crew. He'd take her straight to the execution chamber and finish what he'd planned to do years ago. Her crew, loyal as they were, would go down swinging in her name. And then they would all be dead. Just like Kalee.

So Andi simply stood there, gritting her teeth so hard she feared they might shatter, and listened to General Cortas speak.

"You may be familiar with my head Spectre," he said, flipping absentmindedly through a screen on his large desk. He lifted a pale hand, and an egg-shaped servant droid, blue to match the Arcardian flags, wheeled over from the shadows to hand him a pair of ancient eyeglasses on a golden tray. A fashion statement, no doubt, as vision correction tech had been developed thousands of years ago.

The general looked up at Andi as he placed the glasses on. "He took up the position shortly after your trial, Androma."

Beside her Dex cleared his throat and shifted uncomfortably, his eyes looking at the bookshelves that lined the dark paneled walls instead of at the people around him, as General Cortas continued to speak.

"He has been my most loyal aide since you left. These past four years, difficult as they have been, with the loss of my daughter and then my son..." He sighed and leaned back a bit into his plush chair. "Well, thanks to Commander Racella, they have been a little easier on me."

*Commander Racella.*

Andi glared at the general.

He smiled, clearly amused.

She didn't want to believe her father would work for a man like General Cortas after all that had happened, or that the general would want to work with the man who had fathered his daughter's killer. Maybe, as a way of punishing her family, the general had forced her father to work here, day in and day out. Maybe her father hated the general as much as she did.

But he wouldn't look at her, no matter how much she willed him to.

*I'm your daughter,* she wanted to scream. *I am your own flesh and blood. Look at me.*

She opened her mouth to speak, but mercifully, Dex interceded before she could say anything she might regret.

"The attack on Adhira, sir," he said, his smooth voice drawing the general's attention. "Is there an update? When we left, Queen Alara was missing and…thousands of innocents were…"

General Cortas lifted a hand to silence him. "It's been taken care of."

Dex looked like he might collapse from relief.

The feeling swam through Andi, as well, as she remembered the horrors they'd seen.

"The Xen Pterran attack on Adhira was completely unexpected," the general said. "An absolute tragedy, of that I have no doubt. I'm grateful you managed to get my son out alive— though, in all honesty, landing on a planet with little to no military presence was not a choice I would have had you make." He glanced at Andi when he said this, as if *she* had caused her own ship to malfunction.

The general continued. "A small Soleran fleet has already conquered the rogue Xen Pterran forces, recovering complete control of the situation."

"Did they come because of Valen?" Andi asked. "Because of…" She cast a sideways glance at Dex. "Because of us?"

"That information is classified," General Cortas said.

"The hell it is!" Dex growled. "We were there on the ground, risking our asses so we could get your son out alive!"

"Careful, bounty hunter," the general warned. "A *Guardian* should know his place."

Dex did a very un-Dex-like thing and stepped down from the fight she knew he wished to continue. Andi knew he wouldn't risk forfeiting the status that had once been so precious to him, just like she wouldn't risk her crew.

General Cortas didn't just have her in his pocket—he'd placed Dex in there, too.

The general sighed and motioned to Andi's father. He leaned

in close, and the general whispered something into his ear. Her father nodded, then rushed past Andi and Dex toward the office doors.

Andi caught a whiff of his scent as he passed. *Honey drops and Arcardian coffee beans.* It made her throat ache with wanting, with desperation to be a child again, curled up in his protective arms.

He didn't even glance her way as he walked out.

Her emotions changed like the wind as the need to hurt him and the desperation to be comforted by him warred within her.

"You are aware of the weakened state of Xen Ptera, yes?" the general asked as another Spectre entered the office, assuming her father's post. General Cortas had always had a team of them to guard his back at all times. "It is quite likely they sent every able soldier they have left to Adhira for the attack. The Soleran fleet has wiped them off the map, and all the efforts the Olen System has made to sway the galaxy in the direction of fear have already been crushed. I'm sure it took years to scrounge up their weapons, years more to find a single citizen willing to fight after such a devastating loss in The Cataclysm."

"But why *now*?" Andi asked. "And why Adhira? What about the peace treaty?"

General Cortas raised a brow. "War never really ends, Androma. The desire for revenge is often too strong to forget."

"And the queen?" Andi asked, desperate for an answer for Lira—and Lon, should he recover.

"Safe," the general said. "She intends to be here for the Summit, as is required of each leader of the Unified Systems."

"Cancel the Summit," Andi said suddenly.

The words slipped from her tongue without a thought, too quickly for her to pull them back in.

The general laughed as if she'd just told him she was going to be his successor. "Why would I do such a thing?"

She was going to dive across his desk and drive her fist into his sagging face.

"Because if there was ever a perfect opportunity for Olen to attack, it would be on this planet, at the Summit. Adhira's Revalia Festival was just a small taste of what's to come this week, and with every single leader across Mirabel in attendance…it would be the perfect time to start another war."

General Cortas drummed his fingertips across his desk, as if trying to keep himself entertained while she spoke. "You were a child when The Cataclysm ended, Androma. You lived here, on my planet, surrounded by bright lights and glittering smiles and enough soldiers to make you feel protected at all times. Never, in all of your years growing up here would you have been afraid. Am I correct in saying that?"

Andi's face heated. She didn't answer, so the general went on.

"Arcardius is an iron cage. There is no person, no army in all of Mirabel that can enter it without a key." He leaned forward, hands splayed on his desk. "I hold that key. I say who enters and who leaves, and the day the Olen System successfully mounts an attack on this planet, the stars will fall from the sky. The Intergalactic Summit is a way of preserving the peace and unity between the Unified Systems, Androma. We're showing Olen that we will not bend and we will not break. Queen Alara will back me in this."

He flicked an imaginary bit of fuzz from his shimmering coat and smiled to himself, as if he'd proven his point.

"We delivered your son safely back to you, as requested," Dex said suddenly. His tone held the calm calculation of a man trying to hold himself back, as if he, too, was fighting to rein in the fury that bubbled just beneath the surface. "Now, I believe we are both owed payment."

General Cortas removed his glasses and set them down on the desk. "I've decided to lengthen the terms of our contract."

Andi's stomach felt full of lead. *"What?"*

The general nodded. "Despite what I've said, the events that played out on Adhira cannot be ignored entirely. My son has only just returned home. I can't risk his safety during the Summit."

"What does that have to do with us?" Andi asked.

The general smiled at her.

Her insides crawled.

"You may have delivered him home safely, Androma. But that does not mean I am ready to let you go. You will remain here until the Summit is over and all parties from the Unified Systems have returned to their respective planets." His voice was wicked, a devil hiding behind a soothing smile.

"I decline," Andi said, crossing her arms.

"The payment, General," Dex added.

The general ignored their dissent. "You and your crew will be my son's hired guards for the Ucatoria Ball following the Summit meeting. You said yourself how dangerous it could be." General Cortas chuckled as he turned to his Spectre. "Please escort these two to the guest quarters to join the others. Ensure that they have ample time to rest in their rooms, with *no* disturbances." He smiled at them both. "They've had quite a journey thus far."

"You don't own us," Dex protested as the guard made his way around the desk. "If we say no, we say *no*."

The general shook his head. "You're quite wrong on that front, bounty hunter. I have access to all your funds—*and* your Guardianship title, which I can alter as I please. And you, Androma. I don't just have your crew—I believe, in fact, that I also have access to your ship."

"Take the Xen Pterran ship," Andi snarled. "I don't give a damn about it." She hated that he could use her crew and ship to restrain her without physical bonds.

General Cortas chuckled and placed the glasses back on his face. "I'm talking about the *Marauder*, Androma."

Andi's blood turned to ice.

"My ship is on Adhira."

"For now," the general said. "But if Queen Alara wishes to

enter my system for the Summit and prove to the galaxy that Adhira will not bend to Olen's attempts to instill fear…" He waved a hand before him. "Ah, well. I am quite certain she will agree to my terms of entry."

He was going to take the *Marauder*, just like that.

Andi felt herself careening back into that place of darkness. Her cuffs, heavy on her wrists, ached to become weapons, to swing and collide with his face.

"This wasn't part of the deal."

The general did not smile this time when he turned his gaze on her.

"Neither was being delivered a box of my daughter's remaining bones after you left her to burn in the wreckage of my transport ship. You will stay, continue to do my bidding until the Summit is over and only then, if I am pleased with your work, will you be allowed to go free. Remember, girl. I don't just have your crew and ship. I also have your life in my hands, and I can easily do away with all three if you don't comply."

Each word was a jab she couldn't block.

Her breath left her lungs in a hiss.

He was playing with her as he would a puppet.

"And the payment?" Dex asked.

"Still on the table," the general said. He looked down at the screen on his desk. "I'm offering you free room and board and medical care for the Adhiran Sentinel you brought with you. Don't make me regret my kindness. Now…I'm a busy man, as you may well know. Go now, the both of you, before I change my mind."

With that, they were dismissed.

Andi turned to Dex, who was already staring at her, lips pressed tightly closed.

General Cortas had them bound up in his will, simply for the fun of it. To prove that he was above them, and always would be.

"Move along," the general added, just for good measure.

She could kill him now, as easy as breathing.

But Andi knew her crew was now trapped within the confines of Averia, and she'd been the one to lead them in. She hated the thought of telling them they were stuck here, still on this stars-forsaken job.

Bending to the general's will, so far backward that they might break.

*It's almost over*, Andi told herself, trying to stay calm.

"Let's go, Androma," Dex said, placing a strong hand on her shoulder. He gripped it tight, as if he knew the thoughts assaulting her. As if he, too, wanted to fight back. He tilted his chin, sniffed the air and grimaced. "This office smells like a home for the elderly."

Despite herself, Andi smiled as they left the office, trailed by the general's Spectre.

# CHAPTER 70
## LIRA

WHEN LIRA WAS A CHILD GROWING UP IN THE wilderness of Adhira, she couldn't travel more than a few feet away from her twin brother without his fingers gripping her wrist.

Without him rushing to join her side, always the protector. Always the faithful guide.

Everywhere she went, he went. Everything she did, he did.

Their mother had never been there for them, and so Lon had filled that gap for her, and she for him. They'd shared countless memories, days spent exploring the quadrants of their planet, getting lost in its glorious splendor.

They'd been inseparable, two parts of a whole.

Until, one day, Lon stopped following her. He'd grown out of his need to be near his sister, to follow her motions as if they were his own. He turned his attention toward other things.

Like standing guard near the doors of Rhymore, trying his best to imitate the older Sentinels.

Lira had turned her eyes to the sky, while Lon kept his feet on the ground, his greatest wish to be an Adhiran Sentinel, a protector of the queen whose greatest desire was peace.

It was why, of all people, Lon did not belong in this Arcardian hospital bed, his eyes still shut, his vitals being monitored by a medical droid.

"I'm so sorry," Lira whispered as she held Lon's hand in hers. It was warmer than it had been on that horrid journey across the skies, Lon lying on the cold floor of the Xen Pterran warship. His condition was improving.

Soon, he might even wake up.

Lira wanted to run, to be anywhere but here when she told Lon the news of what had transpired on their planet. When he discovered that he wasn't there guarding their aunt, as he'd sworn to.

His chest was bare, the fresh wrappings on his skin pulled taut as he lay in the bed. The gunshot had just missed his vital organs, but he'd lost nearly enough blood to kill him.

And though he'd survived, after he learned how many had died...

Lira guessed Lon would wish himself dead.

So she sat by his side for endless hours, until the warm clutches of sleep stole her away.

In her dreams, she imagined she was riding atop an Adhiran darowak. The massive winged beast, with scales that burned bright like her own, carried her across the skies of Adhira.

The wind pounded fiercely against her, causing her eyes to water, her hands to shake.

Still, she urged the darowak faster.

At top speeds, she felt she could outrun her fears. Her sadness. Her shame.

The beast banked left, its wings snapping like taut fabric. Lira leaned into its neck, gazing down at the ground below.

Rhymore was bathed in black smoke.

They trailed upward, spiraling into the sky and soaring through a bank of clouds. They came out the other side, sputtering, and as Lira looked down over the darowak's outspread wings, her heart froze at the sight.

Adhira was gone. Where the planet used to be, the dry husk of Xen Ptera sat in its place. A bare orb bathed in darkness, a skeletal casing of a world once thriving with life.

*"No,"* Lira gasped. Her heart began to crack. Fissures spread through it, reaching cold fingers through every valve until Lira felt darkness stealing her away.

She fell from the creature's back, screaming.

Tumbling downward, into the endless pit where Adhira used to be.

Lira woke to a soft hand grazing her cheek.

"Don't cry, Lirana."

That voice, so soothing, so full of calm.

Lira opened her eyes, the sticky wetness of tears obscuring her view. But she saw the beautiful woman standing before her clearly enough, a delicate face she knew and loved, despite the differences between them.

"Aunt Alara," she gasped.

Lira leaped from her chair and fell against her aunt. Their arms encircled each other. Tears fell freely from Lira's face, but for once, her scales didn't heat. Instead, cool relief overcame her.

"I'm so sorry," Lira sobbed. "I'm so sorry, Aunt Alara. I didn't know, I never could have known that—"

"It's not your fault, Lirana. Hatred, and the desire to spread fear, is *never* your fault."

"I'll come back home after this," Lira said. "I'll make up for it. I'll do anything. I'll agree to your terms, if you'll only forgive me for bringing Valen there."

"You'll do no such thing," Alara said, pulling back to look into Lira's eyes. "The only thing you will do is follow your heart."

She pulled Lira back to her chest as she cried.

Lira didn't let go of her aunt until the tears dried up. Until they sat down on either side of Lon's bedside, held his hands and spoke of happier times. The beauty of a family that could come together, broken, and still find a way to become something whole.

It wasn't until later that Lon woke, groaning, the scale on his cheek flaring with his pain.

"Lira? Aunt Alara?" he asked, his voice raw. He looked down at his bandaged chest and winced. "What happened?"

Lira was about to speak, to try to explain the horrors that had transpired on Adhira, when her aunt placed a warm hand over hers.

They shared a knowing glance across Lon's body.

"There was an attack," Alara said.

She told the terrible tale, bearing the burden so Lira didn't have to.

# CHAPTER 71
## ANDROMA

ANDI EMERGED FROM THE WOMEN'S BATHING chambers wrapped in a pristine, warm white robe, a fluffy towel protecting her freshly combed hair.

Two hours she'd spent submerged in a pool full of blossom-scented bubbles. She'd scrubbed every inch of her body with asteroid coal, removing the grime of the past few days little by little, until she felt like she could breathe again.

For two hours she'd lost herself in the luxury of solitary silence, not a single person there to ask her questions or wait for commands or—Godstars be damned—bring up what had happened during Revalia, when Andi had danced with Dex.

Her feet were bare for the first time in weeks, a strange feeling as she unlocked her private quarters and padded onto the plush carpet inside.

The room was decadent, plucked straight from the pages of an Arcardian luxury feed. The four-poster bed was large enough for three, the mattress so soft it was like diving into a sea of spun sugar. Across the room, shimmering gold satin drapes hung over an entire wall made of windows. An attendant had pulled them back to reveal the sun setting, the two moons just beginning to brighten in its place like watching eyes.

To anyone else, it would have been a dream to be here. An honor to live in the heart of the general's estate, with its bustling servants and straight-backed soldiers. To be at the headquarters of the Summit preparations during the most exciting time of the galactic year.

Once, she'd been caught up in the spell of this place, a willing victim to its splendor.

But now it only felt like a cage, made worse by the fact that there was an unwanted guest in her room.

It seemed her father had been waiting for her to arrive.

He sat across from her now in a plush red armchair, his blue Spectre uniform edged with shimmering strands of gold that shone in the light of the crystal chandelier overhead.

Andi sighed and moved past him to sit on the edge of her bed, legs crossed beneath her, hands folded in her lap. Her swords, usually strapped to her back, lay beside her on the bed, freshly cleaned, ready for new tallies to be scratched into the metal, to represent the Xen Pterran soldiers she'd slayed on Adhira. She could still remember the feel of each moment, each second as she chose to steal another life. Her stomach ached, thinking of all the impossible choices she'd had to make.

The silence in the room was sharper than her blades. From the moment she'd entered and seen him waiting, she'd refused to offer him a word. He could start the conversation, no matter how awkward the silence became or how long it took for the ice to break.

After a time, her father cleared his throat.

"You've grown," he said. His voice was softer than it had been when he greeted her and Dex earlier. "It's been…quite a while, hasn't it?"

"Four years," Andi said. "Though I guess you've probably forgotten with how busy the general must keep you."

She'd spoken the words like they were light bullets loosed from a gun. Now that they were out, she couldn't take them back.

Her father didn't move. He only worried his hands together, his chest rising and falling with even breaths.

"His head Spectre?" Andi asked. In a whisper, she added, *"Why?"*

His gray eyes met hers for the first time since she arrived. Beneath his gaze, she wanted to break. She wanted to crumble and fall to the floor, begging him to explain himself. But she wasn't a child anymore. She wouldn't crumble. And she *never* begged.

"It's a long story, Androma," he said, sighing. "And I'm not sure you'll like what I have to say."

She glanced at the door that she'd made sure to lock behind her. "I have plenty of time. The general says he's going to pardon me, once this job is said and done."

He pressed a hand to his ear, nodding absently to whatever voice had spoken into his com. He likely had one similar to hers, but she was sure he hadn't had to travel to some dusty moon and find a black-market doctor to install it.

He looked back to Andi, his expression overcome with sadness. But sadness for what, she wondered? The years they'd lost? The mistakes they'd both made?

He looked so much older now. Four years had passed, and yet it seemed like ten.

Had he missed her? Had he wanted to find her after she'd run?

As she looked at him, the memory of their final moments together took shape.

★ ★ ★

*He'd come to visit her in the holding cell, in the southern sector of the capital city. She'd been nearly starved for three days, and her energy was growing faint.*

*"It's happening tomorrow, Androma," her father said.*

*She'd barely been able to look at him without wanting to cry. But she had no tears left. "Will it hurt?" she asked.*

*He'd glanced over his shoulder to where the guards waited several paces away down the hall.*

*When he looked back at her, his expression was haunted. As if he were already looking at his daughter's ghost. "The injection is painless."*

*Andi had nodded then. His words felt so unreal, they hardly registered.*

*Tomorrow she was going to die.*

*"Where is Mom?" Andi asked. "Is she coming to say goodbye?"*

*Tears streamed down his cheeks. "No," he whispered. "She's not well, Androma."*

*As she looked at him, she felt hollow. The guards approached then, telling them that time was up.*

*"Just a final goodbye," her father told them. "I…won't be able to do it, tomorrow."*

*"Make it quick, Oren," the soldier in charge said. He glanced at Andi, equal parts sadness and disappointment in his face. Andi's father had been a soldier his entire life, was as close as family to these comrades who worked the barracks. The soldier ushered the others a few paces away to give Andi and her father space.*

*"We don't have much time," Andi's father whispered. "You need to listen to me."*

*Andi wanted to reach for him. To hold on to him and never let go. She didn't care, in this moment, that he hadn't defended her in the trial days before. He had always represented safety and strength and warmth.*

*After tomorrow, she'd never see him again.*

*Tears poured down her face. "Please," she begged him. "Please, don't let them take me. It was a mistake, Daddy." She was a child, sobbing in a cell meant for a cold-blooded killer. "Please."*

*He crossed the cell in a few strides. Knelt before her until their gazes were level.*

*"Look at me, Androma," he urged. His hands gripped her cheeks, brought her gaze to his. She tried to blink away the tears, to memorize every line of his face. "You're strong. You always have been." His lips were wet with tears as he pressed them to her forehead in a kiss.*

*"Oren," the soldier outside said, more insistent this time. "Come on. It's time."*

*"I'm coming, Broderick," her father growled over his shoulder.*

*He leaned forward and wrapped his arms around Andi. She couldn't hug him back, her burned wrists too painful and fresh. But she felt his warm hands touch the bandages around her wrists, where the burns were still fresh and aching.*

*As he pretended to kiss her cheek, his next words were so low, she barely heard them at all. "Bay Seven. Tomorrow at dawn."*

*Without another word, he slipped something beneath her bandages. Something cold and solid. A key.*

*When he pulled away from her, his eyes burned like coals.*

*"Any last words?" the soldier outside said.*

*"Goodbye, Androma." Her father nodded once. Wiped a tear from his cheek and turned away from her, never looking back.*

*The soldiers locked her cell.*

*In the morning, when the general and his executioner came for her, the cell door was wide open, the cell itself empty as a tomb.*

*Androma Racella was gone.*

"You were always so strong-willed," her father said now. His voice nearly cracked, but he swallowed and it came back stronger, the lines of his face fading as the commander he'd become took the place of the father she'd loved. "I remember the day you were born. You came out kicking and screaming so loud I thought you'd make everyone go deaf. Your mother and I used to joke that you might never stop." He smiled then, a look that made Andi's chest ache. "When you got older, and you started dancing, we were so proud. You used to twirl for hours in the living room, not stopping until you'd gotten every move perfect. Then, when you became a Spectre… You could've gone so far, Androma."

His eyes took on the shine of someone lost in the past. He was looking at her, but it was like he was really seeing the girl she used to be.

The girl she never could or would be again.

So many years had passed since he'd freed her from death. She no longer knew the man before her, and he had no idea who she was now. They were like two strangers—together in this room, but galaxies apart. It made Andi wonder if they could ever rekindle the relationship they had in the past.

"I wrote to you," Andi said suddenly. "Did you…did you get the letters?"

She'd sent so many messages back to Arcardius once she'd had a safe way to do so. Dex had helped her with that—finding messengers to deliver her letters, and scaring the living hell out of them to ensure that they'd stay and wait for any word that her parents wanted to send back in return.

But nothing ever came.

It had helped to harden her heart. To remind her that even though her father had given her a chance at escape…he'd moved on. It proved to Andi that no one, not even family, could be expected to stay close when the sins of life came to tear them apart.

"I couldn't respond," he said. "You know I couldn't."

She'd seen the headlines on the feeds, the suspicions about who had freed Androma Racella before she could pay for her crime.

Her father stood and began to pace. "I had to protect myself. I was being watched, all the time. Anyone who'd ever known you was under scrutiny. Classmates, professors, drill instructors. Your mother and I were at the top of that list. Any tiny mistake,

Androma, and we would have been found out. Marked as traitors, too. I couldn't live with that."

They had never had a chance to discuss what had happened. After Andi had awoken in the hospital, she'd tried to tell them. But all she could do was cry. Then she'd sunk so deeply into herself that no one could speak to her; no matter how loudly they yelled. How desperately they wished for an explanation. She was drowning, not entirely in shock as the doctors thought, but in despair.

She knew exactly what had happened.

She knew exactly how guilty she was.

"We had to live, all these years, without you. Pretending to the public that we loved our daughter, but not the girl who'd murdered Kalee Cortas. That we *never* would have helped a traitor run free."

Silence filled the room.

Andi closed her eyes, realizing in the darkness that though he'd saved her life that day…he'd destroyed many parts of her soul.

She opened her eyes and looked at him, standing there in his Spectre uniform.

"Why didn't you come with me?"

Her father was as still as stone.

"Everyone makes mistakes," Andi said. "Some are bigger than others. It doesn't mean we can't forgive them. That we can't move on. I was a *kid*. Kalee was, too."

Again, she asked him, "Why didn't you come with me? We could have run together. As a family."

He nodded, and for a moment, she thought he was going to embrace her. Tell her that she'd made a horrible mistake, but every mistake could be fixed, could be forgiven. Maybe he'd wrap her up in his arms, tell her that he was sorry, that he should have stood by her side. That she'd done a terrible wrong to the world, but that he had, too, when he hadn't gone with her.

Her heart leaped a little as he did stand.

But instead of coming toward her, he took a half step away. Toward the locked door.

"Was it truly easier?" Andi asked. "Pretending that you never had a daughter at all? It's what you've done all these years, isn't it?"

Suddenly she *was* that little girl again, desperate for her father's approval. But when he turned, his eyes weren't those of her father. He looked like someone else—a man with gray hair and a sagging face, seated behind a desk too small for his massive ego.

He looked like General Cortas.

"You ruined the family name that day," her father said. Every word was a dagger to her gut. Every breath, a stab to deepen the previous wound. "Your mother and I...we worked our entire lives to become honorable members of Arcardian society. We nearly lost that, after I freed you. And if we'd gone with you? A life on the run, as fugitives? That isn't what I promised your mother when I married her and swore to take care of her."

Inside, her mind was screaming *no, no, no.* This wasn't how their reunion was supposed to go. And yet, her father kept digging and twisting the blade.

"We kept you alive, Androma," he whispered suddenly. "We kept you alive, and all it's done is tear us apart from the inside out."

"You sent me out into the galaxy *alone,*" Andi said. "I could have died!"

"But you didn't," her father said. "You survived, Androma. Because we helped set you free, even though no soldier who'd committed such a heinous crime had ever been set free before."

"What's done is done," Andi said, looking past her father at the holo clock on the bedside. "You've made it quite clear that you no longer care for me."

"I know you don't understand my situation, and I would never expect you to," her father said. "The general offered me this position as a mercy. He's a generous man, willing to save your mother and me, even after the destruction you caused for his family. For ours. I took the job, not because I had to, but because I wanted to. To serve our planet in the most honorable way. It was the only way to show the world that we weren't the monstrous parents your actions made us out to be."

Andi let the truth sink into her, heavy as a rock.

Even though he'd saved her life, he'd never forgiven her.

She doubted he'd ever tried.

"So this is how it is now," Andi said, surprised to find that her voice was strong and steady. That with each word, she felt bravery pouring back into her. "You never were on my side, were you? Your own daughter."

Her father reached the door, placed his hand on the scanner and waited for it to unlock. When he looked back, his eyes were haunted in the same way they'd been back in her holding cell the night he'd come to give her the key. She realized now that she'd misread his look then.

She'd always thought he was mourning the years he knew they would never share together, the struggles she would face out alone in the world.

She was wrong. His words confirmed that now.

"As far as I am concerned," he said, glancing back to meet her eyes, "my daughter died in the crash alongside Kalee Cortas. The girl I freed from that cell was not my daughter. Whether or not she knew it at the time, she had already been stolen by the Bloody Baroness."

He stepped out the door. It slid closed behind him, locking her in silence.

She waited for the tears to come. But they never did.

Instead she sat alone, adding more tallies to her swords. Dancing with the dead inside her head.

Later, Andi strapped the swords across her back and climbed out her bedroom window. She snuck out into the night, feeling for all the world like a nameless ghost.

# CHAPTER 72
## NOR

NOR SOLIS HAD DREAMED OF THIS MOMENT for years, dreamed of the empowerment and relief that she would feel when her dark night finally came to an end.

Soon she would leave this place.

Soon she would take her army and conquer the stars.

The attack on Adhira had been a swift one, a wish she'd granted one of her commanders. It was a last-minute decision when she had learned from a source that the Arcardian general's son was there.

Nor smiled.

It was only the beginning.

The sky was mercifully still tonight, the acidic rain swept

away with the sighing of the wind. It had taken skill to escape her palace walls without anyone noticing, without someone following on her tail, an onslaught of questions thrown at her back.

Nor should be pleased.

But now, as she stood upon the dark remains of her former palace, the only emotion she felt was sorrow. It was as if a gaping wound had opened inside her chest, draining all the happiness from her like a black hole.

She couldn't understand why. She should be proud that her weapon was complete, that she and her army could finally take command of the galaxy that had once exiled her system, killing millions of her people and leaving the rest to die slowly and painfully.

From here, Nor could look around and see all of Nivia. The crumbling capital city surrounded her like a shadow of lives once lived. The ancient buildings, long ago vibrant with color and life, now stood as empty shells, monuments to what they had once been.

Nor was dressed in a traveling cloak, the dark cloth flowing to the ground like a river of onyx. She smoothed the fabric as she settled down on a broken bit of stone that must once have been a garden bench.

Some of its former beauty was still evident on the stone, elegantly carved designs that she knew her mother had once loved.

This was where she used to come and sit with Nor as a child. Where she'd rock her gently in her arms, sing sweet songs to her as she gazed out at the flourishing sea of flora.

Nor had come to the old palace alone a handful of times over the years, to seek wisdom from its ruins, to gain strength when she was weak. It was easy for her to see past the destruction, to imagine a bright film laid over the entire landscape. To see what once was and pretend she was still a part of it.

A tiny princess dancing among the smoke lilies, her fingertips grazing the delicate petals as she imagined one day becoming queen.

Tonight, however, she couldn't summon that happy image. Nothing soothed the sadness that seemed to grow within her soul—not even the closeness of her old family home.

Nor looked around the city as if it were the last time she would ever see it. The streets were barren, and the ground rumbled occasionally as a quake hit miles away.

The planet was hanging on, but not for long.

The citizens of the capital were all inside their ramshackle homes. The previous night Nor had issued a mandatory curfew for their protection. She wasn't doubting her plan—*hell forbid* a ruler who did—but if something went wrong, she knew her planet would be targeted once again. Hiding inside their homes wouldn't protect her people, she knew, but it would give them a false sense of security.

Sometimes illusions were better than nothing at all.

Looking off into the distance, she could see green fog rolling in over the cracked mountains. It drifted toward the city, flowing over the ground like death. One could always see it coming, but the fog took its time arriving.

Nor was so transfixed by the sight that she almost cried out when warm hands grazed her shoulders from behind.

*"Nhatyla."* Even though Zahn said only one word, his deep voice soothed her.

"Zahn." She turned toward him, grasping his hands as if he were an anchor. As if, should she ever let go, she would drift toward the green fog that seemed to be waiting to devour her.

Zhan looked at their interwoven hands and furrowed his dark brows.

"What's wrong, my beautiful *Nhatyla*?" He brought her hands to his lips, kissing her knuckles, including her gold prosthetic.

He'd accepted her as she was, from the very start.

And never once had she tried to compel him to be anything but himself.

"I don't know," Nor said, exhaling a long, deep breath in the hope that it would expel the sadness. "I should be overjoyed that today has finally come. We've worked so hard for this moment, Zahn. For years, I've imagined it. But now that it's here, all I feel is anguish."

Zhan leveled his gaze at hers as if he saw her soul. She allowed him. It was the only way she was certain she still had one.

"They would be so proud of you, Nor," he said, and she knew Zhan was talking about her parents.

He'd grown up in this crumbling palace beside her, before the bombs went off. A young guard's son hiding in the shadows, watching her with his knowing eyes.

She'd never truly noticed him until after the bombs had dropped. Until he had pulled her from the rubble, dust coating his dark hair and skin, blood dripping from his mouth.

*You'll be okay, Princess*, he'd said. A boy of ten, his voice soothing, the only thing she could focus on as the world burned around them. He'd wrapped her mangled hand in his own coat. Shortly after, she lost consciousness from blood loss, and when she'd finally woken, days later in a dark underground bunker, her hand missing, her father *dead*, Zahn had been there.

*Stay*, she'd begged him.

He had that day, and all the days that followed.

Her silent strength. Her shoulder to lean on in the shadows, when the pressure of being the queen of a damned world became too much to bear. When her nightmares tried in vain to destroy her.

A silent tear rolled down her cheek now as she thought of the past. Her father's bright smile, her mother's gentle touch. She hadn't truly known her mother; she had only fragmented memories of a woman who looked just like her.

Yet, strangely, it was her mother's voice that visited Nor so often in her dreams. Stranger still that Nor found solace when her mother's distant voice entered her mind, echoing on that fateful day of Xen Ptera's destruction.

SASHA ALSBERG & LINDSAY CUMMINGS

*I'm sorry. I'm so sorry.*

"Nor," Zahn said, drawing her back to him now. "Tell me what you're thinking."

He sat down beside her on the ruined stone bench.

"I'm afraid," she whispered. Her heart clenched, and she wished now more than ever that she could defeat the Unified Systems with her parents by her side. What would Xen Ptera have become if they had survived? If they had all put their strength together and destroyed the worlds beyond as one? "What if I fail?"

"You won't," Zahn said. He chuckled, the sound out of place in this ruined land. "Do you remember what you said to me once?"

"I've said a lot of things," Nor admitted.

He tugged playfully at her hair. "When you were twelve, you took me to the highest room of your tower."

"To see if we could find the stars," Nor said, remembering that night. She'd finally fully healed from the explosions. It was her father's birthday, and she wanted to honor him by searching for his favorite constellation.

"When we got up there, the sky was so thick with fog that we couldn't see them at all," Zahn said. "You threw a fit that drew the attention of the entire palace. And then, once Darai came up to calm you down, you ended up standing with your back to the glass, the entire planet as your backdrop as you gave a speech worthy of a queen."

Nor smiled at that. She'd been so young then, so rash. "What does this have to do with my fear of what's to come?"

He kissed her cheek and chuckled again, his breath hot on her face. "You stood there all by yourself, your chin high, and you told the entire palace staff that someday you'd give them back the stars. *'They'll be so bright, you'll hardly be able to look upon them.'*"

He pulled back to watch her closely. His eyes shone with all the love in the world. She felt it deep within her, a soothing

434

tincture that touched her soul. "You will, *Nhatyla*. You'll give us all back the stars and more."

A tear slipped down her cheek.

He kissed it away.

He was too good for her.

Too pure.

"This is the fulfillment of your promise to your parents. To your people," Zahn said, taking her hand in his again. "Ever since we were young, I have seen you mourn your losses, but at the same time, you grow from them. Vengeance has been a driving force in your life, and now that it is within your grasp, you're left feeling empty. But not for long, my queen. There are plenty of ways to fill the gap." He pulled her into his strong embrace. His heart beat to the rhythm of hers as he whispered, "This part of your life may be coming to an end, but a whole new adventure is starting."

"And what of your future?" Nor asked, gazing at him. "What will you do, Zahn Volknapp?"

She could nearly taste him on her lips as he drew closer.

"You are my future," he whispered. "I will follow you, from this world and to all the others beyond. I'll be there by your side as the people bow before you and sing your name."

He nipped her ear with his teeth.

Lust tumbled through her.

"And in the quiet moments, when we are alone," Zahn whispered, drawing her ever closer, until she was on his lap, his mouth against her lips, "I will bow to you, too, my queen."

"What about now?" she asked.

In that moment, she could feel the sadness slowly leaving her body, power taking its place.

"Now?" Zahn echoed.

His lips moved down her neck, igniting a fire inside of her.

"Now, my queen, I think I am tired of words."

# CHAPTER 73
## ANDROMA

THE NIGHT SKY WAS MORE BEAUTIFUL THAN Andi ever remembered it being. It lay over the land like a blanket of stars, and on a night like this, crisp and clear, she could make out the nebula that surrounded the system. It was a wash of pinks, light and dark, with stars accenting it like delicate jewelry.

Growing up, Andi's mother frequently told her tales of how the galaxy had formed. There were once ancient Night Spirits that lived in the darkness, feeding off the truest of evils. Their counterparts, known as the Light Bearers, kept the darkness at bay. They brought hope back to the worlds they watched over, restoring tranquility to the universe. It was always black and white between the two entities, until one day, everything changed.

A Light Bearer fell in love with a Night Spirit, a unity that was never meant to be, thus creating a cataclysmic event that changed the course of life.

Their love created a monstrous black hole, something so dangerous and untouchable that it was seen as evil incarnate—until the galaxy started to form around the beast.

But the galaxy wasn't the only thing to form from their union. It also gave way to the creation of the Godstars, all-knowing beings with the power to give and take, the perfect mixture of darkness and light.

"It shows us that everyone has a balancing act teetering in their souls," Andi's mother had told her. "We all stand in harmony between the two. It is up to you which side becomes stronger."

Andi thought often about this story, and wondered if it was possible to be as good as the Light Bringers, but also shaded in the darkness of the Night Spirits. She felt as if a war was always going on within her, both sides constantly fighting one another, no matter how hard she tried to keep both at bay.

Tonight in that room with her father, Andi had felt the Night Spirit within her take a hold.

As she walked, Andi took in the view that spread out from the Cortas estate. The distant shine of the city far below, with its glass spires and rigid, straight-backed citizens. Every plant and blade of grass across the planet had an iridescent glow, as if lit from within. From the skies above Arcardius, the shimmering flora made the planet look ethereal, as if the Godstars themselves resided here.

Arcardius was the first planet inhabited by the Ancients hundreds of thousands of years ago, and many believed that the Godstars must have given the settlers this gift to welcome them to their new home. But whatever the reason, Andi was grateful for it. She didn't want to be in the presence of darkness after everything that had happened. She needed to clear her mind of all that had been clogging it since the beginning of the rescue job.

Andi ran her fingers over the moonlit roses. Huge groups of them had been placed around the pathway that led deeper into the gardens. She watched as a flutterwing darted past her, leaving a trail of sparkling pollen in its wake.

Her feet led her down a few more paths lined with flowers and resting flutterwings that looked like little fairies in the hue of the plants' glow. Even with no planned destination, her feet seemed to have a mind of their own, because she suddenly found herself in the middle of a small clearing. In front of her was one of the miniature floating rocks that dotted the skies of the planet.

This one had a small waterfall streaming from its edge into a pool below. Surrounding the perimeter were huge *Gajuai* flowers, their petals growing over one another to create a natural patchwork pattern.

"A wonder, isn't it?" a voice asked behind her. Andi jumped and cursed herself for letting someone sneak up on her.

This planet, and its illusion of safety, was making her lose her touch.

She hardly recognized Valen now that he was cleaned up. His brown hair was cropped short and, skinny as he was, it made his strong jaw more pronounced. Everything about his oncesoft face was now hard edges. No doubt, with some more meat on his bones, he would be striking.

The boy she remembered from years ago had now become a man.

Damaged as he must be on the inside, at least his physical wounds would heal. The awful things he had experienced at the hands of Xen Ptera would hopefully become a distant memory, as well, and more bearable with time.

"You're looking better," Andi said as he approached her, his hazel eyes burning through the darkness like embers. He held a portable easel in his arms, along with a silver box that Andi recognized as his old kit of paints.

"Thanks," he said. "Mother and I installed this garden shortly after the trial, in honor of Kalee."

Andi didn't know how to feel about that revelation. Suddenly the garden around her seemed to darken. She'd felt called here, as if she'd needed this place.

Maybe Kalee's ghost truly was alive, following her through the Cortas estate. Still, Andi didn't feel as if she deserved to be in Kalee's garden.

"I should go," Andi said. "You probably want to spend some time here alone."

"Actually," Valen said, as she turned to leave, "I was going to paint the gardens. But it would be nice to have a living subject to paint. And to talk to someone who won't try to coddle me. Believe it or not, Mother is so afraid to leave me alone, she nearly followed me into the bathroom earlier."

Andi almost laughed as she imagined Merella fussing over her now-grown son. She couldn't imagine the relief she must feel now that Valen had returned.

Andi paused for a moment. "Did you want to paint me?"

Valen nodded. "The way the moonlight catches the metal on your cheekbones and the purple in your hair. It's colors like these, with dimension and depth, that I've missed."

"You used to paint Kalee," Andi said.

Valen nodded. "She loved being the center of attention. She was always so different from me in that respect." He pointed past Andi, to the edge of the clear pool. "You could sit there. On the rock."

Neither of them spoke at first as she sat down, the cool rock beneath her. Valen set up his easel, placing a blank canvas on it, his motions practiced and full of ease. He unlocked his box of paints, setting them out one by one before he dipped his brush into the first, a soft white the color of her hair. It was peaceful, this silence between them, and the trickle of the waterfall beyond.

"I've missed this," Valen said.

"I can tell."

He looked content as his brush slid across the canvas, his eyes flitting back to her every so often. "Someday, I'd like to paint every landscape in Mirabel," he said.

Andi smiled. "I'd like to visit them all."

She thought of her room on the *Marauder*. All the images of the many corners of Mirabel scattered across the glass walls.

They were silent again for a while as Valen worked. As Andi allowed herself to simply sit for a time. To rest in the moment.

"Do you want to see something neat?" Valen asked suddenly, his gaze now fixed on hers. There was a fleck of red paint on his cheek. It reminded Andi of the Valen she'd once known, before everything changed. "That is, if it's still there... I could use a break." He looked at his paint-stained hands.

"Sure, I guess so." Andi shrugged her shoulders. She smiled as she added, "As long as it's not Jumping Mud."

Valen laughed. "I'm still not sorry about that."

Years ago, Valen had brought Andi and Kalee to a garden similar to this one and talked the girls into touching a pile of brackish sludge. It turned out the sludge was nicknamed Jumping Mud by the local kids because some microorganism within caused it to explode in their faces. The two girls had marched back to Kalee's room covered in filth, fuming as they traded fantasies about getting revenge on her older brother.

Hesitantly, Andi agreed, and she followed Valen to the opposite side of the pond.

A small, floating staircase led to the top of the gravarock.

"Kalee used to wish she could climb up to one of the rocks instead of being flown there," Valen explained. "In a weird way, this is for her." He looked over his shoulder at Andi as he began to climb. "Come on."

The stairs stopped at the top of the rock, and Valen led the way onto its surface. A soft layer of glowing green moss had grown there, soft as a blanket. Valen and Andi settled down on it, side by side.

"This used to be the only place I wanted to spend my days," Valen said.

Andi let her gaze drift over the view before her. It was enchanting. Everything was glowing, fields of light from the garden below mixing with the blue and red of the moons above. It all melted into a soft purple.

"I've missed this," Andi admitted.

"Me, too. While I was in Lunamere, I almost forgot what this place looked like."

Andi had, too. The years she'd spent away from home had stolen many of her good memories of Arcardius.

"Do you think you'll ever be the same?" Andi asked.

Valen toyed with the moss between them. He lifted a brow as he turned to her. "Do you?"

"No," she said. "And I don't know that I want to be."

"I learned something, in my time away," he said, leaning back, arms crossed behind his head.

Andi leaned back, too.

The stars stared down at them. The nebula seemed to loose a sigh as it swam far above their heads, sparkling as if it were made of dancing glitter.

"We've been through darkness, Andi," Valen said. "But that doesn't mean we can't still live in the light."

He closed his eyes, and Andi was left to ponder how much his words echoed her own thoughts from earlier, about the balance between the light and the dark.

They stayed there for a time, silence threading between them.

"Hey...Andi?" Valen said as he lifted himself on an arm and turned to her. "This may be overstepping, and I completely understand if you say no..."

His words trailed off, and she nodded her head in encouragement for him to continue.

"Tomorrow is the Summit, and after that is the Ucatoria Ball. Even though I just got back, my father expects me to make an appearance. I know it's safe here, that everything will be fine, but…I think I'd feel better if, perhaps, you and your crew came with me."

Andi couldn't bring herself to tell him about his father's demand. That she and the girls and Dex would already be there, forced to remain until General Cortas decided he would release them.

So she nodded, still staring up at the sky.

"Yes, Valen, we'll be there."

From the corner of her eye, she could see him still watching her. She turned to face him.

"Was there something else?" Andi asked.

Valen's face paled. "I'm required to dance."

Andi laughed at that. Every year, the Summit took place on a different planet. The Ucatoria Ball was always opened by that planet's future successor dancing with a partner, a tradition that had lasted since the first official Summit fifteen years ago.

"I'm not interested in dancing with a girl," Valen said. "So…I thought…maybe I could dance with you?"

Andi let out a single laugh. "I'm a girl, Valen. In case you'd forgotten."

He cursed. "That's not what I meant!" Then he sighed. "I just meant that, at these things, normally, one dances with a romantic interest, and…I'd rather just dance with a friend."

*A friend.*

He said the word as if he really meant it. As if, somehow, despite what they'd been through, the horrors they'd shared, Valen had begun to think of Andi as a *friend*.

Other than her crew, she hadn't had one in years.

A smile, tentative at first, grew on her lips.

"So?" Valen asked. "Do you think…would you want… I'd ask one of your crewmates, but quite frankly, they terrify me."

Andi laughed again. "It's alright, Valen," she said, sitting up and facing him. "I'll dance with you."

The relief on his face was palpable. He smiled, a real, genuine one this time.

"My father won't be pleased," he said.

"Good," Andi said. "Neither will mine."

They shared a soft laugh.

"Let's go back down," Valen said. "I want to finish the painting."

She nodded and glanced one last time at the view before her as she stood. It was breathtaking, rivaling all the places Andi had seen on other planets far from here.

*Friends*, she thought.

She followed him down the stairs, back into the garden below.

# CHAPTER 74
## ANDROMA

EXHAUSTION SWEPT OVER ANDI LIKE A BLAN-
ket as she made her way through the winding halls of the estate
to the guest quarters.

The hallways at this time of night had more traffic going
through them than was normal. The household servants were
working hard day and night to make the estate look even more
extravagant than it already was. To Andi they seemed to be
wasting time by shining already spotless mirrors and windows,
and she wouldn't be surprised to see one of them picking up
microscopic lint from the carpet.

"That horrid horned fellibrag is going to be the death of me," a woman muttered as she picked up the tattered remains of a shredded rug. Andi smothered a laugh and hurried past.

Just as she was about to turn into the corridor where the crew's rooms were located, a commotion stopped her.

"I don't know what happened, madam," one of the servant droids was explaining to the head maid, his antenna wobbling from side to side.

Andi crept closer, curious, as she watched a group of droids and maids hauling away bits of torn metal and glass, large scraps of computerized bits and wires. They dumped them into a large wheeled bin, sighing as they went about their work.

"The general won't be pleased," the head maid said, tapping something onto a holoscreen in her hands. "He's grown rather fond of that AI."

Andi's stomach sank.

Her curiosity was strong enough to draw her around the corner. "What happened?"

The overseer let out an exasperated breath. "Nothing for you to worry about, miss. Just hurry along now."

Andi shrugged and was just turning away when a white, round object caught her eye.

She gasped. *"Alfie."*

One of the maids dumped his dismembered head into the waste bin with a sickening *thump*.

"What happened to him?" Andi asked, surprised to feel a twist in her gut. The AI had been annoying at times, but he'd been loyal to the crew. He'd saved her life on Adhira, and he'd even remembered to bring Havoc for Gilly's sake.

The maid shook her head sadly as she said, "We're looking into it. The AI served the general well all these years. It's likely he got in the way of a cleaning machine, or ran into some of the kitchen droids who didn't appreciate his cooking tips. Now, if you would excuse us, please," she said, ushering Andi along.

Andi wasn't sure if she believed the woman, but the cleanup was nearly done, and she couldn't do anything to help Alfie now.

As she turned to leave, a small, shiny object on the floor caught her eye. Quickly, Andi reached down and palmed it while the maid wasn't looking. She didn't know much about AIs, but the object in her grasp looked like a memory chip.

"What are you going to do with him?" Andi asked casually.

The woman shrugged. "We'll replace him with another. They've developed newer models since he was created."

The maid turned, clearly done with the conversation.

Like it or not, Alfie had become a part of her crew after what he'd done on Adhira. As she stood to leave, Andi slipped the smooth metal chip into a compartment inside her cuffs.

It could be nothing, a useless memento, but her gut told her something different. She'd look into it later.

She passed several other workers as she walked, all of them averting their gazes as if she were a ghost haunting the halls. One they would rather not bother, for fear that she'd soon come to haunt them personally, too.

She came upon the fork in the hallway that marked the half-way point of Averia.

Left would lead her to the guest wing.

Right would lead her toward the residential quarters.

Her old room was in that direction. She knew the path, could already see it in her mind, the hand-painted portraits from Valen that she'd pass, the smell of Kalee's perfume wafting from her always-open door.

Something changed in Andi as she stood there.

*Go right*, her mind whispered. *Go and face your own ghosts.*

Before she could decide otherwise, Andi turned right and headed down the hall.

# CHAPTER 75
## DEX

DEX PRIDED HIMSELF ON THE FACT THAT HE hadn't lost his ability to become one with the shadows.

He'd been following Andi from afar ever since he'd seen her walking back from the gardens with Valen, both of them silent and looking content.

Dex had to talk to her before it was too late.

He'd almost approached her in the hall, but he'd been distracted by the mess the workers were cleaning up. When he'd discovered it was Alfie, he'd stayed behind to ask his own questions after Andi moved along.

A few minutes later, as he caught back up, he'd just barely

seen her turn the corner into the residential wing of the estate, walking confidently as if she knew the route.

This place had once been her home. Of course she knew where she was going. He'd followed her, curious about what she was doing, until she'd stopped before an unlocked wooden door at the end of the hall. Glancing quickly over her shoulder, she'd slipped inside and shut the door behind her.

Dex had spent half the day imagining how this conversation with Andi would go.

There were plenty of potential outcomes, few of them good.

Whether he liked it or not, their time together was coming to an end. He had to talk to her, put his feelings on the line before she soared away from here when the job was done, never to be seen or heard from again.

With a deep breath, Dex opened the door and slipped inside.

The room was massive.

Moonlight danced through two towering windows on the opposite end, casting the rows of shelves in strange shadows. Books filled each shelf, the ancient kind with pages that could be flipped through, containing entire worlds that one could fall into if they weren't careful enough.

Dex had never been a reader, and he knew Andi wasn't much of one, either.

But he remembered her saying that Kalee was.

"The general scoured the galaxy for this collection," Andi said suddenly.

Dex turned. She stood near him in the dark room, softly lit by a beam of moonlight. The sadness in her eyes could almost be felt, like a tangible thing.

"You said Kalee was a reader," Dex said. He laughed softly. "I didn't know she was *this* much of a reader."

"She loved exploring," Andi said. "The general loved keeping her close. And so she turned to books for her adventures."

She turned and walked past the first row of shelves, running her fingertips across the old spines.

Dust swirled into the air at her touch.

"I guess no one's used this room since…" Andi said.

She stopped talking then and continued to gaze at the books. Dex gazed at her, his mind telling him to talk, his lips choosing silence instead.

"What is it about memories," Andi said suddenly, walking back toward him, "that gives them the ability to hurt us so badly?"

Dex shook his head. "The past is powerful. I think you and I both know that."

She finally looked into his eyes. "I'm tired of letting the past control me, Dextro," she whispered. "Aren't you?"

"It's easier said than done," he said back.

She was standing close to him. Close enough that he could see the scar on her neck from an old sparring accident between the two of them. Close enough that, if he closed his eyes, he could almost imagine her heart was beating as quickly as his was now.

There was a deep, brutal scar on his chest, stretching toward his neck, and it had come from her.

She reached up, slowly, and placed her hand over it.

"I never thought I'd see you again," she said. "That night, on the moon… And yet somehow, you survived."

His body felt like melted wax. Useless beneath her touch.

"Andi," Dex started, but she shook her head.

"Don't say anything. Not yet." She swallowed and pulled her hand away. "I've never felt so wounded, Dex, as the night you betrayed me."

He closed his eyes. He felt the pain in her voice as if it were his own.

"I deserved what you did to me. Many times after that night, I wished I *had* died by your blade." She wasn't looking at him anymore. He stepped closer. "Andi."

She glanced up.

"I'm sorry," he said. And though he'd already told her back on the *Marauder*, it felt like he was apologizing for the very first time. "I'm so sorry for betraying you. I'm so sorry for choosing..."

"Dex."

She touched his chest with both hands now. His heart threatened to burst from within.

"I'm sorry, too," she said.

Each word was like a gift he hadn't known he'd been so desperate to receive.

"All these years," Andi said, "I've held on to my hatred of you. And when you showed back up and you told me the truth...I don't know what I feel for you anymore."

He loosed a breath. "I don't know what I feel for you, either."

Andi laughed softly. "We're terrible together, you and I."

"Are we?" Dex asked. "There was a time when we were great together."

He realized that her hands had dropped to find his. That their fingers were suddenly intertwining, and she was pulling him closer to her, until their bodies were almost touching.

"Andi," he whispered. But his words were lost.

She angled her head up to meet his, and when their lips touched, Dex felt a spark so intense it made him feel as if he were electricity itself. Her full lips slid against his, enticing him with such wanting, he couldn't resist the lure.

Then she was tugging at his shirt, yanking him closer. Their limbs tangled together as their chests breathed as one. He lifted her up and spun her so that her back was up against the bookshelves.

Their kisses became insistent. Hungry. The world around them ceased to exist. All that mattered was this moment and nothing more. His tongue teased at her breathless lips as she ran her hands through his hair.

This moment was familiar as much as it was foreign. They

weren't the same people they used to be, but somehow, with her in his arms, his lips against hers, Dex felt as if he was coming home.

They kissed until they couldn't breathe. Until Dex's body ached with wanting, but he knew they had to stop. When they parted, he kept his eyes closed as he rested his forehead against hers.

They stayed like that for a while, in shared silence.

"Dex?" Andi asked.

He pulled away from her so he could look into her eyes.

"We can't… This won't ever…"

"I know," he said.

And in his heart, he knew that it was true. Their two worlds were never meant to become one. That even through the forgiveness, even with the unavoidable feelings that echoed between them, they could never share a future. They had already had their chance, long ago. They'd both ruined it in their own ways.

"What will you do, after this?" Andi asked.

He shrugged. "I'll become a Guardian again. I'll do whatever is asked of me, go wherever my orders tell me to go."

"And the *Marauder*?" Andi asked.

This part Dex had already thought of, and it was what had surprised him the most. "She's yours," he said. "You earned her through sweat and blood."

She laughed softly. He'd miss that laugh. Someday she'd share it with another man, someone who would give her the love she deserved.

"If you ever need a crew," Andi said, "you can call on us."

He knew it was her way of thanking him. He nodded, sighing as exhaustion swept over him. But he didn't want to go.

"It's late," Andi said. "We should probably try to sleep before tomorrow."

*The ball*, Dex remembered suddenly.

As they stood, straightening their clothes, he took her hand in his.

"I've never done this before," he said. He felt foolish. Like a boy again, hoping for the attention of a beautiful girl. "And I know that we don't have a future together, after this is over. But I think…I'd like it if…if you…"

"Oh," Andi glanced at the ground between them. She shook her head, a sad smile on her lips. "I'm already going with Valen."

Dex laughed bitterly. "I never was good with timing, was I?"

She sighed. They turned to leave, walking in silence to the library doors. Before they parted, Andi placed a hand on his arm.

"It was good, Dex," she said. "The time we spent together, before. I wouldn't take any of it back."

She leaned forward and placed a kiss on his cheek.

When they parted ways, Dex couldn't help but feel as if he were seeing Androma Racella for the very last time.

# CHAPTER 76
## ANDROMA

*HER DREAMS WERE WILD, FULL OF SHIPS* spiraling out of control. A tattooed man made out of stars with a handsome, devilish smile took the throttle as they spun endlessly into the black.

It wasn't his ship, and somewhere in the darkness, she heard the screams of her crew. Lives she'd sworn to protect, to keep safe no matter the cost.

"Give me the throttle before you kill us all!" Andi tried to stop him, but when she reached out, his tattoos turned to tallies.

Hundreds of them.

Always, the tallies, countless numbers of those she'd struck down in years past, and the ones she would in years to come.

There was one that stood out the most, a dark mark on his forehead, right between his eyes.

*"The first kill is always the hardest, Baroness," he whispered.*

*He turned into Valen, and his eyes, once hazel, turned to gold and began to drip red with hot, steaming blood.*

Andi woke to the kiss of sunlight on her skin.

And the too-sharp claws of a horned poof as it pounced onto her face.

She yelped and skittered backward, slamming her skull against the headboard as Gilly appeared in her open doorway, laughing as she scooped up the hellish creature and wrapped it in a tight embrace.

"That *thing*," Andi said, as she rubbed her throbbing head and glared at the orange fellibrag sticking out from under Gilly's arm, "deserves to be skewered."

Gilly stuck her tongue out. "You have no heart."

"I do have one, actually, and I'm convinced that monster wants to consume it." She frowned. "What are you doing in here anyway, Gil?"

The door to her room was cracked open. Servants rushed by outside, hauling boxes, sweeping the floors, speaking in hushed but excited tones.

Gilly yanked the covers from Andi's body, then grabbed her hand and practically ripped her from bed. Havoc hissed in defiance, and Andi sneered back at it. Someday, she'd kill it. Accidentally. With her bare hands.

Gilly's eyes flashed with excitement as she bobbed up and down on her toes. "We're going to become beautiful today! It's time for the ball!"

Before Andi could answer, Gilly tugged her along, out the open door and across the hallway, where another door stood ajar. She could hear Breck's voice inside, yammering away, colorful curses spilling out into the hall.

Gilly kicked the door, and it swung wide, revealing the girls inside.

Breck stood before a large mirror, holding a billowing yellow gown to her chest.

"This," she said, turning to look at Andi and Gilly as they entered, "was made for a *queen*."

"And tonight, you'll be one," Andi said as she yawned and shut the door behind her.

Breck sighed and began to sway, hugging the shimmering fabric.

"Not that one," Gilly said. "I told you, I want to match."

"Matching gowns, Gil? There is nothing less fashionable in all of Mirabel."

"Well, tonight, I say we match." Gilly ripped the dress from Breck's arms, giggling as she curled it into a ball and tossed it across the room. It landed on the bed, where Lira sat, her legs dangling over the edge.

When she saw Andi, a slight smile came onto her face.

"How are you?" Andi asked. "I heard Lon is recovering well." She crossed the room and settled down on the bed beside her pilot while Gilly tried to recruit Breck to her matching-gown cause, and Breck howled about how she would only agree if Gilly got rid of her bloodthirsty little devil beast.

"Lon will heal," Lira said. "And Alara has arrived safely on Arcardius. We had a bit of a reunion last night, the three of us."

"I knew he'd survive," Andi said, as she tugged on a silver tassel on one of the pillows. "And I'm so glad that Alara came through the attack unscathed. How are *you* though?"

Lira tilted her head.

"Since our conversation, on the way here," Andi said. If she closed her eyes, she could almost taste the lingering flavor of Griss. The thought alone made her want to vomit.

Lira looked down at the scales on her arms. "It is customary, on my planet, for us to mourn for three days upon the passing of our loved ones."

Andi wanted to reach out and touch her, but she wasn't sure

how Lira would react. Lira was calm and calculated most of the time. But she also felt things deeply. Sometimes, it was as if Lira's heart was not kept inside her chest, but held in her hands.

"It will take time to move past what happened on Adhira," Andi started, but Lira held up a hand.

"My three days of mourning have passed. Lon's and my aunt's, too. Now we, and the others who lost loved ones during the attack, must give the lost spirits to the stars, to the trees, to the wind."

Lira never spoke openly about her beliefs. They were things she treasured, and kept close. Just like the reality of her aunt's true career, and what she'd offered Lira long ago.

"How will you know if they've been given up?" Andi asked.

"We will know." Lira smiled softly. Her gaze swept to the window, where sunlight was trickling in like a golden river. "We will feel them." She smiled then, a genuine, glittering thing. "I have a surprise for you all."

Andi quirked a brow at her friend.

"Well, it's not exactly my surprise, but a surprise from my aunt."

Andi secretly hoped Queen Alara had brought them a bottle of Jurum, because she would need a glass or two if she was going to survive the night.

"Despite her feelings on the matter, she knew how much I love piloting the *Marauder*, and how having to leave it behind hurt us all." She looked at Andi. "So…she brought it with her."

Andi couldn't believe what she'd just heard.

"No way!" Gilly screamed, while Breck's jaw dropped.

"It's here? On Arcardius?" Andi questioned in amazement.

"It sure is." Lira smiled at her friend. "And fully repaired. Believe me, I'm as surprised as the rest of you."

Andi pulled her into a hug. She would have her ship back after all, no matter what General Cortas had to say.

"Thank you," she whispered to Lira. Then she turned to

her gunners. "Get your stuff together. Before we leave for the ball, we'll pack up the ship, so we can get the hell out of here the moment it's done and the general wires us our funds. And Gilly, that includes Havoc. But I want him caged if he's to be on the *Marauder*."

Gilly sighed before mumbling in agreement.

"Is it okay if Lon gets transferred to the *Marauder* during the ball?" Lira asked. "He's not well enough to attend, and after I would like to take him home myself. I know it's an extra stop, but…I figured, after this is all done, we won't be in a rush to get to another job anytime soon, with all the Krevs the general is about to give us."

"Of course, Lir."

"Ladies," Breck said, smiling at the news. "After tonight, we're going to be rich."

The mood in the room lightened tenfold.

The girls sat together for a time, enjoying the peace of each other's presence. They had always been this way, like the many parts of a whole. The captain and her pilot, the sounds of Breck and Gilly in the background like music to soothe their souls.

There was a knock at the door, and a red servant droid rolled in, clawed hands holding out a silver box.

"For you, miss," the droid's robotic voice spoke. "From Mr. Valen Cortas." The droid placed the box on the bed beside Andi, bowed once and rolled out of the room.

"What's in it?" Gilly asked.

She set her beast down, and it immediately began to claw at the thick plush blankets, tearing a hole the size of Andi's fist in the fabric.

"Gilly," Breck breathed out, her teeth gritted. "Take the monster back to its cage."

Gilly ignored her, gently nudging the creature from the bed. It scurried past Breck's feet, and the giantess leaped onto the mattress, causing the box's lid to tumble over.

"Damn," Gilly said as she peered inside.

Lira smiled, her lips pressed together. "It would seem, Androma, that Valen intends to make you a centerpiece at the ball."

"Not the kind you're thinking," Andi said. "We talked about it last night."

She was about to reach into the box when a knock sounded at the door.

"That had better be the matching gowns I ordered," Gilly said. Breck groaned.

The door slid open, and three workers entered, their loose skirts fluttering around their ankles, boxes of makeup and hair products held in their arms.

"We're here to assist Madams Lira, Gilly and Breck in their preparations," the tallest of the women said.

"The Godstars must be real," Breck responded with a sigh, staring longingly at the Arcadian beauty products. "Come on in, friends."

Andi stepped aside to let them pass, smiling as she watched her crew. They deserved this morning, deserved this small gift of normalcy.

She was about to leave the room when another woman slipped inside. A white hood lined with tassels hung over her face. It fell back as she stopped before Andi, her blond ringlets glowing as bright as her smile.

"My, how you've grown," she said, her voice delicate as a blossom.

It couldn't be *her*, not after everything Andi's father had said the night before.

She stood frozen as her mother wrapped her in her arms.

Glorya Racella had always had the power to make anyone feel comfortable in her presence.

Her voice was like music, her scent as sweet as the finest

Arcardian petals and her smile, always present on her face, lit up her features like the moons lit the night sky.

Andi sat in a chair, staring into the mirror as her mother stood behind her, running a brush through her hair.

So many times growing up, they had done this—shared secrets during their quiet moments together, Andi relaxing as her mother's fingertips gently pulled at her scalp. It should have soothed her like it always had in the past.

But today she felt frozen in a memory, like the subject of a photograph or a painting. Clearly visible, as if she were truly alive, but not quite.

And yet, as her mother spoke, Andi couldn't catch even a glimpse of brokenness in her tone, in the sparkle of her eyes. In the way she drank a glass of bubbling pink liquid that a servant drone brought in for her.

"All the things you've missed," her mother said as she gently tugged the brush through a knot at the back of Andi's head. "There's so much, I can hardly consider which to tell you first. Dahlia Juma, from your Academy year, do you remember her?" She waved a hand, her polished nails sparkling like her dress as she tossed back her golden head and laughed. "Of course you do—you two were always at odds with each other. Well, she's engaged to the son of the head strategist on the general's team! You'll see her tonight, I imagine."

Her words faded away as memories took their place. Andi lost herself to them.

*Andi's mother, rummaging through her massive closet, flipping through dress after dress as Andi stood in the doorway, begging her mother to tuck her into bed.*

*"I'm busy, darling. There's a ladies' banquet tonight at Rivendr Tower, and I'd so love to be seen. Perhaps tomorrow."*

*The memory fast-forwarded to Andi sitting at the glass kitchen table, silent as her mother shared the latest society gossip and her father flipped through his holoscreen, nodding absentmindedly at Glorya's words.*

*Andi, on stage at her dance recitals, watching as her parents arrived late, shuffling their way to the front of the crowd.*

*Andi, seated alone in the Academy office, sporting a bloody nose and facing down another punishment.*

*General Cortas coming to greet her. Offering her a chance to become a Spectre.*

*Andi and Kalee together at a military ball. Andi's mother, parading around the room, making sure everyone knew who she was. "That's my daughter," she'd said. "The youngest Spectre in Arcardian history."*

*Andi, cuffed at her trial, watching her mother sob silently into a silver kerchief. But when it came time for them to stand up in her defense, her mother's tears had stopped. She'd never lifted a hand, never spoken a word to protect her daughter.*

*Later, in Andi's cell, Glorya hadn't come to say goodbye.*

"Darling?" Her mother's voice drew her back to the present. "I asked if you'd like to attend the luncheon with me next week? Only the best of the society girls will be there—"

"I won't be here next week," Andi cut in. "I'm leaving as soon as this job is done."

Her mother laughed. "Nonsense, Androma. According to your father, once the Ucatoria Ball is over, the general plans to lift your punishment. It will take time, I'm sure, for people to get past what you did, but surely your rescuing Valen will help them along." She gently patted Andi's cheek, frowning at the metal implants. "These don't suit you, darling. What*ever* have you done to yourself?"

She sighed, then bubbled over with words again. "No matter. Imagine the suitors you could have. Why, you might even find yourself betrothed to the general's son. Think of the headlines on the feeds! *A romance to defy the stars.* There will be plenty of negotiations, of course. Your father will have to speak to the general, see if he can land you a public interview after your pardon, perhaps even with your father and me there, as well, so the people will—"

Andi stood suddenly, cutting her mother off.

"Did you get my messages?"

Glorya looked momentarily caught off guard. Then she smiled, took a sip of her drink and shook her head. "Oh, you know how those things go, dear. Busy schedules. Hard to keep up with them. I did *so* want to respond, but your father...he advised against it. For our own protection."

"But you got them," Andi said. "You saw how badly I needed you. I was starving. I was stealing scraps from garbage piles."

Her mother wrinkled her nose. "Now, that's a silly thing to do."

Andi's mouth fell open. "You're screwing with me, right?"

Her mother looked like she'd been slapped. "A lady does not speak in such a way, Androma! I know I raised you better than that!"

Heat grew in Andi's face, rising from her neck to her cheeks, soaking down into her skin, turning her words to fire. "You didn't raise me at all, Mother. You let me waste away, alone, halfway across the galaxy, while you attended parties. While you drank your bubbling concoctions and shoved the truth down deep."

She slapped the pink drink from her mother's hand.

It dropped to the floor, where the glass shattered. Broken the way Andi's heart had been the very last time she'd seen her parents' faces in the crowd. Turned away from her. Ashamed of their own blood.

She understood their reasons. She *knew* the Arcardian ways, and yet she had never actually been faced with the reality of them. The harshness with which her planet was run.

"Androma." Her mother lowered her voice. "Calm down. This is a special day."

"It's not special at all," Andi hissed. She took another step backward, realizing how taken in she'd been. How *stupid*, to share even a moment of her time with this woman after all her father had said.

But she'd wanted to believe. She'd wanted a chance to get one of her parents back, even if losing the other hurt.

"You abandoned me," Andi said. "You let me escape this planet alone and afraid after what happened. I could have died, just like Kalee. She was more to me than you ever were. She accepted me for who I was without dressing me in diamonds or pearls or throwing me on a stage in a glittering costume to dance for all the world to see. Now she's *gone*, and I'm still here. And you're acting as if nothing ever happened. As if this," Andi waved her hand between the two of them, at the ever-widening gap, "could ever be anything real. The two of you turned out to be just as traitorous as I was, by letting me go free. What would your precious Arcardian society think of *that*?"

Her mother was now taking steps toward the door, that smile still plastered on her face, and now Andi realized that her father had been right. Her mother truly was broken. Glorya Racella was completely swept up in her fantasies about the world. *Andi* wasn't the subject of a painting or a photograph. Her mother was. *All* of Arcardius was, too, like a beautiful, shimmering diamond, tempting to touch, but sharp enough to cut like a knife when you actually pressed your fingertip to it.

This was not her home.

This woman before her was not her family.

"Father said I was dead to him," Andi said. Her mother reached the door, the smile finally slipping from her face. "But I'm beginning to realize that, despite all that's happened, the day I left here was the day I finally came to life."

"What have those beastly girls been pouring into your brain?" her mother tried again. "Really, Androma…"

Andi held up a hand.

Her mother could insult her and belittle her and ignore the

past as much as she liked. But no one in all of Mirabel was allowed to speak ill of her crew.

"That is not my name," Andi whispered. She allowed the darkness to come up into her voice, the mask of shadow and steel to sweep across her face. "My name is the Bloody Baroness. And if you or *Commander Racella* ever so much as utter a single word toward me or my crew again, I will personally strip the skin from your body and wave it like a flag from my starship."

Glorya let out a soft squeak.

Andi snarled with all of her teeth.

It was then that Havoc dashed out from the shadows of the room, yowling as he chased the cap of a perfume bottle that had rolled across the floor. The beast pounced, landing at Glorya's toes with his claws outstretched like tiny daggers.

Andi's mother screamed, sprinting from the room, shouting for the general's Spectres.

When the sounds of her shrieks faded, Andi slumped back into her chair, picked up the brush and began to smooth out the ridiculous ringlet curls her mother was so obsessed with.

She liked the way she styled it better anyway. In a braid that could lash like a whip.

Havoc curled up at her feet, a loud purr rumbling in his throat. This time, Andi didn't mind the sound.

If Gilly had accepted the creature, then Andi could, too.

Family did things like that, made sacrifices when it wasn't the first choice they wished to make. And now Andi knew, perhaps better than she ever had, that the Marauders were more than just a crew of skilled space pirates.

They were family.

She was theirs, and they were hers.

Andi continued to brush her hair as Havoc chomped on the shattered remains of her mother's broken champagne glass.

# CHAPTER 77
## ANDROMA

ANDI NEVER MADE IT TO BAVISTA, HER COMING-
of-age ball.

When Arcadians reached sixteen years of age, young women
and men alike attended a ceremony that they'd dreamed of since
their early years. A way to show their fellow citizens that they
were willing and able to become adult members of society.

She could still remember seeing the otherworldly dresses and
suits float by her on the feeds as she watched the girls and boys
glide into the A'Vianna House in the Glass Sector. They seemed
light as air, full of pride, bursting at the seams with excitement.
Once inside, they would be greeted by members of the Priest
Guild, who would award each young person three items.

The first was a vial of water from the Northern Ocean, symbolizing strength. For growth, they accepted a single leaf from the oldest tree on Arcardius, known as The Mother, which was said to have been planted when the Ancients first arrived. Lastly, they were given a single floating pebble, no larger than a child's fingernail, chiseled from the very gravarock where the Cortas estate was. It represented the wisdom of rising above.

If Kalee hadn't died, if she hadn't been branded a traitor and forced to flee Arcardius...she and Kalee would have joined their peers at Bavista the year they came of age. Instead, she spent it hiking to the top of a Soleran mountain. Staring at the cold world below through a rifle scope as she and Dex waited for a glimpse of an enemy crew.

She hadn't really thought about how she'd missed her Bavista ceremony until now, as she waited for Valen to arrive at her door.

The girls had gone on ahead, too eager to wait. Andi had allowed them, relishing another few moments of peace before Valen arrived.

She stood in front of a full-length, ornate golden mirror, gazing at her reflection.

A gorgeous stranger stared back.

As much as she hated to admit it, the dress Valen had chosen for her did look nice. The bodice was a dark purple that hugged her curves down to the ground, and the sides of the dress had an intricate mesh paneling that flowed into a sweeping train. Her favorite part of the dress, however, were the sword holsters she'd managed to have the dressmaker include. They were formed to her back, and the bodice fabric was thick enough to cover any ridges. It was perfect.

The dressmaker had also accented her gown with a sparkling necklace full of jewels that Andi didn't plan on giving back.

The gems alone would go for thousands of Krevs on the black market.

The hairdresser had loosely curled her hair so the blond and purple strands melded together in soft waves down her back. Andi had seriously contemplated asking the woman if she would like a spot on the crew. Her skills bordered on the magical.

The makeup artist, a frail-looking woman with deep ebony eyes that matched her close-cropped hair, had brushed a shimmering shadow over Andi's lids, followed by a dark wing that made her look almost feline.

Admitting to herself that she looked pretty was something Andi kept private. She didn't want to give her crew the satisfaction of knowing her true thoughts about fashion. How even though she was a fierce, hardened criminal, she could still appreciate the joy of a beautiful, impractical ball gown.

A knock sounded at the door just as the sun was dipping below the horizon, casting Andi's room in a deep golden glow. She took one last look at herself in the mirror before she made her way across the plush carpet, careful not to step on her gown or breathe too deeply, lest the bodice split.

When she opened the door, Valen was standing there, hands stuffed into the pockets of his suit. It was white and pure, at complete odds with Andi's darker gown. Valen's gold eyes widened as he took her in.

"You look great, Androma. I can't wait to see the look on my father's face when we take to the dance floor together."

Andi gave him a smile, taking his outstretched arm as he led them down the hallway.

"You know, you don't look too shabby yourself," she said. "All eyes across Mirabel will be on you."

"I'm counting on it," he said.

"Valen the Resurrected."

He stopped to look at her, brows raised. "What?"

She shrugged. "It's what the press is calling you in all the feeds."

Valen let out a deep chuckle.

"It's good to be back, Androma." He resumed his pace, and

for a moment, Andi let herself dream of what it would have been like to grow up here beside him.

If Kalee was here, too, her arm linked through Valen's. The three of them against the world.

"Something tells me things are about to change for the better," he said. "I'm ready to see it all happen."

Andi wondered what he would do now that he was home with a whole planet at his disposal.

He deserved to have some fun.

With that thought in her mind, they moved down the halls of the Cortas estate, toward the south end, where the ballroom awaited.

# CHAPTER 78
## ANDROMA

IT LOOKED AS IF STARS WERE FALLING FROM the heavens when Valen and Andi entered the ballroom. There was no roof on this section of the estate, only the clear night sky, illuminated by two full moons and the Dyllutos Nebula above. Abstract sculptures sat upon the high-top tables that dotted the room. At the head of the ballroom, the flags of each Unified System hung above an elaborate, pearly stage set with four extravagant seats, one for each system leader.

Although the other decorations were enchanting, it was the floor that awed Andi the most. She wasn't sure how they did it, but below her feet were the swirling colors of a royal blue nebula.

It was as if they had bottled it up just to release the nebula below them, so the partygoers could dance atop the skies.

As Andi took in the space, she felt as if she were looking out the varillium sides of the *Marauder*.

"Are you ready?" Valen asked.

Andi glanced sideways at him. "Are you?"

He nodded curtly, and together, they entered the crowd.

The ballroom was a melting pot, filled with hundreds of people from all across the galaxy. People with many arms and legs. People with horns sprouting from their hairlines. Tenebran Guardians with constellation tattoos like Dex's and the tall, billowing forms of Sorans milled about the crowd. They passed a Soleran woman whose expression was so sharp, it looked like she was carved from ice. Her dress was transparent as an icicle, sparkling with each step she took to reveal her body beneath. The woman momentarily glanced at Andi with white irises—a product of body modification, no doubt.

She spotted a man with technicolored skin that swirled and sparkled and changed shades at random, as if his whole body was covered with one migratory tattoo. He wore a red tunic that was tied at the waist with sparkling diamonds.

People of all races, backgrounds, ages and careers streamed around her as if they didn't have a care in the world.

As if one of the Unified Systems wasn't attacked mere days ago in a bloodbath drawn by the Olen System.

The wealthy citizens of Mirabel didn't stop for anyone. A party was a party, no matter what hell was raining down around them. Money was the ultimate protector. As long as it was available in plenty, they would always feel safe.

Valen came to a stop near a high-top table toward the back. Andi was keenly aware of the stares and whispers that followed them like a shadow through the room. They saw a pirate and a prisoner, a decorated son and his sister's killer. Andi had expected this, so she ignored them.

SASHA ALSBERG & LINDSAY CUMMINGS

Valen, on the other hand, looked like a caged animal.

"Just ignore them," Andi suggested. "It will only make you look stronger."

She wasn't that great at soothing others' nerves—had never truly been able to calm even herself—but she tried her best with Valen as his eyes darted to different locations in the room.

His gaze finally settled on a group in the middle of the crowd. He smiled.

"They seem to be enjoying themselves."

The music was soft and elegant, but Breck and Gilly were dancing wildly, arms and legs flying everywhere so haphazardly that the nearest dancers were at least five feet away. Andi choked back a laugh. They had their matching dresses on.

Lira was off to the side, talking to an Adhiran official. Her brows were scrunched together like they always did when she concentrated on something serious.

"Valen!" a voice called from behind them.

They both turned to see a plump man approaching, a shock of wine-red hair styled like a wave atop his head.

"Is that—" Andi started, cocking her head toward the approaching figure.

"Alodius Mintus," finished Valen. "Yes, I believe it is. It has to be. He still has that mole above his left eye."

Alodius, an old classmate who'd always been interested in Kalee, stopped in front of them, releasing a huge sigh.

"Good Godstars, man," he said, grabbing Valen's hand from the table and clasping it in his own. "I'm so happy you are home. I thought I'd never see you again!" He playfully swung two fists at Valen's shoulder. "You gave those Xen Pterrans a good pummeling, didn't you, Cortas?"

Andi wanted to cringe at his bad joke, but she resisted as his eyes drifted to her.

"And who do we have here? Already getting the girls, am I right?" Andi wanted to laugh, not at his second attempt at a joke, but because he tried to wink at her and ended up failing, scrunching his entire face instead.

Andi cocked her head. "What, you don't remember me? I thought for certain you would, since you always asked me to pass your disturbingly intimate love poems to Kalee." She felt immense pleasure as his smile dropped. Even his carefully coiled red hair seemed to go limp on his forehead.

"Alodius, you remember Androma Racella," Valen offered.

Alodius opened his mouth, as if he was going to say something, but then thought better of it.

Valen and Andi watched as he started to retreat into the growing crowd of people.

"I have to… There's someone… Oh, look at the time!" he squeaked, giving them a little wave before turning on his heel and nearly tripping as he disappeared into the crowd.

"Well, then," Valen breathed. "That certainly improved my mood."

For the next little while, he smiled as old friends, and those intent on becoming new ones, greeted him. The look on his face was genuine. Andi watched him closely, surprised to see that he'd fallen easily into the role he had to play. Valen the Resurrected, returned home from the horrors he'd faced, yet still with all the poise of a general's son.

But his expression changed when the announcer appeared on stage and called for the official start of the ball.

"This is it," Valen said, turning to Andi.

On stage, General Cortas's face twitched as Valen and Andi stood together and swept onto the now-empty dance floor. A few gasps broke out, then whispers, trickling throughout the room like bugs.

Valen's palms shook as he placed a hand on her waist and grasped her left hand with the other.

"Relax," Andi whispered. "Let's give them something to talk about."

She flashed him a wicked grin as the music began.

And as Valen spun her into the first move of the dance, Andi saw Dex standing on the fringes of the crowd, an expression of longing clear on his face.

# CHAPTER 79
## DEX

DEX WONDERED WHY THIS WAS HAPPENING again. Either it was a very strong form of déjà vu, or a cruel joke being played just for kicks.

Here Dex was, dressed to make the ladies swoon, but all he could do was watch Valen and Andi waltz on the dance floor to the melodic music, wishing he could take Valen's place.

He'd told himself he wasn't going to do this.

That last night, after their kiss, they had said their goodbyes. He'd carefully placed his feelings into a locked box deep in the confines of his mind, then thrown away the key.

But Godstars above, she was striking, her beauty every bit as deadly as her fists.

He had seen her wear various types of clothing in the past—and sometimes nothing at all—but she'd never worn a smile so easily. Never truly danced in the way she'd spent her life training, and tonight, she was impossible to look away from.

He'd thought that the time they shared last night would be enough.

But now, as Valen dipped her, and Andi laughed...

He couldn't take it. He still wanted to be by her side. To be the one whose hands held her, instead of Valen.

*Lucky bastard*, Dex thought.

He turned away, shouldering through the crowd until he found the crew.

"That bad?" Lira asked when she saw the expression on his face, the way Dex slumped into a chair and reached for a glass of bubbling liquid on the table.

"Worse," Dex said.

Gilly sighed wistfully. "I can't wait until I'm in love."

"It's not love," Dex growled. "Not even close."

Breck raised a brow without saying a word.

He sat with them, stewing in his misery, until the song ended and General Cortas took the stage.

# CHAPTER 80
## ANDROMA

WHEN ANDI WAS YOUNGER, SHE'D WATCHED the Ucatoria Ball on the feeds in her parents' living room.

No matter which planet the ball took place on, the room on the feed always shone, as if glitter were cascading down upon the partygoers like a constant, shimmering rain. She'd always turned on the holo feature so that the flickering images of dancers filled the room. It was as if they'd been transported right from the Ucatoria Ball into Andi's home. When the music played on the feed, she danced to its beat and fell into step among the glamorous patrons.

Women in lush gowns danced beside her, while others twirled through the couch at her back. Partners spun atop the coffee table, then glided right through Andi as if she was simply a part of them and they of her.

She'd always dreamed of attending the ball, but when it came time for the dancing to end, and the host system's leader to make his or her speech, Andi had always frowned, turned off the holo and found other things to occupy her time.

Tonight, she wished she could do the very same.

But the host of this year's Ucatoria was General Cortas, and he wasn't just a holo before her. He was flesh and blood as he stood on the dais at the front of the room, his golden suit blinding in the bright lights over his head. Cameras hovered beside him, catching every detail of the general's face.

He looked ten years younger tonight, as if he'd put on a second skin to hide his age.

But his true self still lay beneath.

"I'm going to need another drink after this speech," Breck said as Andi joined her crew at their table.

"Have you seen Dex?" Andi whispered, glancing around the room.

Breck shrugged her large shoulders. "He said he was going to the bar. I'm sure he's already guzzling his jealousy away."

Her words trailed off as the crowd fell silent. Behind General Cortas, the other system leaders took their places, seated on plush throne-like chairs, the colors of their respective systems woven into the fabric.

"Citizens of Mirabel," the general began. His voice, usually so cold, was dripping with a charm that made Andi want to retch. "Welcome," he said, lifting his arms wide, "to the fifteenth annual Ucatoria Ball!"

The crowd cheered, ladies gently tapping their fans against their palms, joyous laughter ringing across the room like the tinkling of bells.

General Cortas grinned as he waited for silence to wash over the room again. "For fifteen years, the Unified Systems have lived in peace. Tonight, we celebrate that unity!" He gestured toward his fellow system leaders. "Let us extend a warm Arcardian welcome to the leaders of the Stuna, Tavina and Prime Systems!"

The crowd cheered again as the leaders behind the general stood together, hands raised in celebration. Governor Kravan of the Tavina System had hair utterly bleached of color, just like Solera, the ice planet where he lived. To the right was General Polerana of the Prime System. She was a muscular woman who looked like she could split Governor Kravan in half. Beneath her black military uniform, Andi could see constellation tattoos crisscrossing her body just like Dex's, the sign of a Tenebran Guardian.

Andi's eyes then fell on Alara, the most breathtaking of them all. She stood with her shoulders back, her small pointed chin held high in a stance that spoke of Adhiran grace. Her bald head was adorned with a glittering green crown, vines and white moonflowers woven intricately around it like delicate, living jewels.

General Cortas extended a hand in her direction. "An extra warm greeting, my friends, for our dear Queen Alara of Adhira, who has journeyed far to show her people's resilience and bravery during the aftermath of the grievous attack on her planet."

She stood and gave the crowd a slight smile, one that looked empty, almost sad. She touched her forehead, an Adhiran sign of gratitude, before sitting back down.

The general pressed a hand to his heart, sending a look of utmost honor toward Alara. Andi imagined him practicing that look before the mirror today, ensuring that he'd look the ever-concerned leader of Arcardius.

He turned back to the crowd, a smooth smile on his thin lips. "Many years ago, these four systems came together and declared a shared desire for unity. Tonight, we celebrate that unity. We celebrate the fact that the Unified Systems, though light-years apart, are *one* system. One world spread across many."

More clapping. The levitating cameras flashed as the general showed off his practiced smile.

"Together, we remain as strong as we were on that final day of battle over a decade ago. Today, we continue to keep our trading ports open, to share new knowledge between the brightest scholars of each system and to be constant in our communications with one another. Why, just yesterday, I caught my wife sending a com to Governor Kravan's wife. I believe the topic of discussion was how closely they could match their gowns without too many people taking notice."

The crowd erupted with polite laughter.

"I told you matching gowns were all the rage," Gilly muttered to Breck.

Andi's skin itched from this speech. This was a waste of her time.

In a few more hours, she and her crew would go free. She would take off this gown, don her bodysuit and swords and they'd be off to take back the *Marauder*, piloting it toward some other mission. Some distant place, far away from the shimmer and shine of Arcardius.

But for now, the speech droned on and on, and Andi lost herself in watching the crowd instead. Some smiles were genuine, like that of an expectant mother across the room, her hands splayed across her swollen belly as she watched General Cortas speak of the future and an ever-brighter tomorrow for the galaxy.

Across the room, a group of girls clustered together, giggling silently as their parents sent them looks of disapproval. A few feet away, two handsome young Arcardian soldiers, their hair groomed back and glowing under the lights, watched the girls with open interest.

Later, Andi knew, they'd walk up to the girls, try to win them over with their smooth words. Hopefully, if the girls were smart, they'd shut the boys down.

But they likely wouldn't. They'd dance together. They'd plan their futures, set on moving higher and higher up in society until they reached the top, just as Andi's parents had.

Andi sighed and glanced over at Valen. He stood in the shadows of the stage, his mother beside him with a gloved hand on his shoulder.

Maybe, in another life, Andi and Valen would have been the same.

Two young Arcardians with bright futures, possibly joined together as society deemed they should be.

Now Valen was staying here.

And she would be gone, never to return.

Their eyes met for a moment, and the new friendship between them made Andi's chest ache a little. She rolled her eyes and pretended to yawn.

He smiled, as if he wanted to laugh. But then something passed over his eyes, and he looked away, his jaw tight.

"Valen," the general said. "My son. Would you join me?"

Valen approached the podium with his mother in tow. They looked like the perfect family to anyone who didn't know about Valen's kidnapping, the general's devilish dealings and the way Merella often turned a blind eye for the sake of the family's reputation.

Everyone in the crowd craned their necks, eager to get an up-close look at the lost son, returned home at last. Andi watched, too, not because Valen was a spectacle, but because she knew, perhaps more than anyone, that he hated to be on display.

Merella stopped short, and Valen's footsteps were the only sound in the room as he walked across the stage to join his father.

General Cortas placed a hand on Valen's shoulder.

Andi noticed the flinch. Almost imperceptible, but there nonetheless. For a moment, Valen looked stiff and pained, as if the darkness of Lunamere was threatening to appear in this room, in front of this crowd and all the watching eyes across Mirabel.

But then he relaxed, sank into the persona of the smooth politician's son he'd been trained to be since birth.

"We are a resilient galaxy," General Cortas said, staring into the cameras, "fully capable of coming back stronger than ever before." He squeezed Valen's shoulder. "My son is proof of this. Many of you know that Valen, my precious firstborn, was taken by Xen Pterran mercenaries two years ago."

The crowd nodded, hushed sounds of disapproval and sadness sweeping across the room.

The general pressed a hand to his heart as if he was touched by their concern. "Thanks to an Arcardian-born hired hand," he said, pointedly *not* looking at Andi, "he has made it back safe and sound."

The crowd roared, and the general raised his hands, his voice booming into the mic.

"Having my son back home after two years of imprisonment on Xen Ptera is proof of our strength and resilience in even the most trying of times. We will not be broken! We will not bow to fear!" He held a hand out to Valen.

With strange, almost broken steps, Valen moved forward.

General Cortas placed a hand on his son's cheek and smiled.

Valen did not smile back.

# CHAPTER 81
## VALEN

THIS WAS HIS MOMENT.

The crowd was loud, the cheers meant for him booming over the sound of his father's voice on the loudspeaker. As Valen looked out across the packed crowd, he saw the looks of adoration in their eyes, people pressing kerchiefs to their faces to wipe away freshly fallen tears, others clapping and waving beneath the glorious skies.

He'd dreamed of this, people calling *his* name, their sights set only on him. Not because of his father, and not because of his last name. Just Valen, standing with his sister, watching the world appreciate them, worship them.

"For you, my son," his father said now.

Valen nodded and plastered a false smile on his face, but it was all a lie.

These cheers *weren't* for him—never could be, because nobody truly knew him. Nobody truly understood the things that Valen had been through.

His father's hand felt like a flaming whip on his cheek.

"My son," the general said, the mic sending his voice out across the crowd, where it echoed back and into his ears and his brain. Valen wanted it *out*. He never wanted to hear that voice again. "Welcome back to Arcardius. Welcome home."

The crowd roared louder, a wave that was cresting, ready to break on top of him.

Valen had made it back to Arcardius, that much was true.

But he wasn't home. He was far, far from it.

Lunamere had been full of terrors, but those terrors had given way to his salvation.

In the back of his mind, he heard a young woman's voice, tender and loving, yet full of power and presence as she spoke to him. He saw golden eyes, dark hair and a heart intent on bringing light back into the galaxy.

It was time.

Valen felt it, as much as he felt the tainted blood pumping in his veins, as much as he felt the separation between himself and the man who stood before him now, pressing a too-hot hand to his cheek.

In Lunamere, Valen had learned of the true darkness his father harbored. A soul as black as the night with secrets as sharp as thorns. They may have shared a lineage, but that was only half of who Valen was.

The other half had taken over him, helped him to become who he had always been beneath the surface.

It all began tonight.

*Home*, his father was saying. *Home*.

"This is *not* my home," Valen said as he stared into the eyes of the man he'd once been so desperate to be loved by. "It never will be."

Valen's hand was steady as he retrieved the blade from the inner lining of his suit pocket.

*I am Valen Solis*, he told himself. *Vengeance will be mine.*

He smiled and drove the knife into his father's chest.

# CHAPTER 82
## ANDROMA

FIRST THERE WAS THE SILVER FLASH OF A KNIFE.

Then there was blood.

Andi watched, frozen in horror as it bloomed like a crimson nebula on the general's chest.

He staggered back once. Twice.

He reached for Valen with a trembling hand. The knife was soundless as Valen pulled it from his father's chest. General Cortas tumbled to the stage with a sickening *thump*.

A woman's scream pierced the air.

Andi saw Merella, Valen's mother, fall at her husband's side.

Then an explosion rocked the ballroom. Glass shattered as the walls were blasted open.

All around her, soldiers clad in crimson began to swarm through the crowd, the symbol of Xen Ptera painted on their armored chests.

A young man screamed as he pointed them out. Then another scream came, and another, and another, until the entire room had erupted into terror.

When the first shot rang out, Andi already had an electric dagger pulled from her thigh holster, the blade sizzling with electricity, eager to protect, eager to *kill*.

# CHAPTER 83
## DEX

XEN PTERRAN SOLDIERS SWARMED THE ROOM.

One second they weren't there, and the next, they were *everywhere*, all around the crowd, black rifles held before them like beacons of death. It was Adhira all over again.

Onstage, Valen still stood over his father's body, knife held in his hand, a strange, absent look on his face as on-duty Arcardian soldiers lifted their own rifles and readied themselves for battle.

They'd only taken down a few enemies when Valen gripped the microphone.

He turned to face the Arcardians, his hand raised in a lazy gesture.

*"Stop!"*

The soldiers froze, accepting the command immediately. Their limbs were unmoving, and their eyes were vacant in their slack faces.

"Lay down your rifles," Valen said.

The Arcardian soldiers dropped their weapons.

Then Dex saw the purple crackle of electricity as Andi's dagger appeared in her hands.

"Wait!" he yelled.

But she sprinted past him, heading straight for Valen.

# CHAPTER 84
## ANDROMA

ANDI DIDN'T THINK; SHE JUST *MOVED* AS HER feet carried her across the room toward Valen.

Her grip tightened on the dagger as she reached the stage, leaping onto it and skidding to a stop in front of Valen, prepared to do what she had to.

He spun around just in time, arm held before him with the knife still clutched in his fist.

"Why?" Andi asked. "*Why* would you do this?"

Behind Valen, six Patrolmen stood frozen, still as statues, midstride, their weapons discarded on the floor. And yet they did not move. Not even to blink. They only moved when six gunshots rang out, and they all fell to the floor in a heap.

General Cortas lay a few feet away, gasping as Merella pressed her hands to his wound, screaming for help, her voice ragged as all around the room, soldiers from Xen Ptera fired their guns. Andi watched as a woman dropped, her head hitting the floor with a sickening *thump*. Her arms splayed out against the swirling floor, limp.

Andi couldn't see her crew, could barely see *anything* in the chaos.

"Androma," Valen said. She whirled back to him. The knife in his hand shone red with blood, all the way to the handle.

Time froze around the two of them.

"I had to do it," he said. She could barely hear him above the screams. What could only be bullets flying from the guns, striking partygoers and shattering glass. Merella was still screaming as Xen Pterran soldiers angled guns at the other system leaders, who sat stunned in their seats, arms raised in surrender.

"He's still alive," Valen said. A smear of blood was trailing from the general as he gasped and tried to crawl away. Valen sighed. "I have to finish the job." He turned, twirling the knife so that he held the blade like a paintbrush, ready to render death upon his own father.

Andi slid past him and stood in his way. "Valen. Stop."

Whatever the reason, this was *wrong*. This wasn't Valen standing before her—not the sensitive boy she'd known, nor the sad, broken man she'd found in Lunamere. This was a killer, cold and heartless.

This was someone like *her*.

Valen's jaw twitched. "Move."

Andi remained in position. "You don't have to do this," she said, her heart hammering. She frowned at him. "What did they do to you in Lunamere? What did they say?"

"The truth." He closed his eyes, rolled his neck from side to side, a small frown on his lips. When he opened his eyes, they were full of an evil she never would have believed him capable of harboring.

"*Please*, Valen," Andi said. "You don't have to do this."

"You're wrong, Androma," Valen said. His eyes fell on the dying man between them. "It's all I've ever had to do."

"I'll stop you," she whispered.

"No." He tightened his grip on the knife and stepped forward. "You won't."

# CHAPTER 85
## DEX

SPARKS FLEW AS STEEL CLASHED AGAINST STEEL.

Andi and Valen were a blur as they fought on stage, too far away for Dex to jump in. The crowd roared around him, people sprinting and bodies falling, their extravagant clothing tripping them up as they tried to escape the chaos.

The Xen Pterran soldiers shot heartlessly, their bullets striking down everyone in their path. It was Adhira all over again, despite what the general had said, despite Arcardius's so-called invulnerability.

Now General Cortas was dying, by the hand of his own son.

Valen the weak.

Valen the painter.

Valen the murderer. It didn't add up.

A man screamed as a soldier began raining bullets in his path. The weaponry was older, outdated, and yet the ammunition was not. Dex saw the moment the man was shot. He watched, horrified, as a silvery substance splattered against the man's forehead where the bullet had gone in. The liquid shimmered and sank beneath his skin, like water into a drain.

The man crumpled to the ground, where he lay faceup, staring up at the sky.

*Move*, Dex told himself. *Get the hell out of here.*

He could see the exit, a perfectly straight path to freedom, with only a few bodies in his way.

But he couldn't leave Andi behind.

Then he heard her scream.

It was a sound he knew like the beat of his own heart, like the roaring of the blood in his ears. He whirled around, his vision tunneling to focus on her.

Andi was down on one knee before Valen. Blood dripped from her collarbone, seeping from a deep wound.

Andi's knife was on the ground between them, the electricity crackling a single time before it winked out.

She grabbed it and shook it once, like the snap of a whip. The electricity fired back up, swimming across the sharpest edge.

Dex was close enough now to hear her voice.

The shots were fewer, lessening to the point that he knew they had no time. That in seconds, he would probably be next.

But he couldn't look away.

When she stood, somehow hauling herself up on shaky feet, Dex knew that Valen would die.

Because it was not Andi who rose, but someone else in her place.

The Bloody Baroness.

# CHAPTER 86
## ANDROMA

ANDI FOUGHT LIKE VALEN WAS HER PAST COME back to haunt her, and with every swing of her blade, she saw the chance to erase him.

But he was too quick. Too skilled. Too *other*.

Not the Valen she'd grown up with, not the Valen she'd rescued.

*Lies.*

*Betrayal.*

*Take him down, Androma, take him down.*

It was not her voice, but Kalee's, that called to her mind.

She advanced on him with fire in her heart, pain lancing through her veins like a poison. The shaky friendship they'd built was gone. She wasn't even sure if it was ever real.

"Kalee wouldn't have wanted this!" Andi screamed. "She wouldn't have…"

Her words trailed off as she saw a flash of blue in the crowd. Lira, rushing toward her, Gilly and Breck just beyond.

She opened her mouth to yell at them, to tell them to run.

Her words were cut off by a gunshot.

The horrible, heart-shredding sound of Lira's scream as she fell face-first to the floor. Another two shots. Another scream, this time from Andi's own lips, Breck howling along with her as she and Gilly fell.

A soldier stood behind them, rifle aimed, blue smoke trailing from its barrel like a demon's hot, hateful breath.

"You can't win this battle, Androma," Valen said. His lips were close to her ear, but his voice was far away. As distant as the safety of the stars.

When Valen dug his knife into her chest, she didn't even feel the pain.

"You shouldn't have gotten in the way," he said.

Andi fell to her knees. She gasped, looking down to see the hilt of his knife sticking from her chest. She pulled it out. Dropped it to the floor and fell beside it into a pool of her own blood.

Valen's image blurred as he walked away from the stage.

The last thing Andi saw was Dex's face in the crowd.

Then the darkness arrived and swallowed her whole.

# CHAPTER 87
## DEX

HE WAS TOO LATE.

For a heartbeat, Dex thought she was dead.

All around him, the room was growing quieter, the screams dying down.

A few more shots here.

A few more there.

The *thump* of a body hitting the floor.

The *click* of another silver bullet sliding into a rifle's chamber.

Dex reached the stage. The system leaders were huddled together in their chairs, bodies of Patrolmen littering the ground around them. But Andi was the only person he had eyes for.

"Hang on," Dex said to Andi. His fingers found her throat. A tiny heartbeat fluttered beneath her skin. "You just hang on."

He saw his hands moving, instinctively ripping off his jacket and pressing it to her chest. He'd kill Valen for this. He'd kill him slowly, bring him back and kill him again.

Her breaths were ragged. She was losing too much blood.

In the crowd, he saw Lira, Gilly and Breck among the fallen. Dex's body shook.

This was a nightmare. One he couldn't wake up from. It had to be.

A few partygoers still stood around silently, frozen in shock. One man huddled in the far corner of the room, arms wrapped around his chest, eyes wide.

"I'm getting you out of here," Dex whispered to Andi as he wrapped his arms around her and lifted her up. "Now."

He could hear the faraway rumble of a ship tearing through the skies, coming ever closer. But what was the point?

These people were beyond saving now.

Bodies were spread across the floor like a carpet, eyes open to stare into the darkness above. Blood staining…

Dex paused.

With a strange sense of clarity, he took in the scene a second time. It was then that he noticed there *was* no blood.

Well, there were a few splashes of red or green or blue, from the soldiers the Patrolmen had managed to stop before the Xen Pterrans gained the upper hand.

But other than that, the room should have been flowing in rivers of steaming colors with the deaths of these men and women from all across Mirabel.

And yet the ground, the gowns, the suits, the ties…they were all completely dry.

Valen had crossed the room, walking over bodies with his head held high like a king of criminals, a lord that delivered loss.

The soldiers, now grouped together near the ballroom doors, stood at the ready before him. As if…as if *he* was their leader.

A shiver ran through him.

*Run now, Dextro. Run, before it's too late.*

The sound of the ship was growing closer. He could see its lights in the sky, and instinct told him it wasn't help. There would be no help tonight, not after this.

He knew there had to be another way out of here. Dex had heard of secret passageways built on the leaders' estates, to help them escape in the event of an attack. He simply had to find one.

Dex cautiously carried Andi off the far side of the stage. As he tucked himself and Andi into the shadows behind a nearby bar, all around the room, the dead began to rise.

# CHAPTER 88
## VALEN

A TWITCH. A CURL OF THE FINGERS, THE clenching of a fist. The blink of freshly opened eyes.

Valen watched it all happen before him, as promised.

He closed his eyes, imagined the little glowing blue thread in the back of his mind. It had always been there, something he'd seen and felt since he was a child.

Only after his time in Lunamere had he fully understood the meaning of it. The raw, pure power he had.

He focused on the thread and *pulled*.

The warmth of her mental presence arrived at once, just as it had when they'd landed on Adhira, and he'd called upon her. Valen sighed, relief flooding into him as their minds wove together, no longer two separate threads, but a shared tapestry. Here, in this intimate space between them, was where he belonged.

It was his birthright. His past and his present and his future all coming together. Everything finally made sense.

She'd given him the keys to understanding, and now he was whole.

*The change is happening, Sister,* Valen thought.

He could almost feel her smile, something so rare for her. As the feeling passed through him, his own mouth quirked at the corners. They'd had so little to smile about until recently. But all the months he'd spent in Lunamere had been worth it.

For this.

*Have them ready for me when I arrive,* she replied.

For a moment, there was silence between them, the space in his mind empty of her warmth.

Then her voice came again. *You did well, Brother. My faith in you was never misplaced.*

She was glorious. But it was more than that. She was victorious, a soldier standing on a blood-soaked battleground, watching the last of her enemies fall.

Valen closed the link, the tapestry gone, the single thread all that remained.

For a moment, he felt cold. Lifeless.

Then he saw the first body stand back up. A Patrolman, unmarred on the outside from the engineered bullets. Like beacons in the crowd, others stood around him. Women, children.

The ones who'd turned, surely ready to join the cause, looked fresh and alert, as if waking from a restful sleep.

The others, the unaffected anomalies who were immune to the substance the bullets carried... Valen knew he'd have to take care of *them* soon enough.

*Like Androma,* he thought with a twinge of sadness. He'd seen that bullet hit her, but she did not fall. She was unaffected by

Zenith. So many times, he'd tried to compel her, only to feel a wall come up in her mind.

One of the soldiers approached Valen. "She's landing, sir."

"Good," he said. "Take care of the remaining unaffected. I don't want her to have to lay eyes on them."

The soldier saluted, slapping a fist to his heart, then rushed off into the crowd as more people began to stand and wake from their stupor. The unaffected were easy to spot. There weren't many, perhaps ten. They walked in circles, blinking, calling for their loved ones.

"A shame," Valen said to no one.

They would all die.

He heard the ship landing, felt the vibration of the ground beneath his feet. His heart raced, and his mind whispered, *family, blood, truth.*

The shattered glass from the doors crunched underfoot as another set of guards arrived.

He turned and made his way to the stage.

There was a wet, red smear where his father's body had been. Valen clenched his jaw.

*Andi*, he thought.

Her body was gone, too.

*Dex*, he thought right after. He couldn't see them, but he knew they hadn't escaped. Not in Andi's condition. And not with his guards blocking every exit.

There were other, far more important things to attend to at the moment, however.

The crowd was just beginning to brew with the sound of voices. Questions. People staring at others around them, wondering what had happened, why there were soldiers guarding the doors. And yet, thanks to the bullets, they stayed mercifully calm.

Valen scanned the faces again, his eyes falling on Lira, the pilot. She stood beside Gilly, both of them staring silently.

Again, the tug at Valen's mind came, and he knew his sister was close.

He faced the crowd, spreading his arms wide. *"Look at me."*

His voice rang out steady and true, and when they looked at him, it was everything he'd ever dreamed of. Not quite adoration…but acceptance.

Valen without a shadow. Valen without the stain of his father beside him.

All eyes were on him, rapt with attention as if his voice was a magnet, and they were helpless to resist its pull. Behind him, the guards brought forward the leaders from the Tavina, Prime and Stuna systems. They stood to Valen's right, silent as night.

"The time to choose has arrived," Valen addressed the crowd. "Today, in this room, we will change the course of the future. We will turn our eyes to the one true ruler, instead of these feeble impostors."

He lifted a hand toward the system leaders of Mirabel.

The room was silent, like the moment before a blade was drawn, before a bullet was loosed. Before a life was taken hold of and remade.

Before Valen asked the question, he already knew, with confidence, what their answer would be. He pulled his shoulders back. He took a deep, steadying breath and looked down at the people.

"Who is the rightful ruler of Mirabel?"

The answer came from a young child, standing closest to the stage.

"Nor Solis," the child said.

Her mother patted her on the head. Her father smiled.

Other voices rang out, one at a time at first, then stronger, filling the room with the sound of the one true name. Valen saw Andi's pilot and the young gunner, Nor's name on their lips, as if it had been there all their lives.

The doors behind them opened. Valen heard the crunch

of boots on broken glass. Soldiers jerked to stand upright as a hooded figure appeared, hands reaching up to pull the hood back and reveal red lips, dark hair and eyes as glorious as the setting sun.

"Bow to your queen," Valen said.

The crowd bowed, reverent and ready, as Nor Solis, the Queen of Xen Ptera, the Savior of Olen, the new ruler of Mirabel, arrived.

# CHAPTER 89
## NOR

HER BROTHER HAD DONE HIS JOB PERFECTLY.

A fine test for his first mission out in the field. She'd been wise to keep him in Lunamere for so long, tortured to near death. It had unlocked his compulsion ability, his true self. His birthright. That was when she had begun to visit him daily in his cell. Training him, guiding him, gaining his trust.

As Nor entered the building now, her two armies were already waiting. One dressed in the colors of Xen Ptera, red to match the horrors they would spread across Mirabel to those who rebelled. The other, her new army, adorned in gowns and suits and all manner of fineries that Nor would do away with.

Such fine things would be for *her* people, and hers alone.

SASHA ALSBERG & LINDSAY CUMMINGS

They all bowed before her, heads tucked close to their chests, breath held as if she were a holy relic. She glided past them without fear, knowing that none would lift a finger to harm her.

Valen waited for her on the stage.

"Sister," he said.

Nor stopped herself from curling her lip at the sight of his figure. Too thin, too angular, too *pained*. No member of the Solis family deserved such treatment. But it had to be done, to ensure that his survival instincts would kick in, to force his powers to unlock.

She would reward him later for his loyalty, perhaps with a crown of his own.

He was a prince of darkness. Her long-lost brother, finally come home to her side where he belonged.

But never her equal. She would rule alone.

"You have done well, Valen," Nor said.

"The final step remains," Valen said, inclining his head in thanks. "Should I leave the honor to you?"

Nor raised a sculpted brow. "I enjoy watching you work, Brother. I can't have all the fun."

He smiled at her, a new thing that had begun to pass between them only recently. She enjoyed seeing that smile.

He turned back to their new army. By now, all across Arcardius, a wave would be spreading as time-released explosives full of the silver liquid went off, bringing more to her cause.

"Followers of Queen Nor," Valen said, his voice ripe with the new power she had unlocked in him. "We must eliminate the traitors to the crown." He looked specifically to the old leaders of Mirabel. *"Kneel before your queen."*

Their faces were calm as the three leaders knelt before Nor. She reached into her cloak and removed a freshly sharpened knife. Nor had used the whetstone on it herself, then polished the blade to a gleaming perfection.

"Your sacrifices, my queen," Valen said as he stepped aside to give Nor space.

The words made her warm, light as air. She felt her lips pulling into a beautiful grin as she approached the leaders of the Unified Systems.

One by one, she ran her blade across their throats. Each leader that fell was a gift to her people.

*Revenge*, her heart sang.

And in that moment, Nor knew that her rule had begun.

# CHAPTER 90
## LIRA

LIRANA METTE FELT REBORN.

For so long, she had been blinded by darkness, by the lies of the Unified Systems. For so long, she had been unable to see the light.

The moment she rose to her feet, she heard a lingering whisper in her mind.

*The True Queen*, it said.

It sounded like Valen. The boy they had not rescued, as she'd previously believed, but stolen away from his queen. She knew Valen belonged at Nor's side, just as much as she knew that the Unified Systems were her enemy. That her aunt would be a worthy sacrifice to the cause. She looked to Gilly and Breck beside her, knowing they also heard the voice in their own minds.

*The True Queen*, it said again. *Protect her, honor her, worship her cause.*

Lira's eyes had been opened, after all this time.

She turned to look at Nor Solis, the True Queen of Mirabel.

The light had finally begun to shine.

# CHAPTER 91
## DEX

THE NIGHTMARE HAD NOT CEASED.

The system leaders of Mirabel were dead. The queen of a system once thought defeated stood above their bodies, smiling as if she'd conquered the galaxy. Dex had watched her arrive, watched her speak to Valen as if they were kin. He'd seen, with perfect clarity, the way she'd slid her knife across the leaders' throats. Lira and Gilly and Breck, the crew who had accepted him as one of their own, turned to face the queen as if they belonged to her now.

And all Dex could do was hide like a coward behind the bar.

He'd managed to sneak back onto the stage and retrieve the general while Valen was distracted. Now he and Andi were on the ground beside him, both bleeding, both dying. A bartending droid, its humanoid torso sprouting from a single wheel, sat silently to Dex's left, awaiting his command.

But what command could he give? The droid couldn't save them from their fate, and Dex surely couldn't, either.

The blood trail outside the bar led straight to them. They'd be discovered soon.

Gone was the bravery Dex had always felt as a Guardian. Gone was the confidence he'd found as a bounty hunter.

Fear had seized Dex in its icy grip, and no matter how hard he tried to break away, the terror surrounding him would not release him.

There was nowhere to go. No escape. The madness continued as Nor addressed the crowd, and her soldiers shot the few who still seemed to have control of their minds.

Then they began to fan out across the ballroom.

The terror intensified with every footstep the soldiers took, every second drawing them closer to discovering Dex's hiding place.

*Run*, his mind whispered. He could scarcely hear the word over the terror that had dulled his senses and kept him rooted to the spot.

Andi lay motionless on the floor beside him, her hand growing colder as Dex gripped it like an anchor. She would not die. She *could not die*, because if she did, Dex would lose his heart with her.

Beside her, the general's eyes were open as he lay on his side, slowly bleeding out. He stared at the wall, lips fluttering with words that Dex couldn't hear.

The soldiers were getting closer. Soon they would discover him. Dex gripped Andi's hand tighter, and through his fear, through his hopelessness, a sudden realization emerged.

He would stay with her until the end.

If it was the last thing he ever did in his life, Dex would die defending Androma Racella. He wouldn't go down until he knew he'd done everything in his power to save her.

The general's mutterings became more insistent.

Dex crawled forward, had nearly placed a hand over the general's mouth to silence him, when the words drifted into his ears.

*"The tunnel."*

Dex shook his head. He wanted to scream. He wanted to claw his way out of here, get them to safety…but there was no good ending to this nightmare.

*"The tunnel,"* General Cortas rasped again. Blood dribbled from his lips, shockingly dark. He lifted a trembling hand and pointed past Dex to the dark shadows beneath the bar top.

Dex squinted into the darkness. At first he saw nothing, but as his eyes locked onto a small seam in the wall, something Andi had said drifted into his mind.

*I remember every little bit. Even the hidden escape tunnels that the general installed. He loved to put them in closets, bathrooms, under the bars…*

Hope blossomed in his chest as he reached forward and ran his fingers along the seam. It was a small door, just large enough for someone to crawl through. Dex leaned his shoulder up against it. *Pushed* with all of his might.

When the door popped open to reveal a dark tunnel beyond, Dex almost wept.

*Run*, his mind said again.

He set to work at once, feeling coming back to his limbs, clarity warming his mind.

"Help me," he whispered to the droid. The blessed thing grabbed the general by the collar and hauled him away like a tray of heavy drinks.

By the time the Xen Pterran soldiers discovered the blood trail behind the bar, Dex, Andi and the general were already gone.

In the docking bay of Averia, inside the *Marauder*, Dex ignited the engines and angled the ship toward freedom.

He'd never been more grateful for the darkness of the night as he left Arcardius behind.

# CHAPTER 92
## ANDROMA

*SMOKE EVERYWHERE.*

*It was in her eyes, curling into her lungs.*

*The transport ship was in flames. The crash had happened so fast. One moment, they were soaring through the skies. The next, fire.*

*Pain.*

*A scream tore itself from her throat.*

*Now her ears rang. Her heart slammed against her ribs, and fear ripped through her. She had to get out. She couldn't breathe.*

*"Help...me."*

*Andi turned in her seat. Through the haze, she saw Kalee's outstretched hand. Her body, turned at an awkward angle in the flickering firelight. Her friend was covered in blood. A piece of metal protruded from her stomach like a sword. With each breath Kalee took, it wobbled.*

*"Oh, Godstars," Andi gasped. She reached out, tried to pull the metal from Kalee's stomach. But the girl screamed, and Andi shrank away, hands trembling, her own vision growing dim. "Hang on, Kalee. Just hang on."*

*Panic seized Andi as she tried to kick open the transport door. But it was stuck, dented in so far that it trapped her leg against the seat.*

*She couldn't move.*

*"Help," Kalee murmured again.*

*There were tears in her eyes, and a trickle of crimson slipped from her pale lips.*

*"I'll get help," Andi said. "Just hang on." Shards of glass were embedded into her arms. Her skin was blistering in the heat before her eyes. She began to sob as she slammed the emergency button on the dash, but no light flickered on.*

*"Come on!" Andi screamed.*

*She slammed the button again, and again, but the ship was lifeless around them.*

*And no one was coming to save them.*

*Beside her, Kalee had fallen silent.*

*She wasn't breathing. Her eyes closed. Her head lolled to the side.*

*"No," Andi said. "Kalee, wake up!" Pain tore her chest open. She coughed again, the smoke and the heat unbearable. "You have to wake up!"*

*She tried to wriggle herself away, but pain exploded from her leg, from her wrists. She was trapped.*

*She knew, suddenly, that she was going to die.*

*The front of the crumpled ship was nearly an inferno now. In seconds, the flames would reach them.*

*"Kalee!" Andi said. "Please don't do this. Please don't leave me."*

*The girl had stopped moving. Blood trickled from her stomach like a crimson river, slowing now. As if she'd run out.*

*"No! You'll be okay, you'll be okay," Andi sobbed, trying again to*

*pull herself from the seat. Her leg wouldn't move; the door wouldn't free her.*

Please, *she begged.* Please, no.

*Andi had done this to her. Oh, Godstars, she'd done this. The crash was her fault.*

*She was Kalee's Spectre, sworn to protect her with her life.*

*And now Kalee was…*

*Andi's head swam as she looked at her charge, the friend who was as close as a sister.*

*Kalee was* dead.

*Andi sobbed, her entire body trembling as her mind screamed,* You killed her, you killed her, you killed her.

*The fires raged, and Andi felt torn from her body as the transport door suddenly groaned and fell away.*

*Cool night air washed in.*

*"I'm so sorry," Andi sobbed as she looked at her friend. Kalee almost looked peaceful, as if she were only sleeping.*

*Andi couldn't leave her. How could she leave her?*

*She had never felt as alone as she did in this very moment.*

*The fire swept into the small space, so close now. The metal shard in Kalee's stomach had gone straight through her, pinned her body to the seat. Andi couldn't free her, couldn't drag her from her grave.*

*Fear swept over Andi like a poison, caused her to tear herself away from the transport as the flames raged.*

*She crawled away from the inferno, coughing smoke from her lungs, her eyes burning so badly she could scarcely see.*

*She blinked through her tears, fighting the darkness as it threatened to overcome her. This wasn't happening. This wasn't real.*

*Kalee couldn't be dead.*

*Andi looked back for a final glimpse of her friend.*

*The last thing she saw was Kalee's eyes, bright blue as the moon, opening wide to stare at her.*

Alive, *Andi's mind screamed.* She's alive.

*Andi reached for the girl, desperate to save her.*

The transport exploded in a final blast of raging, furious light, catapulting Andi backward.

As Kalee burned, tendrils of black slipped into Andi's mind and stole her away.

# CHAPTER 93
## DEX

DEX PACED IN THE MED BAY OF THE *MARAUDER*, watching the life force drain from the general's eyes.

"Tell me what you know!" Dex yelled.

The general was a lost cause. Without doctors or med droids, Dex was helpless to save him. The damage Valen had done was too severe. It was a wonder the man had survived this long already.

On the table beside General Cortas, Andi was still holding on to life. She was pale, cold, her chest wrapped in bandages that Dex had wound around her himself.

He hadn't been trained in medicine or healing. The bartending droid who'd helped him haul the general here wasn't programmed to heal, either.

But Lon Mette could.

Dex hadn't been aware of Lira's plans to move Lon onto the *Marauder* before the Ucatoria Ball, but he was thanking the God-stars now that the Sentinel was on board.

When Dex had shown up with only Andi and the general, both of them dying from their injuries and blood loss, Lon had asked him to choose. Along with his scales, Lon had inherited something else from his radiation-affected ancestors: he was a universal donor.

"I can't save them both," he'd said. "I only have so much blood to give."

When Dex chose Andi, Lon had accepted his decision without question. He helped to stabilize the general as best he could. Then he'd gotten to work on Andi. He sat beside her now, a tube connecting his arm to hers, as his blood flowed through to her. Giving her a chance at life. The silent droid held a cloth to Andi's forehead with humanoid hands, doing its best to help.

The ship was on autopilot, soaring through hyperspace as it carried them toward the only place Dex knew to go. Back to the place he'd learned his skills, back to Raiseth's headquarters outside Tenebris. The one place where they might be safe, where someone would be able to help Andi.

The knife had gone so close to her heart.

Dex tried to calm himself, but anger raged through him.

He needed information. Needed to know why, of all people, Valen Cortas had sided with the queen of Xen Ptera.

They had all been so wrong about him. How had they not seen the signs? How had they not *known*?

"Tell me!" Dex yelled at the general.

At first the dying man didn't answer. Dex knelt down next to him, gently lifting the general's head so he could speak without blood pooling in his mouth.

It took him a moment to find his voice.

"I didn't know this was—" he cleared his throat, a line of blood dripping from his lips "—going to happen."

He paused, once again taking a shaky breath.

"Tell me what you *do* know," Dex growled.

"He is dying," Lon said. "He deserves peace."

"He may be the only man in the galaxy who knows what the hell just happened back there," Dex said, voice rising. He looked back to the general. *"Tell us."*

General Cortas's face was already paling, white as the stars that streaked by. He looked down at his bleeding chest, as if he could still see Valen's hand digging in the blade.

"I knew he had evil in him." He coughed again. "Because of that demon who was his mother."

"Merella?" Dex asked.

"Not her." His teeth were red from blood. He grimaced. "Oh, Godstars, what have I done?"

"Tell me," Dex pressed, because he knew that when the general died, the truth would die with him. "You don't have much time."

General Cortas closed his eyes, and Dex was afraid he was already gone.

But then they opened again, blue as a summer sky. The light in them was slowly fading. "I've held on to this secret for years." He swallowed, tears slipping from the corners of his eyes. "So listen closely—not for my sake, but for Mirabel's. I don't think I have enough strength left to say it twice."

# CHAPTER 94
## KLAREN
## YEAR TWENTY-SIX

*SHE WAS A MOTHER AGAIN.*

*Not a mistake this time. Rather, a plan that fell perfectly into place.*

*Her second child sat in her arms, staring up at her. A boy this time, with dark hair and hazel eyes.*

*He was gentle, this one, but he was strong.*

*Stronger even than her daughter, Nor, had been.*

*The queen could feel it when she held the boy, like a spark that jolted from him to her. Sometimes, when she asked him not to cry, he carried on. Sometimes, when she asked him to sleep, he stayed awake for hours, glaring up at her. Screaming until his face was sunset red.*

When his father held him, he squirmed as if he, too, hated the man as much as she did.

"Someday," the queen said, as she looked down at her young son, "you will learn who you truly are. And you will understand why I did everything."

The baby cried.

She did not love him.

Not in the way she had loved Nor.

"Take him," she said to the servant beside her. The many-armed woman took the baby into one set of her arms, rocking him gently. "I am going to see Cyprian."

She swept out into the halls, passing by servants who cast their eyes down.

They had begun to fear her since Cyprian had given her free rein of the estate. Since the place on his arm was no longer taken up by his wife, but instead by the woman he'd ripped away from the battleground on Xen Ptera two years ago.

She found him in his office, seated behind his desk as he pored over the maps of the galaxy. Deciding how best to attack Xen Ptera and the other small planets in the Olen System in the coming days.

"Cyprian," she said as she entered the cavernous room.

He stiffened. Something he had been doing all too often at the sound of her voice.

She gritted her teeth, forced herself to speak with more strength. "Come to me, my love."

He stood, his chair scraping back. When he crossed the room, his body was stiff, as if he didn't want to be near her. He kept his eyes downcast until she placed a gentle finger below his chin and angled his gaze to hers.

"Kiss me, Cyprian," she whispered.

He pressed his lips to hers in a deep kiss that had him groaning, wanting more. Always more.

She steeled herself as she pulled away and spoke again.

If he obeyed…it would change everything.

"You will take me home tonight," she said.

*Cyprian's head jerked upward. "What?"*

*She nodded. Nerves pricked at her senses.*

*If she could do this, if she could get him to take her back, with their new son in tow…*

*"I wish to return to Xen Ptera," the queen pressed. "My husband… he will surrender."*

*"Your husband," Cyprian hissed. "He does not care for you, fool queen." He shook his head and ripped himself away from her. "I cannot allow this. You have seen too much. Heard too much." His shoulders rose and fell as he inhaled and released a breath. "You are bound to me now, Klaren. Through our child."*

*"Which is why I wish to take him, too," she said. She swept closer to him. "Cyprian…look at me, my love."*

*He spun around, eyes flashing. "I will not allow you to bewitch me again."*

*"Bewitch you?" She put the power into her words, where her compulsion was strongest. Put the power into her gaze, too.*

*She could feel it working on him, but only for a moment.*

*Then she hit the wall.*

*Little by little, Cyprian had begun fighting back, building a wall within his mind. As if there was something inside of him, some hidden power that he, too, bore.*

*"You will send me and Valen to Xen Ptera," the queen said. Her body shook with the power she urged into her words. "Tonight."*

*Cyprian was motionless as he watched her.*

*"You will send me and Valen to Xen Ptera," she tried again, sweat beading on her brow.* "Tonight."

*"Tonight," Cyprian said, and she felt the wall in his mind begin to crumble.*

*Exhaustion had made him weaker.*

*It was why, each night, she kept him awake with her kisses, her touch, her false love.*

*"My husband will allow us entry," she said, still using her power on him, compelling him to obey, "as long as you propose a cease-fire.*

*From both sides. For one day. You will release Valen and me to Xen Ptera, and you will forget that we existed. You will remove us from your memories and from your heart."*

Cyprian looked up.

*This time, when he locked eyes with her, she saw that she had finally won.*

*"Pack your bags, my dear," he said. "Tonight, you will board a ship. It is time for you to return home."*

*"And then?" she pressed.*

*"And then," Cyprian said, his jaw tight as her power flowed into him, "I will remove you both from my memories and my heart."*

*"Good," she said. "We leave at nightfall."*

*As the prisoner queen left Cyprian's office, her steps light and bouncing, she could not help but smile at everyone who passed.*

*Every fool, unaware of her plans. Her time on Arcardius had been hell. A necessary one, but a hell all the same. It had taken years for her to truly understand the magnitude of what was at play.*

*Tonight she would return to her Xen Pterran throne. Back to her husband, back to her daughter, to introduce them to her newborn son.*

*He was asleep when she went to him, the many-armed servant standing guard as promised.*

*"You look pleased, mistress," the servant said, anxiously twisting her many hands together, like a tangle of knots.*

*"I am pleased." The prisoner queen smiled, because she knew the truth. "Perhaps for the first time in a very long while."*

*Freedom was within her grasp. And when her children met, when they combined the strength of the abilities that she'd felt in both of them...she could almost feel the distant Conduit tremble, even from here.*

*The galaxy did not stand a chance.*

# CHAPTER 95
## KLAREN
## YEAR THIRTY

*FOUR YEARS HAD PASSED SINCE THE QUEEN*
*had commanded her captor to take her home.*

*Cyprian had managed to outwit her that night. Flying high with her*
*triumph, she'd never expected him to turn on her.*

*Somewhere along the way, he had discovered her compulsion ability.*
*Somehow, he'd been the only man to ever discover the difference she held*
*in her blood. And so he'd kept her locked up for four years, refusing to*
*see her when she called upon him, ignoring her pleas to return home to*
*Xen Ptera. Denying her the right to see her son.*

*And yet he always came crawling back, unable to pull her from his mind.*
*She'd embedded a deep obsession within him, and it was her only hope.*

*Just days ago, he'd entered her quarters, saying that her husband had agreed to a truce. That she'd finally be able to go home to the family she hadn't seen in six years.*

*Now, finally, she was nearly back where it all began.*

*She sat aboard a starship, staring out at the darkness of space. Far in the distance, the glowing orb that was Xen Ptera hung like a tiny, waiting gift.*

*On its surface, her daughter, Nor, waited.*

*Around her, the ship buzzed with soldiers rushing about. Polished boots thudded on shining Arcadian-mined metal. The captain, with his clawed hands, was busy speaking in hushed tones over the com system. Each time he spoke, Klaren could hear the clacking of his massive teeth. The low, deep-chested rumble of a growl as he communicated with Xen Ptera, where she knew she would soon walk.*

*So many years she'd been away.*

*Now, it was nothing like the planet she had left behind.*

*On that fateful day she'd last seen it, Xen Ptera was already dying, but the surface was still a livable place, its citizens able to grow food and harvest water from great wells. Now it was a dead, barren wasteland that hung limp in the cradle of space.*

*"Home," the queen whispered to herself.*

*Heavy footsteps approached behind her now. A hand caressed her bare shoulder. Lips touched the nape of her neck beneath her piled curls.*

*"You lied to me all these years," she whispered. "You said they were holding their ground, still fighting. But that was never true, was it?"*

*"They weren't lies, my dear Klaren," Cyprian hissed in her ear, his warm breath sticking to her skin. "I just didn't tell you the full truth. You are still my enemy, no matter the things we've been through together these past years." His fingertips trailed farther down her neck and onto her arms, where they squeezed tightly enough to make her gasp in pain.*

*"When?" she asked. "When will I be on the ground?"*

*"As soon as you sign the treaty," Cyprian said, lowering a holoscreen to her lap, the contract she'd requested ready for her signature.*

*"You'll stay true to your promise?" Klaren asked as he knelt beside her, steadily avoiding her gaze. "You'll leave Xen Ptera alone?"*

"Sign the treaty, and you and your planet will be free." Cyprian ran his fingertips down her arm, then took her hand in his.

Slowly, he lifted it to his lips.

"Swear it," the queen said.

Without a moment of hesitation, Cyprian agreed.

Her heart pounded against her ribs. Perhaps it was because freedom was in her grasp. Perhaps it was because finally, after so many years trapped on Arcardius, she would be reunited with her husband.

Her daughter.

Her precious, precious Nor.

That thought, along with the hope that she hadn't failed her mission just yet, was what made her place the palm of her hand on the scanner, initiating the peace treaty that would end this war once and for all.

The holo beeped as her print was recorded.

"Your turn, Cyprian," the queen said, passing the holo to him.

She waited for him to sign the treaty, to seal Xen Ptera's fate—and the Conduit's, far beyond. But instead of placing his hand on the scanner, he stood and walked toward his red-uniformed pilot.

"Is the fleet ready for engagement?" he asked, handing the holo to a nearby soldier.

"Yes, sir," the pilot responded. Cyprian glanced at her without a hint of emotion written on his face, then back to the pilot.

Klaren went still.

"Cyprian," she said. "Where is Valen? You said he would go with me. I will not leave without my son."

She could see his jaw working, see his body go rigid at the sound of her voice. He started to turn toward her, but at the last moment, he stopped.

"Cyprian, come here," she tried again, but her voice had lost its cool calm, replaced instead by a trembling, pathetic note. "Come, and let me look upon you one last time."

Footsteps sounded behind her.

Hands grabbed her shoulders, and Klaren cried out as her head was yanked back against the headrest.

Then she felt the cold, unfeeling grip of a strap locking around her throat. Forcing her to stare ahead, out at the distant planet.

"Release me!" she shouted. "I am the queen of Xen Ptera!"

The strap tightened in place. So tight that she could scarcely breathe.

"Cyprian!" she gasped. "Release me!"

All around her, soldiers were moving to action, tapping on dashboard screens, speaking into coms from which distant voices responded.

But the queen could only stare ahead, eyes widening as she saw a fleet of ships soar past. Massive, hulking black warships, the largest she had ever seen.

"Cyprian!" she cried again, her voice breathless.

His voice came from beside her. She twisted, fighting against the restraint on her throat. Then she froze in horror as he said, "Ready the weapons."

Ice flooded through her.

She knew she'd been fooled, saw her mistake in an instant.

He had bested her, discovered a way around her powers. Discovered a way to fully overcome her compulsion.

The treaty was all a ruse to get her here, to pause the Xen Pterran soldiers while their queen hovered in the sky overhead, about to be returned home.

They wouldn't mount a defense, fearing for her safety.

And now...now, they would all die.

"Please," she begged. "Cyprian, stop this at once. I'll do anything you wish. Please, spare them!"

His deep rumble of laughter sent a cold spike into her chest.

Then his lips were at her ear again. His hands were in her hair, yanking at the strands as he whispered, "Fool queen. You will bewitch me no more."

He stood and gave the command to attack.

Frozen in place, she watched as the ships opened fire on Xen Ptera.

The retort was enough to shake the ship. To sink into the queen's bones and cause her to cry out as she watched blazing, furious orbs of light soar through the darkness, heading straight toward the planet below.

In that moment, the queen knew she had failed.

*All she could see was her daughter's face.*

*Nor, alive and well, her eyes on the sky as she watched her death barrel toward her from the fringes of space.*

*The queen reached deep into her soul. She found that tiny, shimmering thread within, and with mental fingers, gripped it tight.*

*"I'm sorry," she whispered. She begged the connection to work, begged for her daughter to hear her.*

*She sent forth an image of two ancient, bloody handprints pressing against a cold glass tower. Bodies lying beside her bare feet. The faraway Conduit, swirling and bright. The journey. The pain. The constant, trustworthy Darai, always willing to tell her the truth. To keep her in line with the light.*

*Before the bombs reached the planet, the queen sent forth an image of Valen's face as she'd last seen it four years ago, tiny and screaming and so much like her own. "You are not alone. You have a brother," she whispered.*

*She could almost feel the planet shake as the bombs hit. Like a bolt of lightning, fingers of blue fire stretched across it, weaving their way around every piece of the land.*

*With it, a scream erupted from the queen's throat.*

*Xen Ptera went dark.*

*She screamed until she heard Cyprian's voice beside her ear, his lips hot and wet against her skin.*

*"Scream, Klaren," he said. "Scream, and see the proof that you have lost."*

*She kept screaming, even as his soldiers gripped her head tight, and the tip of an electric blade appeared before her.*

*Her voice went ragged as they sliced her tongue from her mouth.*

*She finally fell silent as they unlocked her bindings.*

*As they dragged her limp body into a pod, sealed it shut and sent Klaren Solis, the Failed Queen from afar, barreling endlessly into the cold black skies.*

# CHAPTER 96
## NOR

AS AN ELEVEN-YEAR-OLD CHILD, PRINCESS NOR
lay in the rubble of the palace, her father's corpse beside her. Around
her, fires burned and people cried out in agony. Her world was gone.

Then, just as she had lost all hope, she heard a woman's soft voice
in her head, slowly growing stronger.

It was familiar, a voice she knew but did not know all the same.

It belonged to her mother.

Ten words were all she said before the connection was cut. Ten words
that gave her not just hope, but a drive to fight back against the oppres-
sors who did this to her planet.

"I'm sorry," the voice had said. Then, "You are not alone. You
have a brother."

*The voice disappeared, but Nor knew in her bones that her mother was dead. It was as if a line was cut between them that she never knew existed until this very moment.*

*But the message was enough to fuel her need to escape the rubble and give her a new mission: find her brother.*

*Thirteen years later, Nor's men finally kidnapped Valen from Arcardius and successfully delivered him home.*

*When he arrived, he was a selfish Arcardian-raised boy, scared and frail, not the warrior Nor had hoped to find. At first he didn't seem to share the family's gift of compulsion, but Darai told her to be patient. He promised a way to bring it forward. Not in the same way Nor had accessed her abilities, but through a harsher, bloodier method.*

*She gave the orders Darai recommended, and threw her only brother into Cell 306 on Lunamere.*

*She had him tortured, day after day, until—driven by pain—his mind latched on to the compulsion ability he never knew he had.*

*Nor could still remember the words she'd said to him after he stopped his torturers.*

*She'd knelt before him. Their eyes had met, and she'd felt the power as their telepathic link sidled into place.*

*She'd spoken to him with her mind.*

*"You will join me, Brother, and together, you and I will take back the galaxy."*

# CHAPTER 97
## VALEN

NOR WAS AN ANGEL OF DARKNESS SPRUNG from the most illustrious black hole in the universe. And soon everyone would know her name. She would be worshipped, a goddess who walked among the stars, the ability in her grasp to destroy whole systems with one glance.

Valen looked upon his sister, her elegant midnight gown flowing down her subtle curves like a river of darkness. Power like no other radiated from her.

He would do anything for her. She was his family, his queen, his everything. If she asked him to kill, he would oblige. He would destroy every other being in the universe if it pleased her.

She'd sworn that if he killed the general, they would never

be apart again. He would be by her side as they ruled the galaxy together. Brother and sister, together always.

No one could defeat them.

He shivered with pleasure as he remembered the way his weapon sank into Androma's chest. The look of pure shock on her face before a curtain of pain replaced it.

Pretending to be the Valen that Androma had once known was easy, just as Nor had told him it would be. But he'd shed his past self when Nor found him. The pain Lunamere had inflicted on him opened his mind and led to so many discoveries.

He would happily go through it all again if she asked. He had been given a new chance to protect a sister he never knew he had, a chance at redemption after he'd failed to keep Kalee safe.

He would not waste the opportunity this time.

The only difficulty had been pretending to forgive the monster who had killed Kalee. It wasn't an accident; Androma had killed his sister in cold blood, and it delighted Valen that he'd played Andi like a puppet on strings.

Valen looked down at his hands, covered in the dried remains of Andi's and Cyprian's blood. It was beautiful, the color a deep matte red. He brought his hand up to his face, and his tongue tasted the blood of his enemy. The blood of the man who'd kept Valen from his true mother, the monster who'd lied to him his entire life about where he'd really come from and what he could do.

The sharp, metallic flavor seeped into him.

Revenge did taste sweet. It tasted like justice.

He returned his gaze to his sister, who stood surrounded by her advisers. His gaze met hers, and she lifted her golden hand, motioning him forward.

His feet couldn't move fast enough as he entered her inner circle, standing on the ballroom stage.

"Valen, my brother," Nor's heavenly voice said when he approached. "Darai and Zahn just gave me some wonderful news.

We have successfully established control over Arcardius and will soon have dominion over the remaining capital planets."

Valen nodded; this had always been the plan. The Adhiran attack had been a bit of a deviation, but crash-landing on the planet had allowed for Valen to contact Nor through their bond and given her an excuse to have some fun. To wage war in the bloody ways of old, in a place where he knew she would win. They'd given the people of Adhira something to distract them from passing along the knowledge of Valen's altered DNA.

The only other flaw in their plan had been the general's obnoxious AI, who *had* noticed the change, along with the Marauders. The crew, Valen knew, were to be destroyed during the ball. The AI, however, he'd silenced himself, before it could deliver the message to the general's doctors and destroy the mission before it began.

It was fortunate that Dex and the Marauders hadn't thought to mention it to the general, either—there would have been no way to eliminate them before the ball without arousing suspicion. They had likely assumed that Alfie would pass along the news to the medical team looking after Valen, since the AI had been charged with his care.

Valen looked to Nor again as she spoke.

"Will the Bloody Baroness pose a problem?"

Valen thought of how his knife had met its mark when he sunk it into her chest.

"No. She's dead."

Nor's rouged lips lifted at the corners.

# CHAPTER 98
## DEX

"SO NOW YOU KNOW THE TRUTH," GENERAL Cortas said.

Dex sat back on his heels, staggered at the revelation. "So Valen is…half–Xen Pterran?" he asked.

"Or something else," the general said, coughing. "There was something strange in Klaren's blood…something I'd never seen before."

"That's why you never named him your heir," Dex said, realization dawning on him. "You didn't think he could be trusted."

"And I was right," General Cortas agreed. "But Arcardius… the Phelexos System still needs a leader." He paused, gasped for air. "Get me a holo, boy," the general said faintly.

Dex fetched a holo from the storage room and brought it back to the dying general.

"What would you like me to do, sir?"

"I need to get into my files on the Arcardian database. Do as I say quickly because I can feel our time coming to an end."

The general guided Dex through the various steps that bypassed the Arcardian servers. A few moments later, General Cortas let out a breath.

"Place my right hand on the screen."

Dex did as he said, watching the general scan his clammy, ashen palm.

"Now have it scan my left eye."

Once again, Dex followed his command, and when it was done, he waited for further instructions.

"Now do the same to Androma—hurry."

Dex wasn't sure he trusted the man, but the general seemed so determined. He followed his orders, scanning Andi's palm and eye as quickly as he could.

When he returned to General Cortas's bedside, the man took a moment to speak. Using up his remaining strength, he finally told Dex what he'd done.

"The fate of the galaxy is at stake. The leaders are dead, and I'm sure their successors soon will be, as well."

He took in a ragged breath. "What I just did goes against every bone in my body. But Androma is the only Arcardian on this ship once I die." He coughed, and blood wetted his dry lips. "I cannot let my personal feelings about the girl overcome my duty to my planet."

He paused as he tried to regain his breath. "If she survives, she will lead Arcardius upon my death."

Dex was sure he must have misheard. "Sir?"

"When I die—" General Cortas looked up at Dex with his fading bloodshot eyes "—Androma Racella will be my successor. She will be the rightful General of Arcardius."

Before Dex could ask him any more questions, the general let out a bloody, wet cough.

Dex had seen people die before, many times. But seeing the light fade from General Cortas's eyes marked the end of an era.

And the beginning of another. One with a dark, unknown future.

All across Arcardius, silver explosions rained down from the skies.

At first, the Arcardians were transfixed by the sparkling orbs that came from the clouds. But when they touched the ground, sank into their skin, their minds were altered in a way they could not have foreseen.

The enemies of Xen Ptera turned their eyes to the sky, smiling as they thought of their new queen.

An evil, long thought dead, had been reborn.

A queen without power had taken up her new throne, a prince of compulsion at her side.

And far away, hidden within the swirling colors of a nebula, a general in a glass starship died.

The Bloody Baroness took his place.

★ ★ ★ ★ ★

# ACKNOWLEDGMENTS – SASHA ALSBERG

TRANSFORMING FROM A GIRL WHO STRUGGLED with dyslexia and couldn't read to a woman who wrote a book is, to me, a miracle. My own kind of fairytale.

To my magical co-author, Lindsay Cummings, for being my friend and teaching me the secrets of being a writer. It is surreal that four years ago I was in your acknowledgments, and now we are writing acknowledgments for OUR book!

To the woman who believed in me and my career, Joanna Volpe—words cannot express how grateful I am to have you as my agent. Seriously, I'm at a loss for words. Thank you, thank you, thank you!

To Peter Knapp—so happy you joined our team as Lindsay's agent. You complete our four musketeers!

To the fearless members of #TeamZ…

Harlequin TEEN: Lauren Smulski, Siena Koncsol, Bryn Collier, Amy Jones, Evan Brown, Krista Mitchell, Aurora Ruiz, Shara Alexander, Linette Kim, Natashya Wilson and Erin Craig.

New Leaf Literary & Media: Devin Ross, Kathleen Ortiz, Mia Roman, Pouya Shahbazian, Chris McEwen and Hilary Pecheone.

And to everyone at Park Literary & Media.

To JD Netto for being not only a great friend over the years, but also the talented artist who made our gorgeous cover. *heart-eyes*

None of this would be possible without the love and support of my family. To the man who never fails to brighten up my day: Dad, you have inspired me every day to live out my dreams. You are my cheerleader, and without you, I would be lost. Mom, you jump-started my love for reading during a time when I didn't believe in myself. I love and miss you so much. To my amazing twin, Marisa (we are fraternal, if you're wondering), and my lovely sisters Jennifer, Nicole and Stephanie. To Marina and Aunt Marcia, I am so grateful to have mother figures like the two of you in my life. To Fraser, you are a menace, but you're my menace. To Myles, Oliver and Kolin, you are my little puppers of joy.

To my amazing friends: Gabby Gendek, Jackie Sawicz, Ben Alderson, Annmarie Morrison, Sam Wood, Natasha Polis, Zoe Herdt, Connor Wolff, Tiernan Bertrand Essington, Hannah Sun, Theresa Miele, Kaitlyn Nash, Gemma Edwards, Casey Davoren, Regan Perusse, Christine Riccio, Jesse George, Kat O'Keefe, Emma Giordano, Jenna Clare, Rebekah Faubion, Kayla Olson, Carmen Seda, Emma Parkinson, Francesca Mateo and Molly and Anna Gottfried. I wish I could name all of you, but you know who you are!

To Sarah J. Maas, Roshani Chokshi, Susan Dennard, Victoria Aveyard, Danielle Paige, Adam Silvera, Val Tejeda,

Alexandra Bracken, Renee Ahdieh, Elizabeth May, Laura Lam, Soman Chainani, Dhonielle Clayton, Kerri Maniscalco, Adi Alsaid and Amie Kaufman, for inspiring me as a writer and just for being wicked cool people.

To Scotland—yes, the country—and to Sam Heughan, for being devilishly handsome as my phone wallpaper.

And, of course, thank you to the moon and back to all my subscribers (aka my YouTube family) for being the best support a girl could ask for. Without you, none of this would be a reality. You are my motivation and I love you. <3

# ACKNOWLEDGMENTS – LINDSAY CUMMINGS

HAS IT REALLY BEEN SEVEN YEARS OF AUTHOR-dom for me? Someone help me… I'm getting old.

I'll start the way I always do: I want to thank God for getting me through another novel. The time period surrounding *Zenith*'s creation was thrilling, for all the incredible fun and laughter and amazing things this book has done for my career. But it has also been the hardest two years of my life. While writing *Zenith*, I sunk so deeply into depression, I was afraid I'd never make it back out. You saved me, just as you always do. You gave me the gift of writing, and I couldn't be more blessed by it. You have carried me through, even now, and you always will. I love you. I pray I will always put you first.

To TEAM Z, which includes my fearless agent, Peter Knapp

at Park Literary: You are an absolute JOY to work with! You champion my work like a prizefighter, but you always do it with class. I'm so glad we picked each other. Here's to more adventures, Alfie!

To Joanna Volpe, and everyone else at New Leaf Literary: Thank you for supporting *Zenith* and helping get it to where it is now. This would not have happened without you all.

To my husband, my parents, my sister and my brother-in-law: Thank you for calming me down when I get too overwhelmed about publishing. Maybe someday, I'll relax about it all (but probably not). I love you. I know what true love is because of you.

To my husband's family: Thank you for putting up with me these past two years while we've been living at your place. Most days, I'm a wreck. Other days, I'm sarcastic or plotting something evil. Every day, I'm thankful for your support.

To the entire team at Harlequin TEEN: I've told you a million times, and I'll tell you again...you know how to make an author feel wanted and loved. I'm forever grateful for your kind hearts and overall excitement for *Zenith*. You've given me a renewed joy for writing books.

To Cherie Stewart: Thanks for always being in my court. I'm forever grateful for your support and wise words and fellow appreciation for exhaustion.

To JD Netto: You are the best cover designer in the world. I'm not biased. You're just that talented. Thank you for your creativity and hard work on this series from the beginning.

To the rest of the worship band at church: Sundays get me through the week, especially during stressful deadline times. Thank you for your hearts and your prayers and your music.

To Rebekah Faubion (I miss you!), Kayla Olson, Roshani Chokshi, Sean Easley, Victoria Scott (Come back to TX!), Nicole Caliro, Brenda Drake, Emily Bain Murphy, Susan Dennard, Danielle Paige, Gregory Katsoulis, Stephanie Garber, Zac Brewer, Justine Larbalestier, Scott Westerfeld, Ryan

Graudin and any and all bookish friends I have inevitably forgotten. Thank you for supporting me. You may not even know why you're in here, but I know why, and it means the world to me.

To my readers: You have continually followed me from YA to MG and back, from bloody dystopian, to happy fantasy, to space operas and beyond… With you on my side, I'm not afraid to write what's in my heart. I adore you, #booknerdigans.

Lastly, to my co-author, Sasha Alsberg. Without you, this book would not be a book. Promo events would be lonely, I wouldn't have spent a month in Scotland (sharing a room because we were too afraid of the dark) and I'm pretty sure I'd still be forced to talk to strangers on airplanes. Thank you for showing me how to YouTube and introducing me to your dad's killer cappuccinos. Thank you for saying YES when I approached you about writing a book together. Most people would have run away screaming, and yet here we are, with a giant shiny book that has our names on it! It's actually real.

# HQ Young Adult
# One Place. Many Stories

The home of fun, contemporary
and meaningful Young Adult fiction.

Follow us online

 @HQYoungAdult

 @HQYoungAdult

 HQYoungAdult

 HQMusic